groves, ancie...
setting for romance!' she ...
lush tropical heat of the Caribbean—par...
by a silver sand beach lapped by turquoise water…
What more could lovers want?'

...iniseries

...urprise Love-Child
...y Wedding Charade
...den Italian

...y Cathy Williams

04 ...0

To renew, find us online at:
https://prism.librarymanagementcloud.co.uk/bromley
Please note: Items from the adult library may also
accrue overdue charges when borrowed on
children's tickets.

In partnership with
Bromley

BETTER
the feel good place

Discover more at millsandboon.co.uk.

BOUND BY A NINE-MONTH CONFESSION

CATHY WILLIAMS

DESTITUTE UNTIL THE ITALIAN'S DIAMOND

JULIA JAMES

MILLS & BOON

First published in Great Britain 2022
by Mills & Boon, an imprint of HarperCollins*Publishers* Ltd,
1 London Bridge Street, London, SE1 9GF

www.harpercollins.co.uk

HarperCollins*Publishers*
1st Floor, Watermarque Building,
Ringsend Road, Dublin 4, Ireland

Bound by a Nine-Month Confession © 2022 Cathy Williams

Destitute Until the Italian's Diamond © 2022 Julia James

ISBN: 978-0-263-30091-8

07/22

MIX
Paper from
responsible sources
FSC™ C007454

BOUND BY A NINE-MONTH CONFESSION

CATHY WILLIAMS

MILLS & BOON

To Hannah, for being a lovely and encouraging editor.

CHAPTER ONE

'*WHAT?*'

It had taken a few seconds for Celia to register what her client was saying.

'What do you mean, you've decided not to get married after all…?'

She levered herself up from where she had been kneeling, meticulously pinning the hem of the dress she was making.

A wedding dress.

Not in the traditional white because this was marriage number two for Julie Raymond. This was a pale lilac creation, exquisitely beautiful and threaded with hundreds of tiny pearls, each of which had been laboriously sewn on by hand.

Three months of toing and froing over the design, four months of time-consuming putting together with dozens of fittings, at each of which something had had to be changed. Then there was the time spent sourcing just the right fabric from just the right factory with just the right eco-friendly credentials.

Not so much a labour of love as a rollercoaster ride underlaid with simmering panic that the creation in the making might not come to fruition in time for the big day because of the number of roadblocks that kept appearing on the journey.

But here they were, with the wedding a week away and…

Celia stared up at her client in consternation, her green eyes urgently questioning. The expression on Julie's face was enough to slam shut the door on any notions that she might have misheard. The wedding of the year was being called off.

Should warning bells have started clanging months ago? Should she have paid more attention to throwaway remarks that had become more persistent over the past few weeks?

It wasn't as if Julie hadn't confided in her, snippets about her past and the loveless marriage she had endured for four years. She had wed an earl only to discover that with the title came the expectation that he be allowed to continue his womanising bachelor ways, untroubled by the humdrum monotony of married life. The divorce had been protracted and exhausting, Julie had confided bitterly.

So yes, Celia had had insights into her client and slowly they had formed an easy camaraderie, a closeness that sometimes happened between people whose lives ran on different railway tracks. It was the closeness between one with a need to confide and another with an ability to listen, two people who didn't share the same social platform. It was a safe place for Julie because confidences shared never risked being leaked to mutual friends.

'I can't go through with it.'

Celia rested back on her haunches and waited until Julie had stepped down from the squat box on which she had been standing. Then she ushered her upstairs into the tiny kitchen, away from the main body of the shop with its fitting rooms and racks of clothes in the process of being made and the busyness of her two assistants with their clients.

Julie Raymond was an absolutely stunning and statuesque blonde. A dream of a model who could have worn a bin bag and still looked spectacular.

She towered over Celia, who was secretly in awe of her, from her well-behaved, sleek, shiny bob to the impeccably manicured perfection of her fingernails.

The long-sleeved wedding dress, lovingly hugging a willowy body, trailed half pinned and in miserable disarray along the ground, picking up dust along the way.

'You're just a little nervous,' Celia soothed, seamlessly segueing into agony aunt mode. 'The wedding is only a few days away and life as you know it is going to change but, Julie…you mustn't let your past ruin a wonderful future. I know you had a…um…*disappointing* first marriage, but that was years ago and I'm sure that…er… Leandro will be a wonderful husband…'

'Maybe.' Julie laughed with carefree abandon and rested the mug of tea that had been handed to her on her lap. 'But definitely not to me.'

What could Celia say to that? How could she wax lyrical about the virtues of someone she had never met?

Not once had the adoring husband-to-be arranged to collect his fiancée so that he could whisk her off to a romantic meal after one of her very many late evening fittings.

Nor, come to think of it, had Julie mentioned him very much at all and, when quizzed, had been conspicuously mealy-mouthed on the subject of the love of her life.

She had vaguely hinted that she had known him for absolutely ages and if she had failed to follow this up with the usual glowing reports of how wonderful he was, then, camaraderie or no camaraderie, that was not Celia's business. At the end of the day, she was being paid to do a job and an important one. A huge job for an extravagant wedding where her dress would be the star of the show and, for three young girls climbing the career ladder in the competitive world of fashion design, a real opportunity.

'You wouldn't understand,' Julie said gently, and Celia frowned.

She could see the faintest of tea-ring stains from the mug on the pale lilac.

'Of course I do,' she said. 'You have cold feet. It happens. One minute you're looking forward to a shiny bright future and the next minute you're terrified that you'll be giving up all the freedoms that come with singledom…'

'And have you ever been there, Celia? Torn between the shiny bright future and the allure of singledom?'

Celia flushed and, for a few seconds, she felt the breath leave her body.

Had she ever been there? On the brink of marriage with all its glorious possibilities and dreams and hopes?

Yes! Once upon a time when she'd been just nineteen, engaged to the boy literally only a few doors away, the boy she had known for ever. He'd been her best friend, her confidant and then, when they'd both turned sixteen, her boyfriend. In the little village where they'd both grown up, deep in the heart of the countryside, they'd simply drifted into sealing a union that had been expected of them by both sets of parents.

Celia knew now that the best thing Martin had ever done had been to break things off but still…it had hurt. She'd smiled at the time, and held her head high until her jaw had ached. She'd assured her parents that it had been a joint decision, that they were both way too young anyway, that they'd rushed into things…and wasn't it a blessing that they'd seen sense before it was too late?

But she could still remember the tightness in her chest and the sadness that the wedding dress she'd been making, a labour of love because she'd just nailed her sewing course and had been excited to try out her newly qualified skills, would never be used.

It was neatly folded in a bag in a cupboard, a permanent reminder that when it came to giving her heart away, she would only do so with a clear head. A reminder that what you thought was love was all too often disguised as something else and if you got taken in, you ended up with an unused wedding dress gathering cobwebs in a cupboard. For her, the thrill of being engaged and planning for a wedding had papered over the blunt reality, which was that she and Martin had never been *in love*. They'd been a couple of kids who had allowed the tide to drift them this way and that.

Martin had found someone else in record time, someone athletic and into all the outdoor pursuits he had loved and which Celia had stoically endured. He had found his soulmate, had even asked Celia to attend his wedding, which she had politely declined. He had moved on. But for her? It didn't matter how much she told herself that she was in a better place single than she would have been in a marriage that would have ended in bitterness and acrimony. The scales would have fallen from both their eyes and reality would have eventually intruded on their youthful, impossible bubble and they wouldn't have remained friends, that was for sure! And what if a child had been involved? How tangled would *that* have been?

But Celia knew that the experience had taken that carefree side of her and curdled it. She was so careful now, so cautious…and Julie's throwaway question seemed to have brought it all to the surface. Briefly.

'We're not talking about me, Julie.' She smiled stiffly, eager to swivel the focus away from her. 'So don't try to change the subject.'

Actually, now that she happened to glance at Julie's finger, the engagement ring appeared to have been well and truly ditched. When had that happened and how had she failed to notice?

Celia felt an uncharitable spurt of irritation and banked it down.

Yes, Julie's first marriage had been a disaster. But she had moved on to find someone else, someone she presumably loved enough to accept his marriage proposal, and here she was now, washing her hands of it all in a couple of airily nonchalant sentences. Not a remorseful tear in sight.

'I've worked with many brides-to-be, Julie, and there's always some nerves beforehand.'

'I haven't actually been nervous about getting married.'

'What does Leandro have to say?' Celia swerved away from all non-starter chat about her client's lack of pre-wedding nerves, her refusal to consider the most likely reason for her calling off the marriage at the eleventh hour. 'He must be…heartbroken.'

Did she care about the now fast-vanishing prospect of her stunning wedding gown getting the coverage she had so hoped for? Maybe propelling them into the big league?

Yes, she did.

But more than that, Celia came from a traditional family. She and her brother both did. Their parents had married young and were still in love decades later. A straightforward life with a straightforward outcome. When she thought of the grief and unhappiness opening up at Julie's feet, at Leandro's feet, she felt a wrench of sadness for them both.

How was it that Julie seemed so blithely unaware of the ramifications of her snap decision?

Couldn't she see what she was casually tossing aside? Didn't she know how very lucky she was to be with a guy who loved her? That you didn't get love just to throw it away on an anxious whim? Because you figured that something better might be just around the corner? Didn't she realise that there were women out there with unused wedding dresses stuck in the back of cupboards, melancholy testament to dreams that had never come true?

'If you met Leandro,' Julie said thoughtfully, 'I'm not sure *heartbroken* would ever be a word you could use to describe how he might feel in a situation like this.'

'But I've never met him.'

'He's a very busy man.'

Celia frowned, tempted to pry further but conscious that she had no role to play in Julie's decision. She wasn't a counsellor, and it wasn't her job to try and talk anyone out of anything!

But what a shame and what a waste.

She'd worked with wedding dresses for years. She'd ironically thought how odd it was that from her own abandoned wedding dress, lovingly sewn in anticipation of the big day that never came, had come an absolute love for the intricacies of making wedding dresses.

The attention to detail…the little personal requests some brides-to-be asked to be sewn into bodice tops, under lace…once in the lining…

She had never once felt in the slightest bit envious that all these dresses, made by her and her team, would usher in lives filled with hope and happiness while for her…who knew when her own day would come?

But as she listened to Julie kindly telling her how much she loved the dress, plucking at the expensive fabric and frowning with an expression of mild dismay at the faint mark left by the mug she had rested on it, Celia couldn't help but feel a wave of self-pity. She had chosen to tread carefully, which meant that she was on her own now as much as she had been when she and Martin had broken up. Being on her own seemed to have become a career choice. And here was Julie, wedding dress already stained and soon to be ditched, tossing aside her chance at happiness with a shrug.

'You'll be paid for it, of course,' her client was expanding now. 'You've done an amazing job and I'm going to recommend you to all my friends. You'll have so much lovely business, Celia, you'll be rushed off your feet!'

Celia smiled weakly and gave up on trying to play agony aunt.

She felt drained. Memories had jumped out at her just when she didn't need them and now she wanted to close the shop and head back to the small house she rented in Shepherd's Bush.

'I'm really sorry, Julie,' she said gently, removing the mug, taking it to the sink and then remaining there, standing, waiting for her client to do likewise, which she didn't, until Celia prompted, 'It's nearly time for me to be closing up for the evening.'

'I should mention that I've met someone,' Julie blurted out with sudden nervousness.

'You've *met someone*?'

'Um…'

'But when? How? I had no idea! Not, of course, that it's any of my business, although maybe you should have thought about breaking things off with Leandro earlier? Look, Julie, I really need to close the shop now. We can sort all the details about the dress later. There's no need for you to tell me the ins and outs of your private life. It's very sad that you won't be marrying Leandro but it's your life and, of course, I wish you well.'

She purposefully wiped the kitchen counter and headed to the door, her body language signalling the end of the conversation. She could feel a headache coming on.

'It's the real thing, Celia. I can tell from your expression that you disapprove but, honestly, this guy…? He's the real deal.'

'I… I'm happy for you, Julie, I really am, but—'

'And there's something else I think you should know…'

'Really?' Celia raised her eyebrows. She wondered what more could possibly be on the agenda. A final fitting had turned into the confession to end all confessions and her brain hurt when she thought about not just Julie's poor fiancé but the sheer nightmare of unpicking what had been touted as the wedding of the year. Where did you even start on that?

'The guy I'm seeing? It happens to be your brother…'

Celia was still reeling from that shock announcement two days later as she began putting away stuff in the workshop, ready to lock up and head to the Underground.

Knocked for six and frantically thinking that she surely must have misheard, she had listened with mounting horror as Julie had given her a brief synopsis of her life-changing fling with Dan.

From standing in a purposeful manner, she had collapsed like a rag doll right back into the chair from which she had earlier risen.

How on earth had her brother crept into this scenario?

She had found out fast enough.

Yes, they had met. Quite by chance, as it happened. A couple of months ago, Julie had turned up for a fitting and Dan had been there, in all his good-looking glory. He had rocked up on his motorbike to hand-deliver a book he had promised Celia.

Celia remembered the day quite clearly because she had done her best to hustle him out. She adored her older brother but life, for him, moved on his own timeline and she had been rushed off her feet with a list of things to get through before she left.

Had he and Julie chatted? Sure. Celia had barely noticed. Julie was a besotted bride-to-be. Why would Celia have paid a scrap of attention to the fact that her brother had hung around for longer than he should have, chatting?

Dan was a chatty person! Five years older, he was completely different from her...from looks to personality.

Tall to her short...dark-haired to her red...and carefree in ways she had always envied and admired.

Had Julie fallen for that?

She'd said that Leandro was something of a workaholic. Had Dan's breezy insouciance delivered a mortal hammer blow to a bride whose head had been filled with sudden, last-minute doubts about the guy she was marrying? Had the guy who had gone freelance because he spurned the tyranny of a nine-to-five work schedule charmed the woman destined to wed a man chained to a desk?

Had opposites attracted in what had been a perfect but temporary storm?

At any rate, she had been swamped with guilt. If Dan had never been there, Julie would still be going ahead with her marriage and whatever nerves she was experiencing would have fizzled out like dew in the summer sun.

Instead...

Celia had tried to get hold of her brother, but he had gone underground and when she'd carefully tried to find out whether her parents were any the wiser, she had quickly realised that they weren't. 'You know your brother,' Lizzie Drew had said with maternal indulgence. 'Never one for the details of where he is!'

Celia was beginning to wonder whether she knew her brother at all.

Absorbed in the same train of thought that had been cluttering her head for the past two days, she was only aware of the doorbell ringing downstairs after it had gone from staccato bursts to one long, insistent, demanding and intensely annoying buzz.

She hurried down the short flight of stairs into the display area of her shop, banging on the lights at the bottom.

It was cold and dark outside, and the January air was heavy with the promise of snow, predicted but thus far yet to fall.

A miserable time of thick cardigans and coats and

waterproofs and the dreary daily trudge, fighting the elements and the crowds to get to the Tube.

The Closed sign was on the door, clearly visible to anyone with twenty-twenty vision.

She pulled open the door, mouth half open to state the obvious, hand raised to indicate the sign on the door, and then it fell back.

Startled eyes travelled up and up and up to a face that was so absolutely perfect in its olive-toned symmetry that her mouth fell open and for a few seconds her head went completely blank.

Leandro stared back at the redhead in front of him in silence.

So this was the woman whose name had been mentioned with increasing regularity for the past year. Not quite what he had been expecting although, to be fair, he hadn't had any clear image of anyone in his head.

'Can I help you?' She pointed to the sign that he had seen and ignored. 'I was just about to head off…perhaps whatever you want could wait until tomorrow morning? I'm here most days by eight.'

He detected a thread of annoyance in her voice and conceded that she had every reason to be annoyed but needs must. He didn't want to be here any more than she wanted him here. 'I'd rather not,' he drawled.

'You'd *rather not*?'

'I'd rather not.' He tempered his bluntness with something of a smile, although it was damned difficult because this was no smiling situation. Not by a long shot. He raked his fingers through his hair, glanced away with a frown and then added, carefully, eyes pinned to her face, 'Believe me, I don't make a habit of showing up unannounced anywhere…but I assure you, this is important and it's urgent I talk to you.'

He watched carefully as she digested what he'd said. She had a remarkably transparent face. A useful asset in a wedding-dress designer, he imagined, programmed as he was from a young age to be cynical. A bride-to-be would want an emotional and empathetic listening ear at an emotional and exciting time. All those happy-ever-after endings in sight…all those fairy tales about to turn a corner and come true…what better than someone pinning and sewing with an encouraging smile and appealing, puppy-dog eyes?

Appealing puppy-dog eyes the colour of green glass washed up on a beach?

Everything about the woman oozed just the sort of softness that would encourage a bride to open up and share her secrets.

Leandro, who had received a three-sentence message from Julie two days previously, was in no doubt that, whatever was going on, the small redhead in front of him would have the explanation and he wasn't leaving until he got it.

Where the heck was his fiancée?

He'd thought he and Julie had a pretty good understanding of the situation. No blurred lines or room for error. But he'd been wrong.

I'm so sorry but I can't go through with the wedding, Leandro. It's not you. It's me.

What the hell did *that* mean?

Nor had she graced her father with anything more

illuminating and that in itself had infuriated Leandro, because the old guy deserved better.

Were there dots waiting to be joined? Had he missed the link somehow? He never missed links and he was excellent when it came to joining dots so what was going on here?

'You're interested in commissioning a dress... Mr...?'

'I'm interested in the whereabouts of someone who's recently commissioned a dress from you, Miss Drew,' he said quietly.

'Who *are* you?' Celia's heart was thudding. She wasn't used to the impact of a guy on her like this and she didn't like it. It made her feel exposed, because she had spent so long distancing herself from involvement with the opposite sex, happy to bide her time until the right guy came along. She'd been hurt once and she could still remember how that had felt, could remember it enough to know that if she held back, if no one could really get to her, then she would never be hurt again.

She hadn't budged from where she was standing, blocking entry to the shop.

The man, whoever he was, commanded her full attention, pinning her to the spot. An aura of dark danger emanated from him.

She wasn't used to this sort of powerful, self-assured and masculine presence.

'Let me in, Miss Drew. Please.'

'Sorry, but no.'

'I really need to talk to you and it's a conversation that can't be conducted on a pavement.'

'In that case, you can always make an appointment

like everyone else. Like I said, I'm here from eight most mornings.'

'I need to talk to you about Julie. My name is Leandro. I'm her fiancé. Or...' he smiled wryly '...should I say *ex*-fiancé? I seem to be caught in an evolving situation.'

She was staring at him, lips pursed, arms folded, welcome mat fully retracted.

In every respect, she was as far removed from the women he was accustomed to as chalk was from cheese. Her clothes were comfy, shapeless. A pair of loose trousers, an extremely baggy shirt, an even baggier cardigan and a tape measure around her neck, which he assumed she had forgotten about in her haste to get the door.

Everything seemed to be in various shades of grey and black, but she was rescued from inevitable plainness by the amazing vibrancy of her copper-coloured hair, the way it rioted around her heart-shaped face in rebellious disarray, and crystal-clear green eyes that were framed by sooty dark gold lashes. And, of course, freckles. A lot of them.

'*You're* Leandro...'

'Will you let me in, Miss Drew? It *is* Miss, isn't it? Julie never clarified so feel free to correct me if I've jumped to conclusions?'

'Yes, I'm *Ms* Drew, Celia, and okay, I guess you'd better come in.'

'I appreciate that,' he told her. 'It's dark. You're in the process of locking up to go home. You don't know who the heck might be knocking on your door, so thank you for trusting me. Like I said, I wouldn't have descended on your doorstep if it wasn't important.'

Her breath hitched as he swept past her, bringing in the cold air with him.

Under the glare of the overhead lights, she now had an up-close-and-personal view of just how spectacular the guy was.

He towered over her, at least six-three to her five-four, and his hair was raven black and cut short, which emphasised the harsh contours of his face with its sensual mouth, straight nose and slashing cheekbones.

'You'd better come upstairs.' He still made her heart skitter inside her and her nerves were all over the place, but something about him, something about the sincerity of his words, made her realise that the guy was to be trusted.

And what did she imagine he was going to do anyway? She was as safe as houses around a guy like him. Just one glance at his elegant, beautiful fiancée and any fool would be able to work out that he was a man who liked tall and elegant. Not petite and far too sensible.

She spun round on her heel and headed up, acutely conscious of him behind her, as stealthy as a jungle cat.

This was not what she'd been expecting.

When she'd eventually shown Julie the door two days previously, she had been too shell-shocked to ask detailed questions about what plans she and Dan had made. The Dan connection had been enough to blow all those obvious questions out of the water. She had just gaped in silence like a stranded goldfish as Julie, liberated from having to keep everything under wraps, had opened up with enthusiasm about the thrilling journey of her wonderful affair.

Celia had assumed that her brother was diplomatically ducking the worst of the fallout for as long as he could

She'd, however, taken it as a given that Julie would have been more forthcoming with the guy she'd jilted, yet here he was now, seeking answers to questions.

Of course, he would know about her own personal connection to the messy, sorry saga. Did he intend to lay the blame at her door? Somehow? None of it was her fault but she knew that, in times of extreme stress, it was normal to divert all blame onto the shoulders of someone else. The alternative would be for him to look inwards and try and question his own role in what had happened and, judging from what she'd seen so far, this guy didn't seem to be the sort who spent too much time soul-searching.

'I have tea or coffee,' she said, reluctantly turning to face him and struck once again by the sheer beauty of his perfectly arranged features. He dwarfed the tiny kitchen and seemed to suck the oxygen out of the air so that she felt breathless and addled.

'Coffee. Black. Shall we do away with the chit-chat? What exactly did Julie say to you?'

'Say?'

Leandro raised his eyebrows in wry questioning, utterly relaxed in the chair he had taken. 'The one name that's crossed my ex-fiancée's lips for the past few months has been yours. It seems that she's built up some kind of bond with you, which in turn leads me to conclude that you know where she is, and I would very much like to find that out.'

No beating about the bush. Celia could feel the prized self-control she had learned to exercise begin to slip away, buffeted by the sheer force of his personality.

Did he think he could breeze in here and prise information out of her? Information his fiancée, for reasons

Celia might not be able to fathom or condone, had seen fit to withhold from him?

She fiddled with her hair, twirled the ends between her fingers. 'Why would I tell you if I knew where she was?' she eventually asked. 'If Julie hasn't told you where she's going, then perhaps it's because she doesn't want you to know, and if she doesn't want you to know, then it's not up to me to go against her wishes.'

But how could she understand the questions he must want to ask, questions only Julie could answer, which was why he had shown up here on her doorstep? Hadn't she spent days and weeks analysing her own break-up? Even though she and Martin had talked about it, even though she'd known why it had ended? It was basic human nature. Leandro had been about to walk up the aisle only to find that the woman he was in love with had decided to do a runner with another man. It was heartbreaking, really.

He wanted answers and, because Julie had failed to provide them, he had come to Celia seeking some sort of balm for his aching soul.

Granted, as they stared at one another, his dark, saturnine face coolly remote and watchful, as she felt a shiver of something steal through her body like quicksilver, she couldn't help but think that he didn't look at all like a guy with an aching soul.

Still…

She sighed, prepared to give him the benefit of the doubt.

'I actually don't have the answers to your questions,' she confessed. 'I wish I had, but no. I have no idea where Julie and my brother have gone. Not a clue.'

Leandro stilled, sat forward and looked at her with laser-sharp concentration.

'Your brother? What does *your brother* have to do with this…?'

CHAPTER TWO

LEANDRO WATCHED THE slow burn of colour invade her cheeks. She might have thought that he was in the dark about Julie's whereabouts, but it was obvious that, whatever she'd been thinking, it hadn't occurred to her that his ex-fiancée might have vanished withholding the most important piece of information in the whole, sorry scenario.

Another man.

Not even on the very edges of his consciousness had another man featured in Julie's disappearance. When it came to the opposite sex, she had had her fill of men, or so she had assured him on countless occasions. Wasn't that why their arranged marriage had seemed such a good idea at the time? No unrealistic dreams to be shattered. Just cool, practical reasoning to create a solution for a problem that had arisen out of the blue with her father, like the sudden onset of a storm rolling in from distant horizons, bringing with it the promise of catastrophe.

And for him? What would he be sacrificing by a marriage of convenience? Dreams of everlasting love with a good woman? Starry-eyed, romantic notions of fairytale happiness? No. Far from it.

Leandro had learned from a young age that love was a weakness to be avoided at all costs. Lust and hot sex? Yes. Those were things he could control, but love? No. Love was pain and loss and vulnerability, and he had seen from a young age what that side of the happy-ever-after coin was all about.

He didn't remember his mother, because she had walked out when he'd been a toddler. One minute there, the next minute not. She'd dumped his dad for the glitter of jangling gold coins in a rich man's pocket. He knew that she'd been a beautiful woman, because his father had hung onto all the pictures that he'd taken of her that used to sit on tables and shelves until, at the age of eight, Leandro had methodically gathered them all up and dumped them in the bin. Had his father rescued them? He would never know because they'd never again reappeared on the tables and shelves. Perhaps he'd known that if he'd ever brought them out again, Leandro would have done the same thing all over again, because what child needed to be reminded that he'd been abandoned by his own mother?

His father had never managed to patch up what had been left of his broken heart. In later years, he had told Leandro about the dreams he and Isabella Diaz had had and that, in the end, he just hadn't been rich enough for her. He'd been clever and handsome, but a clever and handsome workman on a ranch hadn't stood a chance against a rich, young guy who had come to visit and had ended up leaving with his pretty young wife.

By the time Leandro was old enough to understand the ways of the world, he had learnt a valuable lesson. His father had shown him the things he wanted to get out of life—financial security and complete control of his destiny—and the way to get those was to avoid the pitfalls of handing your heart over to anyone.

He and Julie had had an understanding and he'd liked the arrangement they'd had.

But now, a man had entered the equation and he intended to find out just how that had come about.

There wasn't a shred of gullibility in him and, for the first time, he looked around, really taking in his surroundings.

What did he see here? A talented seamstress working hard to make a decent living. One who had suddenly found herself working on a wedding dress for a confiding client with a lineage as long as your arm and a family pile in Northumberland.

Was it coincidence that her brother had appeared from nowhere?

That Julie, in the space of a few days…or weeks… was suddenly smitten enough to disappear with a guy she barely knew?

Was money at the root of it all?

Suspicion was so much a part and parcel of Leandro's DNA that that was the very first route he felt he needed to explore, because he was having a hard time marrying the image of his lovely but ice-cool fiancée caught in the throes of illicit passion with a virtual stranger. It made it all the more impossible to believe that this improbable whirlwind fling was anything other than a clever con-man working on a vulnerable woman.

'So…' He sat forward now and pushed the mug of coffee to the side with one finger so that he could rest his arms on the table, narrowing the space between them. 'I'm intrigued. Where does your brother fit into all of this?'

'What did Julie tell you?'

'I've never been much of a fan of anyone who answers a question with a question,' he murmured drily, his dark eyes watchful and speculative. 'And I don't want to waste time playing games. I'm guessing that Julie and your brother have embarked on some kind of affair?'

'I'm sorry.'

Leandro waved that aside, his mind galloping towards an explanation. 'When? When did it all start?'

'I honestly don't know.'

'Sure about that?'

'What do you mean?'

'Tell me about your brother.' Leandro abruptly pulled back from voicing his suspicions. He wanted a clearer picture, and it was beginning to seem that the brief question-and-answer session he had had in mind wasn't going to go down the predicted route.

But attack wasn't usually the best way to elicit information. Everyone deserved a fair hearing even though, in true Hansel and Gretel style, the trail of crumbs seemed to be heading in a very predictable direction, directly to the gingerbread house.

He tilted his head to one side and watched as she softened, and half smiled. An indulgent, loving sister who seemed to be in awe and admiration of an older brother who, from the sounds of it, was the sort of free spirit Leandro, personally, really didn't get.

Momentarily distracted, he halted her in mid flow and said, with genuine curiosity, 'You admire the fact that he doesn't own anything even though he's...what? Pushing thirty?'

Celia smiled. 'He's a free spirit.'

'And what's there to admire about that?' The *free*

spirit, it appeared, used a motorbike as his primary mode
of transport and lived, by choice, in rented accommo-
dation because the harsh realities of getting a mortgage
represented just too much of a headache for someone
who refused to be ruled by all the normal things that
most people set their compass by.

'Haven't you ever wanted to be free of…a nine-to-
five job?'

'I don't actually have a nine-to-five job.'

'No,' Celia mused thoughtfully. 'You're a workaholic.'

'Is that what Julie told you?'

Celia flushed. 'She wasn't being critical,' she inserted
quickly. 'She was just being honest.'

'But moving back to the subject of your brother…'
He absently wondered what it was about the woman that
threw him. Was it because there was something refreshing about her? Something that made him think that she
was being utterly honest in her responses even though so
much of him was primed never to take what anyone said
at face value, especially in circumstances such as this?

If her brother had made a play for Julie because of the
family fortune he believed she had, then was his sister
complicit in any way?

For once, he hesitated to pursue cold, hard suspicions.
That said, he'd never shied away from anything in his
life before and he wasn't about to start now.

His dark eyes didn't leave her face.

'What I'm thinking is that all of this has happened
very, very suddenly. Along comes your fun-loving
brother with his disdain for all things material, and
in a matter of seconds he's swept my aristocratic fiancée off her feet and whisked her away to who
knows where. Is it just me or does that feel a little…

suspicious? Maybe I'm being over-cynical, but there's a lot of truth in the saying that money makes the world go round...even to a fun-loving free spirit who doesn't care about the cost of a loaf of bread...'

His accusations filled the space between them, and Leandro watched as she paled, absorbing what he was saying and probably reading between the lines to what he wasn't.

'How dare you?'

'I had no idea Julie was involved with someone else.'

'My brother would never...*never*...get involved with someone for the wrong reasons!'

'You're very trusting when it comes to human nature. From experience, I've found it wiser to steer clear of blindly believing what I'm told.' He sat forward, his expression suddenly urgent. 'It's important that I find Julie, Miss Drew.'

'Celia...' Her voice was distracted, her expression tense; she was dismayed by the accusations that were rolling around in her head.

But wasn't there a part of her that could understand, not only why he had shown up here, but why he had jumped to the conclusions that he had?

He'd accused her of being trusting, but wasn't she just the opposite? She'd been burnt once and no amount of cool-headed reasoning about the narrow escape she'd had had been able to stop her from building walls around herself when it came to men.

The last thing she was was *trusting* and yet she knew that, underneath her own heartbreak, she still believed in love. It would never have occurred to her that something as tawdry as money could ever influence someone's behaviour, and certainly not Dan's. But the wealthy were often objects of pursuit, so why wouldn't he immediately jump to the conclusion that a guy who was a self-confessed free spirit might find the temptation of a rich and beautiful woman irresistible? He was wrong about her brother…but that didn't mean he might not have grounds for suspicion, did it? Especially if he was suspicious by nature.

She wondered what those experiences were that had made this man so cynical. People were shaped by what life threw at them, and as their eyes met and tangled she felt a sharp stab of curiosity that was momentarily powerful enough to sweep away the raw anger at his accusations.

There was no place for curiosity, though. This was a straightforward situation, insofar as she had no idea where Julie and her brother had gone. When she glanced at her watch, it was to find that more time had gone by than she'd expected.

'I'm very sorry about what's happened… Mr…'

'Leandro.'

'Yes, well, I'm sorry that Julie has run off with my brother. I did try to talk her out of it, tried to tell her that it was just a case of pre-wedding nerves. But she'd made her mind up. I know that's probably not what you want to hear, but…' She hesitated but then figured that if he felt free to say exactly what was on his mind, whether it was offensive or not, then why shouldn't she? 'People fall in love and it might just be the case that Julie and Dan have fallen in love, in which case what's the point in trying to find them? What will you hope to gain? And if you're still keen to track them down…' she shrugged, hardly believing that the cool, controlled man staring at her with such brooding intensity could be capable of the sort of wild passion that would propel him to hunt down a woman who had jilted him '…then surely you can just hire someone?'

Leandro looked at her in silence for a few seconds, then he stood up and moved towards the door.

'It would seem that that's the last remaining option,' he murmured and then he smiled and, just for a moment, Celia felt the breath whoosh out of her because she had a glimpse of the sort of devastating charm that could knock a person off her feet. 'And just for the record…' his voice was dry and amused '…this isn't about love. This is much bigger and more important than that. My apologies for showing up on your doorstep, Celia. I'll see myself out.'

Which was the end of that, so why, she wondered, as she waited to hear the shop door slam before treading quietly downstairs, did she feel a certain disappointment? Was it because, for reasons she couldn't explain, he'd sparked an interest in her even though that interest was one hundred per cent inappropriate? Even though he was just the sort of guy she personally didn't like? Work-oriented, tough and way too arrogant and self-assured?

It was a relief she wouldn't be seeing him again. She didn't need to start questioning the choices she had made. She was perfectly content to keep her distance until the right guy came along. She was older and wiser now.

Leandro pulled to kerb, killed the engine of his Range Rover and, for a few seconds, he reclined in the seat, eyes narrowed on the bank of terraced houses on the opposite side of the narrow street. His car was wedged between a skip and an e-scooter that appeared to have been abandoned in haste, and it occurred to him that, in his rapid climb up the greasy pole of success, he had almost forgotten what the world on the other side of the tracks looked like.

A thin fall of snow had begun hours earlier and was trying hard to gather pace.

Finding out where Celia lived had been a piece of cake. He could have used one of his people to find out, but that felt like a distasteful invasion of privacy. Instead, he had gone to the shop and one of her assistants had been more than happy to provide the information. And why not? His ex-fiancée had been one of their biggest clients. Why would they withhold information?

That had been a day and a half ago.

He could have bypassed Celia and just headed up to Scotland himself, but with a man involved…

Things had become complicated, far more complicated than Leandro could ever have predicted when he and Julie had embarked on their joint plan to save her father from penury while salvaging his pride in the process.

He owed Charles more than money could buy and this had been his way of repaying the debt to the best of his ability.

And Julie, who had left her first marriage and had resolved never to go there again, had seen the sense of their arrangement.

But love?

Was that what had happened?

Leandro found it incomprehensible. What was the point of a learning curve if you didn't learn from it? Julie had been embittered by her first awful marriage. Why would she want to test the waters again when it came to her emotions?

Leandro was proud of his resolute stance when it came to harnessing all emotion. He could value the love he had for his father, mingled as it was with pity for the chances he had never taken because he had allowed the past to dictate his future. He could appreciate the depth of affection he had for Charles, who had been instrumental in helping him in his education. But he couldn't begin to understand, particularly after a bruising experience at the hands of someone else, why anyone would want to voluntarily go there again.

He, thankfully, had been smart enough to make sure he'd protected himself from the folly of losing his head to any woman and he was genuinely puzzled as to Julie's abrupt departure from lessons learnt.

Celia's enthusiastic and admiring descriptions of her brother as someone who scorned the trappings of routine and preferred the call of adventure had got every pore in Leandro's body bristling with justified scepticism, and the very view of this row of terraced houses staring at him now should have consolidated the suspicion that here were a likely pair of con artists, but no.

Something about Celia, something about the honesty in those amazing green eyes, had opened a door to the notion that she might just be right.

Julie might well and truly have fallen in love. Or else, *thought* she had fallen in love.

Which would scupper all their well-made plans to help her father, to rescue him from the financial bind now wrapped around him like tentacles.

But that was not why he was here, important though

it was to at least try and find out what exactly was going on and find a way to a solution by hook or by crook.

He was here…because fate had decided to lend a very unhelpful hand.

With a sigh, Leandro slid out of the car and felt the sting of bitter cold working its way through his jeans and jumper and cashmere coat.

The house where she lived was neat, the tiny front garden tidy. They all were. There were lights on inside and he wondered what he might have done had she not been in. Driven a couple of blocks and then returned, he presumed, but in this weather it was a relief that he wouldn't have to, and he banged on the knocker, two raps, and waited.

From nowhere, he had a vivid image in his head of her—those expressive green eyes, the freckles, the riot of red hair, unrestrained, no pretence at elegance. He closed his eyes for a few seconds, feeling the stir of something inside him he didn't want to identify.

He was hardly starved of sex. He had had one very discreet and short-lived relationship on a three-month stint in New York while he and Julie had been engaged, for theirs was to be a respectful but sexless union, and sensible rules had been put in place for obvious reasons.

But all of a sudden, his libido had kicked into gear and, just as fast, Leandro put the brakes on that. With all inappropriate thoughts swiftly uprooted at source, he lounged against the doorframe and waited.

It was a little after six. Snow was falling outside and Celia, barricaded in her cocoon of warmth, was guiltily relieved that she wasn't going anywhere, even though she should have been, really, because it was Saturday night and she was young, free and single.

Plus, after that nerve-wracking encounter with Leandro, she had started thinking that she had to do something, had to venture into the world of dating, of finding someone.

The fact that he had managed to get under her skin the way he had had been a bit of a wake-up call.

If a guy like him, someone who did not meet any of the internal checks she had in place when it came to the opposite sex, could *get to her*, then something had to be done.

Very soon.

When the weather improved, she had resolved, gently turning down the offer of an evening out with the girls she worked with.

Who wanted to tramp through the snow to get to a crowded bar in Soho for drinks?

At least for this one evening, she had been very happy to stay in. So the sharp peal of her doorbell was annoying and, while she contemplated ignoring it, she stuck on her bedroom slippers and padded out to get it.

She was programmed never to ignore someone at the front door. When you spent all your formative years in the countryside where everyone knew everyone else, you never let your doorbell ring without answering it, and old habits died hard.

The last person Celia expected to find standing outside was Leandro Diaz and as she looked up and up and up, until their eyes met, she felt the breath leave her in a rush, felt the world narrow down to just him, tall, dark and stupidly handsome.

He was wearing black jeans and a black jumper, visible under the open lapels of a tan cashmere coat, and had a black scarf round his neck. He looked ridiculously elegant and very, very expensive and all those things flashed through her mind before the more prosaic thought... *What on earth was he doing on her doorstep?*

'What are you doing here?'

'I've done it again, haven't I?' Leandro said apologetically. 'Shown up unannounced on your doorstep. My apologies. I would have telephoned to warn you of my arrival, but I had a vague suspicion that you might have taken steps to avoid seeing me and I really had no choice but to see you.'

'You *had* to see me?' Celia belatedly remembered that he had accused her and her brother of being gold diggers and, now that the shock was wearing off, she resuscitated the anger she had felt at the insult. 'And you're damn right I would have taken steps to avoid you! In case you've forgotten, you accused Dan of targeting Julie for her money. You implied that I might have had a hand in it!' She remained firmly planted by the half-opened door, barring entry. She had every right to be furious at him showing up and invading her personal space *again*, but instead she felt a heat coursing through her that had nothing to do with anger. The same intense physical awareness that had gripped her two days ago was squeezing tightly now again.

Was it because it was such a novel sensation? She had cared deeply for Martin but, even in the height of their teenage romance, she had not felt anything like this, had not been *aware* of him as a living, breathing, *sexy* male...not like this.

Lack of experience, she told herself urgently. She glared at him with barely disguised hostility, but she had to force herself not to let her disobedient eyes rove down the length of his body.

'How did you find me, anyway?' she demanded.

'Celia, I simply went to your shop and asked one of your assistants. Considering my relationship with Julie, she didn't think that dispensing the information was beyond the pale, and why should she?

'Please let me in and I'll answer whatever questions you have.' Leandro looked briefly around him. 'It's freezing out here.' He scanned her, taking in the bedroom slippers, the light jogging bottoms, the baggy cotton jumper, clothes that weren't designed for long conversations conducted outside in freezing conditions.

'What more do we have to say to one another?'

'I've located Julie and your brother.'

'You've *found them*?' Had he come, the bearer of bad tidings? Had they been in an accident? He had the information he had come to her for, he'd managed to find out where they were, so why was he here now if it wasn't to deliver news she didn't want to hear? News that could only be imparted face to face? That could only herald bad news. It was on a par with the phone that rang in the early hours of the morning. Celia fell back, allowing him to sweep past her. The small hallway seemed to shrink to the size of a matchbox as he turned to face her.

'Are they okay?' she asked tersely. 'Has there been some sort of terrible accident? Are they...?' Her mouth trembled and she blinked, while worst-case scenarios had a field day in her head.

'Alive and well,' Leandro interrupted hurriedly to prevent what looked like a descent into just the sort of emotionalism that was alien to him and unwelcome. 'To the best of my knowledge. The last purchase made was the

day before yesterday and it's safe to say that they're e⟨
route to my house in Scotland.' He looked at her waril⟨
and she shot him a narrow-eyed, baleful and accusator⟨
look from under her lashes.

'In which case, why scare the living daylights ou⟨
of me?'

'Come again?'

'If you've managed to find them both and they're fin⟨
and dandy, then why come here and lead me to believ⟨
that there was something wrong?'

'Did I do that?'

'I suppose I should offer you tea or coffee now tha⟨
you're here.' She propelled herself towards the kitchen
acutely aware of the smallness of the house and annoye⟨
with herself for wondering what he might be thinkin⟨
of his surroundings.

Following in her wake, Leandro vaguely noted wha⟨
was around him. It was a small house painted in uni⟨
formly bland colours but the prints on the walls wer⟨
quirky covers of old Parisian fashion magazines, nicel⟨
framed, and as he glanced to one side he saw throug⟨
the semi-opened door a wooden mannequin being use⟨
as a frame for a half-finished wedding dress and an ease⟨
on which a large sheet of paper was clipped—presum⟨
ably a picture of what the dress in progress was destine⟨
to look like.

He paused, pushed open the door and stepped inside
curiosity taking him towards the easel to look at th⟨
drawing, and he turned around when she angrily aske⟨
him what he thought he was doing and how *dared h⟨*
make himself at home in her house.

'You're very talented,' he commented, ignoring th⟨

heightened colour in her cheeks and the spitting fire in her eyes and the hands placed squarely on her hips.

'You can't just come in here and nose around!'

She began moving towards the easel but he beat her to it to stand in front of the accomplished drawing, one hand resting on the paper so that she couldn't flip it away.

'Is this one of your commissions?'

Celia wanted the ground to open and swallow her up. He was being complimentary, but she was too aware of him, too sensitive to his overpowering personality and too conscious of the fact that he wasn't *a friend paying her a visit* to appreciate the compliment. She could barely think straight as she stared up at him. His eyes were so dark and so deep that she had to fight a drowning sensation. Somewhere at the back of her mind, she knew that he was the sort of guy to find this extreme reaction amusing and she made an effort to put things in perspective.

'Yes,' she said tightly.

'Did you think up the design?'

'Yes.' She lowered her eyes and was aware of her laboured breathing. Her heart was beating like a sledgehammer and she folded her arms and took a step back. 'Edith wanted something a little more severe, but I managed to persuade her otherwise. She didn't have the figure for the style she was after and as soon as she saw what I had in mind, she was thrilled.' She shot him a look from under her lashes, expecting boredom and finding interest.

'I know Julie loved what you did.'

'Even though she won't be wearing it,' Celia muttered, brought back to reality after that short breathless moment when time seemed to have done weird things as he'd gazed down at her. 'Perhaps we could continue this conversation in the kitchen... Mr...er... Leandro. You can tell me what you're doing here and then you can be on your way.'

'Plans for the evening?' Leandro asked conversationally as she spun round on her heel and began heading out of the room, making sure, he noted, to firmly shut the door to her study behind her.

Celia was very glad he couldn't see her face as she shrugged, her back to him, and casually told him that it had been a long week.

'So...'

'Coffee would be good. Black. No sugar. I told Julie's father about the development with your brother. He'd been as much in the dark about what was happening as I was when I showed up at your shop two days ago. I thought it was only fair that he not cling to any unrealistic hopes about last-minute nerves. The last thing I wanted was for him to be under any illusions that Julie might materialise out of thin air just in the nick of time.'

Celia looked at him in silence, her head tilted thoughtfully to one side.

'You love him, don't you?'

'Love isn't a word that exists in my vocabulary.' Leandro flushed darkly and looked away. 'But yes, I happen to be very fond of him.'

'What did he say?' *Why was love a word that didn't exist in his vocabulary?*

'That's the problem.' Leandro waited until there was a mug of coffee in front of him, waited until she was sitting opposite him, waited until the silence started to become borderline oppressive. She didn't try and hurry him into an explanation, for which he was grateful because he was still processing the situation himself. 'Yesterday I received a call that Charles has been admitted to hospital with a stroke.'

He looked away. Celia saw the tic beating in his tightly clenched jaw and the rigid stillness of his posture and she reached out to place her hand gently on his arm.

'It's not your fault. I mean, for telling him.'

Their eyes met as he firmly pulled his arm out of reach.

'I don't believe I said anything about it being my fault, did I?' But he rose to his feet to restlessly pace the kitchen before sitting back down.

'No, you didn't,' Celia murmured.

'I've come because I need to tell Julie what's happening, and I need to try and persuade her to revise whatever plans she's making with your brother. Or at least to work with me at finding a place where she can temper the truth for the sake of her father's health. I… I judge that it would be a more successful trip if you were there with me to likewise talk to your brother.'

'You want me to…'

'Come to Scotland with me. It would be a matter of a night or two, at the very most.'

'No!'

'I would make it worth your while financially.'

'Do you honestly think that you can get whatever you want by throwing money around?'

Leandro shot her a thin smile. 'You'd be shocked at how often it works.'

'Absolutely not!' She fidgeted in the chair, stood up, walked towards the kitchen window to peer out at the tiny darkened back patio overlooked by a bank of houses just beyond the border of her fence. When she swung back round to face him, it was to find his eyes pinned to her with a mixture of strange hesitancy and reluctant resignation.

'There's more to it than that,' he said quietly. 'Of course, it's vitally important that Julie know about her father's state of health, vitally important that he doesn't have any continued stress that might exacerbate his situation…and perhaps you'll change your mind about Scotland when I tell you what my marriage to Julie was really all about…'

CHAPTER THREE

LEANDRO GRIMACED. CONFIDING was not in his nature. In fact, it was so much *not* in his nature that he was temporarily at a loss as to where to begin.

Her eyes were curious, her mouth parted and there was a puzzled expectancy in her expression. Of course there was. She was an incurable romantic. It shone in everything she said and in her sympathetic misconception that he was somehow broken-hearted, having been dumped by his ex.

On every level, she was unknown territory. Leandro had always made sure to steer clear of women with romantic dreams because he knew that he was incapable of fulfilling them. The thought of becoming entangled with someone who wanted more than he could give brought him out in a cold sweat. A woman in search of love had no place in his life. His speciality was an ability to shower lavish gifts and open doors to experiences only afforded to the uber rich.

But she deserved to have the full story because he needed her co-operation and it was unfair to keep her in the dark, that being the case.

'You think that Julie and I are...in love...'

'I don't know. I did, to start with, but I'm beginning

to think that maybe that wasn't the case. But if that's so, then why would you get married in the first place?' She frowned. 'I know that you two go back a long way...'

Leandro could see her trying to work out how anyone could make a leap from friendship to marriage without the middleman of *Love* being at the party.

Looking at her now, Leandro suddenly felt a hundred years old. There had been no gullible staging posts in his life. He had made the leap from boy to man at a young age. Too young? He'd never asked himself that question. He'd grown up associating love with pain and loss. He'd never hankered for kids because he knew his limitations and respected them. Love wasn't for him and if you couldn't give love then surely any child would be born immediately disadvantaged?

'Many would agree that a solid friendship is the best basis for a successful union,' he now said, curtly. 'The statistics say it all. Most marriages end in divorce once the shine wears off and reality begins to bite. People walk up the aisle with stars in their eyes but give it a few years and the stars get snuffed out and the next joint venture out is to the divorce courts.'

'That's an awful interpretation of marriage!'

'We'll have to agree to disagree on that one. The point I'm making is that Julie and I had...an understanding. I'm assuming you know about her first marriage?'

'Yes, she mentioned that it wasn't a happy one.'

'We made a joint decision to marry for practical reasons.'

'Children?' Celia asked faintly.

'No.' Leandro paused and marvelled that spelling out the blunt facts behind their marriage, which he had not once questioned to himself, now felt like an act of positive cruelty. Impatient with himself, he shook his head and frowned. 'What we were going to have would have been, essentially, an open marriage.'

'An *open marriage…*'

'There's no need to sound so shocked,' Leandro said irritably.

'But I *am* shocked,' Celia said simply. 'And I don't understand…'

'Julie found out several months ago that her father had, basically, gone bankrupt. She made the discovery quite by accident. Happened to be at home at their estate in Northumberland when her father's bank manager unexpectedly decided to pay a visit. Charles was out but Julie managed to glean sufficient information to form a rough idea of what was going on. Mountains of debt… and a supply chain to his outlets that had ground to a halt because suppliers were owed money.' Leandro sighed and raked his fingers through his hair. 'I could go into the details of when what happened and what the knock-on effects were, but, to sum it up, he was in deep financial trouble with creditors banging on the door and threats of the family estate having to be dismantled to pay debts.'

'How awful,' Celia said softly. 'Where do *you* fit in, if you don't mind me asking?'

'I…' Leandro paused. So much of his life was accessible and out there on the World Wide Web, the bare bones of the road he had travelled to get from A to B, but this? No, this was a part of him that had always been firmly barricaded behind No Trespass signs. His thoughts and feelings about the life he'd led and the debts he owed.

'Yes?' Celia prompted. He didn't like talking about himself. He was intensely private and she could tell that parting with whatever information he thought she was owed was going to be difficult. She got that. In a way. She had never discussed the business of her break-up with Martin with anyone. She had smiled and offered anodyne explanations, but she had largely kept her feelings private.

The fact that he felt obliged to open up with her, more than anything else, showed her just how much he wanted her to go to Scotland with him because Dan was there and suddenly, because of that, she had become part of the equation.

'When I said that Julie and I go back a long way, I should clarify by adding that our fathers…grew up together in a manner of speaking…'

'What does that mean? In a manner of speaking?' She felt as though she were being asked to swim through a river of treacle to get to what he was trying to say. 'You grew up…in…'

'Argentina.' He sighed, fidgeted and then muttered, lowering his eyes, 'I don't make a habit of doing this.'

'Confiding?'

'All that touchy-feely stuff normally has no place in my life…but in this instance…'

Just for a split second, there was something so incredibly *human* about him that Celia was shaken.

'My father worked on a ranch for a guy called Roberto Suarez. He was a dogsbody, but he became close to Roberto's son, Fernando, and then, along the way, with Julie's father, who had been to university in Oxford with Fernando and used to come over to the ranch for the long summer vacations. They were all roughly the same age. They hung out. My father was an excellent horseman and I suppose they bonded over that.'

He shrugged. When he was much younger, Leandro had been scathing about the quality of this so-called friendship, which he saw as one based on pity because how could the masters ever feel anything meaningful towards the servant? But time had proved him wrong and he had never really forgiven himself for that brief period of resentment. He'd been young.

'When my mother…was no longer around…they took my father under their wing, so to speak, and much later, as the years rolled on…well, my father had an accident. He was thrown from a horse and was bedridden for a time. When it transpired that he was not going to be able to work in the capacity he'd worked in previously, Fernando, who was now in charge of the ranch and with a family of his own, ensured that my father was secure in his house…'

'And where were you at the time? Did your mother… pass on?'

'My mother passed on or, should I say, continued her onward journey in life with a very rich house guest who had visited the ranch to talk business with Roberto Suarez. She never looked back. I was a toddler at the time.' Leandro moved on quickly from that statement of fact even though, as he looked at her, there was a gentleness in her gaze that almost made him want to break the rule-book and elaborate. He didn't, of course. Not his thing.

'When my father had his fall… Roberto gave him, as I said, permanent residence at the place he had always called home and Julie's father…took care of every aspect of my education. He paid for me to attend a private school in Buenos Aires. My father had been saving for years but the accident reduced his income. It was a mess, as I came to understand. Later, Charles took care of every single bill that came my way, when I gained a scholarship to study at Cambridge. During the holidays, he paid for my flights back to Argentina and when I wasn't there, I stayed at his country house, sometimes for weeks on end.'

'It's how you know Julie…'

'Correct. We met from a young age but became good friends once I began studying in England. I was at her wedding, as it happens. I was the first and only person she told about her father's financial situation. I would have been happy to have simply handed over the cash to sort out the mess but he's too damned proud for his own good…'

There was affection, indulgence and frustration in Leandro's voice.

'I get it,' Celia said softly. 'You and Julie decided on a marriage of convenience to bail her father out without him seeing it as an act of charity.'

'Charles fondly thinks that he's giving me the cachet of being absorbed into one of the country's oldest families. He doesn't know that I don't give a damn about any of that.'

'But what about love?'

Leandro shrugged. 'What does that have to do with anything? I'm repaying a debt, doing what any man of honour would do. There's no place in this scenario for misty-eyed daydreams.' He leant forward with a sense of urgency. 'This is why I've come here. Of course, I can't drag you off to Scotland with me. But I think that if for some reason Julie fancies herself in love with your brother, the two of us together might stand a better chance of at least trying to find a way to salvage the situation.'

'I barely know you,' Celia said, without thinking, and his eyebrows shot up in obvious amusement.

'What do you think I'm going to do?'

'Nothing!' But she was bright red. 'But…the thought of just taking off with a stranger…'

'I wouldn't ask if I didn't think it was important. Charles is in hospital with a stroke. Not only will Julie's disappearance be a major cause of worry for him, but he will now be having to come to terms with the fact that he might be looking at losing everything that has been in his family for centuries. Either that, or he, as you put it, accepts charity from me, which would cut to the quick for a man who is kind and generous but too proud for his own good.'

'Yes, I get that…'

'You're one hundred per cent safe with me,' Leandro said earnestly, and Celia felt as though, somehow, he had a direct hotline to her thoughts and was having a private laugh at her unfounded misgivings. Not that she wasn't well aware that her misgivings were unfounded, but she had led a sheltered life where impulse had always taken a back seat to common sense and it was hard not to fall back into that mindset even though she could see where he was coming from.

Dan had been the impulsive one. He had been the one who lived outside the box, always willing to take risks and explore options.

Celia, on the other hand, several years younger and born after her mother had suffered two miscarriages, had been raised with kid gloves, protected by loving parents who no longer had the mindset to let her run wild and free, as they had her brother.

That was the only basis for her hesitancy, she feverishly told herself.

The fact that there was a treacherous sizzle of something disturbing in her responses to this man had nothing to do with anything.

'Celia…'

'I'm not suggesting anything…it's the way I am… I suppose I'm quite a careful person…' She fell into an erratic explanation for her reluctance before lapsing into silence, mesmerised by the dark eyes pinned to her face as he listened to her rambling.

'You're not my type.'

'I beg your pardon?'

'I'm not being at all…insulting when I tell you that you're perfectly safe with me because you're not my type.'

Celia was mortified. She had no idea how to respond to the bluntness of his statement, and the fact that he genuinely hadn't said it to offend her, because she could see the gentle sincerity in his eyes, somehow made his casual remark all the more offensive. Yes, she was short with freckles that had once been the bane of her life, but it still hurt to have her physical shortcomings pointed out by a guy with killer looks.

By *anybody* it would have been bad enough, but with someone as devastatingly good-looking as Leandro, it was positively humiliating.

'I realise I'm not a catwalk model,' Celia began stiffly, and Leandro grinned and waved his hand in airy dismissal.

'Nothing to do with looks,' he asserted. 'You're a romantic, Celia. Am I right? You don't really understand why I would want to get married for any reason other than love.'

'I see why you feel indebted to Julie's father,' Celia stammered, still red-faced but slightly mollified by what he had just said.

'But for you, marriage is something that goes hand in hand with love. For me? I have no such illusions, and when I say that you're not my type? My type of women aren't looking for permanence, at least not with me. Scotland will involve a helicopter flight and then two nights at my estate, where your brother and Julie are currently hiding out.'

'How do you know for sure?'

'Because Julie has a key and it's the only place they are likely to be heading. Trust me on this.' He looked around him and then said, as though the thought had only just occurred to him, 'I haven't asked, but I'm assuming that you would be able to take two days off from your commitments?'

'Work?'

'I was thinking of commitments of a more personal nature. Boyfriend? Girlfriend? No dogs at any rate…'

'I…no, I don't have a boyfriend,' Celia said stiffly. 'Not that that's any of your business.'

'It is if I think it's something that might influence your decision.'

'I would never go out with someone who's autocratic enough to disapprove of me being away for a couple of days.'

'With another man. Apologies, forgot we'd established that I don't fall into that category.' Leandro grinned but then said, seriously, thoughtfully, 'You'll be gone for two days at the very most and I would want to leave first thing in the morning. I can't force you to accept any financial compensation from me for the inconvenience, but every year I get several tickets for front seats at the London Fashion week. This year, it's a winter spectacular according to the blurb.'

'You like that kind of thing?' She knew that he was cleverly tempting her in a way that showed just how adept he was at getting what he wanted. Would she want to go to the show of the year for a dress designer? Just thinking about the chance made her feel faint.

'Oh, I try to avoid that event at all costs,' he murmured silkily, 'but I imagine the opportunities for you could be considerable. I could even put a word in about your…er…designs—from what I've seen, you've got a great deal of talent, which could end up going to waste without the right exposure.'

'Are you trying to bribe me?'

'I'm trying to persuade you.'

'Will you let me think about it?'

Leandro smiled slowly and sat back. 'Of course. The last thing I would want to do is force your hand. I'll call you…' he glanced at his Rolex then looked at her '…in precisely two hours.'

He would send a car for her and it would deliver her to an airfield, where he would meet her shortly after lunch.

Celia had squashed her apprehensions and agreed. She'd been swayed by her conscience. If someone were to suffer a misfortune because of her, then how would she ever be able to live with herself? If Julie's father, on the brink of financial collapse, were to suffer a fatal stroke through the sheer stress of the situation, then no amount of reasoning would have persuaded her to conclude that walking away from the situation had been okay.

She also wanted to find out what was going on with Dan. Leandro's assumption was that if anyone was going to be hurt, it would be Julie for having been targeted by someone who was after her money. Money she didn't have, as things stood. Was he still of the opinion that her brother was guilty of being a gold digger? The topic had been shelved. He'd decided that he needed her input and so had tactfully pulled back from anything contentious.

From Celia's point of view, what if her brother was the one at risk of being hurt if Julie had absconded because of a sudden attack of to-be-expected pre-wedding nerves? What if she had second thoughts and decided to get back together with Leandro? There were compelling reasons for her to do just that and where would that leave Dan? Footloose and easy-going he might be, but, like her, he was a solid traditionalist at heart. He'd been out with countless girls, but he'd never come close to asking any of them to marry him. What if *the one* turned out to be a mistake? She could remember her own hurt all those years ago when the blinkers had been pulled from her eyes and she wouldn't wish that on her brother.

And then the dangling carrot of that ticket to the fashion show…

He'd known just how to tempt. He'd been smart enough to drop all talk of money changing hands and instead had offered her something priceless. A golden opportunity to climb the career ladder and to see, first hand, what was happening in the fashion world, to have a possible audience for her calling cards.

They stood on opposite sides of the fence on pretty much everything. He was cold, tough and driven to make money and she could never like a guy like that, but she'd agreed, and even if the misgivings hadn't been completely put to bed she managed to put a lid on them as, the following afternoon, she was duly delivered to the airfield in gathering gloom.

The helicopter was a dark shadow against the velvety sky, as still and as ominous as a giant, watchful, waiting insect.

Snow had gathered apace overnight though not enough to settle. The chauffeur-driven car slowly pulled to a stop just as the door to the helicopter was flung open and there he was, a commanding silhouette, barely visible in the semi darkness.

She had her overnight bag with her, stuffed with thick clothing and a selection of thermals and her computer in its waterproof case. Now, as the driver fought the sleet and snow to open the car door, Celia took a couple of seconds to review her situation. The darkness and Leandro's commanding presence didn't do much for her nervous system, which suddenly went into sharp overdrive.

Her heart began a steady thump as she headed towards the helicopter, with the driver bringing up the rear with her cases.

If she'd ever secretly mourned the predictability of her day-to-day life, then no one could accuse her of not being wildly and scarily unpredictable now.

'Good. On time.'

The helicopter door slammed behind her. She'd never been in a helicopter before. Her life didn't include such adventures.

Just the two of them in a tiny little bubble with sleet and flurries of snow gusting around them.

She was shaking as he strapped her in but, even

though she was in a state of anxious meltdown, her eyes skittered to him. He was in black, from his shoes to his black polo neck and the bomber jacket. Like her, he was wearing a woolly hat, which he kept on. It was freezing in the helicopter.

'You're scared,' he threw over his shoulder, before opening the throttle so that the eerie silence turned into a cacophony of noise from the rotor blades. 'Don't be,' he shouted. 'You're in safe hands.'

But Celia felt far from safe as the helicopter spun into motion, accelerating sharply upwards and then buzzing at speed over a vista submerged in darkness.

She hadn't thought out what she was going to say to her brother when she saw him and she couldn't think about that now because she was too busy clinging to her seat, eyes tightly shut, breathing all over the place.

Through a haze of fear, she was aware of the helicopter shuddering like a tin can in a tornado, taking for ever, and then the descent, sharp and fast and over in the blink of an eye.

The silence as the rotor blades slowed was as deafening as the noise of them rotating had been.

She opened her eyes to find that Leandro had unbuckled and moved towards her and was grinning.

'Have you had your eyes closed for the entire flight?'

Busying herself with the safety belt, Celia glanced at him and blushed.

'It's my first time in a helicopter,' she muttered. 'How did I know that it wasn't going to crash?'

'Because I was piloting it,' Leandro said with supreme confidence. 'It's pretty bad here. Leave your bags. I'll take them. We can make a dash for the house. Snow here isn't like snow in London. Up here, I find the snow is generally a little less polite.'

'I know,' Celia puffed breathlessly, 'it's the same in Shropshire where I grew up. It comes and then never knows when it's time to leave.'

'Well put. Let me help you.' He cranked open the door to a white, barren and starkly beautiful wilderness.

For a few seconds, Celia looked out in awe at the splendid isolation. Pure darkness encased a wintry wonderland that shimmered under silent, falling snow. She forgot how cold she was, how anxious, how apprehensive. Dark shapes were visible, definitions of the landscape, but they could have landed on another planet.

The snow was thick and vicious, slicing through her clothes as he hoisted the various bags in one hand and propelled her through the darkness towards the looming vast shape of his country estate.

She could *sense* unease in his silence.

They hit the front door at pace. Massive front door. Behind them, the helicopter was a disappearing dark blot and behind that, Celia could only surmise, lay gates and trees and hedges and who knew what else. All the stuff of a country estate.

The actual manor house was so big as they stood in front of it that Celia could barely see where it began and ended through the densely falling snow.

It was shrouded in complete darkness and as they entered, Leandro banging on the lights, flooding the vast hall with light, bitterly cold.

He dumped all the bags and made straight through the hall, bypassing the grand staircases to the left and the right and towards the bowels of the house.

Celia followed. She had to half run because he was

moving at a brisk pace but, even so, she still managed to take in the opulent grandeur of the surroundings. Pale walls, marble, exquisite panelling and chandeliers and paintings that looked as though they cost a fortune.

There was an urgency to his purposeful stride that ratcheted up her nervousness and, sure enough, when he flung open a cupboard to fire up the central heating and turned to her, she knew what he was going to say before the words could leave his mouth.

'There's no one here.'

Their eyes tangled and a frisson swept through her body as the ramifications of that simple statement took root.

No Dan. No Julie. No safety net of other people around, however thorny the atmosphere might have been. Just her and Leandro rattling around in his sprawling mansion with a snowstorm raging outside. One night here? Two? Or more?

As he'd said, the snow in this part of the world, as it was in Shropshire, was not polite. It didn't fall for a couple of hours before packing it in. It outstayed its welcome.

What did that mean? What if they were stuck here?

Celia didn't want to dwell on worst-case scenarios but as she stood there, in front of him, they filled her head, swamping all rational thought until she could feel her pulses racing and her body prickling with panicked perspiration.

She was as safe as houses with him, whatever the circumstances. She wasn't his type and he wasn't hers.

But those killer looks...

She could breathe him in, the smell of cold mingled with woody aftershave. It made her feel unsteady on her feet and she automatically took a couple of steps back, breathing in deeply and gathering herself.

'If they're not here, then where are they? You said that they were going to be here!'

'It's obvious they started in this direction.' He began walking, throwing over his shoulder that she should follow him, that there was no harm in checking all the rooms. 'But…' he picked up where he had left off as he led the way up one of the grand staircases, which ascended to a huge galleried landing '…with the last leg to go and travelling by car, they must have decided not to brave the weather.'

'So what do we do now?' Celia dashed past him and then spun round so that she was ahead of him, looking down the staircase to the marble-floored landing and the richness of the paintings on the walls. From this vantage point she was almost on eye level with him and for a few seconds she regretted her move because they were so close, close enough to see the flecks of gold in his midnight-dark eyes and the lush thickness of his lashes. She breathed in sharply, heart beating like a sledgehammer.

'We check all the rooms and then decide in the morning.'

'Is that *it*?' Celia cried.

'What more is it possible to do at this hour in the evening? There's no way I'm going to attempt to make the journey back in this weather.' His eyes were as cool as his voice. 'I'm not jeopardising your life nor am I jeopardising my own because you're panicking about being here with me.'

'That's not it *at all*!'

'You're tired and hungry, but getting over-emotional about this situation isn't going to help either of us.'

'And what if we're stuck here for longer than one

night?' Celia demanded. 'Will you be able to fly the helicopter back in the morning if it continues to snow overnight?'

Leandro met her blazing green eyes with a remote, un-readable expression.

Her cheeks were flushed, her copper hair tangled around her heart-shaped face, her full lips pursed. She oozed fury. How could that be attractive? It couldn't. He loathed this sort of extreme emotionalism. What was the point of overreacting to something that couldn't be changed? And yet, as he stared at her, he was discon-certed by the tug of something strong, swift and primal. She was the very essence of lush, tempting femininity and as he looked away, impatient with his response to her, he could feel a telltale tic in his jaw, a potent re-minder that his lofty reassurances that she was utterly safe with him might have a few holes he hadn't foreseen.

But a lifetime of iron control came to his rescue. He had never been ruled by his body and that was some-thing that was never going to change.

'Pointless question,' he said smoothly, moving to step past her, feeling the warmth of her body close to his as he brushed past and sensing the hurried, breathless shift of her body to let him pass by. Now, he was gazing down at her, her face upturned to his, and again, that uninvited intrusion of a libido that was always kept under control. 'In the morning, we'll see what's happening with the weather and take it from there. For now, I'll show you where you can sleep, and we'll have something to eat. Tomorrow, as I've said, is another day.'

CHAPTER FOUR

HOW WAS LEANDRO to know that those glibly spoken words that *'tomorrow is another day'* would come back to bite him? Tomorrow *should* have been another day. It should have been the day they returned to London, where he would pick up the search for Julie, having first begun the business of sorting her father's financial woes, never mind about the old man's misplaced pride. He and Celia would part company, she the better for tickets to the fashion show. Despite what he had said to Celia, he had been privately convinced that, with no Julie or Dan there, making the trip back by helicopter the following day would have been a certainty.

That was four days ago.

He knew that when snow fell in this part of the world, it meant business. He had awoken to the silent force of a snowstorm the morning after they'd arrived and realised that any hope of getting the helicopter up was out of the question.

In his meticulously ordered life, where there was no place for surprises, the weather had decided to blindside him.

They had sat opposite one another at the vast table in his kitchen, which was a marvel of what money could buy, from the four-door cream oven to the high-tech seldom-used gadgets and he had seen exactly what she'd been thinking as clearly as if her thoughts had been emblazoned across her forehead in neon lettering.

Get me out of here.

She couldn't have looked more horrified if she'd glanced up to discover that the sky was falling down.

She'd been prepared to be polite for a night or two, knowing that she would be rescued from having to be alone with him because they would be greeted at the house by Julie and her brother.

The prospect of them both sharing space for longer than that without any convenient chaperones or a helicopter on red-alert standby had appalled her and she hadn't bothered to disguise her reaction, even though he had spent at least an hour assuring her that the house was so vast that they could get lost in it and, besides, he would remove himself during the day to carry on working from the office that was set up in another wing of the manor house.

'You won't notice I'm here,' he had said. 'We can meet in the evenings for dinner, but you'll find your quarters comfortable enough for you to stay put all day while we're here. You'll have your own suite, with a television and a dedicated space if you want to work…'

'Good,' she had said with visible relief, and so here they were, several days later, their time together reduced to an hour or so in the evenings over dinner.

Where he had always had a short attention span when it came to listening to people talk about their feelings, he found, to his intense irritation, that her silence on the subject got on his nerves. Where he was used to zoning out, his mind veering off to work-related issues when meandering anecdotes from dates turned into search-ing questions designed to elicit confidences he had no intention of sharing, he found himself encouraging her to open up. Thus far his success rate hovered around the zero mark.

And in this scenario, how was it possible that his li-bido moved into fifth gear every time he looked at her? How did that even begin to make sense?

Was it the novelty of being in the company of a woman who didn't spare him a second glance? Or did those lush curves appeal to him in ways that bypassed his brain and went straight to his groin?

Or maybe it was just the stark isolation of their cir-cumstances...

He banged his fist in seething frustration on the desk where he was now forced to abandon work because the Internet had decided to crash, and scowled.

It was a little after three in the afternoon. Through the window, the swirling snow against a darkening sky made for an eerie landscape.

There was an afternoon to fill and an evening to get through. For a workaholic, the prospect of idling in the slow lane indefinitely was the stuff of nightmares.

Defeated by the lack of Internet and not caring for the direction of his thoughts, Leandro vacated his office to wander in the direction of the kitchen.

The size of the place had naturally lent itself to subdi-vision, with one half reserved for friends and family as and when they chose to visit, which was not often, and the other half devoted to work-related gatherings, which had been far more frequent over the years.

It was not unusual for entire high-performing teams to be given all-expenses-paid time there where they could enjoy first-class service and idyllic surroundings with their family.

Connecting doors could slide seamlessly into place, separating one side from the other completely. It was a marvel of advanced engineering and Leandro had personally oversaw its implementation.

Now, making his way through the vast house, absently contemplating the prospect of Celia and his wayward responses to her and wondering, yet again, what the hell was going on with him, he glanced through the windows of one of the rooms he swung by and there she was.

Outside!

What was she doing *outside*?

Was this what she got up to mid-afternoon when he was in the office, sitting in front of a computer, linked up to half the world for his uninterrupted hours of virtual meetings?

Having walks outside in driving snow? Or was this her first venture out to make a change from the horror of being cooped up in a luxury manor house the size of a small castle?

Leandro didn't give himself time to dwell. Instead, he sprinted to the front door, grabbing the house keys en route, not bothering to hunt down his wellies from the boot room behind the kitchen.

The freezing cold hit him with the force of a body blow. He gasped sharply but didn't slow his pace, moving swiftly through the snow and oblivious to the physical discomfort.

He could handle black runs in the most challenging of conditions and ergo he could handle anything.

Not least a stubborn woman who should know better than to put her life at risk by venturing out in hostile weather conditions!

He reached her at speed, aware of the slushing of the snow in his loafers and the bitter wind stinging his face.

She was so small against the vastness of the landscape, a vulnerable little dot, and he fought against an urge to pull her against him.

She was huddled into so many layers of clothing and her woolly hat was pulled low over her eyes and his heart clenched with a surge of protectiveness that took him by surprise.

He reached out to circle her arm with his fingers, turning her to face him because she hadn't seen him approaching from behind her.

'What the hell do you think you're doing out there?'

The sudden fear and panic that had gripped him when he'd spotted her outside made him sound harsher than he'd intended. But he wasn't going to apologise because it was sheer crazy recklessness to be out in these conditions, where the darkness and the falling snow concealed a multitude of potential danger zones.

'What on earth are you doing?' Celia, alone with her thoughts and enjoying the peace of not being in the house where she seemed to be on constant alert to the sound of his approaching footsteps, stared at Leandro in astonishment.

Shouldn't he be working?

It was all he did! He worked from the early hours of the morning to late in the evening. Either he had a limitless amount of things that couldn't possibly be deferred for a day or two or else, more likely, he was intent on doing everything within his power to avoid her.

She couldn't blame him. Why would he want to be stuck out here with a woman who had come along for the ride as a matter of necessity? This was the sort of wildly romantic place he would choose to come with a lover. She could picture him, the Lord of the Manor, with an icy beauty, strolling hand in hand through the ruggedly untamed countryside, stopping only to lose themselves in one another.

Instead, he'd found himself closeted with a woman he barely liked, reduced to small talk when it just couldn't be avoided.

Conscious of that fact and not wanting to be a bother, Celia had been at pains to be in his company as little as possible. They ate together and she was surprised that he was as good a cook as he was, turning down her offers to help because, surprisingly, he enjoyed it.

Watching and listening, enjoying the sight of him moving confidently around the well-equipped kitchen and knowing that her disobedient eyes were just fanning the flames of an illicit attraction that no amount of common sense could squash, Celia hung onto every word that left his lips.

She knew it was wrong. It wasn't as though he were sharing anything with her that he wouldn't have shared with anyone else who happened to be there at the time he just happened to be throwing a few things in a pan! She was very careful to keep herself to herself, which wasn't difficult because whenever she was around him, she became curiously tongue-tied. It had been easier to argue with him when he'd first shown up on her doorstep with his accusations and arrogant assumptions about her and Dan.

But out here, there had been a lull in hostilities, and

she had been treacherously aware that, within the lull, she had glimpsed a multifaceted guy with a sharp sense of humour and a charm that she couldn't have predicted.

Not the kind of man who was her type, because their worlds were just so far apart, because she would always need someone so much more normal and down-to-earth. So she was as safe as houses on that front...but he was still so physically attractive that what woman wouldn't feel her insides go just a little bit squishy in his presence?

She tried to yank her arm free, sensitive to the heat pouring from him straight into her.

'I'm rescuing you,' Leandro gritted. He began tugging her back in the direction of the house and, rather than resist, she hurried alongside him because the force of the snow didn't permit extended arguments to be conducted outside. Not without hypothermia kicking in.

'Rescuing me?' she all but shouted once they were inside the house with the front door firmly shut against the elements. She'd leapt back and now she glared at him, hands on her hips, fuming green eyes clashing with equally fuming black ones. 'You were *rescuing* me?'

Leandro wondered what the world was coming to when an act of pure chivalry could be met with open hostility.

'Don't be bloody-minded,' he growled. 'Have you any idea just how dangerous it is attempting to venture out in this weather anywhere near that loch?'

'I *know* where the loch is, Leandro! I've been having an afternoon walk every day since we've been...been... cooped up here!'

'I get it this isn't exactly what you'd bought into!'

'Is it what *you've* bought into?'

'It could have been a damn sight worse.' Leandro was

so aware of her pulsing, throbbing, sexily alluring feminine anger that he was driven to stare, knowing even as his eyes rested on her that what he *should* be doing was looking away. Cutting the conversation dead—if she wanted to berate him for being a gentleman, then that was her problem.

However, he couldn't tear his eyes away. She'd yanked off the woolly hat and he wanted to reach out and push her tangled hair away from her face, gather her into his arms and kiss her senseless.

No...he wanted to do more than that...he wanted to take her to his bed, see her naked, that wild hair strewn across his pillow...he wanted to touch...

'I wasn't in any danger.' Celia's voice hitched in her throat and she stumbled a couple of steps back.

'I could do without any more complications if you'd fallen in,' he muttered, looking away but only for a second. 'This is a pointless conversation.'

'I grew up where snow was something that happened once a year!' Celia snapped, patches of bright colour staining her cheeks. 'I know how to handle being in it! Which *you*,' she added, 'evidently do not!'

'Meaning?'

'*Meaning* that when you decided to do your knight-in-shining-armour routine and rescue the damsel in distress, you didn't stop to think that braving a snowstorm in some cotton track pants and a jumper and...and shoes without socks might not have been the best idea in the world!'

But he *had* played the knight in shining armour, hadn't he? And whatever he'd said about only rushing out to save her from her own carelessness because he didn't want the hassle of her breaking a leg on him, she *knew* that he had reacted on instinct. The instinct to protect someone he thought might have been in a vulnerable situation. That was who he was, whether he wanted to admit it or not, and when was the last time she had laid eyes on *any* knights in shining armour?

Celia knew that her one disappointing experience with Martin, her youthful mistake of being in love with the idea of being in love without the maturity to delve deeper into her headlong rush into an engagement with a guy she'd liked but not loved, had made her cautious, but had her retreat from the messy world of men and dating also made her cynical?

Leandro had been right when he'd told her that she was a romantic, that she wanted the whole fairy-tale happy-ever-after ending for herself.

But was that something she believed for herself because that was just the way she'd been brought up? Did she take the whole business of romance for granted because it was in her DNA to think that she would end up like her parents, in love after so many years, travelling down a straightforward road to a predictably happy destination?

In the meanwhile, had her feverish building of protective walls around herself gradually turned her into someone who had bit by bit been losing the ability to trust? Had holding all men at arm's length, while she waited for Mr Right to magically come along, curdled her natural softness into hard-baked cynicism?

It was easy to dwell on the marvels of True Love from a distance. If you never took risks, then you would never get hurt. Had she drifted towards that place? Safely marooned on her little island, all by herself? Prickly and incapable of just being *nice* to a guy who had hurtled out of this house because he'd thought she might have been in mortal danger?

Even if she was familiar with this sort of inclement weather a lot more than he was?

But he got to her...made her behave out of character...threw up her defences even though she knew she was being silly...

And he was savvy enough to figure out that she was prickly around him!

'I'm sorry,' she muttered, casting her eyes downwards even though her body language was still rigid with tension at the wayward direction of her thoughts. 'You rushed out because you thought I might have been in danger of hurting myself and I appreciate that.'

He didn't reply, instead spinning round on his heel and heading to the kitchen.

'I... I also didn't expect to see you,' she confessed, following him as he stripped off the soggy jumper to the tee shirt underneath.

'I'd better go and get into some dry clothes,' he said, turning to her and raking his fingers through his damp hair.

'You should.' Truce in place. Felt better. She might feel safer when she was angry with him, because that way she could shut the door on inappropriate reactions, but a truce felt better and she realised that, over the past few days, she had become accustomed to not arguing with him about the situation.

She'd grown used to the way he sometimes raised his eyebrows and half smiled when she dug her heels in and argued with him about something and nothing. She enjoyed the absent way he sometimes let slip things about himself without really realising it and the way he had of making her laugh, because, oddly for someone who could be so arrogant and autocratic, he was also very good at doing that.

'You'll get your death of a cold if you hang around for too long in wet clothes.'

'That's an old wives' tale.' But he glanced down at his loafers, which he proceeded to kick off, as though only just remembering that his feet were wet. 'Never had a cold in my life.'

Their eyes collided and Celia drew in a shaky breath, which almost managed to clear her head but didn't quite seem to dispel the sudden flare of crackling tension that had sprung up from nowhere. Was it her imagination or was she reading something in the depths of those dark eyes, something that was thrilling and unsettling at the same time?

Or were her own contraband thoughts interfering with her common sense and making her sense something that wasn't there? She blinked and looked away but she knew that she was flushed and breathing fast.

'Internet's down.' Leandro broke the stretching silence and Celia breathed a sigh of relief at the normality of his remark, something to cling onto to distract her from her misbehaving mind.

'You're kidding. When did that happen?'

'A couple of hours ago. I tried to do as much as I could without it, but it was hopeless.'

'Is that how you managed to spot me outside?'

'I was heading towards the kitchen.'

They had, thankfully, managed to contact Julie via Facebook two days previously, to tell her about her father's condition, even though the conversation had been limited because of the Internet wherever they were falling in and out of service in the continuing poor weather. It had been Celia's idea because Leandro, to her surprise, was not connected on Facebook or interested in any other form of social media that could get an uninvited foothold into his private life.

'I guess you'll have to discover what life is like without being connected to the rest of the world via a computer.' Celia smiled a little shyly and he grinned back at her.

'You can tell me how you manage to make life work for you on that front when I'm back down,' he said drily, eyes still pinned to her face as he hovered by the door, on the verge of leaving but not managing to do so quite yet.

Celia broke the spell by turning away, telling him that she would make them some tea…there were some biscuits she'd spotted in one of the cupboards.

Only when he'd left the kitchen did she sag with relief. She made a pot of tea in a rush, every nerve in her body keyed up to hear him returning while she tried to think of what on earth he was going to do if the Internet remained down and the snow continued to layer everything in a blanket of white.

He still managed to surprise her when her back was turned as she searched through the cupboards for the biscuits. With no one in the place, there had been a shortage of fresh food easily compensated by freezers and larders bursting at the seams.

'So…' his lazy drawl had her spinning round to find him changed into a pair of faded jeans, tan loafers and a black tee shirt, for the massive house was incredibly warm, despite the conditions outside '…you were going to tell me how you busy yourself without the Internet…'

'Was I? Tea? I found the biscuits…'

'Sit and relax.' He moved towards the kitchen counter, threw a glance over his shoulder. 'How are things doing in your shop?'

'I beg your pardon?'

'You've been away…' he brought the pot of tea to the table along with the biscuits '…for longer than anticipated. Do you have reliable people working with you who can pick up the slack?'

He angled a chair so that he was sitting close to her, their knees almost touching, relaxing back with one arm slung over the back of the chair, the other resting on the table as he idly played with his mug.

'They're very good.' Celia cradled the mug with both hands. She was so alert to him sitting close to her that her nerves were all over the place as she tried to relax, telling him about her shop and what was going on in her absence while he listened in silence, head tilted to one side.

'You haven't stopped working while we've been here.' She adroitly changed the subject because his focus was so intense. 'Don't you trust the people who work with you?'

'They're good but when it comes to the crux, the only person I trust for the big stuff is myself.'

'Poor you if that means that you're condemned never to have time off,' she said lightly, eyes flicking to his serious, thoughtful face and just as quickly skittering away.

'But I'm not the only one with a few trust issues, am I?' Leandro murmured softly and Celia's eyes shot back to his face with alarm.

'I trust my colleagues one hundred per cent!'

'That's not what I'm talking about.'

'Then I don't know where you're going with this.' She

jutted her chin at a defiant angle and her eyes widened in shock when he reached out and gently, absently and only for a few seconds touched the beating pulse at the base of her neck.

'Your body is telling a different story.'

He sat back while Celia stared at him, dumbfounded. Where his finger had rested was on fire. The heat started at that small spot and radiated all the way through her, sparking a fire inside her that made her want to leap out of the chair and dive right back into the freezing cold outside.

'Why are you so nervous when you're around me? No.' He held up one hand and half smiled. 'When I surprised you outside, you jumped a mile…'

'I wasn't expecting you! You should have been working—'

'And you're skittish around me…are you going to deny it? To me, that could only mean one of two things.'

'I don't want to have this conversation with you, Leandro. I…it's a pointless conversation and I don't like you…speculating about me.'

'Of course I'm going to speculate. We're here together, "cooped up" as you put it. Speculation is a by-product of the circumstances.'

'Not for me.'

'Liar.' He looked at her in silence just long enough for her to get the feeling that he was somehow seeing straight into her head, rummaging around and finding all those taboo thoughts that were whirling there.

Leandro noted every nuance of pink colour creeping into her cheeks. He registered the darkening of her eyes, the slight flare of her nostrils, and felt a surge of satisfaction that shocked him in its intensity.

How long had he had this urge to take her out of hiding? Had he even recognised his curiosity for what it was? Stronger than common sense? No, because he had never been this curious about anyone in his life before. What was it about her? Was it really just a case of curiosity being a natural by-product of their enforced isolation, as he had told her? He refused to contemplate the notion that somehow, without him realising it, she had managed to find a way to get under his skin. No woman was capable of doing that and many had tried over the years. He was inured against that and he liked it like that.

So this was…fun. More than that.

'Either you're aware of me on a level that's not just about us being here together…' He waited for her to say something but she didn't. She didn't meet his eyes either and discomfort was written all over her face.

He was playing with fire. She wasn't his type. She was a woman who wanted a relationship, a proper, full-blown relationship with the end result of a ring on a finger and a walk up an aisle. He knew that he should steer clear of her. He might enjoy women, but he never set out to break hearts and he wasn't going to start now.

'Or maybe…' his voice was husky and just a little unsteady '…you have trust issues because someone hurt you in the past. Is that it?' But still he played with the tantalising thought that underneath the defensive exterior, she fancied him. It was pointless pretending that he didn't fancy her. From the start, there had been something about her that had pulled him in.

Skewered by those deep, dark eyes and prisoner of a line of questioning she knew could so easily unpick her fragile defences against him, Celia said hesitantly, 'I was engaged once.'

He was shocked. His reaction was so open and so extreme that she couldn't help but smile.

'People do get engaged, Leandro, and sometimes those engagements don't work out. You should know that more than anyone else.'

'They do,' Leandro murmured. 'What happened?'

Celia shrugged. She'd opened a door and now feelings that had been buried for a long time poured through her. She was rusty when it came to talking about it. The last time she *had* had been years ago, in the immediate aftermath, when there had been superficial explanations all round, to friends, to her family, squashing their concern even though she had been hurting inside, feeling like a gullible fool.

She expected to revisit those feelings now but instead she was surprised to find that she wasn't in the least bit sad at the memories of what had gone wrong for her and Martin. It was just something that had happened.

She began telling him, going round in circles and picking up threads of the past and interweaving them, feeling a weight lift from her shoulders.

'You're a good listener,' she finished, embarrassed at how much she had opened up.

'You sound surprised.'

'I wouldn't have expected it of you.'

'You still keep in touch with your ex?'

'On Facebook.' Celia shrugged. 'They post a lot of family shots.'

'Still have feelings for him?'

Celia laughed shortly. 'It may have taken me a while

to get over the hurt, but no, I don't have feelings for Martin, aside from friendship, which was really all there ever was.'

'Yet…he's still influencing how you live your life…'

'We're *all* influenced by our past,' Celia defended stoutly, then she paused and looked at him with speculation. 'Aren't you?'

Leandro flushed and then relaxed back with a lazy, charming smile. 'Absolutely. Are you hanging on to hear more?'

'Well, you *did* just hear my entire backstory.'

'So I did,' Leandro conceded. He hesitated, unfamiliar with anyone asking him about his private life. He was aware that his Keep Off signs were very good at doing their job, at making people know just what lines to stand behind. Yet it felt different sitting here far away from reality, locked up in a bubble with a green-eyed woman who teased his senses as no one ever had. Besides, where was the harm in sticking to the bare bones of his past? For the first time, it hit him that his well-ordered life, where he was the master of his universe and answerable to no one, also had its own hidden drawbacks. An ivory tower might protect against people getting in, but did it also prevent him, in the end, from getting out?

He dismissed that weird bout of introspection. It was no big deal. When they left, they would both return to their lives, two ships that briefly passed in the night. It wasn't as though they moved in remotely similar circles so the chances of them ever meeting again were minimal, unless it happened through Julie, but his friendship with his ex, should this break-up be permanent, would simply resume where it had left off. A one-on-one meeting every so often because of their shared past.

'My father,' Leandro mused thoughtfully, 'had no money. No, I tell a lie. He had a good life working on someone else's ranch, obeying someone else's orders, and the truth is he was happy with that. My mother left, and when she left she took his hopes and dreams with her.' Leandro's mouth thinned and his thoughts swirled around the words he hadn't said. The truth was that Leandro saw as weakness his father's acceptance of his lot, the way he had allowed the collapse of his marriage to tarnish the rest of his life. Too much given away. It would be something he, Leandro, would never allow.

'So when it comes to the past influencing the present? There you have it. I watched my father settle for less that he was worth and I decided that I would never do the same.' In danger of the atmosphere getting a little too serious for his liking, he lightened the mood with the ghost of a smile. 'So here I am. I'm at the top of the food chain and that's exactly where I want to be.'

'And your father?'

'Would you believe he's still living in the same house on the ranch even though I've told him a million times that I can buy him anything he wants, anywhere he wants?'

'Because your dreams aren't his.' Celia felt the intimacy of shared confidences wrap around her in a dangerous stranglehold and she stood up to begin tidying the mugs and biscuits.

She could feel his eyes boring into her. She wanted to ask him about his mother and she wondered whether he was even aware of how much he gave away by the bitterness in his voice when he mentioned her.

He was so deeply, bewitchingly complex and she shivered and slanted her eyes to glance at him, to find that he was staring at her, his expression broodingly intense.

'I should…go and get changed…' she murmured, backing away. She was doing it again…being skittish around him. What conclusions was he reaching? The one she dared not say out loud? That she fancied him? He was dangerous and she loathed the thought of danger so why was she so drawn to him?

'I'll see you later for dinner.' He vaulted upright, strolled towards the window and peered out at a landscape washed in grey and white, then he turned to her. 'With the weather like this and no Internet…we could be spending a lot more time together than we'd anticipated. I hope you don't mind…'

'Why should I?' Celia could hear the brittleness in her voice but she met his languid gaze steadily, challenging her body to let her down. 'The walking is lovely provided you wrap up well, and for me? I'm not reliant on the Internet. I brought my computer for sketching and I can do that anywhere…'

CHAPTER FIVE

CELIA TOOK HER time with a bath. She had a couple of hours to kill before heading right back down to the kitchen and she intended to kill them on her own, getting her thoughts in order so that when she faced Leandro later on, she would be in control.

She dreaded the thought of him wandering the house like a lost soul without his Internet connection to the rest of the world. They had shared something back there in the kitchen and, whatever it was, it had wreaked havoc with her composure.

It was a little after six by the time she made it down to a silent kitchen. There was no Leandro waiting to send her nervous system into freefall, and for an hour or so Celia enjoyed the peace, even though she had one ear out for his footsteps and an eye on the kitchen door for when he pushed it open.

She was puzzled when, at a little before seven, there was still no sign of him. He usually enjoyed the relaxation of cooking but now, fancying that he had maybe become wrapped up in something work-related that didn't require an Internet connection, she began preparing some dinner for them both.

She switched the radio on. It was the one old-fashioned gadget in the uber-modern kitchen and she hummed along to old tunes as she tackled the larder, pulling out rice and beans and some tuna and wondering how creative she could get with the ingredients.

It was only when the eight o'clock news came on that it dawned on her that Leandro wasn't going to show up.

Bitter disappointment swamped any feelings of relief that she wouldn't have to face him.

She *wanted* to see him, wanted to feel the fizz of excitement coursing through her. Why pretend that he didn't excite her? He did.

But maybe he had had time to regret the fact that they had bridged a gap. Maybe he had stopped to think that encouraging anything with her would be stupid because, as he had told her from the beginning, she wasn't his type. He didn't go for the romantic sort. Had he got a little spooked at the idea that she might start getting feelings for him?

Celia burned with embarrassment when she thought about that but what if it was true?

Deflated, she made the most of the meal she cooked. Relaxing on her own no longer seemed to have any appeal. She headed up to her suite, slowing her steps as she passed his bedroom. She didn't want to knock but the impulse was so strong. She *had* to find out for herself whether he was avoiding her for all the wrong reasons. She was in *no danger* of letting her guard slip around him! She had no idea how she could manoeuvre the conversation in a direction whereby she could make that perfectly clear but somehow it felt vital that she do so.

Her hand hovering in front of the door, her mouth dry, the decision was taken out of her hands when she heard a crash and then she didn't bother to knock at all.

Celia pushed the door open and stepped into a darkened room. She had to blink for her eyes to adjust.

Leandro was in the process of pulling himself up onto the bed and, without thinking, she raced towards him, heart beating a mile a minute.

'What's wrong?' she asked.

There was panic in her voice. She circled his waist with her arm, helping him up and then straightening the bedside table, which had crashed to the ground under the impact of his weight.

The feel of him, his skin against hers, burnt into her as she leapt back to look at him with mounting alarm.

He had flopped back onto the bed, half propping himself up on the pillows. He loosely draped a dark-coloured duvet over his body but, save for a pair of boxers, he was completely naked and while she did her utmost not to look, she couldn't help herself.

He was all shadows and angles and absolutely, stunningly beautiful. In repose, he was a work of art, broad-shouldered, lean-hipped, a vision of beauty and strength.

She hovered by the side of the bed and flinched when he switched on the lamp, which she had repositioned on the bedside table.

'I feel like crap,' he rasped hoarsely, opening one baleful eye.

'When? How? You were fine earlier…'

'Got up here, had a shower, had a sudden urge to climb into bed and fell asleep.' He groaned. 'Woke up with a splitting headache, started getting out of bed and that's when you heard me. I reached for the table but ended up toppling it over.'

'You're burning up.' Hand on his forehead, Celia went from being agonisingly *aware* of him to briskly recognising that she had a patient on her hands who would need taking care of.

The distinction was a blessing. She could deal with being Florence Nightingale. It was a lot less stressful than trying to work out how she could convince him whatever effect he had on her was all in his mind!

'Do you have a first-aid kit?'

'Bathroom.'

'Take these.' This when she had returned with some water in a glass she had found on one of the inset shelves by the huge, swimming-pool-sized bath.

'I don't do tablets.'

'In that case—' she rested the tablets on the table, stood back and folded her arms '—you can do a raging fever and aches and pains instead. Your choice.'

Leandro held out his hand and she duly put the tablets into it and watched as he swallowed them before settling back down, eyes closed.

'Are you hungry? Would you like something to eat?'

The question hung in the air but by the time she reached the door, he was asleep.

Leandro slept fitfully for the next couple of hours. Celia checked in on him and when, at a little before midnight, his fever began climbing once again, she repeated her tablet routine although, this time, he didn't argue.

This time, when their eyes met in the darkened room, his were alert whatever the state of his aching body.

He swallowed the tabs but when she turned to leave, he stayed her, his fingers circling her wrist, tugging her gently back so that she half stumbled onto the bed.

'I should thank you for this,' he rasped and Celia, hyper conscious of his fingers on her wrist and the pad of his thumb idly gently stroking the tender sensitive skin, muttered something and nothing.

Celia licked her lips and tried a reassuring smile on for size but those small, stroking movements...

They were flooding her treacherous body with heat. She wanted him to stop, wanted to yank her hand away and rub where he'd touched but she didn't because she was enjoying it too much. She was, oh, so tempted to touch him back and the strength of that temptation terrified her because it was so new.

'For what?' She laughed jerkily. 'All I've done is bring you some tablets and water and checked in occasionally to make sure you haven't...worsened...'

'It's after midnight.'

'I know.'

'You must be tired and yet you've still checked in...'

'Leandro, has no one ever taken care of you before? I mean,' she added softly, quickly, 'when you've been laid up? It's no big deal. My brother's older than me but we both live in London and, honestly, as soon as he sneezes twice, he calls me and begs me to come over and look after him.'

'I thought he was a free spirit.' There was a smile in Leandro's voice.

This felt so good, so relaxed, their voices low murmurs in the bedroom and the curtains letting in just a slither of silvery light here and there.

'He's as free as a bird until he gets a cold.' She smiled back.

'You're very close, aren't you?'

'Yes. We are. Small village close to a small town where kids still play outside without supervision and mostly everyone knows everyone else. We went to the same school and, even though he's older, his friends all somehow seemed to know my friends because they were related or neighbours…so yes…'

'That's why you drifted into an engagement that wasn't right…'

Celia shrugged. She'd already told him about Martin so what was the point in being coy on the subject if he chose to raise it again? She'd opened a door and she didn't regret it because it had felt like a release.

'Like I said…'

'You didn't tell your brother how much it affected you?'

'I suppose I was embarrassed…ashamed that I'd been so naïve.' She looked away and then confessed, in a low voice, 'And Martin found someone else so fast, someone tall and athletic and pretty and really nice as well…'

Leandro heard the vulnerability in her voice and his heart clenched.

It was one thing to admit to a broken engagement, which she had. She could tell him why it had ended, a simple youthful error of judgement, not that uncommon in the great scheme of things. But now, he could detect the place where it had really hurt and it felt like something twisting inside him.

She had lost confidence in her own sexuality because the guy she'd mistakenly thought she'd end up with had found someone else in record time and someone else who was probably, physically, the polar opposite of her.

He reached out to push her hair back and then let his hand linger, tangled in her hair. He felt her breathe in sharply and saw the widening of her eyes but she wasn't pulling away.

She was still in a jumper and her jogging bottoms, hadn't changed into whatever it was she slept in. He wondered what it was she did sleep in. In that suite of rooms so close to his.

'You're still lucky,' he murmured, sliding his finger across her cheek, which was as smooth as satin. 'You have a support system that's been there for you through thick and thin.'

'And you haven't.' Celia was just stating a fact.

'No. Which—' there was wry amusement in his voice '—is probably why I have never fallen ill. I've always known that I wouldn't have anyone around to play nursemaid and mop my fevered brow.'

Celia thought that there would be a long line of women all dying to play nursemaid to Leandro. She figured that he would have to erect a wall of steel to stop them from stampeding into his house, bearing thermometers and cups of tea, able and willing to minister to his every need.

She didn't have to join too many dots to figure out what he wasn't saying.

Leandro didn't *want* anyone to play nursemaid with him. He didn't *want* that level of involvement from any woman because that would have encouraged a conversation about *commitment* that he would never have.

She was here now and what choice did he have when it came to nursemaids?

She was the sole candidate and so she knew that she shouldn't be reading anything into the intimacy swirling around them now.

Logic having asserted itself, Celia knew that she should drily tell him exactly what she was thinking, then she should change the subject and leave because he needed to get some sleep and so did she, but instead she remained silent.

Her body was melting. It was on fire and, deep inside, the bloom of a craving she had never felt before was spreading through her. It made her limbs feel heavy and, between her legs, warm wetness was pooling, liquid heat that made her breathing sluggish.

The dangerous notion that somehow the here and now was *real* threaded a way through common sense and cold reason. After all, hadn't they confided in one another? With the snow falling outside, thick and dense and wrapping them in a bubble? She felt that he'd opened up to her in ways he hadn't foreseen and she'd certainly done the same, telling him about Martin and about how she'd felt when he'd settled down with someone else five minutes after she'd returned his engagement ring. Beautiful, leggy, *nice* Annabelle.

She leant into him and closed her eyes to the kiss she knew was coming, one she wanted so much. The kiss that would clear her head of everything, take her back to a time before disappointment and disillusionment had made their mark. And yet, as his lips met hers, she was still rocked to the very core.

Her hands feverishly smoothed his broad, hard chest, with its sprinkling of dark hair. She didn't even want to come up for air! Who needed to breathe?

As his mouth travelled along her neck, she gasped and sifted her fingers through his dark hair, pulling him towards her.

Her breasts felt heavy and sensitive. She wasn't wearing a bra but under the layers, the thermal vest and the jumper, she could feel the scrape of her nipples against the fabric.

She longed to lose herself completely in the present but, of course, that was not how she had been brought up. She'd been brought up to think about consequences. She pushed him back, but it was like surfacing from a warm, cosy blanket to the bitter cold of Arctic air.

He released her instantly, but when he pulled back she could see that his breathing was as uneven as hers.

'Leandro,' she husked. 'That… I'm sorry…'

'Not your fault.'

'That shouldn't have happened.' She was almost disappointed when, after a moment's hesitation, he raked his fingers through his hair and muttered agreement.

'I… I don't know what…' She laughed self-consciously.

'I would never make a pass at a woman before knowing that there's an invite on the table…the kind of guy who touches what's out of bounds…' Leo said.

Celia thought that the last thing she had been a few moments ago was *out of bounds*. She'd matched his kiss with equal passion, as though the walls of the dam had dropped away and nothing could stop the torrent of uncontrolled water.

'I'll go now…get some sleep.'

'Yes.' Their eyes met. His kiss was still on his mouth and she wanted more.

So she was the romantic type. She would always be the romantic type, a woman who would never allow lessons learnt to warp her vision of *True Love*. He didn't get it, himself, but then no two people were ever the same.

That said…she'd closed herself off from men since she'd returned that engagement ring to the guy who'd

promptly replaced her with someone else. That said...
whatever fairy tales she believed in when it came to
Love, she was too scared to seek it out because of what
had happened. He'd seen those shadows on her face when
she'd told him about her replacement, and he'd known
there and then that the depth of her hurt had come not
just from the bruising of her ego because her engagement had ended in tears. *That* was something that would
have shaken her, but its effect wouldn't have been lasting.
He'd believed her when she'd said that she'd understood
how right the ex had been in calling it off. Too young...
invisible pressure to drift into something everyone expected...in love with the feeling of being in love.

But then her ex had hooked up with another woman no
sooner than he'd finished his *Dear John* or, in this case,
Dear Jill speech to her. And not just that...he'd hooked
up with a woman Celia felt was superior to her physically. Leandro was sure that she couldn't have been further from the truth on that count, but the fact remained
that self-confidence in herself as a *woman* had taken a
beating and *that* was what had held her back.

She fancied him. Leandro had felt it in the urgency
of her mouth against his and the eager caressing of her
hands and, hell, he couldn't remember fancying any
woman as much as he did her.

But, in her head, sex was all tied up with Love and
how wrong she was.

What she needed was to get her self-confidence back,
to know that she was a beautiful, vital woman who could
pick and choose from whatever pond she decided to
throw her rod into.

Without self-confidence, she would remain hiding in
the shadows for ever, waiting for someone to come along

and tick all the boxes, without her having to do any hard work to get there.

'Or…' Leandro let that one word drop into the silence and linger there for a few seconds '…you could sleep here.'

His dark eyes challenged hers.

'Let's not pretend… We want one another. A lot.'

'That's not the point,' Celia stammered.

'Isn't it?'

Celia heard the warm persuasion in his voice and shivered. 'You can't just do as you please in life.'

'Why not?'

'Because…' Her voice petered out. She was rooted to the spot but when he patted the space on the bed that she had seconds before vacated, she felt her trembling legs take a hesitant step towards him, then two steps, then she was perched on the side.

'Because you're scared,' Leandro said gently. 'You're scared you're going to be hurt if you allow yourself to just let go.'

'I…' She shook her head in confusion.

'You've spent years holding back from involvement because you lost your self-confidence when the guy you thought had your back disappeared with another woman in the blink of an eye.'

'Maybe.' She looked at him with angry defiance, but his voice was thoughtful and soft and her anger was skin deep. She'd never had a conversation like this with anyone and it made her feel raw and vulnerable, but he was right, wasn't he?

'You won't be hurt with me,' Leandro told her quietly. 'I'm not your type, remember?'

'No. You're not...'

'We're two adults who fancy one another and, of course, I will completely respect whatever decision you make, so if you choose to walk through that door right now and not look back, then you can trust me that I'll back off straight away. I checked the snow earlier on the way to the bathroom and it's clearing. We will be out of here soon enough and you can pretend that none of this ever happened.'

You won't be hurt with me...'

But, Celia thought, would she hurt herself if she walked away? Would she regret for ever this chance to have just the sort of adventure that might do her so much good in the long run? They weren't emotionally involved...she could touch without fear...she could let herself feel and be a woman again.

She reached out with one trembling hand and cupped the side of his face and then moaned softly when he turned her palm over and kissed it, his dark eyes still on her.

'I want you,' she sighed in surrender and Leandro pulled her against him and buried his head into her neck, tugging her jumper so that he could nuzzle her shoulder.

'But...' she added.

'But...?'

'But are you feeling okay for...?'

Leandro loosed a low, sexy laugh. 'I think the best thing is exercise...'

Half lying on him, Celia laughed and then smiled and hoisted herself into an upright position, eager to get her clothes off but too shy to actually do it.

Leandro sensed her hesitation and understood it. He slipped his hand under the cotton jumper and gently smoothed her shoulder and with each languid motion, the top was pushed further down her arm until, with impatience, she did as he'd hoped and pulled it off with abandonment.

He'd dreamt of a feast and was faced with a banquet, such was the stunning sexiness of her curves. Full breasts pushed against a cotton vest. No bra. He could just about make out the stiff protrusion of her nipples and the sight made him feel faint with desire.

He wanted to tear the vest off and cup those luscious breasts. He wanted to touch and taste and then touch again and keep touching until he knew every succulent inch of a body that was designed to drive a red-blooded man mad.

But he was going to take it slowly. She'd roused something protective in him. It surprised him but he wasn't going to fight it. Something about being in this cold, silent place, as close to the wilderness as he had ever been, was playing games with his common sense and he was enjoying the unexpected journey.

He angled her so that she was astride him. He was sitting up and here, in this position, they were eye to eye, their bodies so close he could feel the heat from hers and her warm breath softly against his face. So close he could pull her towards him and kiss her senseless, which was what he was aching to do. His erection was so steel hard that it was painful and he had to shift a little to relieve the discomfort.

When she tried to snuggle against him, like a little mole seeking the safety of its burrow, he gently eased her back and smiled.

'You're nervous.'

'A little,' Celia admitted breathlessly. 'It's been a while…'

'You're beautiful.'

Celia laughed self-consciously and blushed.

'Whatever feelings you've had about your ex…' Leandro sifted his fingers through her hair and left them there to gently caress and then cup her cheek '…forget about thinking that somehow it had anything to do with how you look, because you're the sexiest woman I've ever shared my bed with.'

'You want to put me at ease…'

'I never lie.' His voice was low and husky as he trailed one finger down the deep indent of her cleavage and then over the vest to circle her protuberant nipples, zeroing in on the stiffened buds and grazing the pads of his thumbs over them. She groaned softly and arched towards him, head flung back and her eyes fluttering shut as sensation replaced thought. 'Although, it's true, I *do* want to put you at ease.'

She was already at ease.

So relaxed that she quivered with longing when he pulled the thermal up and over her breasts, freeing them to the pinch of cool air.

He straightened, manoeuvring them both into a position where her breasts hung heavy and ripe, close enough to almost brush his chest.

He weighed them in his hands and had to close his eyes and breathe deeply just to control himself. He'd never been premature in his responses with any woman, but he was facing a challenge now. Even more of a challenge when he finally looked at her flushed face and her parted mouth and inhaled the scent of pure lust.

With a stifled growl, he replaced his fingers with

his mouth. She had larger than average nipples, each pink disc topped with the stiffened bud against which he rolled his tongue, licking and tasting and tugging until she was whimpering and rocking on him.

How had she managed to find just where to move, rubbing his erection in the sort of way that was sending his body into a slow orbit?

He couldn't keep up the slow tempo any longer. Not if he wanted to emerge with his masculine pride intact.

What remained of their clothes came off in a hurry.

Boxers…vest…underwear…jogging bottoms…all hit the floor at speed. Her nakedness against his, her soft, rounded curves were driving him crazy. And had he really been laid up? Feverish? He couldn't remember. The only fever he felt now was the searing heat of uncontrollable craving.

She was still straddling him. He eased her off. He was desperate to do more than have her rotate her sexy hips and get him so steamed up he wanted to explode.

He nuzzled the soft underside of her breasts while his hand travelled down to cup her between her legs. He pressed gently, felt her wetness and kept just the right amount of pressure there to remind her of the pleasure coming her way.

He didn't have to guide her hand to him. She was exploring him with impatience, curving her body to his and opening her legs to accommodate his hand.

She stroked his spine and then feathered tiny circles at the base and then ran her hand along his waist and everywhere she touched lit him up like a match hitting dry tinder.

When she circled the thick shaft of his penis, he groaned and fell back for a few seconds.

With very little effort, she could take him right over the edge the way those hands and fingers were working and, however novel and enjoyable the prospect was, he had other ideas in his head for where this was going.

With a low laugh, he flipped her and slowly, with devastating intent, he made his way down her body, touching and feeling and moistening with the flick of his tongue.

She responded without inhibition. Whatever shyness she'd felt at the start, when she'd stared down at him with those big green, innocent eyes, had evaporated like dew in the summer sun and every touch elicited a whimper of pleasure.

Leandro kissed, suckled, nuzzled. He circled her belly button with his tongue. He stroked under her arms, along her arms and licked her fingers one by one.

He let his hand drift along her inner thigh and allowed his knuckles to brush against the soft folds of her womanhood in a way that teased and aroused, and only when she demanded more did he dip his fingers in to feel the wet heat of her arousal.

He felt that it had been a long time coming…this… this feeling of wanting to lose himself in someone else.

Physically, of course.

Always just *physically* but even so…it was joyous.

Their bodies were on fire when, at last, he fumbled his way to retrieve a condom from his wallet and entered her. Her slippery wetness welcomed his hardness, wrapped like honeyed sweetness around his shaft and he was alive to her every moan of intense satisfaction as he thrust long and deep into her.

They came quicker than he wanted, but even as his body stiffened and arched and he felt the exquisite shudder of release he was acknowledging that he didn't want this to be the first and last of their couplings.

He held her close.

'Stay.'

Celia, basking in the warm glow of absolute fulfilment, her mind hazy with every pleasure chemical her body had released during an orgasm that had left her weak, swivelled so that she was half draped over him, her arm resting on his chest and her chin propped in the crook of her elbow.

'Huh?'

'Stay. Here. In bed with me. All day and all night.'

Celia laughed but a little bubble of pleasure swelled inside her because his dark eyes were deadly serious even though there was just a ghost of a smile on his lips.

Alarm bells rang in her head. Spend all day and all night with him? Share his bed? For how long? And what happened next in that scenario?

But her heart was safe. This was sex and she'd flung herself headlong into it because, by gosh, it had been a while. *For ever.* To be touched, for her body to be alive again after years buried in deep ice…it had felt *good*, better than *good*.

Leandro had opened a door for her to re-enter the living, breathing, vital world she had left behind.

'I hear the sound of a guy who can't spend all day working…' she teased, but her voice was a little breathless.

'You hear the sound of a guy who's never had such good sex in his life. It's the sound of a guy who wants more. Do you? Want more? Of this?' To emphasise his point, he stroked the curve of her waist and let his hand rest there.

'While we're here...' Celia let that hang in the air between them, willing him to pick up the baton and run with it, to paint a bigger picture than something that would last until the snow melted, but he didn't.

He said in a soft, sexy purr, while he feathered the soft down between her thighs, 'While we're here. The snow's falling and we're locked away here until...who knows when? Even when it stops, it'll be at least a day or so until I can get the helicopter in a fit state to take to the skies. And in the meantime...'

'In the meantime, we enjoy...this...'

'We're on the same page, Celia.' Leandro sifted his fingers through the tangled copper curls that fanned over her face and shoulders in riotous disarray. He traced the outline of her mouth with his finger. 'This is fun. I figure we could both do with a little of that. A little no-strings-attached fun.' He sighed and for a few moments, he fell back to stare at the ceiling and then he held her close against him and said, face averted, 'I thought I had my life sorted when Julie and I got engaged.' He turned to her but still held her close to him. 'You don't get it, but it was an arrangement that worked for me. I can't love and this offered friendship without the complications of anything more, while helping her father, repaying a debt. Yes, we would have had, what you might call, an open marriage, but a very, very discreet one.'

'You're so cynical, Leandro.'

'I'm realistic. I have no desire for children, but companionship? Maybe so...'

'So you have uncomplicated fun here, with me...'

'And then return to whatever awaits on the personal

front. Charles, at least, is sorted as far as his finances go. The rest he will have to come to terms with. And you, my darling…' he smiled a little more '…you get to let go of whatever demons you've had and return to London refreshed. The perfect guy awaits you out there. Maybe you won't be afraid to take up the challenge of trying to find him.'

Celia thought that that felt about right. Didn't it? He should have sounded arrogant in assuming that this brief sojourn was somehow doing her the favour of setting her on the right path of finding true love, that, thanks to him, she was now freed from her demons. He didn't. He sounded sincere and she was confused because she wasn't sure whether she liked that or not.

But of course she did, she told herself stoutly.

And she sure as heck still wanted this man. Fiercely and passionately and for as long as she could have him. She curled against him and smiled back, at peace with her decision.

'Yes, Leandro. While the snow falls…'

CHAPTER SIX

'There's a Celia Drew to see you.'

It was not a call Leandro had expected to take three weeks after he returned to London.

He sat back in his swivel chair, surprising his PA by telling her to send up his unexpected visitor and to cancel his morning meetings until he told her otherwise.

He vaulted out of his chair and strolled to the bank of windows overlooking the dank, crowded streets several stories below. So, she'd had second thoughts. Maybe she had revisited his offer and decided that taking him up on it might not be such a bad idea after all. He perversely hoped so because he would then be able to tell her that it was now off the table.

Which it most decidedly was.

Leandro's lips thinned at the unsavoury recollection of how their stint in Scotland had concluded.

A week living in a bubble. It had felt as though he had found himself inside one of those snow globes—shaken it and watched the white swirl of snowflakes covering everything for a few breathless, magical seconds.

He had gone to get a job done and had persuaded her to come because he'd needed her there. His objective had been simple—confront his runaway ex-fiancée, fill her in on what was happening with her father, remind her of the agreement they had reached to safeguard his financial future in a way that would salvage his pride, and to check out for himself what was going on with her mysterious lover who had bounced along and screwed everything up.

Simple.

Unfortunately, there had been no runaway ex-fiancée to confront and, instead, he had found himself trapped in his snow globe with a woman who had utterly bewitched him. For the first time in his life, well-laid plans had veered off-piste at dizzying speed.

Just thinking about it now made his teeth snap together with impatience and frustration.

He should have known that the temptation to touch would have been too much. He should have known because he'd sensed something intensely, sexually compelling about her from the very first minute he had clapped eyes on her.

She broke all the rules when it came to the sort of woman he tended to go out with. She had appealed to him on some weird level he hadn't quite been able to understand and, maybe the second he'd clocked their isolation, he'd known that lurking in the safety of his office would not have been enough to kill off his very inconvenient attraction.

He'd wanted her and she'd wanted him and somehow he'd let her get under his skin.

The sex had been mind-blowing.

He'd stepped out of time, forgotten the rules and regulations that governed his uber-controlled life. Why? How had that happened? How had the walls he had constructed with such painstaking care been so easy to breach? And why on earth now did it feel so liberating?

Liberating enough for him to lose sight of the fact that what had happened between them had been a moment in time.

He had offered her more. When that snow had melted and the helicopter had signalled the return of normality, instead of shaking hands and saying *Goodbye...it's been nice...look me up if you're ever in the area...* he'd asked her to carry on.

'This isn't over yet,' he'd husked, basking in the warm glow of post-coital satisfaction and knowing that she was as well. *'Why call it a day when we're still hot for one another?'*

It hadn't crossed his mind that she would turn him down. Why would it have? She'd known the enticing benefits that came with dating him. He hadn't needed to spell them out and front-row tickets to a fashion show had been just the tip of the iceberg.

And if she wasn't interested in weekends at Lake Como or prime seats at the theatre or eating in the finest restaurants that money could buy? No problem. He would happily have ditched the lot, closed the front door and whiled away the hours between the sheets.

Still, it hadn't troubled him when she'd very politely but very firmly thanked him for the kind offer and declined.

Now she was here.

Had she had second thoughts?

He wouldn't blame her. She'd taken him up on the tickets to the fashion show. He knew that because he'd checked. Had that opened her eyes to what she might enjoy if she had a change of heart about his offer?

Or maybe she'd just realised that she still wanted him, plain and simple. Maybe she'd spent the past three weeks tossing and turning at night in bed, thinking about him and wishing that they were tossing and turning together.

It was galling for Leandro to think that he had laughed, shrugged...*you win a few, you lose a few...* and accepted rejection with nonchalance because, face it, there were plenty of other fish in the sea, only to find that she was still in his head three weeks later.

Leandro didn't know how that computed but now that she was here, now that she had shown up out of the blue, he was feeling good for the first time since he'd locked the front door of his place in Scotland.

He was ready, waiting and half smiling as his dividing door was pushed open, as she was announced by his PA, at which point he spun round on his heel and headed back to the chair behind his impressive mahogany desk.

Celia, having weathered the worst week of her life, had been gripped by a sense of inevitability as she had stood, hovering and indecisive, in front of the towering glass spire in which Leandro's offices were housed.

It had taken every scrap of moral fibre not to turn tail and flee.

Unfortunately, there was no choice in the matter. This was going to be step one of a journey she had not anticipated and the prospect of all the other steps to follow made her feel sick.

She'd wondered whether he would even agree to see her at all and had worked out what she would do in that eventuality.

The bald fact of the matter was she had turned down his suggestion that they carry on seeing one another when they were back in London. Until such time as it came to a natural conclusion. He hadn't had to say that in so many words, but the implication had hung in the air between them like the sword of Damocles.

So much tantalising promise, dangling in front of her eyes like a banquet in a famine and, oh, how she had longed to jump at his offer. How she'd yearned to keep the door firmly shut against reality and continue to live in the delicious bubble they had constructed for themselves.

She had been deep frozen and he had brought her to life. That was how it had felt out there in the middle of nowhere, with the snow locking them in and making it easy to pretend that what they had was real.

It wasn't. Not for him. It was real for *her*. She'd gone into a situation with her eyes wide open and yet had been totally unprepared for the consequences.

Again!

She'd cheerfully told herself that he wasn't her type, at least not on any level that counted for anything. Yes, he was utter physical perfection and, sure, she reacted to him as any woman would, but there was no way sleeping with him could get complicated. Complicated was when emotions entered the equation and she was older and wiser and well able to recognise the sort of guy who could introduce complications.

But he'd touched her and she'd melted and he'd kept on touching and holding and captivating her and, bit by bit, the ground had shifted under her feet without her even realising.

She'd gone from hostile and suspicious to enthralled in supersonic speed and when the snow had finally petered out and London had beckoned, she'd been horrified to realise just how hard she had fallen for him.

Not just *fallen*. Fallen somehow implied she could pick herself up and dust herself down as she had with Martin, even though at the time she hadn't realised just how easy that had been. She'd been too busy feeling sorry for herself and humiliated because he had found her replacement in record time.

No, she had lost herself in Leandro and she'd known that finding her way back from that place was going to take strength she wasn't even sure she had.

And the only way she could even begin to do that was to walk away from him.

He hadn't even bothered to hide the fact that, as far as he was concerned, whatever they had wasn't going to last. It would run its course and come to an end, probably when he got bored with the novelty of having her around.

At which point, he would pick it back up with the sort of women he was really drawn to.

But fate had had other ideas.

It had been bad enough dithering outside the impressive building, but it had been ten times worse when she'd stood in front of that granite counter, with the bustle of city professionals swarming around her, and been told that, yes, Leandro would see her.

'Hadn't expected to see you.'

Leandro's dark, sexy drawl snapped her back to the present and Celia blinked as the door behind her gently clicked shut.

She'd barely paid any attention to her surroundings as she'd been shown up to his office and she hardly noticed them now. She was one hundred per cent riveted to Leandro's face, to the lazy sprawl of his big body behind the desk and the uncanny way he had of looking at her as though he could see right down to her very soul.

How could she have forgotten just how powerful his presence was? How shockingly good-looking he was? Darker, harsher, more forbidding than she remembered, but then they were no longer in the same place, where they were relaxed and laughing and all over one another, eager to get back in the bed as soon as they were out of it. Sometimes, not even making it to the bedroom. He was back to the guy she'd first met when he'd shown up unannounced at her shop.

'I hope I'm not disturbing you.' Celia hadn't moved one inch from the spot to which she was rooted by the closed door. 'I thought I'd try and catch you before you left.'

'What are you doing here? Just passing by? Thought you'd swing by for old times' sake?'

Leandro had thought, when they'd parted company, that the snowbound isolation of their situation might have exaggerated her sexual appeal, but the second she'd walked into his office he'd known just how far off target he'd been in that assumption.

He was grimly aware that his libido, which had done less than zero on the two occasions he had opted for distraction tactics and got in touch with a couple of women he knew, was now hale and hearty and ready to party.

He shifted uncomfortably in his chair and scowled.

'Sit.' He nodded to the chair positioned in front of his desk and couldn't help the fall of his gaze on her breasts, swaying under the…whatever it was she was wearing. What was she wearing? Some kind of suit and a jacket and some furry ankle boots.

She was nervous as hell, that much he could see, and it occurred to him that if she'd come to fling herself in his arms, then she surely wasn't dressed for the occasion. Not, he thought with a kick of masculine appreciation, that she didn't look as cute as hell in her get-up. Her hair was clipped back but, with almost no leap of his imagination, he could picture it as he had seen it so many times, in wild, copper disarray around her face.

Leandro breathed in deeply and half closed his eyes and fought against a bombardment of powerful, graphic images.

Watching him, stomach twisted with nervous tension, Celia couldn't help but notice just how unwelcoming he was. How fast he'd gone from the guy who'd gruffly but sincerely asked her to carry on what they had because he still wanted her to someone who was clearly put out that she'd shown up unexpectedly at his workplace. It hadn't occurred to her, but now she wondered whether he'd met someone else.

She walked to the chair on wobbly legs and fell into it but then she quickly gathered herself and looked at him.

'You're wondering what I'm doing here.'

'Is it to do with Julie? Your brother? I'm guessing not because everything seems to be roses and sunshine on that front.'

'Yes.' Celia grasped the lifeline of innocuous conversation because it gave her time for her nerves to steady. 'I don't know how Julie's father feels about it because I haven't spoken to her face to face yet, but I know Dan's over the moon and so are Mum and Dad.'

'So…if you're not here to discuss family matters, then why exactly are you here?'

Her silence, Leandro thought, was telling. He wanted her still so badly that it *hurt* and that, as much as anything else, enraged him because it signified just the sort of weakness he had spent a lifetime protecting himself against. A simple request, nothing more, and yet it felt like a stake of trust being driven into the ground, a vulnerability with someone else of the sort that should never happen. Had never happened.

His eyes cooled and his expression hardened.

'If you've come,' he inserted quietly into the awkward, lengthening silence, 'because you've decided that you want to pick up where we left off, after all, then I'm sorry to say that that window has closed.'

Uttering those words didn't give Leandro the satisfaction he'd expected but there was no way he had any intention of taking them back. He was, however, bemused by the expression on her face, which went from puzzled to incredulous to downright angry. Colour flared in her cheeks and she half rose from her chair only to abruptly sit back down.

'Believe it or not, that's *not* why I've come to see you, Leandro!'

'Then why?' Leandro asked.

'I'm beginning to wonder that myself,' Celia said in a driven undertone. 'I wouldn't have bothered you if I'd had a choice. I know that I turned you down and I know I probably…offended you…'

Leandro laughed with incredulity.

'Offended me? How? I thought we might have had a few more weeks of fun but the fact that you weren't interested in that option hardly tore my life to ribbons!'

Hearing that hurt and Celia felt the sting of tears push behind her eyelids.

'I'm here to tell you that I'm pregnant, Leandro.'

It still sounded surreal to her own ears. It would. Bearing in mind she hadn't said a word to anyone. It was something she was still holding to herself and coming to terms with as her whole world was turned upside down.

She'd barely been aware that her period was overdue until she developed an aversion to her usual morning cup of coffee and then, just like that, it hit her that her body was behaving differently and it wasn't just the coffee aversion. Her breasts had started feeling weird and she'd almost nodded off a couple of times when she'd been doing some sketching for a commission.

She'd known, *deep down*, but it had still come as a shock when that little stick had confirmed her worst fears.

She'd scrabbled around in her head trying to work out the when and the how, but everything had become a blur and the only thing that had become clear during those horrendous few days when she'd walked around in a daze was that she had to tell Leandro.

They might not have anything left between them but a handful of memories, and he might very well slam the door in her face when she broke the news, but she *had* to tell him because that was the person she was.

'You can't be.'

'I'm sorry.' Her eyes slid away from his ashen face to the window behind him. 'I know this is the last thing you want to hear but I had to come and tell you. I haven't come here to ask anything of you, just in case that's what you're thinking. I know what we had…er…ended a couple of weeks ago but I didn't think it would have been fair on you if I hadn't…filled you in. Well, you would have probably found out anyway, because of your connection with Julie…'

'How? How did this happen?' He waved one hand and then rubbed his eyes with his fingers and for a few seconds he said nothing at all, then he looked at her. 'No need to answer that. We…had a lot of fun and sometimes it's possible that I wasn't as careful as I might have been.' He sat back and briefly closed his eyes. 'Are you sure?'

'I did more than one test, Leandro. Of course, I'm more than happy to do a few more, but there's no doubt that I'm having a baby.' But his willingness to accept at least some of the responsibility was a weight off her shoulders.

All the attendant problems now crowded in on her and she blinked, suddenly vulnerable under the onslaught.

Before she could react, he had swerved around the desk and positioned himself next to her, half stooping so that they were on eye level.

'This isn't the right place to be having a conversation about this.' He raked his fingers through his hair but didn't take his eyes off her face.

'It's a shock, I know.' She began standing. Her legs were still wobbly but it was a relief now that she had said her piece. 'I'll leave you to mull things over.'

'What?' Leandro said sharply. *'Mull things over?'*

'Yes. We can always talk again soon.'

'No, no, no. I think you've got the wrong end of the stick here, Celia. There's nothing to *mull over* that's going to propel me into reaching any kind of alternative conclusion. You're pregnant and it's my fault.'

'It takes two to tango.'

'We need privacy for this conversation.' He was already moving towards a concealed door, pushing it so that it sprang open and reaching for a tan coat in the softest of cashmere.

'Where are we going?'

'My place.'

'What? No!'

'Why not?' Leandro strolled in front of her, invading her space for a couple of seconds, hands shoved deep in the pockets of the coat. His dark eyes ensnared her and the silence stretched taut.

Leandro's eyes drifted down, remorselessly drawn to her stomach, and it hit him hard that this was more than just a theoretical discussion about what happened when faced with an unexpected pregnancy.

She was carrying his child.

He felt shaken to his very foundations. Nothing in life had braced him for this eventuality. How had he ended up being cavalier, at least on one occasion he could remember when the distance from kitchen to bedroom to get protection had been a little too far, and not foreseen the consequences?

And yet now, as he stared down at her, what should have horrified him, didn't.

What should have filled him with resentment, didn't. He didn't feel the walls closing in. He felt…a surge of protectiveness that knocked him for six.

Where did *that* come from?

He'd never factored children into his life. Why would he? He'd seen the damage parents could do, he'd lived the unspoken sorrow born of growing up with the whiff of abandonment because, although he'd had his father, what child would not be affected by a mother who left him when he was barely out of nappies?

So having kids? Never been on the horizon. Easier to shelve that whole issue than take the risk of being an unwitting cause of hurt to a kid who hadn't asked to be born. He worked all the hours under the sun. That, for starters, augured badly for the sort of family lifestyle children needed.

And yet...

Leandro had an insane desire to whip this woman away, wrap her up in cotton wool and protect her because she was now the mother of his unborn child.

He stepped back, looked away, shaken to the core but channelling her up and then out, barely aware of telling his startled PA to block out all meetings for the remainder of the day.

Urged on by Leandro, Celia felt as though control had been whipped away from her.

She'd come to tell him what had needed to be told but after that? She'd vaguely assumed that a billionaire who had been frank about his views on commitment and marriage and everything that went with it would hardly have flung down the welcome mat at what she had to say. After that? Who knew? After that, her mind had been taken up with the ensuing way forward, breaking the news to her mum and dad, absorbing their disappointment, which would be hidden beneath their loving support. They would ask themselves how it was that she had made mistakes not once, but *twice*, and, this time, a mistake with long-reaching consequences.

They would wonder how it was that they had brought her up to respect the tradition of marriage and to value love and commitment only to get involved with a guy who had no interest in any of that.

The tangle of thoughts had stopped at Leandro's office door, like a messenger ringing a doorbell to deliver a package and then leaving.

So she was in a daze as she was ushered to an underground car park where she vaguely noted three high-end cars, all black, parked alongside one another.

He took the middle car, a low sleek sports car that purred into low-throated life as he slowly manoeuvred it out of the car park and into the London traffic.

'When did you find out?' Leandro glanced across to her before refocusing on the stop-start traffic.

'A couple of days ago,' Celia said unevenly.

'And have you told…anyone yet? Your parents?'

'I'm…working myself up to it. I thought…you should be the first to know, considering you're the father.'

'Thank you for that.'

'For what?' Celia laughed humourlessly. 'For being honest with you? Look, I'm not sure how much there is to talk about, Leandro. You forget we spent time together…long enough for me to know that this must be your worst nightmare come true. I've already told you that I don't expect anything from you.'

'And for that,' Leandro said quietly, again glancing across at her.

'For what?'

'For telling me that you don't expect anything from me.'

That stung. Celia's eyes glazed over and she stared out of the window in absolute silence, digesting what he'd said.

Of course he was grateful that she wasn't going to make a nuisance of herself. Did he think that she might have turned clingy and needy? She loved him but he

didn't know that and he never would. She might have
lost her heart to him, but she hadn't lost her dignity and
she never would.

She almost laughed out loud when she thought about
how he would have reacted if he'd known, not just that
she was pregnant, but that she was in love with him! He
would have strapped rockets to his ankles in his hurry
to see the back of her.

So was he whipping her away to the privacy of his
house to try and come to an arrangement whereby they
worked out how she could become invisible?

No…even as Celia thought that, she knew, deep down,
that that just wasn't the guy she had fallen for.

'We're here.'

Celia shook herself and took stock of the electric
gates opening to a pale grey courtyard fringed with
impeccably manicured grass. By London standards,
it was huge for a house within easy reach of the city.
The house itself was as modern as his manor estate
in Scotland had been old and established, a marvel of
sharp angles and banks of glass, all protected by high
walls even though it was a quiet and tree-lined resi-
dential street.

She was ushered into a vast, cleverly arranged open-
plan space, the sort of uber-sophisticated bachelor pad
that would have cost a small fortune. The kitchen, to the
left, looked over an island the size of a skating rink and
behind which sat a vision of metal and chrome and marble. Ahead were various rooms, some behind doors and
the living area was a sunken space sparsely furnished
with pale tan leather and a white rug. A galleried landing, where the bedrooms were, she assumed, overlooked
everything on the ground floor.

'Celia...' he guided her to the sitting area and waited as she gingerly perched on the edge of one of the immaculate leather sofas '... I thank you for telling me that you expect nothing from me because I can't think of any woman who wouldn't see this situation as a passport to asking a great deal from me. What can I get you to drink? Tea? Coffee? Are those things off limits for pregnant women?' He squatted next to her, then swerved to sit so close that his thigh was pressed against hers. 'Surely you know that the last thing I have any intention of doing is *nothing.*'

'What do you mean?'

'I mean you can trust me to do what needs to be done. I am a man of honour, as you know, and I have every intention of doing the honourable thing. Neither you nor our child will want for anything. I'll take care of that.'

'You'll take care of that...' Celia parroted.

'It's a pretty scary time for you,' Leandro murmured as Celia continued to gape at him. 'You haven't told your parents and I'm guessing, when you say that you're *working up to that*, that you're privately apprehensive about what their reaction is going to be...maybe scared at what you might think will be inevitable disappointment.'

Celia dragged her eyes away with some effort. 'You have no idea what's going through my head, Leandro.'

Except he did, right down to the last detail, from the sounds of it.

'I might not have seen this coming,' Leandro admitted, 'but you're pregnant and there's no other option than for us to be married.'

Celia, who had been gaping before, now uttered a strangulated sound of complete shock. Her eyes widened. 'Get married? Get *married*? No! Leandro, we're not going to *get married.*'

'We are,' Leandro countered quietly and without a shred of doubt in his voice. 'I could give you a thousand reasons why. I could write a book on how beneficial it would be for our child to be raised with financial security and I speak from a position of experience. I could tell you that your traditional parents would welcome their only daughter getting married and settling down to raise a family, not having to go through the heartache of disappointment and anxious that they may have failed to provide you with the wherewithal to make sensible life choices. But the only reason that counts is this: when you have a child, it becomes time to put selfish concerns about your own happiness behind you because there's no room for that. Something else—' his voice hardened as he rose to his feet '—I learnt on my travels through life. I don't intend to be an absentee father because I don't happen to fit the bill when it comes to the life partner you had in mind, because this is not what either of us signed up for.'

There was intent behind his words but, more than that, a sincerity that made her realise that he would do everything it took to fulfil his fatherly obligations. He was a man who had no problem with a marriage of convenience. He had just left one behind. This was more of the same, if for a different reason.

How far would he go for the sake of honour and was that something she wanted to find out?

And how much would *she* sacrifice because she was in love with a guy who didn't love her back? The happiness of her own baby? Because she might not be able to deal with daily contact with Leandro? Was that something *she* wanted to put to the test?

'Can I think about it?' Celia murmured.

'You can think about it—' his voice was deadly serious '—but there will only be one answer I'm willing to accept…'

CHAPTER SEVEN

'I CAN'T BELIEVE IT. Have I said that already? Yes. I have. But it's…well, pet, you know the old saying…you spend a lifetime waiting for a bus and then two come along one after the other. First Dan and lovely, lovely Julie and now you and Leandro. You know your dad and I couldn't be happier…'

Celia made a game effort to smile. She and her mother were in the kitchen clearing away the dishes. Leandro and her father had remained in the sitting room for a while, bonding over a glass of port, which, for her father, could be classified as a celebration after-dinner drink, and had then retired for the night. Leandro had swanned into the kitchen, given her mother a hug and a peck on the cheek, effusively thanked her for the best roast dinner he had ever had, and announced that he would be heading up.

It had taken a little over a week for her to summon up the necessary courage to make the trip to Shrewsbury so that she could break the joyful news to her parents.

A husband-to-be…a baby on the way…love at first sight…every romantic dream rolled into one with dizzying speed.

They had both patiently explained the situation with

Julie and her engagement to Leandro as soon as they had arrived several hours earlier but, as it turned out, both her parents were already aware of the backstory.

Dan had told them all about the engagement of convenience and how it had crashed and burned when he and Julie had fallen in love.

'I would have told you,' Lizzie Drew had said sheepishly, 'but we'd only just about found out ourselves and I thought it best if Dan and Julie told you themselves. Cleared the air. I know they planned on meeting Leandro, but they wanted to reassure Julie's father first that he had nothing to worry about. It all seemed a bit of a muddle for me to start trying to dissect down the end of the line but now that you're both here…and, well! What a wonderful turn up for the books!'

As far as her mum was concerned, Celia discovered very quickly that her fairy story of meeting the guy of her dreams was every bit as romantic as Julie and Dan's had been.

The fact that Leandro had been prepared to marry a woman so that he could rescue her father from pain and penury already spoke volumes. There was already a halo on his head by the time they'd rung the doorbell.

And Leandro had not failed when it came to keeping the halo in place. He had gone full throttle with the charm and, over the course of dinner, Celia had watched her parents visibly melt.

If they had been favourably predisposed towards Leandro to start with, then, by the time the sticky toffee pudding was eaten, they had become full-time members of his fan club.

Not for one single second had either of them had any doubts that she and Leandro were in love.

The pregnancy had said it all.

They had such faith in her, and were so disingenuously convinced that their daughter would never fall pregnant unless love was involved because that was how she had been brought up, that the entire evening had been filled with teary-eyed smiles and congratulations and enthusiastic wedding planning.

Now, with the last dish finally washed and at a little after eleven, Celia felt as exhausted as if she'd run a marathon. She looked around the sparkling kitchen and wondered whether she could hang around for another couple of hours pointlessly wiping the counters, because arrangements on the sleeping front all seemed to be a bit of a nightmare.

'You go on up, Mum,' she said faintly as her mother headed to the kitchen door. 'I'll stay here…er…' she looked around her at the spotless kitchen with a hint of desperation '…and unload the dishwasher. You and Dad are leaving first thing in the morning for your cruise— you don't want to come down to a full dishwasher…'

Quite rightly, her mother looked a little startled at this suggestion.

'I wish you had come sooner, darling. I so would have liked to have spent longer going over all the wedding plans…you know… Dan's getting married but there's nothing like a mother and her daughter when it comes to weddings.'

'Well, like I mentioned, Mum…it's going to be a small wedding…all under the radar…literally just you, Dad, Dan and Julie and Julie's dad…piled into a register office…'

She smiled brightly while wondering how her life had

veered so wildly off course from what she had always planned for herself.

The girl who had been saved from marrying the wrong guy was now marrying the wrong guy.

The girl who had thought she'd learned lessons had ended up learning nothing at all.

The girl who'd dreamt of a big white wedding, with all her friends and relatives there, was looking forward to a register office and an event that would be a formality, just a piece of paper signed legitimising the union she had been persuaded into. Not that it had taken much persuasion. Not only could she see things from Leandro's point of view...not only could she empathise with his need to provide two parents for his child where he had had one, but from her point of view, yes, a child should never pay for the mistakes of its parents.

If, in the years to come, their situation became insupportable, then that was another matter.

For the moment, as he had pointed out, they got along very well indeed and how, he had inserted deftly, would she ever be able to explain to their son or daughter that they had been denied the advantages of having both parents because she'd decided that she wouldn't give it a go?

Celia had seen the harshness on his beautiful face and had known what he had been thinking. That his own mother hadn't been bothered and look at the legacy she had left behind.

But she knew that she had wandered into a minefield because everything had changed.

She hadn't been able to fault him. For the past week and a half, he had seen her three times and together, like business associates, they had hammered out their way forward.

He had listened to her concerns and had answered all of them, fairly and gently and with understanding. She had told him that there was no way she wanted to live in London.

'I can't imagine bringing up a child in the city,' she had admitted, looking around his spartan, urban space and wondering whether there could possibly be anywhere less suited to a child. 'I grew up in the country and I know it would be inconvenient, but if we get married, then we need to find a solution to that.'

He had agreed with alacrity. There was Surrey…there was Berkshire…there were countless towns and villages where she could find the space she needed, which would also be commutable to London.

'You can keep your shop here, in London,' he had said thoughtfully. 'Maybe leave the running of it to your assistants? And start afresh wherever we settle. I imagine the provinces might prove a very lucrative market for wedding dresses unless, of course, you want to pack in working altogether, which would be absolutely fine with me.'

Celia had hurriedly turned down that suggestion. The thought of being dependent for ever on someone who didn't love her and was only with her for the sake of the child they had conceived didn't sit well.

There were moments when she almost wished that he weren't quite so nice because *nice* was not what she wanted. She missed the Leandro who had looked at her with simmering passion, who had made love to her until she'd wanted to scream with pleasure. She missed the sexy, sensual familiarity that had grown between them during those magical days in Scotland, when they had been prisoners of the weather.

Now, he gave her respect and she didn't know what to do with it.

The guy who had huskily asked her to continue what they'd started when they returned to London had gone for good.

In his place was the guy who, undeniably, wanted to do the right thing and quite frankly would turn out to be a great dad.

But he no longer touched her. He kept his distance and that hurt even though she knew, in a muddled way, that touching would just add to the complications.

Was he assuming that, because this was a business arrangement for him, what they would have would be along the same lines as what he had agreed with Julie? An open marriage of sorts where she would discreetly overlook any misdemeanours?

Or was he just biding his time? He might genuinely believe that two parents were better than one, but maybe, subconsciously, he also knew that a divorced guy had a lot more rights than one who had never married.

Was he playing a waiting game? He certainly no longer had any interest in her on the physical level.

It was a subject Celia dared not broach because of the worms that might start crawling out of the can.

Did she really want him to kindly tell her that she wasn't his type after all? That what they'd had had worked in Scotland, where reality was something they had left behind? That it just wasn't something, on reflection, that could survive the light of day?

Did she want him to know how much she missed him? No, she didn't.

They would marry and who knew—it was possible that seeing him up close and personal all the time would put paid to the hold he had over her. How long could one person carry on loving someone who wasn't interested?

The house was quiet by the time she made her way up to the bedroom that her mother had lovingly made up for them, right down to flowers in the vase on the chest of drawers and some kind of scent that filled the room with the smell of cedarwood.

She quietly pushed open the door to a semi-darkened room and Leandro on the bed and, suddenly, she was on red-hot alert, her senses quivering with forbidden excitement. The horse might have bolted and it might have been futile trying to bolt the stable door, but right now there was no comfort in the fact that they had been lovers.

She felt his dangerous presence and shivered.

'You're on the bed.' Celia folded her arms and stared down at Leandro, who returned her gaze, unperturbed.

He was half naked and she hoped that the nudity didn't extend beyond what she could see because she didn't think her blood pressure could take it.

'Where else am I supposed to be?'

'Leandro,' she muttered, but she could feel her fingers digging into her arms, 'this isn't going to work.'

'Why not?'

'Because…because this isn't what we're about now!'

No, Leandro thought. Under normal circumstances, wouldn't this have been a good outcome? A marriage of convenience, admittedly, but one with the bonus of hot sex. With or without the hot sex, however, it was a union he had been determined to cement. The fierceness of what he felt for this unborn baby astonished him, but he wasn't going to pretend it didn't exist, and, that being the case, his mind had leapt several steps ahead, to a scenario in which they went their separate ways, sharing custodial rights.

A child toing and froing from one house to another. Different wardrobes in different places, treading a thin line between what was diplomatic to say to one parent in the absence of the other.

Eventually, another man would come on the scene. How long before that other man became central to his child's life? How long before *his* flesh and blood started calling *another guy* his *dad*?

Right there and then, Leandro had known that no way was that ever going to be allowed to happen on his watch. And more than that…more than all those plausible scenarios was the uneasy recognition that she was pulling away from him. Hell! He didn't want to care but he was finding that he did. He didn't want her distance. He wanted…what? Could it be the ease of connection they had had before things had become complicated? Before a future he had never considered became the present with which they both had to deal?

Now here they were.

'This room,' he told her, voice cooling, 'is the size of a matchbox. You want me to sleep on the ground? I'll sleep on the ground.' How ironic that they were now in the most intimate situation possible and yet she couldn't bear the thought of sharing her bed with him. 'And what if they poke their heads in and find the pair of love birds not sharing the same bed?'

'They're leaving at the crack of dawn tomorrow morning. They'd never know.'

'Fine.' Leandro shrugged and made to fling aside the duvet.

'Okay. No. They…it might be hard to explain if they popped in to say goodbye before they left.'

'Yes. After the effusive welcome we received, there might have been disappointment all round if they thought we'd ended the evening on a raging argument serious enough to send us shooting off in separate bedrooms. What's the problem with sharing a bed? Have I tried to lay a single finger on you since you came back into my life? Have I given you any reason to believe that I'm anything other than a decent guy trying to do the decent thing, which doesn't include forcing himself on a woman who's not interested?'

Their eyes tangled, his darkly brooding, holding her gaze until she was the first to look away.

If he'd hoped to force a response from her, then it hadn't been forthcoming and he was annoyed with himself for trying to corner her into saying something, *anything* that would let him know what exactly was going on behind that guarded exterior.

Foremost wasn't the crazy issue that he was still attracted to her. It wasn't even the realisation that he had become the very man he had always sworn he never would…a man vulnerable to someone else's decisions. First and foremost and the only thing that mattered was the knowledge that she was having his baby and he was going to marry her, going to be a full-time father with none of the hopeless complications associated with any kind of joint custody.

Sure, joint custody would always be a damn sight better than what *he* had had as a kid, but it still would never be in the same league as a child having both parents there.

He noted the tic in her neck and the steady blush that

invaded her cheeks and he wondered whether she was trying to work out how to knock him back without getting into a pointless war of words.

'No, of course you haven't.' Celia tilted her chin at a mutinous, defensive angle. 'I just thought that it might be a bit awkward… It's not a very big bed…'

'Feel free to barricade yourself behind the cushions but trust me…if our bodies touch during the night, then I assure you it will be purely accidental.'

Which, Celia thought with such a sharp stab of pain that she momentarily felt faint, pretty much said it all. Accidental touching where before there had been touching with intent, with intent and passion and desire and, she'd sometimes thought, more affection and tenderness than he was probably even aware of.

'I would never,' Leandro said gravely, his voice warmer, 'do anything that might make you feel in the least bit uncomfortable. If it would make you feel a little…less awkward, I can head down to the kitchen and spend a couple of hours working, give you time to fall asleep in peace.'

'It's okay,' Celia muttered, flushing. 'I'll get changed and of course it's not a problem sharing the bed. I… I apologise for—'

'Forget it!' He waved his hand dismissively. 'This is new for the both of us. Let's put this kind of thing down to teething problems.'

She did.

She took her time showering unnecessarily and then she took her time applying some night cream and then doing a few deep-breathing exercises before she returned to the bedroom in the most conservative nightwear she

had, long bottoms and a short-sleeved top firmly buttoned up.

She slept. Soundly. If their bodies *accidentally*
touched, then she wasn't aware of it.

She woke at five, her senses alert to her parents up
and about and trying to be as quiet as they could.

Next to her, Leandro was still asleep, the covers half
off, his muscular, bronzed body so compellingly beautiful that she remained frozen and in awe, drinking in the
sight and luxuriating in the freedom of appreciating him,
of not having to hide her love because he was sleeping.

Then she slid off the bed, tiptoed out of the bedroom
and only detoured via the bathroom to shove on her
bathrobe so that she could go and wish her parents a
good holiday.

They might have been in a state of simmering excitement about their departure but not so excited that they
didn't have time to repeat the mantra of how wonderful
they thought Leandro was. So much better suited to her
than Martin had been, for all Martin's sterling qualities.
Celia marvelled that her parents could both misread Leandro so completely but, then again, the guy could charm
the birds from the trees and he had dazzled them both,
maybe just the way he'd dazzled *her*.

It was nearly an hour before she headed back to the
bedroom but still only just after six in the morning and
she half expected Leandro to still be asleep, but when
she quietly pushed open the bedroom door, heartened
by the fact that the lights hadn't been switched on, she
was shocked to find that the bed was empty and Leandro
was perched on a chair by the window. He had pulled
open the curtains just enough for her eyes to quickly adjust to the fact that he had changed into jeans and a tee

shirt. His long legs were stretched out at an angle and next to him...

Draped half on, half off the stout chest of drawers she had used ever since she'd been a kid...

Celia's mouth dropped open and she took a couple of faltering steps forward.

'What...what's this doing out?'

'Tell me about it.'

'You've been rummaging in my wardrobe?'

'Hunting down a face towel. Thought there might be a stash there. You never said you'd hung onto your wedding dress from years ago.'

'Because that was none of your business!' But she walked towards the dress, covered in its voluminous mothproof cover, and gazed down for a few seconds at it.

When she rested her hand on it, she didn't flinch as he covered it with his own.

Leandro watched her closely.

He'd vaguely been rooting around for a face towel but the truth was that he'd heard her sidle out of the bedroom and had known that she'd been heading down to chat to her parents before they left on their holiday.

They'd slept in her bedroom. There was stuff everywhere, from the pictures in the frames on the dressing table to the old board games in a stack on the shelf above the chest of drawers.

He'd leapt out of bed, slung on some clothes and taken his time looking at the pictures, stories of a happy childhood. He'd only peered into the wardrobe because he'd just happened to be standing in front of it and his curiosity about Celia had been piqued by the mementoes all around him.

And the wedding dress had been impossible to miss because it was the only thing in the cupboard and it took up so much space.

He knew that she didn't pine for her ex. She might have been hurt but she had never registered any lingering pain when she'd mentioned him.

But that didn't mean that the experience had killed off all her dreams. She'd planned for the big white wedding and she'd hung onto the dress because it had been a reminder of what she had longed for.

In a flash, Leandro realised just how much she was willing to sacrifice for the sake of a child neither of them had reckoned on.

Not just her hopes of finding Mr Perfect, after she'd almost married Mr Imperfect, but all the other things that went with that. The courtship…the planning for the big day…the confetti and photos and speeches and the driving off to the romantic honeymoon. The way she now rested her small hand on that dress and the wistful look in her eyes said it all and something inside Leandro twisted.

'I'm not going to force your hand,' he said roughly. Their eyes met and he nodded at the wedding dress. 'If you're still holding onto dreams, then I don't want to be the one to trample all over them.'

'That's not what you said to me a few days ago. A few days ago you made it clear that marriage was the only solution as far as you were concerned.'

'It still is but I have no intention of getting what I want by using a whip.'

Celia raised her eyebrows at this change in tune, then she sighed, thought of what life would look like without him in it, now that she had reconciled herself to marrying him.

It wasn't an attractive picture.

Disentangling her parents from the happy-ever-after fairy-tale ending was just the cherry on top. The truth was that she had guiltily found herself painting unrealistic pictures in her head about life with Leandro.

Of course he didn't love her! Good heavens, he no longer even wanted to come near her physically! There were so many problems associated with those two things, but hadn't there been just a tiny bloom of *possibilities* cutting a forbidden path through all of that? Hadn't a little voice carried on saying, however much she'd tried to shut it down, that who knew what lay around the corner…?

'You're not,' she confessed. 'So I really didn't think that we would end up…well, *here*, when I came to tell you about the pregnancy, but I agree that two parents are usually better than one and you've met Mum and Dad. That was how I was brought up. So you're not forcing my hand. If I really and truly didn't want to go through with it, then I wouldn't. And for the wedding dress? I hung onto it…' She paused and glanced down, noting with surprise his hand on hers and quietly slipping hers free '…because it was the first one I ever tried my hand at after I finished my course. I…it's not even properly finished, so it isn't as though I could sell it…'

Her voice petered out and the silence hung heavily between them for a few seconds.

She didn't know where this was going and she had no idea what was coming next, so she was shocked when he said, voice low and even, 'We've talked about a lot of things, by which I mean, we've gone through all the reasons why we've decided on…doing what needs to be done for the sake of this baby. We've agreed on where we could live and the money side of things…but on a less… formal level, you're going to be giving a lot up for this.'

'As are you.'

'We also,' he said neutrally, 'find ourselves in the unique position of being in the most intimate situation possible without the benefit of really knowing one another.'

'I…' Celia was hurt because she'd thought they'd got to know one another well over that short space of time. She'd told him things she'd never told anyone else. Had she been a complete fool in thinking that perhaps it might have been the same for him? Just a little? 'I…yes, I suppose you're right…'

'To make this really work, maybe we should take some time out together.'

'You think that because I didn't tell you about the wedding dress you don't know me?'

'How much do we know one another?' His voice was a low, lazy drawl.

In truth, Leandro realised that he had been more unsettled by that wedding dress in the cupboard than he'd thought. Of course it had made him realise what she was giving up, all the intangible things she was saying goodbye to.

He patted himself on the back because that showed a magnanimous side to him of which he was proud, even though the emotional response was unusual enough to floor him.

But now that he considered it in a little more depth, he wondered whether her nostalgia for romance would leave ajar a door through which she would eventually be tempted to enter. Would she want to see what was on the other side?

He would take things back a bit, he'd determined. They'd skipped a lot of steps in the process she'd probably spent her whole life looking forward to. He'd met her parents, had been charmed by them, had seen them for the traditional sort who truly believed in the power of love. He didn't get it, but what he *did* get was the power of sex and that was something they had had in abundance.

So she had given him the cold shoulder when he'd suggested they continue. Maybe she'd had big dreams of walking off into a rosy sunset arm in arm with some guy who probably didn't exist, whom she might or might not meet one fine day and to whom she would give her heart.

But they were here now and something about her alarm at sharing the bed with him the night before had nudged something inside him. Was she as indifferent to him as she wanted to be? Or was there still the same simmering attraction inside her that, if enticed, would blow hot and fierce as it had done before?

She might not welcome a reaction that didn't suit her ideals but if they were to be married…? Then the world turned on its axis, didn't it?

Thoughts of seduction, let loose from the cage in which they had been confined, roared out with the power of a sudden burning conflagration.

Seduction rarely involved the prosaic. They had done prosaic, insofar as prosaic could exist in their current situation.

'Once we're married, whatever the timeline, the pregnancy will be further along,' he murmured. 'You might even find it difficult to travel anywhere…'

'Travel anywhere?' Celia looked at him with open bewilderment. 'I know my car is small,' she said, 'but, actually, I *will* still be able to get around in it! Even if I grow to the size of a barrage balloon, I can just push the seat back a bit and travelling isn't going to be some kind of dicing-with-misfortune experience, Leandro. I'm not going to be an invalid just because I'm having a baby!'

'What's the state of your passport?' he mused, by way of response, and Celia frowned.

'I have one. Why do you ask?'

'I may be realistic,' he responded wryly, 'when it comes to finding solutions to problems, but I'm not completely without finesse. Most married couples go on honeymoon.'

'We're not most married couples.'

'In the eyes of your parents, we are, wouldn't you agree?' He waited a heartbeat knowing that there was no argument she could use against that. 'They would hardly expect us to get married, as the loved-up couple they believe us to be, for me to promptly return to work without even paying lip service to my new bride…'

There were so many words in that sentence that were at odds with what actually existed between them that Celia's head was in a whirl and yet, treacherously, she clung to those words with the desperation of a complete idiot. *Loved-up couple…new bride…a honeymoon befitting those things…*

He was only stating the obvious, wasn't he?

They *had* put on a united front. They had come as the bearer of glad tidings and her parents had not doubted otherwise. Many times, Leandro's arm had rested across her shoulders…around her waist…his fingers lightly feathering her wrist…his thigh brushing hers as they had sat together on the sofa in the sitting room.

She had been unbearably *aware* of each and every one of those little intimate gestures because she was so unbearably aware of *him*. Her parents, of course, would have been equally aware of each and every one of those gestures. Her mother was eagle-eyed when it came to things like that.

Celia was sure that her mum would be nursing some disappointment about the size of the wedding. She would have wanted planning and hats and showing off her daughter to all her friends in the village. But she hadn't said a word. However, if there were to be no honeymoon and nothing at all to mark the event as something joyous and to be celebrated, then how would she feel?

Would a pretence of a honeymoon be necessary?

'I suppose we could pretend to do something.' She frowned, staring off into the distance, and Leandro did his best not to grit his teeth in pure frustration.

Was there a woman as challenging as the one now chewing her lip and staring off as though waiting for divine inspiration? Was it utterly arrogant and egotistic of him to think that there were very few women who wouldn't have leapt at everything he had offered instead? The ring? And all the benefits that came with that? Which, quite frankly, were more than generous?

'We could. What,' he asked with an edge of genuine curiosity, 'did you have in mind?'

'Well, we could hide out at your place…'

Leandro burst out laughing and, when he'd sobered up, he gazed at her with amusement. 'When this breaks, there'll be some press coverage. I'm a billionaire. I'm not saying the paparazzi are going to be stalking us in the hope of a juicy story, but I'm well enough known in financial and society circles for some interest. If they discover that we've put it about that we're heading off to exotic climes on a pre-baby-being-born honeymoon only to discover that we're both lurking under the bed at my London place, then I can't think what will be made of that.'

'Exotic climes?'

Leandro shrugged. 'The world is full of some exceptionally lovely outposts.'

'So you're thinking we actually go somewhere.'

'Leave it to me. I'll sort everything out.' He grinned. 'And you can relax. You're pregnant. Pregnant women are supposed to take it easy. I'll make sure you don't have a minute's stress.'

Celia gaped and blinked. Was he kidding? A honeymoon with this guy so that they could *get to know one another* and he was guaranteeing her a stress-free experience? What planet was he on?

But of course she knew.

He wanted to make sure they entered this new arrangement as friends, and friends surely didn't stress about spending time in one another's company. Did they?

Except for her...

When she thought about being away with him, she felt faint, but he was already rising to his feet, getting ready to start the day, and she knew, with a sinking heart, that what he wanted he was going to get.

CHAPTER EIGHT

CELIA'S IDEA OF the perfect honeymoon involved white sands and blue sea and lazy cocktails on a beach and being somewhere where you could easily imagine that the rest of the world didn't actually exist. Even after she and Martin had parted company, she could remember guiltily and longingly gazing at faraway destinations in magazines, where sun, sea and sand were the only 'S's to be had, without that other one, *stress*, rearing its ugly head and spoiling everything.

By the time they'd returned to London the previous afternoon, *stress* at whatever Leandro had planned had definitely been high on the agenda as she'd churned over in her head the prospect of going on a pseudo honeymoon with him.

She'd made an effort to find out what he had in mind, but he had told her to just make sure her passport was up to date and her summer wardrobe was up and running.

Then he'd looked at her, a quick, sidelong glance as his powerful car ate up the motorway miles, and said thoughtfully, 'I think a shopping trip might be in order.'

Why fight it?

The consequences of accepting his offer of marriage had been beginning to sink in.

The altruistic *rightness* of doing the best for the baby they now shared hid a network of uncomfortable realities.

His wealth was staggering and while she had every intention of continuing her own business, adapting and adjusting as necessary, she would essentially be the recipient of immense financial comfort.

How could she dig her heels in and fight that? He wanted the best for his child and she would be tugged along in the undertow.

'Really?' She'd greeted his pensive observation with a half-hearted lack of enthusiasm. 'I have summer clothes.'

'What?'

'I said I already have perfectly fine summer clothes.'

'No. *What* summer clothes do you have?'

Celia had bristled, but had then remembered what her summer wardrobe consisted of and said, truthfully, 'I think I have some shorts and a couple of dresses.' The truth was that she had the sort of clothes designed to hide behind. Baggy shirts and loose-fitting dresses and everything in muted colours that allowed her to fade into the background.

'We're going to be getting married,' Leandro had pointed out. 'You're going to have to dress the part.'

'*Dress the part?* Do you think I'm some kind of Barbie doll, Leandro? What world do you live in where you really imagine that women should dress to fit in with a guy?'

'Actually...' Leandro had been sidetracked '...you'd be surprised how many women enjoy shopping for expensive clothes. They rarely have to be forced into it kicking and screaming. But,' he'd continued reasonably, 'that wasn't what I was getting at.'

'No?'

'If we go anywhere expensive, you're going to be ill at ease in clothes that make you feel self-conscious. Besides, has it occurred to you that I might actually want to treat my bride-to-be to a new wardrobe? Jewellery? Holidays? A new car...?'

Bride-to-be in name only, Celia had thought. 'I don't need a new car.'

'Stop arguing with me all the time.'

'If I don't happen to agree with what you're saying, it doesn't mean that I'm arguing with you.'

At which point he'd burst out laughing and told her that he would collect her the following morning at ten sharp from her house.

So here she was now. She was no wiser as to the destination of this honeymoon and locked into a morning shopping with Leandro.

She was far from beginning to show yet but, even so, her first words as she settled into the back of his chauffeur-driven car were, 'It's silly to spend a lot of money on clothes that are only going to fit me for a few weeks— by the time summer rolls round over here, I'll be as big as a whale.'

'And a good morning to you as well, Celia. Good night's sleep? I wouldn't have to do this trip out if you'd simply listened to me and moved into my place. It's not like your parents' house where you would be forced to share a bed with me. You would be able to have your pick of rooms.'

When he had suggested that, Celia had instantly turned him down on the grounds that there was no need.

'Where are you taking me?' she now asked and he grinned.

'You make that sound as though I'm ferrying you for a day out of pure torture.'

'I hate shopping.'

'I believe you've mentioned that to me once.'

'Have I?'

'It may have been post-coital conversation in the early hours of the morning when we were in Scotland.' His voice was husky and amused. When he thought of those intimate moments in the stillness of a snowy night, when they had talked about anything and everything, he could feel his libido rising to the occasion and reminding him of just how much he was going to enjoy seducing her back into his bed.

More and more, he got the tantalising sensation that what she wanted to box away was still there, a simmering physical pull that matched his. Why was she so keen to deny it? Was it because she'd come to the conclusion that to indulge in sex with him was no longer acceptable despite the situation they were in because she needed an emotional attachment he was incapable of giving? Had she succumbed once and decided that once was enough? Had she thought it through at all? Underneath all that speculation lay the uneasy notion that she subconsciously saw herself walking away from a marriage in search of the fairy-story ending, maybe not immediately but sooner rather than later.

Was he being over-imaginative? Leandro didn't know because she was the very essence of everything that was mysterious about the opposite sex even though she could be as transparent as a pane of glass.

If she wanted to lock those memories away then he'd determined that he wasn't going to let her and he wished he could see her face now as he dropped that perfectly innocuous remark in a voice that was easy-going, casual and reeking of innocence, but he didn't want to make a point of it.

'Don't worry. I guarantee you'll enjoy the experience and to answer your question—Selfridges.'

Celia lapsed into silence. Post-coital conversation… She wished he hadn't reminded her of those because how she had luxuriated in them, loving the darkness and the quiet and the lazy chat that was so easy and languid in bed, naked bodies pressed together, warm and content.

Overwhelmed by a sudden wave of sadness for having made the mistake of falling crazily in love with a guy who was incapable of loving anyone, she blinked and stared out of the window at yet another grey day.

She wasn't aware of Leandro reaching out until she felt the curl of his fingers around hers and when she swung round to look at him, she was bowled over by the gentleness on his face.

'It's going to be okay,' he said roughly.

In that very instant, Celia made her decision.

She would never find the love she wanted with Leandro but she *would* have support and affection. It might not have been on her wish list when she was young and filled with dreams about her future, but she was going to marry him and they were having a baby and it could have been a whole lot worse.

And if he didn't and never would love her?

The option of pulling back, of trying not to go further down the road of giving him her heart, now seemed naïve and futile. What would happen in that scenario? He would eventually drift away from her. He would turn to other women to find physical closeness. She had debated telling him that she wouldn't marry unless he promised not to stray, but had known that that would have been crazy unless they became lovers once again. Not knowing what to do, she had remained paralysed, but now…?

Those fingers entwined with hers would have to be enough. She would never tell him how she really felt because she would always want to hang onto her dignity, but she could no longer fight the hold he had over her.

Was it the same for him?

He hadn't come near her since they had left Scotland, but if she didn't risk finding out whether there was any semblance of attraction left between them, then she would regret the omission for ever.

She squeezed his hand without looking at him and then left her fingers linked with his. Finally, she turned and smiled weakly.

'If you say so.'

'We're here.' He nodded to the busy entrance.

Celia breathed in long and deep and together they headed into the department store.

She'd reached a crossroads and was going to make the very best of where she was. She was going to love this man and if he hurt her, then she would accept the body blow.

They went directly to the designer floor. Celia had only been into Selfridges a couple of times and never anywhere near the designer section, which was out of bounds moneywise for her.

He held her hand and moved with confidence, ignoring eager looks on salespeople's faces, asking her what sort of things she liked to wear and then telling her that anything baggy was out of the question.

'Why?'

'Why would you hide your figure?' He slid appreciative eyes across to her and she blushed. 'It's amazing.'

She remembered the way he'd made her feel. Sexy and beautiful and provocative. He'd opened up a whole new side to her and it was exciting to think that she might go down that road again.

Would she?

She could feel his body language and it made her bloom somewhere deep inside with the slow burn of desire.

'Can I ask you something?' Celia stopped and looked up at him, suddenly anxious to find out why, having been so scrupulous in avoiding touching her ever since she'd shown up, he was now giving off signals that he wanted her after all.

Had he reconciled himself to taking what he thought might now be on offer? Even though he might have been happy to shrug her off before? Easy come, easy go?

She wanted him. She was in love with him. But was she so in love and did she want him so much that she would be happy to be considered as better than nothing? Would her self-esteem ever recover? But then she thought of them living separate lives, growing more and more distant from one another over time, holding herself in a state of frozen limbo because she didn't want to have sex with someone who couldn't give her the love she craved. How satisfying would that be?

There were few people around them, but she still shuffled him away from the main drag and towards the side.

'Do I have a choice of answer?' Leandro asked cautiously and Celia chewed her lower lip and shook her head, which was honest enough.

'You haven't…come near me ever since I told you about the pregnancy…'

'Come again?'

'I got the impression…that…er…' His look of bewil-derment made her stumble over her words but then his expression cleared and he looked at her seriously.

'You made it clear that you weren't interested in pro-longing what we had,' Leandro said bluntly. 'I got the message loud and clear so when you showed up, I was hardly going to take that as a green light to start mak-ing a move on you, was I?'

He tilted her chin so that she was looking at him, her clear green eyes hesitant.

'Do you know what my mission in life is?' he asked, his voice teasing, which brought all sorts of tingly sen-sations racing through her, making her squirm in a very pleasurable way.

'What?' Her voice was breathless and she was mes-merised by the glint in his eyes.

'To just get you to feel more confident about yourself.'

'Of course I'm confident!'

Leandro looked at her wryly. 'How could you think that I would want you one minute and then be so turned off you the next that I don't want to come near you?'

Celia shrugged. 'Men change their minds.'

'I don't. There's such a thing as respecting someone's choices.' He was tempted to ask her why *she* had found it so easy to dismiss what they'd enjoyed but he already knew. She'd been looking for Love and happy to relegate the fun they'd had to the history books.

Except fate had had other things in mind.

But he still turned her on and maybe she was seeing things from his point of view now. A baby and a mar-riage and the bonus of great sex to keep the wheels oiled.

Love might not be part of the equation but that didn't

mean that everything then became a lost cause. Life was seldom a case of all or nothing.

She'd forgotten the value of fun somewhere along the line and he was surprised at how relieved and frankly *overjoyed* he felt at the thought that she had come round to his way of thinking.

'So,' he purred silkily, 'shall we get down to the drudgery of shopping for an entire new wardrobe for you? Money no object?' He wagged his finger sternly at her. 'And don't even think about quibbling about that one…'

Celia had always loathed the business of buying clothes. Of course, Leandro had a point. When you lacked confidence in your body, when you looked in the mirror and mostly saw room for improvement, then trying on clothes became a chore.

But now she was imbued with such a sense of heady sexiness that she threw herself into the task with gusto. She forgot about the fact that most of the stuff came with price tags that made her eyes water.

Anticipation at what she had given herself permission to do gave an edge to the remainder of the day. Every sideways glance was thrilling, every brush of his hand against her sent a rush of adrenaline through her system.

Celia could barely remember what exactly she had chosen for herself because her mind had been racing ahead to what lay in store.

A night with Leandro, wrapped in his arms, her body singing to the drumbeat of his love-making.

She knew she stocked up on three dresses, some shorts, some tee shirts that were as soft as silk and even some strappy shoes and sandals. She bought stuff she would never have chosen for herself in a million years, tops that showed off her generous breasts and dresses that skimmed her thighs and delicate shoes that reminded her that she had very pretty feet and slender ankles.

They held hands, had some lunch and, in true billionaire style, he had his chauffeur stop so that the shopping could be dumped in the boot of his car. No inconvenient traipsing through the store weighed down by bags.

They were in the back of his car and heading to her place so that she could *fling a few things in a suitcase and make it quick because he was going crazy* when it occurred to Celia that he still hadn't told her where, exactly, they would be going.

'Dubai.'

'I've always wanted to go,' she confessed.

'It's busy. Had I known that we would...' he eyed the closed partition and lowered his voice to a seductive purr '...be spending a week removing one another's clothing and getting reacquainted with what's underneath, I would have definitely opted for something a little less frantic.'

'Thank you,' Celia said simply, then she looked away because there was way too much her eyes could tell him that her head warned her not to say.

The casual purchase of a wardrobe of designer clothes, a shopping trip where price tags weren't consulted because money didn't matter, should have prepared her for the lavish experience of travelling with a billionaire a mere three days later, but Celia was still shocked at the mind-blowing opulence of luxury travel.

They flew first. People fawned and practically pleaded to bring food and drink, whatever they wanted. There were massages on tap should they want…manicures and pedicures at the snap of a finger…

The sofas strewn here and there in artful symmetry were deep and comfortable and there were USB ports everywhere because nearly everyone in the spacious, airy lounge was a businessperson.

There was an air-conditioned limo with privacy windows waiting for them when they landed and they were ushered out with the sort of respect reserved for visiting dignitaries.

'I guess you come here often? Why do people know who you are?'

'No need to whisper, Celia. We're not in a library. And this is just the level of service that happens when you get to a certain financial position. Admittedly, I've met the Sheikh a few times in the course of business. You'll be pleased to hear that I've turned down his dinner invitation at his palace. We're here for a week and I intend to spend every second of the week in your company and your company alone.'

Leandro meant every word of that. He had barely been able to focus on work because having her back in his bed had taken up all his waking thoughts.

Sex had never ruled his life. He had never had a problem prioritising what was important, which was the thing that gave him financial security, the thing that saved him from the fate of his father. He had discovered, to his bemusement, that that paled into insignificance with Celia back on the scene.

He felt that it was all tied up with the fact that she was having his baby. No woman had ever occupied that spot in his life before and, while he had never thought about it, he now felt a depth of protectiveness that over-ruled everything else.

He couldn't stop looking at her. Right now, she was pink from the surge of heat outside the airport and her hair was in its usual disarray, rebelling against the clips she had pushed in to control it, begging to be released.

There was not an ounce of artificiality about her. She looked left to right and left to right as the limo left the airport towards the five-star hotel his PA had booked for him.

He reached to clasp her hand and she shot him an open, delighted smile.

'This is amazing,' she confessed. 'There weren't a huge amount of holidays growing up and when I left home to open my business, there just wasn't the cash to indulge in going abroad.'

'I never went on holiday either, as a child,' Leandro confided. 'It's why I never take any of this for granted, however much I'm used to it. I was propelled into private education thanks to Charles and I learned quickly how to survive in that small pond where the rich and famous swim.'

'How?'

'You need to have a killer instinct and when you come from nothing, you need to be better, faster and smarter than the kids who come from moneyed backgrounds. You have to make sure you don't give anyone an advantage over you.'

'A lonely life,' Celia murmured and Leandro flushed and looked away for a few seconds.

'I've never considered myself lonely,' he said crisply, holding her gaze for a moment and then briefly looking down. 'If anything, when I went to boarding school, I would say there were way too many people around.'

Celia half smiled and reached to squeeze his hand. 'I'll bet.'

Her eyes were warm and, suddenly disoriented, Leandro heard himself say gruffly, 'I admit I was lonely… sometimes.' Then he shrugged, astonished at that confidence. 'Kids adapt.' He dealt her a gentle smile. 'I'm just glad ours won't have to.'

'I might need to do a lot of adapting.' Celia laughed. 'I never saw myself living anywhere but a modest little house with a bit of a garden and enough space for a decent workroom.'

So the conversation moved on. They arrived not long after at the resort, which turned out to be a breathtakingly elegant compound located on the crisp white shores of Jumeirah Beach. It was big enough to get lost in and yet they were greeted, once out of the car, with impeccable efficiency. Celia lagged behind, awestruck by the opulence. Acres of marble floor and a dazzling abundance of chandeliers and gold-leaf ceilings nudged alongside warm earthy tones, a visual reminder that this palatial five-star resort owed its existence to the splendour of the sand and desert in which it resided. The searing heat was left behind as it was beautifully cool inside and busy with people coming and going. Many were tourists but many were also locals, wearing the impressive, traditional dress, white tunics and headscarves.

She half listened to the spiel the hotel receptionist was imparting as she went through the formalities of checking them in, then she smiled and said, deferentially, that perhaps Mr Diaz already knew what there was to know as he had been there already.

'And our esteemed Royal Highness, the Sheikh, sends you his best,' she murmured, eyes lowered.

This was like no hotel Celia had ever been in, not that she had been in very many, and she followed Leandro in a daze as he confidently led the way to the bank of lifts purring up and down, disgorging people into the plush foyer and transporting ones on their way back to their rooms.

She could understand why he had chosen this place for a honeymoon that wasn't supposed to have been a real honeymoon. If the aim had been for them to get to at least know one another a bit better, without any atmosphere of romance to muddy the waters, then it couldn't have been better. Lavish and big enough to be impersonal, vibrant without the danger of intimacy lurking in secluded corners and cosy nooks and crannies.

They were whooshed out into a huge, ornately carpeted corridor with just a handful of doors guarding the most expensive of the suites.

'Wow.' That was all Celia could say as the heavy door was pushed open and she walked into a vast open space, all white, from the sprawling U-shaped leather suite to the pale rug on which it sat.

To one side, there was a magnificent circular glass table, big enough to seat eight, and directly in front was a bank of glass to which she was drawn.

The city twinkled far and away and beneath them. She rested her hands on the floor-to-ceiling glass and looked out and then shivered as she saw Leandro's reflection behind her.

He reached, flattening his palms on either side of

hers, locking her in and sending goosebumps racing through her.

The thrill of flirting and the anticipation of where all that flirting was going to lead made her weak at the knees. She turned within the loop of his outstretched arms so that her back was against the glass and she stared up at him, breathing fast, her mouth parted in invitation.

He was wearing a light-coloured shirt, cuffed to the elbows, and low-slung chinos and she undid the buttons of the shirt and pushed her hands to feel the hardness of his chest, roughened with dark hair. She circled her fingers over his flat nipples and felt his sharp intake of breath. She tugged the shirt free of the trousers. His dark eyes held hers and she liked that because she could see the heat of desire burning in the depths, turning her on, fuelling her with the confidence that had been shorn away when she had thought that he no longer wanted her.

'I've wanted to touch you all day,' he rasped, one hand still planted on the glass while the other did to her what she was doing to him, pushed under the silk blouse to find the front clasp of her bra, which he undid with proficiency.

Her breasts fell full and soft, released from their restraints, and Leandro flung back his head, nostrils flared, eyes half closed as he cupped her breasts in his hands and massaged them.

With a groan he roughly undid the buttons, tugged her blouse free of the matching silk culottes, felt her wriggle against him, unzipping and pulling down, as frantic as he was.

They barely made it to the bedroom.

Clothes were shed on the way, a trail of discarded items that followed them into one of the three rooms, which was dominated by a super-king-size bed complete with drapery.

Celia vaguely took stock of all of this. Yes, she was aware of the size of the bedroom, the pale voile at the windows, the lush deep blue of the carpet and the sleek glossiness of the built-in furniture, but that was all on the periphery of her vision.

Really, she only had eyes for the man who was now standing back, looking at her with such hot longing in his eyes that she wanted to swoon.

They were both naked. She dimly remembered kicking off her panties. The cool air-conditioning made her nipples stiffen.

'I've missed you,' Leandro half moaned.

My body, Celia knew. Where *she* missed his familiarity and the wonderful essence of him, *he* missed her body, missed the sex.

It was something she would have to accept and accept it she would.

Her love was so entwined with lust and desire that she knew that they could never be untangled.

She sighed softly and her eyelids fluttered as he curved his hands smoothly over her waist and then he knelt at her feet and breathed her in.

He smoothed his hand over her belly and kissed it and then he gently eased her legs apart.

Oh, how she had missed this!

She arched back and reached out to clutch at one of the wooden posts of the bed. Then she lifted her leg, resting it on the mattress so that she could accommodate his exploring tongue working its way along her clitoris, teasing it into stiff arousal.

Her fingers curled into his dark hair. When she looked

down with slumberous eyes, she was further turned on by the sight of him, moving against her, between her thighs.

He eased a finger into her, two fingers, and between his tongue and his mouth and those fingers, Celia could no longer hold on.

She came fast and hard, spasming against his mouth, her whole body convulsing with the mind-blowing pleasure of her orgasm. She barely recognised the guttural sounds leaving her mouth, but she could feel the hot, prickly flush of the blood rushing through her, as searing as fire.

The strength of her orgasm left her as weak as a kitten but she was still startled when he lifted her off her feet, as though she weighed nothing, and gently put her on the bed.

Their eyes tangled and she could feel her body begin to shift back into gear, could feel that want seep through her. It was an ache between her legs that made her want to rub them together.

'You are every man's dream,' Leandro husked, bending to suckle on one nipple, which turned want back into mindless craving with supersonic speed.

'That's the nicest thing anyone's ever said to me.' She laughed softly and tugged him so that they were looking at one another. Then she kissed him. A long, lingering kiss. 'And it's your turn now because I've missed you too…'

CHAPTER NINE

'I HAVE A surprise for you,' Leandro's voice was low and lazy. He stroked her with one finger, trailing the feathery touch from her cheek along her shoulder blades and then dipping down to her cleavage.

Celia smiled and sighed, enjoying the familiar tingle his slightest touch produced in her.

They seemed to have spent the past five days in bed, a blissful orgy of love-making only interrupted by occasional sightseeing and food.

The sweeping swimming pool had largely remained unexplored and they had only actually gone to the beach once.

'Perhaps not the best of ideas…' Leandro had murmured, toying with her copper hair, twirling strands around his long, brown fingers, 'not with your colouring. You might burn.'

'There's a reason why sunblock was invented,' Celia had responded wryly, 'and, strangely, I tan pretty easily for a redhead. I must have inherited some of Dad's genes there.' But she had succumbed fast enough to the promise of what he had had in mind as an alternative.

She couldn't resist him. She would never be able to resist him. For now, she knew that it was mutual, but how long would that last for him? Surely not for ever, because the sweaty heat of passion always calmed and into that calm came the glory of contentment, but only if there was love as a stepping stone. Without that, there was always the danger that a replacement would be found to fill the vacuum.

Celia tried hard not to project into the future because their future was hardly straightforward with a baby in the mix. He was proving himself in so many ways he was probably not even aware of…proving himself in his kindness and his generosity, and she knew that that would translate into just the qualities that went into great parenting.

And the power of parenthood could be stronger than the tug of lust, especially for a man like Leandro, an honourable man who knew, from first-hand experience, the bitterness of an incomplete home. He was prepared to marry her for the sake of his baby and with that, he would surely realise, would come a curtailment of his freedoms? Once, she had wondered whether he might put their arrangement on a par with what he had had with Julie, but he and Julie had been platonic friends with the understanding written in from the start that they would discreetly take lovers, as need be.

That was quite different from what *they* shared. There would be no open doors when boredom with her kicked in, when he grew tired of the novelty of sleeping with her.

He would risk jeopardising the very thing he wanted to protect if he thought that he could look elsewhere, but would that be sufficient to stop him if and when that time arrived?

And what would she do if she were to be confronted with that situation?

These were uncomfortable questions that Celia thought it best to leave be. Why look for pain in advance? Why not throw herself into what they had and hope that the future was different from the one she predicted?

'A surprise?' she said now, still smiling, making sure her eyes didn't give away the tenderness she felt every time she looked at him. She had learned how to conceal what needed concealing and only revealed her emotions when he was asleep, when she could look at him with unguarded love.

'Last night here and then it's back to London.'

'I know.' She groaned and flung herself back to stare at the ceiling for a couple of seconds before facing him once again, stomach to stomach, their bodies pressed against one another. She grinned. 'I'd forgotten how nice it is being away from the grindstone for a bit.'

'We'll have a proper honeymoon later,' Leandro promised. 'Wherever you want to go.'

That was music to Celia's ears and she smiled. 'I'll start searching as soon as we're back,' she teased. 'Sure you can take more time off work?'

'I own it all. I can do whatever I want. If there's one thing money and power buy, it's freedom. That's all I ever wanted and I have it now, so yes. I can take whatever time I want away from the desk.'

'Were you and Julie planning on having a honeymoon?' Celia wasn't sure whether this question overstepped boundaries and then she decided that, as he was her husband-to-be, she should be free to overstep them. She would never ask him any question unless his answer couldn't hurt her. She would never ask him if he could ever love her...or how much she meant to him...those were lines her own self-defence mechanisms would never allow her to overstep, but everything else?

This was all part and parcel of the sort of *friendship* zone he had in mind, surely.

'No,' Leandro admitted without any hesitation. 'Ours was purely a business arrangement and, to be honest, Charles wouldn't have been too surprised at the lack of a honeymoon. He's always known me for the workaholic that I am. I expect, for the sake of appearances, we might have gone to some city or other for a weekend, but I would have worked and she would have shopped.'

'I guess *we* could have done that,' Celia mused. 'I mean, when you first thought about having one. It's not as though…well…'

'As though we were planning on picking up where we'd left off?' Leandro shifted, thinking that there was no way that *work* and *shopping* were going to be the only things they did. That would have been impossible.

'Tell me what the surprise is.'

'Dinner.'

'Dinner?'

'There won't be any air conditioning where we're going tonight and the views might be slightly different from what you've sampled before, but I'm hoping you enjoy the experience.' He grinned and began easing himself off the bed. 'We're being collected in an hour… so bath time, I think. Although…' his grin broadened and there was a glint of wicked invitation in his eyes '… we *could* have a bit more fun before we get changed…'

Celia took her time in the bath. Leandro was making calls. With the door to the bathroom open, she could dimly hear his deep voice and could picture him sprawled on the leather sofa in the sitting room, lazily telling his army of CEOs what to do and when.

She closed her eyes, wanting to relive everything they had done here since they'd come. She'd always led a sheltered life. Holidays were caravan parks and then, later, a rush of adrenaline when she'd gone on a ski holiday with her class to France. Then, in the blink of an eye, she and Martin were planning a future, heads in the clouds, and holidays were something not even on the agenda because they'd both been young and too broke to even buy a place to live.

She'd rushed headlong from that broken relationship to running her own business and trying to build it into something and, during those years, the very thought of a holiday was a joke.

So now? Overload. She'd managed to pack into a handful of days an entire lifetime's worth of gaping tourism.

They'd dined in a restaurant many floors up in their hotel and, sitting on beaded cushions, she had looked out through elegant arches to the stunning Burj Khalifa, which rose like a needle piercing the velvet sky. She'd been taken for a personal visit to a top falconer and seen how the birds were trained and watched as Leandro had handled one with unexpected expertise. She'd experienced the glitz and glamour of the Dubai Mall and been impressed by the architectural magnificence of the Burj Al Arab, a breathtaking testament to the bold contrasts that characterised the vibrant, bustling city. Everywhere was a fascinating mix of old and new, where the vibrancy of concrete, glass and stone nudged the stillness of the sand and sea.

Celia half guessed where they might be going but she

was still impressed to death when they left the bright lights of the city behind and were driven out towards the open desert, an ocean of dark shapes and shadows, interrupted here and there with occasional bursts of bushes and trees.

Their driver played proud tour guide, told them about the history of Bedouin nomads who once called the land their home. All the while her eyes darted greedily out, shivering at the dark swirls and swells of sand while, next to her, Leandro's fingers curled into hers, setting alight all those forbidden emotions within her.

The utterly private Bedouin camp that greeted them took Celia's breath away. They were ushered into an enclosed area, which was incredible—with colourful rugs and lanterns and huge, hand-woven cushions and adorned with traditional relics.

'We could have spent the night here,' Leandro told her over the delicious hand-prepared meal that was brought in to them with a lot of pomp and ceremony, in various stages. 'There's a very nice and very small boutique hotel just a camel ride away. In fact, we'll go there before we head back so that we can freshen up and you can have a look at the pool. It's quite something. Fashioned to resemble an oasis. That said, I wanted to spend the last night here in our own bed with no one around...'

The lanterns flickered, creating a seductive, mellow atmosphere. The daytime heat had subsided and here, in the ornate tent, the air was fragrant with delicate incense and just the right side of warm. Celia had worn a floaty dress, perfectly buttoned up and respectful of all the dress codes of the country, but underneath the silk and cotton she felt the wetness pool between her legs and she pressed them together. Her mouth parted and Leandro fluttered his finger across her lips, touching her in a way that sent her pulses racing.

'We still have to finish the dessert course,' Celia breathed. 'And we can't leave without sampling the coffee. You know how proud they are of their coffee here…'

'Sadly you have a point, even though I'd like nothing more than to take that dress off you, button by button. Another time and another place…' He sat back with an elaborate sigh of resignation. 'We need to change the subject and urgently or else I'm going to have to make some kind of excuse and skip the dessert and coffee.'

Celia laughed. 'Okay. Tell me about Julie's dad and what's happening now that he's out of hospital… I had an email from Dan and apparently Julie's dad is over the moon at the upcoming wedding.'

'Yes.' Leandro grimaced. 'Julie and I decided that honesty was the best policy. We told him about the reason for the engagement. I'd half expected him to hit the roof, if I'm honest, but she knows her father better than I do and she was right in guessing that, with his finances now in order and presented with a fait accompli, his pride wouldn't be a problem. He's also over the moon that his daughter has found true love, given the horror story of her first marriage.'

Celia looked down and squashed a sudden sharp pang of envy. She'd smiled at many a radiant bride-to-be, twisting and turning and beaming at a fitting, waxing lyrical about The Big Day, but this was the first time she'd ever felt envious at someone else's dream wedding. She knew why. This was the first time she was in the position of knowing that her own dream would never come true even though, cruelly, she was just so close.

The baby…the wedding plans…the man of her dreams…
Just so happened that she wasn't the woman of his…

For the rest of the night, while they finished their
lavish meal, they skimmed the surface, chatting about
all sorts of things. When Celia thought back to the arrogant guy who had shown up at her shop, setting her
teeth on edge, she almost couldn't believe that they were
here now.

Was he equally aware of how far they'd come?

There was a familiarity between them that said so
much. Did he recognise that as well? Or was he so em-
bedded behind the walls he had built around himself that
this was all just part and parcel of the friendship angle
he felt they needed to cultivate? There was *lust* in one
box and *friendship* in another box but there was no box
for *love* because, for Leandro, that didn't exist.

Lust and friendship didn't add up, for him, the way
they did for her to anything more than two separate emotions and the friendship element, she recognised, was
only there at all because of the situation in which they
found themselves.

For what they had to work, they had to get along. That
was the practical approach and Leandro was practical
and solution based.

If she had dug her heels in and refused to marry him
because she wanted to be with someone who loved her,
then she wondered if he might have been tempted to simply approach it from the solution-based angle that marriage would still be a good thing because a child needed
two parents. So what was needed? A wife even if that
wife wasn't the birth mother.

Celia didn't like thinking like that, but she knew that
she had to protect herself somehow and being realistic

was as good a protection as any. She wouldn't beat herself up if sometimes, in her quiet moments or when she was just lying in his arms, she hoped for more. She was only human, after all! She just wouldn't let *hoping for more* overtake *having her eyes wide open*.

'You've gone quiet.' This as they were back in the four-wheel drive and bumping away from the mysterious shape-shifting dunes, back to the bright twinkling lights of the city.

'Have I?' Celia plastered a bright smile on her face but it felt a little strained.

'Tired?'

'And very, very full.'

'Not too tired and full, I hope…?'

Sex was uppermost on his mind, she thought, and, while it thrilled her, for once she would have liked to have told him how she was really feeling and the doubts that were crawling through her like bothersome insects that wouldn't go away.

She pictured his face closing up and the shutters being pulled down. They had an arrangement and, without anything in writing, the terms and conditions of their arrangement were clear.

'It's being pregnant.' She yawned, veering away from the powerful tug of honesty. 'Something to do with the hormones, I guess.'

'Celia, my apologies. It never occurred to me…'

Celia heard the genuine concern in his voice and relaxed. He might never love her, but he would love their child, of that she was one hundred per cent sure.

'It's okay.' She laughed, relaxing. 'I'm pretty new to this as well. I only recognise the symptoms as and when they occur!'

'Okay…so tiredness and easily full…'

'Leandro, the meal was enormous.'

'What other signs and symptoms should I be on the lookout for?'

'I think pregnant women can sometimes get a little over-emotional.' Celia laid some groundwork just in case she needed it to come to her rescue in the future.

'I don't think that's confined to pregnant women,' Leandro drawled. 'Perhaps I should download a book…'

'You would download a book on pregnancy just to find out what you should look out for?'

'Amongst other things…'

'I thought you only read work-related tomes and heavy-duty biographies for light relief?' she teased.

'You make me sound like a bundle of laughs.' He looked at her with an easy grin.

The bright lights of the hotel were ahead of them and suddenly she really did feel tired even though she'd been buzzing all night.

'It's nice that you want to actually read a pregnancy manual. I can't think that many guys would be interested in doing that.'

'Like I keep telling you, I'm not like many guys and, besides, that's what we're all about, isn't it?'

Celia stilled and then was glad for the distraction of the car stopping and the doors being opened by the uniformed porters outside and then hurrying inside the hotel, out of the sticky night-time heat.

'I mean,' Leandro picked up when she'd hoped he might just have left it off, 'this isn't about us, this is about the baby we've made together, so it's only right that I find out as much as I can about the business of pregnancy and giving birth and what I will be required to do. It's new to you and it's new to me as well.'

For once, she wasn't desperate to get her clothes off when they entered their suite of rooms and, strangely, he seemed equally reticent.

She felt sticky and ever so slightly depressed and when she excused herself to go have a bath, he nodded without demur.

'Get you something cold to drink?' he offered, once again the very essence of kind consideration and reminding her, without even having to try, that this was first and foremost what he was about. Her welfare was his concern because she was carrying his baby. 'The apricot juice is excellent. You might find it refreshing. It's been a long evening, perhaps too long given your condition.'

Celia smiled tightly. Irritation surged through her. She knew she was being unfair, but she was still smarting from his casual reminder that what they had was all about the baby yet to be born. None of it was about *her*. He fancied her for the moment but essentially *she* didn't matter.

And the fact that he was now treating her like a piece of porcelain made her even more irritated.

Was this how she would be treated as time wore on and the sex dimmed?

'Apricot juice would be…lovely…'

'Sure you're okay?'

Celia bit back a sarcastic retort that would get neither of them anywhere and might even start erecting the sort of invisible barriers she would later find difficult to dismantle.

'If this doesn't work out between us, Leandro…what happens next?'

'Whoa. Where did *that* come from?' His brows knitted and his dark eyes were a little cooler now, a little more watchful and bemused.

Celia shrugged and looked away.

'I thought we had a good time tonight,' he said slowly.

'We did.'

'I *thought* we were doing a damn good job of getting to know one another.'

'We are.'

'Then where are you now heading with this?'

'Nowhere.' Celia looked at him, held his gaze, her eyes steady and as unreadable as his were.

'I'm thinking,' Leandro murmured, 'that *nowhere* isn't a direction for the questions you're asking.'

'I'm just tired, that's all.' She felt panicked at the box she'd opened because she knew that certain boxes, given their situation, were best left shut.

'There's only so far you can run with that excuse, Celia. That's not the first time this evening you've told me that you're tired and it's beginning to sound like a sticking plaster being put onto something that's really bugging you.' He led the way to the sofa and beckoned her across.

He patted next to him and when she sat down he immediately turned to her, his eyes penetrating and intense, searching her face to get inside her head and find out what was going on.

'So? Are you going to spit it out or are we going to go round the houses playing guessing games?'

'I suppose we've discussed a lot of things,' Celia muttered, one foot hovering over the edge of a cliff she'd been so determined not to go anywhere near. 'We've talked about the practicalities like where we're going to live and what the choices are for me after the baby's born. We've discussed whether we would get a nanny if I decide to return to work and *when* returning to work might be appropriate…'

'But…? Because I can hear the siren sound of a *but*.'

'*And* I think that this has been a fantastic few days getting to know one another…'

'Agreed.' Leandro smiled with wolfish sexiness that made Celia's bones feel like mush.

'But lust and sex don't last for ever…'

Leandro frowned. 'We have yet to put that to the test.'

'Maybe we should try and work out what we might do if and when that time comes.'

'Why?'

'What do you mean *why*?'

'Why pre-empt a situation that's nowhere on the horizon?'

'Because…'

'There are no guarantees in life, Celia.' His eyes were serious and he was leaning into her, which had the effect of jumbling her thoughts until she wasn't sure quite what she'd been trying to say in the first place. Her hands itched to touch him and to smooth over the crease that had suddenly appeared between them, like a ripple disturbing the flat, smooth surface of a lake.

'I get that.'

'We do our best and if problems arise at a later date, then that's the time to try and sort them out.'

'Yes, well…'

'You want to turn this into a list of pros and cons and I don't think that's a good idea. We both know what we have to do, what the right thing to do is…don't we?' He inclined his head to one side and gave her a few seconds to respond, which she did by nodding. Not vigorously but sufficiently for him to nod firmly in return, in agreement with her. 'We've talked at length about this,' he said quietly. 'In the end, there's nothing in life that's one hundred per cent guaranteed. Nothing. The rate of divorce says it all, wouldn't you agree? People walk down the aisle with big dreams and big hopes but two thirds of those starry-eyed couples will see the inside of a divorce court sooner or later. What we have will be sturdier, trust me.'

Celia was the first to look away.

'You're right.' But she had to try and inject conviction into her voice and remind herself of all the reasons why what they had was better than the alternative. She might be greedy for more, but greed was no reason to start unpicking what had been knitted together. When she smiled, there was more warmth and she stood up and told him that she was going to have a bath.

'I have so many baths and showers here.' She did her best to get things back on track.

'It's the heat.' Leandro followed suit and stood up, towering over her, his dark eyes still concerned and still ever so slightly watchful. 'Relax. I'll hunt down some juice for you from the cafe downstairs. It's open twenty-four-seven and I could do with stretching my legs.'

Celia kept smiling even though there was a wariness in his voice that dismayed her. Instead of relaxing in the bath, she opted for a quick shower and then, on the spur of the moment and instead of climbing into bed, she changed into a pair of loose dark culottes and a grey silk top and headed down to the cafe.

She knew where he had gone because it was the cafe that was transformed into the breakfast area in the morning.

There were several five-star restaurants in the complex and the cafe was the least formal of all.

At a little after eleven, it was still busy, with people coming and going. The crowd were all elegant, expensively dressed, and the mix of different languages as they chattered past her made Celia smile. This was a land of such contrasts, a place where people converged from all over the world, rich in diversity and ancient in its heritage.

Which made her think of the perfect evening they had shared at the desert. Leandro had put real thought into doing something special on their last evening in Dubai and he would have been utterly perplexed by the way she had thrown the gesture back in his face.

This wasn't about *him*. This was about *her* and it suddenly felt imperative that she set things back on the right track.

Fired up with a new sense of purpose, Celia almost missed Leandro because she was so certain that she would find him at the long mirrored bar, which was still buzzing with people.

Standing in the doorway, she looked around, taking in the huge room as a whole. It was cleverly divided by tall, leafy trees in huge urns, and circular seating wrapped around marble-topped tables sectioned off private seating areas. Elsewhere, there were low, informal sofas with tables and more formal arrangements for dining.

Mostly people were standing with just a handful of diners sitting at some of the tables, having heaven only knew what manner of late-night snacks.

Eyes flitting then returning to the tall, languid figure leaning against the wall at the back, Celia felt her heart begin to beat fast.

Leandro was holding the glass of apricot juice and he was chatting to a young woman so stunningly beautiful that she took Celia's breath away.

Her hair was short and sharp and raven-black and she was slender as a willow, wearing figure-hugging trousers and a bright red top that managed to be prim and ridiculously sexy at the same time.

She saw Leandro glance at his watch, smile, prepare to move off.

Nothing about his demeanour spoke of anything suspicious at all. He wasn't standing too close to his companion and his expression was polite and friendly, but nothing more than that.

So why did she suddenly feel as though the world were tilting on its axis?

Old insecurities rose up with a vengeance and she was catapulted unfairly back to how she had felt when she had found out that Martin had found someone else, someone tall and beautiful and quite the opposite of *her*.

She'd felt *wanting*. It was the same feeling that hit her now like a wave and she stood there, eyes wide, trembling and trying to kill the feeling because there was no place for it in this scenario.

But she was rooted to the spot.

Leandro, on the other side of the room, was startled because he'd been chatting to the Princess for longer than he'd thought but out of politeness it had been impossible for him to get away.

She'd spotted him and hived off from the group of friends she had come with so that she could tell him all about the latest family sagas, of which there were many.

Leandro had met Leila several times and had helped

her with various university application forms, guiding
her in her choice of subject and giving her the rundown
on what Cambridge as a town was like because that had
been her choice of university.

But even as he'd been chatting, his mind had been
taken up with Celia.

He'd hated her withdrawal. It had made him realise
how much he'd become accustomed to the easiness that
existed between them. The silences between them were
as comfortable as the chat and for Leandro that said a lot,
although he was only now realising how much.

He glanced idly at the exit, ready to make his polite
excuses because a tipsy Princess looked set to talk for
England while her bodyguards, discreetly positioned by
the bar, tried to stifle their yawns.

He saw Celia just as she spotted him and their eyes
met, homing in on each other and eliminating everything
else that was extraneous, from the milling late-night
crowd to the sound of talk and laughter. The expression
on her face was open and honest before she had time to
think about adjusting it.

She was...*hurt*.

'Excuse me, Leila, I really have to go—'

'So soon, Leandro? Come join us for dinner!'

Leandro smiled but he was already straightening and
his eyes were still on Celia. 'I feel my age enough as it is
chatting to you, Leila. Ten minutes surrounded by your
peers and the hair on my head will start going grey!'

He detached himself, headed towards the exit to
where Celia hadn't moved although her expression had
smoothed over, was now polite and distant.

'What are you doing here?' he asked. He ushered her

away from the cafe, back into the lobby and towards the bank of lifts, still holding the juice in one hand.

He didn't do *hurt* from women when it came to his personal life. He never had. He had never welcomed the sensation of being penned in or the irritating feeling that he should be justifying himself in any way. As far as Leandro was concerned, there was a thin line between questioning his motives and nagging him into toeing a line he had never had any intention of toeing.

The claustrophobia of Celia's jealousy, because jealousy was surely what he had glimpsed, fleeting but all too apparent, was not welcome.

He didn't expect or court jealousy in women. He didn't like it because…of what it said. Celia was jealous because she cared. The thought of that was ice in his veins. With the force of muscle memory ingrained for more years than he cared to remember, Leandro's aversion to the swirl of that forbidden emotion rammed into him with the force of a sledgehammer. He wasn't built to return emotion, to return love. It just wasn't in his DNA and the need to repel was as instinctive as drawing breath.

She was walking alongside him, head held high, explaining that having a shower had woken her up and she'd decided to come down and perhaps have her drink in the cafe rather than wait for him to bring it up to her. Her voice was light enough as she repeated the mantra about not wanting to be treated like a china doll just because she was expecting.

But she wasn't looking at him and he wanted her to.

'I expect,' he cut through the chatter just as the lift doors opened to their floor, 'that you're going to ask me who I was talking to…' He could feel himself shutting down inside, sealing himself off because that was just what he was programmed to do. What was wrong with that? What was wrong with self-protection? He'd built his life around it.

Celia looked at him for the first time since he had joined her where she'd been frozen to the spot in the cafe. She had to school her features into a mask of smooth, casual indifference. She was hurting inside so much that it felt as though a knife were twisting inside her, but this was what she had signed up to and she would find a way of dealing with it.

'No,' she said tonelessly. 'I wasn't. You're not a prisoner, Leandro, and, as you've said too many times to count, this is a marriage of convenience. We both know why we're doing what we're doing but I suppose it does bring me back to what I was trying to say to you earlier…'

'Which is what?'

'What happens when the lust dies? Do you start looking elsewhere?' She paused and then said, sotto voce, 'Or do I? We never quite addressed that, Leandro, and yes, it might be good to live in the moment and cross bridges when we get to them but maybe we're being naïve. Maybe we need to deal with what happens…'

CHAPTER TEN

LEANDRO DIDN'T SAY ANYTHING. He nudged open the heavy door to the suite. He could feel a cold thread of something… *What was that emotion? Surely it wasn't fear?* It rippled through him and in that very instant he realised that the terms of the contract had changed.

How had that happened?

He was always the one in control, always the one who called the shots and yet now, as he looked at the cool, determined expression on her face, he knew that the role had been reversed.

Old instincts died hard, though. A primal revulsion at the thought of anyone else having a say over him, over his thoughts and decision, roared into life, obliterating everything else in its path.

'Maybe we do.' He held her gaze for a couple of seconds, then strode off towards the kitchen where he dumped the now forgotten glass of apricot juice so that he could help himself to a glass of cold water. Frankly, he could have done with something stronger.

He felt rather than saw her pace to the kitchen behind him and his pulses quickened.

'You were hurt.' Leandro dumped the empty glass on the pale, glossy counter and folded his arms.

'Yes,' Celia said quietly. 'I was hurt even though I knew that I had no right to be.'

'Why?' Leandro demanded.

'Because I foolishly trusted you...' Celia's heart was beating fast. He had seen her, had seen the expression on her face before she had had time to conceal it and he was astute enough when it came to reading women to know what had been going through her head. All the pitfalls to this arrangement were suddenly laid bare and, while she would much rather have not had to face up to them just yet, maybe it was all for the best that they did. Marriage was a solid commitment and not to be taken lightly. She'd dithered and agonised over what would happen without Love as the glue to bind them, not as parents but as two human beings sharing a life together.

She'd pretended a lot of things to herself from the very first moment she had slept with Leandro. Before even.

She'd pretended that she wasn't attracted to him, and then when she'd faced that one down and accepted the truth, she'd kidded herself that fancying someone was a far cry from having feelings for them.

What a joke!

How could she ever have swept every core value she'd grown up with under the carpet?

And yet that was what she had done. She'd managed to convince herself that she could be like him, that she could detach, and of course she couldn't.

What a mess. How on earth could she have contemplated a life in love with a guy who wasn't in love with her? This very moment was always going to come, the moment when she knew that he would always be attracted to other women. He might not consider doing anything with any of them, not now at any rate, but how long would that situation last?

The very fact that he had no desire to at least defend himself against what he knew she would have been thinking pretty much said it all.

'And what have I done that makes you assume you can't trust me? I've been honest with you from day one, honest about…the man I am…'

'So you have. I don't want to have this conversation standing up here.' She spun round on her heel and padded towards the sitting room to perch, arms clasped tightly around herself. She looked at him as he sat on the chair opposite her but then he pulled it closer and leaned forwards so that he was crowding her.

'I thought I could do this,' Celia said quietly. 'Even when I saw you there, talking to that woman—'

'Friend,' Leandro interrupted, 'talking to that *friend*. I know Leila's father. I've met her a few times in the past and she's like a sister to me.'

Celia blushed but she wasn't going to apologise for jumping to the wrong conclusion because it didn't make any difference.

'Whatever…'

'No!' Leandro all but roared. 'It's not a case of *whatever*!' He vaulted upright, raked his fingers through his hair but just as quickly sat back down, his body language urgent and demanding.

It was late but he hardly noticed the hour.

No deal, however big, no decision, however life-changing, had ever occupied his attention the way it was occupied now.

'It would have happened sooner or later,' Celia told him gently. 'I know we both had the best of intentions going into this and I wish so much that I could carry on believing that those good intentions would be enough to see us through but, for me, they just won't be.'

'Don't say that. You've barely given this a chance.'

'It's…it's not got anything to do with giving it a chance.'

'We get along, Celia. You know we do. And we're one hundred per cent compatible in bed—'

'I was hurt,' she interrupted him bluntly, 'when I saw you with that girl. I suppose I knew in my heart that there was nothing going on there—'

'Then what is all this about?'

'If you'd just let me finish, Leandro…' She breathed in deeply, but it was difficult to meet his piercing gaze. 'I wasn't just hurt when I saw you with…that woman. I was *jealous*.'

Celia's heart sank as she saw him get exactly where she was going with this. Hurt was a very different animal from jealousy.

'And just then, at that very moment,' she continued quietly, 'I realised how impossible life was going to be with you, not despite the fact that we get along and we're compatible in bed. Impossible *because* we get along and we're compatible in bed. If I could treat this like you, as a business transaction, then it would be fine.'

'You make it sound as though it's deprived of all emotion.'

'It's deprived of one essential emotion. At least it is for me.'

'I don't do love.'

'I get that, which is why I'm calling the whole thing off.'

'This is crazy,' Leandro grated, ashen.

'Mum and Dad are going to be disappointed but it's

better for them to be disappointed than for me to face heartbreak every single day because I don't want to face disappointing them.' She paused and then continued, in the same low, even voice, 'And before you tell me that it's always better for a child to have both parents, I would say that you're right but only if both parents are happy. You might be happy but I wouldn't be, not really.'

'You have my word that I would never be unfaithful.'

Celia didn't say anything for a bit because she knew that this would be a big thing for Leandro.

What was he promising her? Were there things being said between the lines?

Hope sprang eternal. Celia knew that. She also knew that, for her own sanity, it wasn't something she should cling to. Besides, what was said now could easily be forgotten in times to come. Leandro was a man accustomed to getting what he wanted at whatever cost. It would not probably even occur to him that he might be toying with the truth when he made a promise like that.

'I'm going to hit the sack now.' She stood up, just about managing to avoid bumping into him. She was already missing him! All her clothes were in the bedroom they had been sharing but tonight she would be sleeping in one of the other two rooms.

She grabbed her clothes quickly, half expecting him to follow but he didn't. When she left the room they had shared, he was standing in the sitting room and as ill at ease as she had ever seen him.

'I'm going to head down to the bar. I need a drink.' He shoved his hands in his pockets and stared at her, but Celia shrugged and mumbled something along the lines of *okay*.

'What time will we be leaving in the morning?'

'We will leave the hotel around eleven.' His mouth

twisted into a parody of a mocking smile. 'That gives us some uncomfortable time to spend in one another's company. Do you think you'll be able to do that or are we to abandon our attempts at friendship on the back of everything you've just said?'

'No!' Celia took a couple of steps towards him. She felt the prick of tears stinging the backs of her eyes. 'This isn't what I wanted,' she cried, stricken. 'It's important that we maintain a good relationship…'

'I feel,' Leandro said heavily, 'that we took two steps forward and then, suddenly, fifteen back.'

'Because I broke the rules and decided to be honest with you?'

'Because you changed the rules halfway through, without warning.'

'I'll see you in the morning, Leandro.' They weren't going to get anywhere, going over the same old ground. Celia turned away, aware of his eyes on her, and she only sagged with relief when the bedroom door was closed, then she leant against it, drawing in ragged breaths.

How had it all come to this? How had she gone from *A bit of Leandro is better than none at all* to *I just can't go through with this*?

Seeing him with another woman. That was how. That was what had brought home to her just how tough it would be to face an uncertain future, always wondering when he might stray, always aching somewhere deep, deep inside, prematurely grieving something that would happen at some point in the future.

Yes, it would be horrible having a lifelong connection with him and watching him move on with his life, but at least she might be able to move on with hers. At least he wouldn't be there, living under the same roof, with a wedding ring on her finger reminding her that this was her life and there was nothing she could do to change it.

Celia fell into fitful sleep, having changed into a baggy tee shirt and the soft shorts she had brought over to sleep in, before sleeping naked had become the order of the day. She wished she'd brought all her clothes across. She should have done that when he'd disappeared for a drink. If she'd done that, she would have been able to kill some time packing to leave in the morning. As it was, she nodded off to the bright light on her phone updating her on what was happening in the news back in the UK.

She wasn't aware, two hours later, of the soft knock on her bedroom door.

On the other side of that door, Leandro waited, torn between knocking again or bailing.

He'd gone for a drink but had ended up on strong coffee instead.

Everything had been going along swimmingly so Celia's revelations had come as a body blow. Of course, he had accepted that life as he knew it had been irrevocably changed the second she had told him about the pregnancy. If he had been a little surprised at how easily he had assimilated that change into his psyche, then he had simply put it down to his expertise at dealing with what life threw at him.

He had been more astonished at how passionately he had felt about the baby she was carrying.

He'd gone from the prospect of fatherhood not being anywhere remotely on his radar to it being the most important thing in his life. Why else would he have agreed with alacrity to sacrifice his way of life? Without question?

But there *had* been clauses, he'd thought, as he'd stared down into his cup of black coffee an hour previously.

He'd brought the same clauses to marriage as he had brought to their fling when they'd been trapped by snow in Scotland. *No love...no emotional anchor being sunk to the bottom of the ocean...*

He'd expected her to fall in line and do the right thing because *he* was prepared to do so. And she had. She'd agreed because she was someone rooted in doing what was morally right. He hadn't had to beg because she was unselfish by nature and traditional enough to acquiesce to the overriding importance of family. She wasn't someone who was trained to put herself first.

Leandro had realised, as the thoughts had piled up in his head, that he had been lazy.

He'd read so much of her and enjoyed it all but he hadn't bothered to join the dots to see the road ahead.

He'd grown accustomed to her openness, her refreshing honesty and that way she had of looking at him that made him feel a hundred metres tall.

He'd sunk himself into their love-making and become addicted to it.

In every single way, he had luxuriated in her giving and her affection and her warm, supportive, empathetic conversation that had seen him open up in ways he never had before, and still he had kept reminding her of the boundaries to what they had. He'd stuck to what he knew without bothering to analyse why. It was who he was and what he did and he hadn't questioned it.

And he'd watched her fall in love with him without considering the ramifications.

Worse, he'd watched *himself* falling in love with her and completely ignored the signs because falling in love had never been in his remit.

Which brought him here now, with his hand raised to knock on the door again.

Except was it going to be too little too late? He would bare his soul, but would it seem too coincidental? Would she think that he was simply playing a card from his hand in the hope of bringing her back on board? Manufacturing his words into what she wanted him to say?

He knocked on the door, this time a little more forcefully, and then he gently pushed it open to stand, framed in the doorway, for a couple of seconds.

Celia had dimly been aware of *a sound* but it was only when Leandro knocked for a second time that she blinked and rubbed her eyes and realised that someone was at the bedroom door and, since there were only two of them in this presidential suite, there was no mystery as to who her caller was.

She sat up, on full alert, and stared at Leandro backlit in the doorway.

Was he drunk? Had he come on the back of several whiskies to try and make her change her mind? She tightened her lips. She wasn't going to start arguing because he was right, they needed to keep their lines of communication open. But she wasn't going to cave in either.

'I'm sorry.'

Those two words were enough to give her a jolt.

'What are you doing here?'

She had left the light voile curtains pulled and the

shutters open and, through the slats, moonlight illuminated the bedroom. He didn't sound drunk.

'I…can I come in? I won't sit on the bed. Don't worry. I can…pull a chair…please.'

Please. Another word to undermine her defences.

'You can't change my mind, Leandro.'

'I… I'm not here to do that. I'm here because I find I have no choice.'

'You're talking in riddles.'

'Let me come in. Please, Celia. If you don't want me to, then that's fine. I will stand right here and say what I have to say.'

'Have you been drinking?'

'Black coffee.' He half smiled. 'I'd aimed for stronger but realised that, when it came to getting my thoughts in order, whisky on the rocks wasn't going to work in my favour.'

The *please* along with the *I'm sorry* had got to her, and, with a click of impatience with her own weakness, she nodded curtly and told him that he could come in but that she was tired and that he shouldn't think for a second that she was going to have a change of mind.

'I do want to change your mind,' Leandro said in a low voice. 'More than anything else I want to change your mind but, even more than that, I want you to be happy and if being happy means letting you go, then I'll do that.'

'You will? Is this…some sort of game you're playing, Leandro?'

'I've never been more serious in my life before. I was sleepwalking, Celia, and it took you telling me how you feel about me to wake me up.'

'I don't need reminding of that,' Celia said stiffly.

'It took guts.' Leandro met her eyes. 'More guts than I've had.'

'Don't say things you don't mean,' Celia whispered. As fast as she tried to squash it, hope flared, a little flame that refused to be extinguished. She hated it yet couldn't stop it.

'I'm saying things… I never thought I'd ever say but you told me you loved me and suddenly everything fell into place. I've spent my life accepting that love and everything that went along with it wasn't for me. It was no great loss. I saw my father's life and I worked out before I even hit my teens that what he had wasn't what I wanted. I heard him crying at night and putting his dreams in a box and throwing away the key because my mother left him. Well, you know all this because I've said as much. Truth is, the very fact that I said that much to you should have set alarm bells ringing in my head.'

'What do you mean?' Unconsciously, Celia was straining towards him. Caution warred with simmering excitement because every word that left his mouth rang with heartfelt sincerity. She weakly tried to remember the dangers of believing what you wanted to believe.

'I made my mind up about a lot of things,' Leandro said quietly, 'when I was too young to know that life isn't something you can plan out like a military campaign. I forgot about nuance. Then you came along and that's what you brought to my life. I didn't want it and I didn't like it, but I was powerless to resist it.' He sighed. 'So, I guess, what I've come to say is this: I'm in love with you.' He held up both his hands in a gesture of weary resignation. 'I know what you're going to say and I can't blame you, Celia. You're going to tell me that you don't believe a word I'm saying and I shall have to accept that.'

'You would do that?'

'I want you to marry me, Celia, for real. For love. I need you to believe me when I say that, but…if I've left it too late then, yes, I will never bother you again, but I will never be the man you made me again. So will you marry me? Be my wife? Grow old with me and have a dozen more kids with me?'

Celia flung all doubt out of the window and threw herself at him, at this wonderful guy she loved with all her might.

'Yes, yes, yes, yes!' She laughed and half sobbed and covered him with kisses. 'Except for the dozen kids…although…' she smiled and this time kissed him tenderly '…who knows what the future holds?'

The wedding, three months later, couldn't have been more perfect.

That first dress would never have an outing, destined to remained preserved behind plastic for ever, a reminder of what, thankfully, had never been.

But the simple ivory dress she created for herself, with the help of her two enthusiastic assistants, was perfect in every detail, from the white soft folds like petals along the hem, that reminded her of the falling snow in Scotland, to the pink delicately woven beads and rosebuds that made her think of the glorious sunrises in Dubai. She got her opportunity to walk up the aisle of the little church her parents attended and all her friends and relatives, past and present, were there for the ceremony.

And if she was showing her baby bump? Leandro couldn't have been more proud. He couldn't take his eyes off her. The honeymoon, which was now planned post baby and when all the settling into their new house was done and dusted, would be to the Maldives.

'Sun,' he had promised two months previously, 'sand, sea and sex. Don't forget the dozen babies you promised me...'

'Let's just get baby number one out of the way first.' She had laughed.

And baby number one was born three days early and arrived with no fuss, although Leandro had been prepared for all and every eventuality.

He had downloaded the latest baby book and had passed many a contented evening squirming at some of the more graphic details.

Yet, when the time came for her to go to the hospital, he was more nervous than she was.

Tomasina Elizabeth Diaz.

His father, Tomas, had been over the moon and so had Celia's mother, Lizzie.

But Lizzie Drew had more than her cupful of joy, for Dan and Julie, whose wedding had been low-key on a beach in Scotland followed by a reception at Leandro's country estate there, were also expecting their first child.

All those strands that had seemed to float in disarray had been woven together.

'Penny for them.'

Strands...accidental meetings and quirks of fate... *Those* were the things that had been occupying Celia's mind as she'd gazed at her six-week-old daughter, who was fast asleep in her Moses basket, oblivious to her parents sitting on the sofa next to the basket, lazily watching telly and sporadically chatting.

What better way to spend an evening, one of their first, in the sweetest cottage they had found in a little village in Berkshire?

'Do you ever think what might have happened…?'

'If your brother hadn't been in the right place at the right time delivering a book to you? If he had never crossed paths with Julie?'

Leandro pulled her to him and engulfed her in his arms before tilting her chin so that their eyes met, his openly loving and deadly serious.

'I try not to think about that,' he told her truthfully, 'but yes. Who can ignore the coincidences that have led us to this place, right here and right now? I'm the happiest man on earth because of you but you're right…if Dan hadn't met Julie…if snow hadn't stopped them from reaching my place in Scotland, hadn't locked us into a bubble and made lovers out of us…if an accidental pregnancy hadn't brought you back into my life.' He paused then added, thoughtfully, 'No… I would still have come back to you, my darling, whether you had returned to my life or not. It might have taken a bit longer because I was a stubborn fool too set in his ways for his own good, but I would have come right back to you because *not* coming back to you would have been unthinkable.'

'Right answer,' Celia said with a sigh of pure contentment.

'Now…while our precious Tomasina gives us a moment of free time, shall we…?'

Leandro stood, pulling Celia up with him and then holding her tight to kiss her long and slow on the lips.

'I can't think of anything better,' Celia gurgled, smiling and hugging him as they headed for the bedroom.

* * * * *

DESTITUTE UNTIL
THE ITALIAN'S
DIAMOND

JULIA JAMES

MILLS & BOON

To JW, my out-going editor.

Thank you for all your help and support over the years.

CHAPTER ONE

SALVATORE LUCHESI CAREFULLY eased his body away from that of the woman who was pressing ardently against him.

'Gia—no...' he began, keeping his voice temperate.

'Oh, Salva! Don't you *know* how crazy I am about you?'

The woman's voice was a mix of cajoling and demanding. She'd turned up uninvited at Salvatore's Rome apartment, pushing in impetuously on the grounds of long acquaintance, coaxed a cocktail from him and was now, quite literally, throwing herself at him.

Salvatore tried not to sigh heavily. *Si, Dio mio!* He most definitely knew how crazy Giavanna Fabrizzi was about him! But even if she hadn't been the daughter of his closest business associate, her dark, sultry beauty as much as her youth—she was barely twenty, if that—was not to his taste at all. His taste in women ran to cool, long-legged blondes.

They, he freely acknowledged, made a perfect foil for his own looks—tall for an Italian, but with the typical olive-toned skin and dark hair and eyes. Plus, he also acknowledged, without vanity, he had the blessing of a face arranged in features that women found highly attractive and a tautly honed body that men envied.

'Gia, *cara*,' he said now, stepping away from her to hold her at arm's length. 'I'm immensely flattered—what man wouldn't be? But you are Roberto's *daughter*—I'd be mad if I dared to mess around with you!'

He tried to keep his tone humorous. Gia was a pain, but she was also notoriously volatile—over-indulged by a doting father—and he did not want to trigger a scene.

Gia's almond-shaped eyes widened. 'I don't want an *affair* with you, Salva!' she cried.

Her scarlet mouth lifted yearningly to his, and Salvatore could feel her pushing forward against his restraining hold on her arms.

'I want much, much more!'

He stared down at her. A bad feeling was starting to form in the pit of his stomach, and at her next dramatic announcement he knew exactly why.

'And so does Papa! He's told me! And he's right—totally right! It would be perfect—absolutely perfect!' She gave a lavish sigh, lips parting as she gazed hungrily at him. 'I want to *marry* you!' she trilled.

The bad feeling in Salvatore's stomach turned to concrete.

Lana's feet hurt in their killer platform shoes as she stood in the wings with the other models, then, as her turn came, stalked out on to the runway to the pounding music. After ten years in the modelling business she could do these shows with her eyes shut.

Did I ever really think all this was glamorous and exciting? she thought with an inward sigh as she swivelled expertly at the end of the runway, hand on hip, holding her pose for the correct amount of time, before stalking back up again. She had once, years ago, but now, with twenty-seven looming, she wanted to call it quits finally.

Except that she could not afford to.

Tiredness lapped at her. She'd been working non-stop with photoshoots and back-to-back shows during this frenzied fashion week, and it wasn't over yet. There was still the after-party for the VIPs to get through, which all the models had to grace.

Some half an hour later she was doing the requisite mingling, wondering when she might be able to make her escape, knowing she had a heavy work schedule the next day. Helping herself to a glass of calorie-free mineral water, she glanced uninterestedly around at the wall-to-wall models, stylists, editors, all the glittering entourage of *haute couture*, clustering around the designer and his top assistants.

Male eyes were coming her way, but she took no notice. Her mouth tightened. The one time she had she'd made the biggest mistake of her life.

How could I have been so stupid? Letting Malcolm into my life.

Mal by name and *mal* by nature, she thought darkly. But she'd not seen it. Wanting only, she knew with a pang in her heart, someone—anyone!—in her life to stop her feeling so alone.

Bleakness fleeted in her eyes. That nightmare time, nearly four years ago now, when both her parents had been killed in a motorway pile-up, had been unbearable. Letting Mal into her life had helped her bear it, helped her blot it out. And her eagerness to have someone had blinded her, she knew with hindsight, to Mal's character. She'd imagined he cared about her—but all he'd cared about was having a model as a trophy girlfriend, to make him look good as he grafted his way upwards as an aspiring actor.

Black fury replaced bleakness in her face. It turned out, though, that there was something else he'd cared about. The flat she'd bought in Notting Hill, paid for out of her savings from years in the modelling business and with what she'd inherited from her parents on their death. Mal had been very interested in that flat of hers...

She gave a mental shake. She was here to mingle, not to brood on Malcolm's perfidy. Resignedly, taking a sip of water, she glided forward again.

Salvatore accepted a glass of champagne from a passing server and took a brooding sip, looking with indifference at the party in full swing going on all around him. As an investor in the fashion house he'd been invited to the London show, but his mind was back in Rome. And the problem he faced there.

Gia—or rather, her father. Because Roberto, just as Gia had declared, saw things his spoilt daughter's way too.

'It's an ideal match!' Roberto had told him fulsomely. 'You couldn't ask for a more beautiful bride,' he'd said fondly. 'And I would be more than happy to entrust her to you, safe from fortune-hunters!' His eyes had narrowed. 'Do you have any objections to marrying my daughter?' he'd demanded, a discernible edge in his voice.

Salvatore had kept his face expressionless.

You mean apart from her being an over-indulged princess, nearly fifteen years younger than me?

'Any man would think themselves privileged to marry my Giavanna!' Roberto's eyes had narrowed again. 'You don't need me to tell you, Salvatore, how closely en-meshed we already are—so many joint ventures between us. Marriage to Giavanna would ensure they continue, make our partnership even closer.'

Salvatore's face had become even more expression-less. So that was what was behind this absurd notion! Well, his response would be adamant and ruthless, and then it would clearly be time for him and Roberto to end the business association that dated back to his fa-ther's days.

It could not happen instantly, however—there were ongoing ventures which either had to be completed, or from which Salvatore had to extricate himself without loss or complication. He did not want Roberto fighting him, or blocking him, by refusing to give up on the idea of his marrying his daughter. Somehow he had to con-vince Roberto it was a non-starter.

Making himself scarce had been the a first step—this impromptu visit to London and the fashion show... unnecessary but timely. He glanced around him, tak-ing another brooding mouthful of champagne. But as he lowered his flute the mass of people parted, shifting his view. And into his sight came someone who stilled the glass in his hand.

Por Dio, but she was fantastic! Golden hair piled high, a racehorse figure robed in a skin-tight scarlet and crim-son evening gown that slithered down her long, slender body and even longer legs. He could not take his eyes from her. The room was full of show-stopping women dressed to the nines. But there was something about this one—

His gaze lingered.

Bellissima...assolutamente bellissima...

The fulsome description fitted her perfectly. Perfect features, high cheekbones, wide-set eyes…and a mouth made for kissing.

He felt his hormones kick in and moved forward.

The blonde's head turned slightly and she saw him.

And she stilled completely.

Lana froze. A man was walking towards her. People stepped aside as he did so, and she knew why. Knew, too, why her pulse had suddenly given a kick—why her head had turned to let her eyes focus straight on him.

Tall—taller than herself—in a tuxedo whose jacket was set superbly across lean shoulders, dark-haired, dark-eyed, and with Latin looks that—

Take my breath away.

Chiselled features, mobile mouth, winged eyebrows over night-dark eyes. And with something about him that effortlessly radiated wealth and power.

A money man. One of those unseen backers of all this, whose money pays for all of us and who collects the profits we make for him.

But she didn't have time to think any more. Or to analyse. Or consider.

He'd stopped in front of her.

And suddenly, out of nowhere, there was no one else in the crowded room except him.

Salvatore stopped. His eyes had never left her. Up close she was even more spectacular. He could see the vivid green of her eyes, like jewelled emeralds—could see, too, with a kick of his hormones, that they had flared wide at his approach.

He lifted his glass of champagne to her.

'Don't tell me…' he said, and his voice was a drawl. He inserted an edge of humour into it. 'You're a model.'

For a second she did not respond. Then— 'Don't tell me,' she echoed. 'You're a money man.'

Deliberately she echoed his gesture too, lifting her glass to him.

Salvatore gave a laugh, short but genuine.

'Well, I'm certainly not one of the birds of paradise here—male or female!' he riposted.

He felt himself relax, settle into the exchange. His hormones were cruising along nicely, and in his head new thoughts were shaping. He could do with diverting them from the problem of Roberto and his pernicious pampered daughter. And this fantastic female here could divert them very, very easily…

'Tell me,' he said, relaxing his stance, wanting to engage her in conversation. 'How will this collection go down, do you think?'

She made a slight face. 'Word is two of the fashion editors here like it—the one from New York is less keen. But the Chinese guy is smiling, which everyone will like, because that market is massive. Which,' she said pointedly, 'you don't need me to tell you.'

'No, but it's good to hear you tell me that he's smiling,' Salvatore said.

It was good just to be in conversation with her. But it was a conversation that was not, to his annoyance, destined to last any longer. Someone was swooping down on him. One of his countrymen.

'Signor Luchesi! *Mi dispiace!* I did not see you there—'

Voluble Italian enveloped him, inviting him to join the exclusive circle around the celebrated designer. Impatiently Salvatore wanted to fob him off, return his attention to the breathtaking blonde, but she was drifting away—accepting, it seemed, that he'd been claimed by those a lot more important than herself.

He gave a half shrug of resignation, allowing himself to be ushered unctuously forward, a fresh glass of champagne pressed upon him. He'd catch up with the fabulous blonde later. He did not intend to let her slip through his fingers.

But some twenty minutes later, when he'd finally extricated himself from the circle around the designer, when his needle gaze threaded through the crowded room it drew a blank. Where had the fabulous blonde got to? A frown formed on his brow. She was nowhere to be seen.

Lana stood on the London pavement, under a bus shelter, relief at her escape from the after-party filling her. There was only one slight regret—if she could call it that.

That man—the money man who came over to chat me up...

Usually when she was hit on at these affairs she never engaged. But this time had been different.

Why?

She stared out into the damp chill night as the ceaseless traffic on the busy street went to and fro. An answer formed in her head and she couldn't dismiss it.

Because he was the most fantastic-looking guy I've seen in my life!

Nothing like Malcolm's blond beachboy look—she was off that look for ever! No, that money man tonight had a completely different appeal. Dark and devastating...

She felt again the kick that had gone through her

as her eyes had met his, during the brief conversation they'd had.

Too brief.

She gave an inner sigh. It didn't matter how bowled over she'd been by him. He'd walked away and that was that. Besides, there was no point in wanting anything more from him. Not with her life in its current mess.

Wearily, she flexed her aching feet again, blessedly in flats now. She was glad to be back in her own comfortable clothes, hair brushed out into a loose ponytail, her face clear of make-up. She looked down the street, hoping to see a bus approaching.

There was no sign of one.

Instead, gliding into the bus bay was a long, silver-grey expensive-looking saloon car. It was driven by a peaked-capped chauffeur, and the rear passenger door was opening on her side. A man in a tuxedo was half leaning out towards her.

'So,' said the lethal-looking Italian money man who'd zeroed in on her at the after-party before zeroing out again, 'there you are!'

His voice sounded deep, accented—and filled with satisfaction.

A kick went through Salvatore. It had annoyed him not to find the stunning blonde model again, and now here she was. He'd recognised her instantly, even with her hair tied back and wearing a trench coat. She was having exactly the same impact on him as when he'd first set eyes on her. And he definitely wanted more of it. More of her.

He undid his seat belt, getting out of the car. 'Why did you disappear?' he asked her.

His eyes raked her over. Yes, even without all the

fancy clothes and coiffure and make-up, she was every bit as stunning as he'd known she would be. And his visceral response to her was every bit as strong.

She was replying to him now, giving a little shrug. 'I snuck off early,' she said.

He smiled. 'Good,' he said. 'Come and have dinner with me.'

A look of surprise crossed her face—and something more. Something that registered at an instinctive level of his masculinity. That increased his satisfaction.

But she was shaking her head. 'I'm calling it a day. Heading home. My feet are killing me.'

Was there regret in her voice? He was pretty sure there was.

He cupped a hand under her elbow. 'Then I'll give you a lift.' He glanced down the road. 'There's no sign of a bus, and you look cold. Besides, it's coming on to rain.'

For a second he felt her stiffen, and then, as a few drops of rain conveniently precipitated out of the murky sky, she let him usher her into his car.

'Where do I tell the driver?' he asked.

She gave an address—a quiet road in Notting Hill—and he relayed it to the chauffeur, who nodded behind his glass screen as he changed direction and set off to cross Hyde Park towards Bayswater Road, instead of heading towards Park Lane and Salvatore's hotel there.

'I hope it's not too out of your way—but you did offer!' The blonde's voice was half apologetic and half not.

'Not at all,' he assured her smoothly.

He smiled across at her. Her face was in chiaroscuro now, as the intermittent light from the street and passing vehicles played across it. He felt that kick go through him again, welcoming it.

'Will you change your mind about dinner?' He turned to look at her as the car moved off again into the traffic. 'There are some excellent restaurants in Notting Hill!' he said lightly.

She shook her head again, and he was surprised. Women did not usually turn down dinner invitations from him. His eyes rested on her appreciatively. In the time since he'd last set eyes on her she had not lost an iota of the impact she'd made on his senses. His eyelids drooped in sensual assessment.

'Thank you—but I really do need to head home.'

Her voice still sounded composed, but he suspected she was not as indifferent as she was making herself out to be.

He was glad of her turning him down now. Perhaps it made sense not to rush things with her. He'd acted on impulse in picking her up as he had, and that was unusual for him. Unusual to the point of his never doing so. His affairs were always carefully considered and of deliberately limited duration, and he chose the women he had them with just as carefully.

So why act on impulse with this stunning blonde?

The question flitted, but he dismissed it.

'Perhaps I could take you to dinner another evening,' he said now. He would happily extend his trip to London to do so.

For a moment she seemed to hesitate. Then she shook her head. This time he was sure there was regret in her face.

'I really can't afford any more complications in my life right now,' she answered.

He honed in on the key word. 'More?' he asked. She didn't answer and he pressed again, an unwelcome thought occurring to him. 'Are you involved with someone?'

If she were, then he definitely didn't want to have anything to do with her. But she shook her head—quite decisively.

'No—thank God! Not any longer!'

His eyes rested on her. He could see agitation in her face now.

'A broken heart?' he asked.

If so, that would be a definite no for him too. He preferred to keep things simple when it came to women—no complicated emotions ricocheting around.

'A broken bank balance!' came the retort. Anger flashed in her face, her voice. 'Courtesy of my ex-boyfriend! It means I have to work non-stop right now.' She looked at him square-on. 'I can't take any time out for... well, for dinner for a start. Or...' She didn't quite look at him now. 'Or for anything else.'

'I'm sorry to hear it,' he said smoothly.

He was, too. In this confined private space she was having a powerful effect on him, from the perfection of her profile to the gold of her hair.

'So am I,' he heard her say, almost *sotto voce.*

That made him speak again. 'What did your ex do to you?'

'He took out a four-hundred-thousand-pound mortgage on *my* flat!' she bit out. 'Then did a runner, leaving *me* to repay it!'

The anger was back in her voice, in her face, in her emerald flashing eyes.

Salvatore's eyebrows rose. For a woman without his

kind of financial background that was a hefty amount indeed.

She broke eye contact with him. 'I'm sorry. I don't know why I blurted that out,' she said tightly.

She looked out of the car window suddenly. They'd reached Notting Hill Gate and were heading down Kensington Park Road.

'Oh, I'm the next cross street after this one. On the left!' she exclaimed. The car was already turning, guided by the satnav, and drawing up outside a handsome plaster-faced house, part of a well-kept terrace.

Salvatore glanced at it. No wonder the ex had been able to raise such a hefty mortgage—property in this part of town did not come cheap.

As if reading his thoughts, she threw a look at him. 'Years of non-stop modelling, plus an inheritance,' she said, and anger was audible in her voice again. 'And the bastard's gone off with half of it!' She shook her head. 'I'm sorry,' she said again. 'I've got no call to dump any of my problems on you!'

Her voice changed and she undid her seat belt. The chauffeur was already opening her door for her.

She looked back at Salvatore as she started to get out. 'Look, thank you for the lift. I'm sorry about dinner, whether tonight or any other time, but…well…' Her voice trailed off and she just shook her head.

Did her eyes linger on him—was there regret in them if they did? But she was getting gracefully out of the car.

She glanced back in. 'I'll wish you goodnight,' she said, and now he was sure he could hear regret.

Well, he felt it too. For himself. He raised a hand in farewell. Should he ask her name? Give her his card?

But she was already crossing the pavement, running

lightly up the steps to the glossy black front door, fetch-ing a key out of her handbag. Then she was inside.

She hadn't looked back at him.

The chauffeur was back in the driver's seat, and Sal-vatore told him to head to his hotel. He would be dining in his suite…alone.

Che peccato.

A pity.

CHAPTER TWO

SALVATORE WAS BACK in Rome, having taken in an extended trip to New York and Chicago after London. He'd been half glad, half reluctant to leave London, and it was because of the fabulous blonde—the one he'd wanted from the moment of seeing her, but who'd told him she didn't have time for him.

Yes, well, he could see why…saddled with that crippling debt she was working all hours to service. He frowned a moment. Had she told him because she'd thought she could get *him* to pay it off for her? After all, he'd admitted to her he was a 'money man'—

He dismissed the suspicion. If his wealth *had* been of interest to her in that respect she'd have snapped at his invitation to dinner—at the possibility of having an affair with him.

He was glad he didn't have to think ill of her in that way. Even though it made it all the more frustrating that she had turned him down.

The phone rang on his desk and he snatched it up, glad of the distraction from thinking about a woman who didn't have time for him…even though he, he knew, would have made a considerable amount of time for someone that stunning and desirable…

But the voice on the line was a distraction he did not welcome. It was Roberto—pressing him to come to lunch. Ostensibly it was to discuss the progress on a joint venture they had both invested heavily in, but when—warily—Salvatore joined him, Roberto was soon back to pushing Giavanna at him.

'She needs an older man, my darling Giavanna… someone to guide her and protect her!'

'But that man, Roberto, cannot be me,' Salvatore retorted.

He could see a mulish expression forming on the other man's face—Roberto liked getting his own way. *Like father like daughter,* he thought cynically.

'Why?'

The challenge came bluntly. Demandingly.

Belligerently.

Salvatore's irritation and annoyance turned to exasperation. He needed something that would stop Roberto in his tracks, yet not put his back up so much that he would make excessive trouble when Salvatore extricated himself financially from him. Something that would be impossible for Roberto to challenge. And only one thing occurred to him.

'Because…' he made his voice sound resolute '… I am involved with someone else right now. Someone,' he went on, hearing the words fall from his lips—hearing them with a disbelief that was echoed in Roberto's face as he spoke them. 'I intend to marry.'

The words were there, pulled out of thin air—and they could not be unsaid.

Just where they had come from Salvatore had not the faintest idea. Only he had a bad, bad feeling that he had just burnt every boat in his possession. And then some—

Lana climbed wearily aboard the bus. She'd been working non-stop all day—three shoots—and was fully booked for tomorrow as well. The following day was lighter—just a single casting. She frowned slightly—it was in an odd place, somewhere in the City. There had been no mention of the client, or what the campaign was, nor any other details. She'd agreed to it because she never turned work down these days. However exhausted and dispirited she was.

I can't go on like this—I'm burning myself out just keeping up with the sky-high interest payments.

Malcolm had not bothered to look for cheap borrowing. He'd simply applied for a mortgage on her behalf, using a fake email address he'd set up for her, brazenly forging her signature on the loan documents. He'd had the money paid into the joint bank account he'd persuaded her to open with him to make paying household bills easier—not that he'd ever paid any—then immediately transferred it to his own account and cleared out of her flat.

She'd come home from a foreign shoot to find him and all his stuff gone—and a letter from a completely unknown mortgage lender setting out just how much she owed them, and what the crippling rate of interest on the massive loan was.

As for Malcolm, probably living it up God knew where, on *her* money, he was untraceable. Her vociferous complaints to the mortgage company, her solicitor and the police had met with sympathy, but if there was no one to prosecute for apparent fraud—well, there was nothing that could be done except what she was doing—working herself to the bone, day after day.

She stared bleakly out of the bus window.

However hard I work, will I have to accept that the only way I can pay off this crippling mortgage is by selling up, taking a massive hit, and then finding some place outside London for half the price of what the flat is worth?

It was a galling prospect, and she felt familiar fury at Malcolm bite again. Her expression changed as she heard in her mind her own voice railing about him to that fabulous Italian who'd given her a lift home after the fashion show two weeks ago.

I just blurted it right out to that man—a complete stranger!

Yet there'd been something about him that had made her want to be upfront with him.

Maybe it's because after what Malcolm did to me— the lies, the deceit, defrauding me—I just want honesty.

After all, the fabulous Italian had been upfront about his invitation to her. Dinner, she knew perfectly well, would have been the first step towards an affair. An affair she just didn't have time for...and she'd been upfront about that straight off.

Her expression became rueful. The first man to have drawn her interest since Malcom had done the dirty on her, and she'd walked away...

But it hadn't stopped her thinking about him. In the four weeks since the fashion show she hadn't been able to forget him. During tedious shoots, holding her poses while photographers argued with stylists, his image— those amazing Latin looks, his dark, long-lashed eyes, his sculpted mouth—had constantly made its way into her head as she'd replayed her encounter with him. Replays laced, she knew, with something she had to admit was very much like regret...

Well, it was too late if so—he'd made no attempt to contact her again. Although he knew where she lived, and it would be easy enough for him to find out her name

from her agency via the fashion house he was an investor in. But he hadn't.

*A man that gorgeous—and that rich!—won't have to
hang around waiting for a woman to say yes to him...*

No, she'd missed her chance with him—and maybe
that was just as well, given her unrelenting workload.

Wearily, Lana got out her phone and checked her ap-
pointments for the next day. Work: that was her prior-
ity—her sole agenda.

Nothing else.

And certainly not some drop-dead gorgeous Italian
whom she would never see again...

Salvatore paced to the window of his serviced office
suite in the City, from where he conducted his London
business. He frowned. What he was contemplating right
now was not business—

More like insanity!

He shook his head. No, it was *not* insanity! It was very
real, very practical, and the more he went through the
advantages, the more sense it made. Since making that
impulsive, even desperate announcement to Roberto, to
stop the damn man in his tracks—which it had, totally
effectively—he'd gone through all the arguments, pros
and cons, exhaustively, in a ruthlessly rational fashion.
And he had come to one conclusion only. The cons could
be limited—and managed—while the pros...

He felt a kick to his system. There was one very definite pro. And it had nothing to do with getting Giavanna
and her father off his case and everything to do with the
woman he had quite simply been unable to get out of his
system. Just why, he still could not account for. It had

been over a month since the fashion show, and surely that was time enough to forget all about her? Yet he hadn't.

And now—

The phone on his desk rang and he snatched it up.

She was here.

Lana followed the svelte secretary from the outer office of this very upmarket office suite in the City, still with no idea what she was turning up for. The brass plate at the entrance had simply said *Luchesi SpA*. Was it some Italian fashion house she'd never heard of?

As the secretary shut the door behind her, she took in a large space with a lush dove-grey carpet, a pair of grey leather sofas and a huge mahogany desk—behind which someone was sitting.

She stopped dead, an audible exclamation breaking from her.

It was the drop-dead, lethal-looking Italian money man. The man she'd turned down for dinner—and anything else! The man whose image she had not been able to get out of her head—now here, right here in front of her.

He was getting to his feet. 'Thank you for coming. Won't you sit down?'

He indicated a leather and chrome chair in front of his desk, then resumed his own. Dark eyes rested on her, as unreadable as his expression, but still she was all too aware of their magnetic effect on her. She hadn't set eyes on him for weeks, but he still had an instant impact on her that she had never experienced before. She could feel her heart-rate increase, but managed, through long schooling, to keep her expression composed and inexpressive, saying nothing yet.

For a moment he just rested his gaze on her, giving nothing away but, she thought, both assessing her and taking stock. His manner, it dawned on her, was quite different from his relaxed demeanour at their first encounter. Now it was formal—businesslike.

Thoughts, confused and hectic, flashed through her mind.

Just what is going on? Because whatever it is, this isn't a casting!

'Before we proceed,' he was saying now, his English accented, as she remembered it, and the low timbre of his voice having the same effect on her now as it had that evening after the fashion show, 'I must ask you to sign this.'

He withdrew a piece of A4 paper from a leather folder on his desk, placed it in front of her. Lana's eyes dropped to it.

'It's an NDA—a non-disclosure agreement,' she was informed. 'What I am about to say to you must remain between ourselves only.'

Her eyes went from the paper to him, but his expression was still unreadable. She leant forward to skim-read the document—which did, indeed, seem to be nothing more drastic than an undertaking, legally binding, by her to make no reference in any way to any person or organisation or representative thereof, to any part or the whole of the content of the discourse about to take place, today or subsequently at any time, via any media, whether voice, written or electronic, et cetera, et cetera.

Her gaze went back to him. This was so different from their first encounter she could not make sense of it.

'Look, signor—' She halted, realising, with a start, that she had no idea who he was.

'Luchesi,' he supplied. 'Salvatore Luchesi.'

There was reserve in his voice, she could hear it. Almost, she recognised, a wariness.

'What is going on?' she asked bluntly. 'My booker told me this was a casting of sorts…'

A mordant expression was in his eyes. 'Of sorts, yes,' he echoed, his reserve still apparent to her. 'If we proceed.'

For a moment he just surveyed her, with that unreadable look on his face. Then he placed a gold-tipped, very expensive fountain pen in front of her, nodding slightly at the NDA. She picked up the pen and signed. Clearly he would say nothing more until she did. She pushed the paper and the pen back towards him. He slid the signed and dated NDA back into its folder and rested his gaze on her again.

His expression was still unreadable, but something, Lana fancied, had changed within it. And across his broad shoulders, so elegantly clad in his bespoke suit— Milan, not Savile Row; she'd recognised that from the off with her practised eye for fashion—sat a new slight but discernible tension.

She waited. His eyes rested on her impassively—so dark, so unreadable, and so unfairly fringed with velvet lashes that, had they been fringing a female's eyes, would not need mascara to thicken them.

But there was tension in his gaze as well. As though, she thought, he might not continue with this exchange after all.

She sat still—she was used to doing so for extended periods during photoshoots—keeping her expression as neutral. Then, abruptly, he spoke again.

'I find myself in a situation…' he drew a short breath '…which requires a certain line of action.'

The accented voice was brisk now, and very business-like. The dark eyes were obsidian, suddenly, the planed cheekbones taut, the sensual mouth a tight line. And the tips of his fingers had discernibly whitened around the arms of his chair.

He's steeling himself.

The realisation was in her head, and a frown as she wondered why that should be so was starting to form on her forehead.

His next words gave the explanation. Bluntly, brusquely and blatantly.

'I wish,' he said, 'to discuss the possibility of a marriage between us.'

Salvatore heard the words fall from his own mouth. In that instant if he'd been able to recall them he would have.

Had he really, truly, gone and said them?

Yes, he must have. The look of extreme astonishment on her face told him so.

His own face set. Too late to backtrack now. He'd launched his bombshell and he must follow it through.

A tight, almost-smile pressed at his mouth. 'Yes, I agree—not what you were expecting,' he commented. He took a breath, deliberately slackening what had become an iron grip of his hands around his chair-arms. 'However, there are sound reasons—indeed, quite sane reasons—for what I have just said.'

She still hadn't moved, let alone replied, but instinctively he raised a hand as if to silence her.

'Hear me out,' he instructed.

For a second he gathered his thoughts. He'd rehearsed his argument countless times since the notion had first come to him, but now it was to be for real.

'I require,' he went on, 'at very short notice, a female in my life whom I can present, for a limited but immediate period, as my wife.'

He halted. She was staring at him as if he were mad, and he could well understand why. He lowered his raised hand and placed it palm down on his desk, pushing his chair back slightly, making himself adopt a more relaxed pose.

It wasn't one that was echoed in Lana—she was still sitting there, completely frozen, completely expressionless.

Yet still stunningly beautiful!

She was dressed in neutral colours: a pair of dark blue narrow-legged trousers, and a grey, close-fitting top with a loose but smart jacket worn over it. Her feet were in heels, but of modest height. Her hair was drawn back into a ponytail, and she wore only light make-up. But she was still far and away the most stunningly beautiful-looking female he had ever set eyes on—and she was having exactly the same impact on him as she had the first time he'd seen her at that after-party.

She refused me then—will she refuse me now?

He crushed down his reaction to her. Time for that later. For now, it was all about the reason he'd just dropped his bombshell in front of her.

He took a breath, short and indrawn, and made himself speak, keeping his voice impersonal, dispassionate. 'I have,' he began, 'a long-standing business partnership with an associate of my late father, who has recently taken it into his head that I...' his voice tightened '...

would make a suitable husband for his daughter. A notion that, unfortunately, his daughter also shares. She, however...' and now his voice was edged '...would *not* make a suitable wife for me! And although I have tried hard to convince both herself and her father of that truth, neither is willing to accept it.' He took another incising breath, felt his jaw tense, his mouth thin. 'It has, therefore, become clear to me that I must...reluctantly...take drastic steps to dispose of a nuisance that has become increasingly irksome...to me. Hence,' he concluded, 'what I have just proposed to you.'

He fell silent, his gaze resting on her, still veiled. For a moment longer she did not move. Then she did.

She got to her feet.

'I'm sorry you went to the trouble of drawing up that NDA I just signed, *signor*, because it won't be necessary. I would *never* make any mention to anyone of this *insane* discussion!'

She made to turn, presumably to exit, but Salvatore was before her. He was on his feet, around his desk, blocking her way to the door.

'Unusual it might be—insane it is not,' he said tightly.

Her head swivelled. 'It's insane,' she insisted.

He didn't argue with her. He cut to the chase instead.

'Whatever you or I choose to call it, I am prepared, should you agree to spend the next twelve months as my wife, to pay you a sum that will entirely clear the outstanding debt your ex imposed upon you.'

His eyes met hers. His were unreadable. Hers were not. They had widened, and in them was a mixture of disbelief and something quite different.

Salvatore stepped away. Behind the mask of his expression he was giving nothing away. But he knew from long business experience that he had hooked her.

'Let us discuss this more fully,' he invited, and gestured to the pair of leather sofas.

Jerkily, but obediently, Lana did as he'd bade.

Relief filled Salvatore. And more than that—anticipation. But that was for later. For now there was the matter of a marriage to be hammered out...

Lana's head was reeling. Numbly, she sat herself down on one of the sofas, sinking down into its depths. Opposite her, on the other one, the man who had just offered, with a flick of his fingers, to lift her out of the bottomless financial pit Malcolm had so callously tossed her into did likewise, crossing one elegant leg over the other.

'What I require from you is this,' Salvatore Luchesi said.

He spoke in the brisk, impersonal tone he'd used since her arrival—which perhaps, she allowed, made it easier to cope with what he was saying...easier to forget that he'd once invited her to dinner, to an affair.

'As soon as it can be arranged, we will undertake a legal marriage. After which you will return with me to Rome, where we will present to the world the appearance that we are normal married couple, following a whirlwind romance here in London.' His voice tightened. 'A wife at my side will dispose once and for all with the wishes of my business associate's daughter and her father's ambitions for closer financial involvement with me. I shall use the duration of our marriage to extricate myself from my various complex high-value joint ventures with him. Once that is accomplished...' his eyes were holding hers, an intent expression in their dark depths '…our marriage can…and *will*…terminate.'

Lana said nothing, still trying to get her head around what he was saying. But he was speaking again.

'At that point we will divorce, and you will receive, according to the prenuptial agreement you will sign before we marry, the sum of four hundred thousand pounds and any accruing interest.'

She swallowed, her head still reeling, and fought to get control of her blitzed thoughts.

This isn't really a marriage—it's a business deal, that's all! A marriage for public consumption only. And when it's over I get my debt paid for me.

And because of that—because he was going to pay off her mortgage for her—of course the marriage would be for show only…nothing else.

Something flickered inside her as if it were a little dart, piercing her.

Nothing else.

Her own words echoed in her head, that little dart piercing again. At their first encounter he'd invited her to dinner—to an affair. She'd turned him down.

Now all he wants is a business deal.

A business deal that would lift the crushing burden of debt from her.

'Well?' The single word fell from Salvatore Luchesi's lips. 'Do we proceed?

For a timeless moment Lana could not answer.

Then she did.

Salvatore stood in front of the bathroom mirror in his hotel suite, adjusting his bow tie, preparing to set off for a livery company dinner in the City.

So he had done it. He had put into motion what surely was the most extreme solution to his infuriating predicament that he could possibly have come up with.

And yet—

His expression changed as he dropped his hands, eyeballing his own reflection. And yet it had simultaneously achieved a very different goal.

Lana was everything he remembered about her and more. Just as stunningly beautiful. He'd sounded brusque, he knew, putting his proposal to her—but he'd needed her to understand right from the off that their marriage was going to be temporary only. Actual marriage—real, lasting marriage—was not for him.

He stared at his reflection for a moment, eyes shadowing. He had his father's looks, he knew—but was that all he'd inherited from him? Grimly, he suspected not.

Transient affairs—that was his style. His preference. He would not risk anything else.

With an abrupt movement, he turned away. Time to head off for his dinner. And tomorrow he would press ahead with expediting all that had to be done before he could return to Rome—with Lana at his side.

CHAPTER THREE

LANA STOOD IN front of the registrar, supremely conscious of the man at her side. The man she was about to marry. All the paperwork had been completed—another, even more comprehensive NDA, and a rigorous prenup. Now there was just the wedding ceremony to get through.

Her eyes dropped to her ring finger and she swallowed. She had already known Salvatore Luchesi was rich—he was a money man, after all—but the glittering diamond-encrusted engagement ring he'd slid onto her finger just before they'd walked into the register office had made her widen her eyes.

'It will be expected that you wear a betrothal ring,' he'd told her.

His voice had been impersonal then and it was impersonal now, as he gave the expected responses to the registrar. Hers was as well. A feeling of unreality had come over Lana, and she clung to it. This was not, after all, she reminded herself yet again, a real marriage—so of course reality felt far, far away.

Whatever had passed between her and Salvatore so briefly, so fleetingly that evening of the fashion show— weeks ago now—had been and gone. What they were undertaking now was reflected both in her own cool, calm composure and in the brisk, businesslike demeanour he was treating her with.

As she stood beside him now, with neither of them looking at each other, only at the registrar, she could catch the faint scent of an expensive aftershave—could feel against her own sleeve the slight brush of his. And she knew that if she turned her head even a fraction she would catch his distinctive profile, the sensual curve of his mouth, the high cheekbone, the sable hair, the strong line of his jaw.

But that was irrelevant.

As was the slight but discernible pang that went through her at the fact that it was so.

He wants nothing else—and I want...

Well, that was irrelevant too. The very nature of their marriage made it so.

That and that alone was what she must remember.

Salvatore picked up the leather-bound menu and tried to peruse its offerings. But his thoughts were on matters unrelated to lunch.

So, it was done. He'd entered into a state of legal marriage with a woman who was barely more than a stranger for reasons which he had resented being imposed upon him in the first place. But there was no point in rehashing all that now, when their signatures were on the marriage certificate.

His eyes lifted briefly to Lana as she sat opposite him, studying her menu with more attention than he was giving his. He felt his sombre mood lift discernibly and allowed his gaze to take in what he was seeing. She was dressed exactly right for the occasion, wearing a cream-coloured suit that accentuated her tall, racehorse figure, and wore her hair up, with a wisp of what looked halfway between a hat and a fascinator. The whole effect was dressy, but not specifically bridal. Only the diamond betrothal ring and the wedding band denoted her change in status since she'd got dressed that morning.

As did his own wedding band.

He could see the light catching at it, and memory slid uninvited into his head. His father had never shed his own wedding ring, however much he'd made a mockery of it.

He pulled his mind away from that thought. Silenced the thought that followed. That he, too, was making a mockery of the ring he was wearing...

Refutation was instant. No, he was not. Okay, so they'd married for reasons that people did not usually marry for, but the point was that they both had good reason to marry each other, and they both knew what that was. Their expectations of this marriage were the same.

Unlike his own parents'.

He silenced the memory again. It was neither relevant nor justified. He dropped his eyes to the menu again, making his choice, then glancing at the wine list.

Time to choose an appropriate champagne for the occasion. After all, he thought caustically, it was his wedding day.

Lana let her gaze rest lightly on the man sitting opposite her as he perused the wine list. He was totally at home in this quietly expensive restaurant in Knightsbridge, to which his chauffeured car had delivered them from the register office. Totally at home in a plutocratic lifestyle that was his birth right.

Luchesi SpA, she now knew, was a top player in Italian investment circles, or so it seemed, and had been so for close on a century. It had been founded by Salvatore Luchesi's grandfather, taken on to greater heights by his father, and now the man she had just married was expanding it even further.

But he didn't spend all his time on business, she had read. In her Internet searches about him his name had cropped up in the Italian tabloids and all the glossy magazines, There had been pictures of him attending glittering events on the Italian social scene—nearly always, Lana had not failed to notice, with a beautiful blonde on her arm.

And now it's going to be me.

It was a strange thought that now she was going to be paraded not just as his latest beautiful blonde, but as his chosen wife.

But not chosen for any reason that people usually choose who they marry. At heart, money is the reason both of us have married—Salvatore so he can extricate his financial affairs from a business partner he no longer wants, and me so I can extricate myself from the mountain of debt Malcolm dumped on me.

She realised the man she'd married for those pecuniary reasons was now asking her, in the same clipped, brisk tones he'd used with her since his car had collected her and her luggage from her flat, what she wanted to eat.

It was on her lips to order what she always ordered in restaurants—grilled fish and undressed salad—when it dawned on her, with an unexpected sense of gratification, that for an entire year she'd have no shoots or shows whatsoever. Not a single damn one. She glanced at the menu again, her eyes falling to a dish she had automatically ignored. She felt her mouth water even at the thought.

She looked up at the waiter who had approached to take their order. 'The chicken breast in marsala cream,' she told him. 'With *pommes parmentier* and buttered green beans.'

She closed the menu decisively as Salvatore gave his own order, and then named the champagne he'd selected. Lana felt her mood lift. There was a definite upside to what she'd done—and it wasn't just because of the mortgage she was going to be free of. She'd also be free of her constant near-starvation diet. That was a definite bonus.

Moments later, when the champagne arrived, she all but thrust her glass out to be filled. Alcohol was a calorific luxury in itself.

As the beaded bubbles blinked at her, gently fizzing in the flute, and the waiter slipped away, Salvatore raised his own glass. 'To a successful partnership,' he said.

His voice was still brisk, but there was something else in it too. A lighter tone. Slight, but discernible.

She lifted her lass, keen to taste the champagne. As she took a careful sip, savouring the soft mousse, a warning came to her.

All this is temporary—nothing more than that. Don't ever forget it.

It was a timely reminder. Everything about the life she had just stepped into was temporary.

Of their own volition her eyes flickered to the man opposite her, casually tasting the uber-expensive vintage champagne.

Including him.

As her eyes rested on him, on his looks as lethal as

the rest of him, she knew with a slight tightening of the breath in her lungs that that was what she must remember most of all.

Salvatore heard the landing gear release and felt the plane move into its approach path to Fiumicino. Beside him in First Class his new bride sat, absorbed in looking out of the window.

'Have you been to Rome before?' he asked. It was something he would be expected to know about the woman he was going to present to the world as his new bride.

His mood darkened. In a very short while they would be in Rome, and the reality of what he'd done was hitting home. A woman who was all but a stranger was to be regarded by everyone as if she really was the woman he wanted to spend his life with—as if a whirlwind romance had indeed taken place. That was the fiction he had to make Giavanna and Roberto believe—and everyone else would have to believe it too. Including his friends. And his household. Everyone who knew him.

They'll believe a lie.

And, whilst he might not care over-deeply about what Giavanna and her father believed, it was different when it came to his friends, to those who knew him well…

Impatiently he pushed the unwelcome thought aside. What was done was done—now he just had to ensure it would work. And if that made him less than relaxed… well, so be it. The situation was inherently stressful, and that was all there was to it.

'A few times,' came the answer, and Lana turned her head to look at him as he addressed her. 'Fashion shoots.

But I never have time to see the places I go to—just fly in and out.'

'Well, you'll have time now,' he replied. Briskly, he went on, 'We'll spend long enough here socialising to show you off—send the message to Giavanna and her father—and then I'll take you off to Tuscany, to the family *palazzo*. Officially we'll be on our honeymoon, so we won't have to entertain.'

The welcome thought lifted his mood. At the *palazzo* he could relax. They could both relax. And there, with Lana at his side, away from everyone else, with nothing to distract him, he could finally focus on her and her stunning beauty exclusively.

It was a pleasing prospect…

The stewardess was gliding by, inspecting their seat belts, interrupting his pleasing thoughts about life with Lana in Tuscany away from the world's eye.

Moments later the plane was on the ground, and shortly after that they were heading into Rome. During the drive he double-checked with his new bride just what she was to tell the people he introduced her to about how they had met and why they had married so precipitately. It was essential their story was convincing.

His eyes slid to Lana, sitting in the spacious passenger seat beside him, long legs elegantly slanted, her stunning beauty effortless in her well-cut wedding outfit, and he remembered how he'd given her a lift back to her flat after the fashion show party. She'd caught at his senses then, just as she was doing now.

His thoughts lingered a moment, then refocussed on what he still needed to tell her.

'We'll have this evening to ourselves, to allow you to settle in, but tomorrow we are lunching with friends of mine and I will introduce you then. That will serve to start the spread of the word.'

He gave her a brief rundown on them, and then moved on to the next essential item on his list.

'As my wife, you'll need a wardrobe to match your position, so use this time in Rome to go shopping.' His eyes glanced at her again in the passing streetlight now fitfully illuminating the car's spacious interior. 'You chose well for today,' he allowed.

'Thank you,' she answered evenly. 'It seemed to fit the bill. I've got something with me that I have in mind for lunch tomorrow. It's not this season—models don't get given those—but it's by an English designer, so not likely to be something your friends will have seen. Would that work?'

'I'm sure it will,' Salvatore replied.

His phone was ringing—the call was from New York and he needed to take it. At his side, his new bride turned her head, gazing out of the tinted window as they drove into the city. Salvatore left her to it, busy with his call, yet conscious that he would rather have gone on gazing at Lana's perfect profile…

Well, there would be time for that—he would make sure of it—but, alas, not right now.

With a mental shake of his head, he switched to business matters.

Lana looked about her appreciatively. Salvatore's apartment in the *centro storico*—the historic heart of central Rome—was huge: two floors at least of an elegant eighteenth-century townhouse set around a spacious interior courtyard. Inside the apartment, beyond the entrance hall, a double aspect drawing room stretched from end to end, overlooking the internal courtyard to one side and a peaceful-looking *piazza* on the other.

It was opulently but beautifully styled, Lana thought as she glanced in, with a mix of antique and more modern pieces. She had no time to take much in, though, as Salvatore was leading her towards another flight of stairs, less imposing than the external ones.

'The bedrooms are one floor above,' he said, as he headed purposefully ahead of her. Gaining the landing, her turned at the door immediately in front of him, which he then opened, flicking on the light. 'This is mine,' he informed her. 'Yours,' he went on, 'is next door. For obvious reasons that has to be so. There is a communicating door between the two.'

He headed for a door inset into the wall, opening it and gesturing for Lana to step through. She paused a moment to cast her eyes around the bedroom of the man whose wife she now was. It felt odd to do so. It was the first personal space of his she'd been into—a very masculine space, with huge pieces of antique furniture in heavy wood, dominated by a vast wood-framed bed with an intricate carved headboard.

Salvatore's bed—the bed he sleeps in...

Almost she could visualise him there...

Hurriedly, she withdrew her gaze, walking across to the open communicating door into the bedroom beyond. She stopped short, giving an exclamation of pleasure.

'Oh, how beautiful!'

She gazed around. It could not have been more different from the heavily masculine bedroom that belonged to Salvatore. Though just as large as his, this was a feminine space, the colour scheme of soft blue and silvery grey, the antique furniture light and graceful.

'It was my mother's room,' came the clipped reply to her exclamation.

She glanced at Salvatore, but his face was expressionless. Was it good that it had been his mother's room, or bad? She had no idea. And it was not her place to ask.

'What was once the powder room—in the eighteenth-century hair powder was applied in a separate room,' he was saying now, 'has been turned into an en suite bathroom.'

He strode to a door inset into the far wall, opening it slightly. Lana got a glimpse of a luxuriously appointed bathroom and abruptly felt the need to take off her shoes, and her constricting outfit, and stand under a refreshing shower after her long day.

My wedding day.

But the thought was impossible to compute. Okay, they'd said words, signed a register, but that hadn't been a wedding. Not a real one. Not one that actually *meant* anything.

Yes, well it does mean something, actually! It means I can get myself free of the crushing burden of debt that bloody Mal dumped on me! That's what it means!

Salvatore was speaking again, as cool and brisk as ever, saying that dinner would be served in forty-five minutes, and she should change into something more relaxed for the evening. He left her to it as a maid entered with her luggage, and Lana headed for the en suite bathroom to freshen up.

An air of complete bemusement took her over. She was here, in Rome, with a man she had married for a year and for four hundred thousand pounds—and it felt completely and utterly unreal.

Salvatore stood at his bedroom window, conscious of the ever-present hum of traffic in the ancient city coming from beyond the quiet *piazza* even at this midnight hour. Conscious, even more, of the woman in the bedroom next to his—separated from him only by a communicating door.

He was not sure what he was feeling. It was…complicated.

That same sense of the enormity of what he'd done that had struck him on the flight came again. Had he really done what he just had? *Married?*

He had the legal proof of it in the marriage licence now sitting on his tallboy, waiting to be filed under 'Personal' in his study. But *was* it personal?

The marriage bit was not—that was simply a means to an end in his business affairs. Separating Luchesi SpA from any involvement with Roberto Fabrizzi now that the latter had made a nuisance of himself.

But his bride?

She was 'personal'—definitely!

His mouth tightened. Except he would far rather, he knew perfectly well, she had remained 'personal' simply as the current woman he was interested in, the way her predecessors—and inevitable successors—had been or would be.

Not as my bride.

He gave a quick shake of his head, as if to dispel the word and the thoughts that went with it. Okay, so it might be complicated that the woman he wanted was also the woman he'd married for the reasons he had. But that was their only connection.

She is a woman I desire, who just happens, for now, to be the woman I have married.

That was not complicated—it was very simple. The way he liked life to be.

He turned away from the window. It had been a long day—and he'd thought about it quite enough for now. As he headed for his en suite bathroom his glance went to the thin communicating door on the opposite side of his bedroom.

Lana was on the other side.

For now, she would stay there. There were things that had to be done before that door could open.

One last thought flickered in his head.

She's in my mother's bedroom. My poor, unhappy mother—

He banished the thought from his head, firmly closing his bathroom door. Leaving the past behind.

Lana paused at the head of the staircase on the landing outside her bedroom. Dinner last night had passed easily enough, though an air of reserve had still emanated from Salvatore, as it had over lunch and their flight out to Rome. Now they were about to set off to meet his friends for lunch.

Nerves plucked at Lana fractionally as she walked down the stairs. Not because she was going to be on show—she was well used to that—but because of the role she had been cast in.

Salvatore Luchesi's bride.

Her task was simple—make his friends believe her to be just that. Well, she would do her best. No point having nerves of any kind. She would just do what she had to do—what, after all, when it came right down to it, she was being paid to do.

Salvatore was waiting for her in the entrance hall and she was all too conscious of his presence there. He looked, as he always did, a knock-out, in another hand-tailored suit, pale grey this time, and radiated the kind of effortless style that seemed to come naturally to all Italians, male or female.

Hopefully, though, she could hold her own. Certainly as she came up to him she saw approval in his eyes sweeping over her.

'You have chosen well—again,' he said, and there was slightly less reserve in his voice.

His dark eyes flicked over her once more, taking in the soft grey jersey dress that draped with deceptive ease over her tall frame, looking both simultaneously understated and eye-catchingly chic.

She was reassured by his praise, but then he frowned. She'd accessorised the dress with a heavy necklace of large haematite beads, but these, apparently, met with his displeasure.

'Wear these instead,' he instructed, fetching a large flat box from a nearby pier table and clicking it open.

Lana's eyes widened. 'Oh, how beautiful!' she exclaimed. 'And absolutely perfect for this outfit!'

It was a necklace of huge coin-flat baroque pearls and a matching bracelet. The price tag would have had a large number of zeroes on it, she knew, having modelled—under strict security conditions—enough expensive jewellery in her time. And modelling this fantastic necklace and bracelet was all she was doing now, she reminded herself, as she removed her own beads. Part of the role she was playing.

'Turn around...'

A moment later she felt the pearls move around her in a long loop, and then cool fingers were at the nape of her neck, fastening the necklace. It was only a moment—the merest snap of a clasp and a safety chain—

yet something had been done to her nerve-endings in the sensitive exposure of her skin to Salvatore's touch. It echoed even after he stepped away, subjecting her to a critical appraisal, and then, with a nod of apparent approval, he handed her the matching bracelet to fasten around her wrist herself.

'Okay, let's go,' he announced.

Lana found herself glancing at him. There had been an audible tension in the brief command. Did he think she wouldn't pass muster with his friends? Eat peas off her knife? Make embarrassing remarks? Surely not.

Even so, she felt a flicker of unease go through her. She was about to be put in front of people he'd told her were long-standing friends, and they were meant to think that a whirlwind romance had so enthralled him that he'd married her on the spot. Wasn't that deceiving? She gave a mental shrug. Well, it was not her responsibility. She would just act her part, play her role to the best of her ability—what else could she do?

She put aside her faint unease, and headed off with him.

Lunch, so he'd already told her, was to be at the famed Viscari Roma, and when they arrived they were shown into a *salon privé* off the main dining room. Inside, four pairs of eyes snapped to her.

Keeping her expression carefully schooled, Lana let Salvatore guide her forward. Swiftly, she took in what was facing her.

The two men were not as tall as Salvatore, but they were both ludicrously good-looking in dark Italian style. The two women were quite unalike. One was an extremely pretty blonde, with a slight figure, a lot of make-up and short hair, wearing a sunshine-yellow outfit which

Lana immediately recognised as the work of one of Italy's glitziest designers. The other female was taller, a long-haired brunette with a full figure, wearing a closely fitting dress that showed it to best advantage.

Salvatore greeted them all in laconic Italian. The note of tension in his voice was gone now. She heard her name mentioned—but only her first name. The man who was with the blonde returned the greeting first. Lana couldn't follow what he said, but she could certainly read the look in his eyes as his glance went towards her with well-practised masculine appreciation.

He came towards them, hand outstretched. Automatically Lana offered hers, and was not that surprised when it was lifted to his lips and kissed with a gesture that was part clearly exaggerated and part sending a definite message.

But not to her. He dropped her hand and said something to Salvatore in a low, throwaway voice that held a wealth of masculine appreciation.

'Thank you, Luc,' came Salvatore's dryly sardonic reply—in English. 'Your vote of approval means everything to me.'

Luc Dinardi—their host, as Lana knew from Salvatore's briefing—gave a low laugh, not in the least put out.

Now the other man was coming forward, also with a hand outstretched. This time, though, Lana's hand was not subjected to any practised Latin Lothario treatment, but simply a brief but firm handshake.

'Vito di Vincenzo,' he introduced himself, speaking English. 'And my wife, Laura.'

The full-figured woman stepped forward, her smile friendly. 'Hello,' she said. 'How lovely to meet you.'

Her English was perfect, and Lana quickly realised she was a compatriot.

Then the blonde was surging forward, her brown eyes alight. 'You look absolutely *fantastic*!' she exclaimed enthusiastically, her English highly accented. 'You absolutely *must* tell me who the designer is! Of course, only someone with your height could get away with it!'

Her bright eyes danced.

'We had no idea Salva was bringing his latest! And there's no need for him to tell us anything about you—you're a model! You just scream it!'

She gave an insouciant laugh and ran on unstoppably.

'Come and get a drink and tell me all about how you and Salva come to be together! I absolutely *adore* gossip and I want to be the first with this! How long has this been going on...when did you meet, and how...and what are you going to be doing in Rome now you're here?'

'Don't let Stephanie drown you with her chatter,' said Luc, the blonde's partner, humour in his voice. 'As you'll have realised, she never lets anyone reply anyway!'

The blonde exclaimed something in indignant Italian, as Luc enquired what Lana would like to drink, indicating the wide choice. Lana was about to give her usual answer of sparkling mineral water, when she abruptly changed her mind, remembering afresh that her starvation diet days were over.

'Sweet vermouth spritzer, please,' she said.

Luc busied himself mixing it for her, and Lana found Laura beside her. The blonde had zoomed up to Salvatore, to interrogate him.

'Don't mind Steph,' Laura said in a low voice, with a smile in her voice. 'She's completely harmless, but...' there was a slight warning in her grey-blue eyes '...she means what she says about loving gossip! And she adores passing it on.'

'I'll bear that in mind,' Lana said. 'Not that there is anything about me to cause gossip. Yes, I am a model— it's a bit of a giveaway when you're my height with my thinness.'

Even as she spoke Lana felt conscious that she was being disingenuous. In fact, there was a whole heap about her presence in Rome with Salvatore that would make explosive gossip. But there could not be a breath of sus- picion about it…

'Not to mention the show-stopping looks!' Laura was saying now, smiling as Luc handed Lana her cocktail. She smiled back at Laura, liking her, and feeling again uncomfortably conscious of the deception being prac- tised upon her…upon all of Salvatore's friends. She was falsely here as his wife. But there was nothing she could do about it except go along with it as best she could.

She took an appreciative sip from her drink as Sal- vatore came up to her. He was smiling at her, but she could see a watchful look at the back of his eyes. He ad- dressed Laura, asking after her little boy. Lana saw the other woman's expression soften.

'That's a fatal question to ask me, Salva,' she said warmly. 'I can go on for hours about just how perfect he is!'

He laughed, and Lana took the opportunity to ask how old her son was.

'Three, going on four, and he is just *adorable*!' Laura enthused. 'I only hope that when—' She broke off, her glance going to her husband. 'Vito, shall we…?'

Her husband came up to her, put his arm around her waist. 'Let's,' he said. He held up his glass. 'My friends, now that Salva has joined us this is the perfect moment to tell you all that Laura and I are hoping to present our perfect son with a perfect brother or sister!'

He'd spoken in Italian, but Lana knew enough to understand what he'd said. Everyone promptly burst into hearty congratulations. Stephanie was particularly voluble in hers, rushing up to Laura to kiss her cheek and exclaim excitedly. Lana felt her elbow taken, and she was guided slightly aside by Salvatore.

'You followed that?' he asked in a low voice, and she gave a quick nod. In the same low voice he went on. 'I won't steal Vito and Laura's thunder right now, but when we sit down I'll make our announcement, so be prepared. No one seems to have noticed the ring on your finger,' he said dryly, 'or mine.' He paused, his expression changing, 'But that is not surprising... Stephanie's absolutely right. You do look totally fantastic.'

'Well, that was the intention,' Lana answered evenly, but the admiring way Salvatore had spoken made her nerves flutter. Then she realised she had better get used to praise and admiration from him—after all, she was his brand-new bride, and it would be expected of him. In public, anyway.

She turned back to Laura. 'What wonderful news for you,' she said warmly to the other Englishwoman.

Laura's smile was warm in return. 'Yes, it is. We're thrilled!'

'How many weeks are you?' Lana asked.

'Just gone twelve, so just into my second trimester now. Because I'm Junoesque—as my dear grandmother used to tell me!—I've got away with it so far.' She glanced at Lana's racehorse figure. 'I hate to tell you this…' she shook her head humorously '…but you won't ever get away with hiding even the tiniest baby bump!'

'Not a chance,' Lana agreed with rueful good humour.

She didn't mind the observation—becoming a mother was so far off in her future that it was unimaginable. She felt herself frown. Not even with Mal had she ever once contemplated having a baby…

Maybe that should have told me something about him and what he meant to me. Or, more to the point, what he didn't mean to me…

It was something she knew she had to be grateful for. As she had blurted out to Salvatore that night he'd given her a lift home, all Malcolm had broken was her bank balance—not her heart.

And I don't want my heart broken—not ever.

She must take care that it did not happen. That she did not fall for a man who did not return her feelings. Who did not want to make his life with her.

Unconsciously, her glance went to Salvatore—the man she had married yesterday morning. Married for reasons that had nothing to do with the true purpose of marriage, which was to unite two people, two lives, in love for the rest of their lives.

Yet again, that feeling of unease went through her, She had married not just under false pretences, but for a reason that marriage should not ever be for. For money.

She shook the thought from her, glad of Salvatore's interjection now.

'Lana, we're taking our seats,' he told her, indicating the table in the centre of the room.

She took her place beside him, opposite Vito and Laura, with Luc and Stephanie, as host and hostess, at either end. A pair of waiters sashayed in, one with

wine and the other with their *primos*. Lana felt her
petite quicken at the herby aroma coming from the ▌
tered scallops in front of her. They proved every bi▋
delicious as they looked, and she ate with unalloy
pleasure, the delicious dish complimented with a fr▋
white wine.

'Are you one of those unbearable women who ◖
eat anything she likes and it never shows?' Stepha▋
asked with cheerful envy. 'I only have to *look* at a p▋
of pasta and I get a kilo heavier!'

Lana shook her head. 'Alas, no. I do have to wa▋
every calorie—or rather I did while I was modelli▋
That's why I'm so glad I don't have to any longer, r▋
that—'

She stopped abruptly. Horrified. Then, suddenly,
felt her hand being pressed, such that she released
fork. Salvatore, at her side, was raising his other ha▋

'I, too, have something to announce,' he said.

Lana felt his long fingers slide into hers on the d▋
ask tablecloth. It was a strange feeling, but she had
time to pay attention to the sensation as he went
speaking—in English for her benefit, she knew.

'For you who know me so well, this will come
a surprise—even a shock…' His voice was dry. '▋
when I introduced Lana I failed to do so complete▋
He paused—for dramatic effect, Lana was pretty s▋
'I now make good that omission. May I therefore ask ▋
to raise your glasses—to Signora Luchesi?'

For a moment longer than the one that had gree▋
her entrance there was complete silence. Predictabl▋
was Stephanie who broke first. A squeal—just abo▋
shriek, Lana thought—of over-the-top excitement b▋

from her. Then there was a cacophony of voluble Italian all around the table.

Lana felt Salvatore's hands mesh more tightly with his.

'We neither of us wanted a fuss made,' he was saying, still in English. 'It was a register office in London yesterday. I wanted you four to know first. Stephanie?' Salvatore's tone of voice was openly, if good-humouredly, pointed. 'I rely on you to tell all of Rome!' He glanced across at Laura and Vito, reverting to Italian. 'I never intended to steal your thunder, you two, so I hope you will forgive me.'

Vito threw up his hands. 'Of course! My God, I can't believe it Salva! You've always been totally allergic to marriage! Understandably, I know. But—'

Then he was being ruthlessly interrupted by Stephanie, who was beside herself with excitement. 'Salva, this is incredible! Just incredible! Tell us *everything*!'

Her eyes were alight, and it seemed to Lana she meant what she'd said. Fortunately, from the far end of the table, Luc spoke.

'Steph, my treasure, believe me. Salva and Lana are *not* going to regale you with the tale of their romance, let alone the details that you would sell your soul for!'

He spoke humorously, but with resignation in his voice. Then he picked up his glass, looking at Lana and then Salvatore.

'Every happiness in the world to you both!' he said.

This was echoed all around the table, most volubly by Stephanie, still visibly bubbling. Lana felt as if she was the opposite, sitting motionless next to Salvatore, who was taking it all in his stride.

Well, of course he is. That's what this is all about. Telling Rome—telling Giavanna and her father—that

Salvatore Luchesi is now a married man, thank you, and off the menu.

And even as she reminded herself of the blunt truth behind the announcement she felt a sliver of…if not guilt, precisely, then definitely that sense of discomfort again. These people were genuine friends of Salvatore—their ease with each other, their familiarity, the warmth of their welcome to her all showed her that. Yet he was deceiving them. Making them believe that he had made a genuine marriage yesterday, however much out of the blue.

But it's just fake. Not real. Not genuine. A show. A deceit—

She tried to shake the sense of discomfort from her to tell herself that the deceit was all on his part, not hers. That she was nothing to do with it…that she was just doing what she was as if it were a business arrangement, nothing personal at all.

But the unease remained. Strengthened, if anything, during the course of the meal. For herself, Lana kept conversation to the bare minimum, especially with Stephanie, simply saying that she and Salvatore had met in London at an after-party, that it had been a whirlwind romance, and that that, really, was that. There really was nothing more to say.

Stephanie rolled her eyes in frustration. 'Well, at least tell us where you are going on honeymoon! The Caribbean, the Maldives, the South Seas…?'

'Tuscany,' Salvatore answered decisively, and Stephanie made a disgusted face at such a tame destination.

'Your *palazzo* in Tuscany sounds more than gorgeous enough for a honeymoon.' Lana smiled at her husband. She made her voice warm, though it felt odd to do so. Oddly intimate. Or perhaps it was the word 'honeymoon' that did that...

Well, obviously it's not actually going to be a honeymoon! It's just a place to stash me after showing me off here in Rome to get the message home that he is off the menu for Giavanna!

'Salva's place is definitely gorgeous,' Laura was saying. 'Do you know Tuscany at all?'

Lana shook her head. The conversation became general again, as they talked about Tuscany and all its cornucopia of cultural treasures, and Lana was glad. Glad, too, when lunch finally ended, well into the afternoon, and the party dispersed, with a lot of hugging and kissing and invitations all round for her and Salvatore when they came back from Tuscany.

As Lana got into the car waiting at the kerb, the same disquieting sense of discomfort about the deceit she was being a party to assailed her. Everyone had been so nice, so friendly, believing her to be their friend's real wife. It did not sit well with her.

Roundly, she admonished herself.

Well, you'd better damn well get used to it! It's going to last an entire year! That's how long you've got to fake this marriage for! And if you make any slip-ups you can kiss goodbye to your four-hundred-thousand-pound payoff at the end!

That was, after all, why she had married Salvatore.

Not for any other reason.

Any other reason was impossible...

CHAPTER FOUR

SALVATORE SHUT HIMSELF into his study in his apartment, settling down at the antique desk that had once been his father's. Out of long habit his mind skittered away from the memories it held, focussing instead on the main problem currently facing him.

Tonight he was taking Lana to a charity fundraiser being held at one of Rome's grandest High Renaissance villas, situated on one of the city's famous seven hills. It was going to be a full-on affair where everyone who mattered would turn out to see and be seen—including Roberto and his daughter.

He'd had an evening gown delivered to Lana that afternoon, from one of Rome's most expensive couture boutiques, together with a diamond parure extracted from the bank vault. She would look every inch Signora Luchesi.

His expression flickered a moment. The last time those diamonds had been worn by a Signora Luchesi—worn at all, in fact—it had been his mother wearing them…

He felt his thoughts skitter away again, as they had from the memory of his father sitting in this very room, at this very desk.

They were gone, both of them, his mother and his father. For a moment—just a moment—he found himself wondering what his parents would have thought of what he had done...marrying a stranger for the reasons he had. His mouth twisted. His father would have approved his choice of blonde bombshell. His mother—

He stopped his thoughts. He knew what his mother would have thought, and he didn't want to hear her voice in his head.

But he heard it all the same.

'Love, Salvatore my darling boy—only marry for love. Love shared and reciprocated! Promise me that—oh, promise me that!'

With a sudden bleakness in his face he reached for his pen, flicking open the file in front of him, ready to make his annotations to the documents printed out within.

Love was the last reason he'd married for. The last reason he ever would.

His mother should have known that.

Lana blinked at the brilliance of the scene in front of her. White marble nymphs framed the periphery of the room, completely unable to compete with their living female counterparts thronging the centre. Fortunately a lot less flesh was being revealed by the female guests than the marble nymphs were displaying, and as for the male guests—they were the usual army of strictly black and white penguins.

Not that the man at her side could ever be castigated in such a way. She'd only seen Salvatore in a tuxedo once before, the very first evening she'd met him, and when she'd seen him again as she'd walked down the stairs to the entrance hall of his apartment the sight had all but taken her breath away.

He really was quite magnificent in evening dress that was superbly cut and tailored to make the absolute most of his height and lean masculinity, and she found herself wondering, yet again, just what it was about dinner jackets, dress shirts, bow ties and winged collars that made all men look so...so fantastic...

But, as she glanced around the throng in front of her now, she knew without a doubt that the man at her side was the most fantastic-looking of all the males here.

Not that it mattered, of course, she reminded herself. He was not here to look fantastic for her—*she* was here to look fantastic for *him*.

And she did, she knew. Around her throat she could feel the heavy diamonds enhancing the ivory silk gown she was wearing, one shoulder bare, the bodice very plain, cut straight across her cleavage, then falling in soft folds to her ankles. Already she could see eyes turning to her as Salvatore guided her forward, hand under her elbow, greeting people to left and right as they made their way towards their hosts.

Then Salvatore was halting in front of a very well upholstered woman in late middle age, with a portly man beside her.

'Duchessa...' Salvatore was taking the proffered hand, kissing it with graceful formality, then shaking the outstretched hand of the portly man, a brief man-to-man gesture, before turning to Lana. 'Duchessa.' He spoke again, in English. 'May I have the honour of presenting to you my bride?'

Lana could see astonishment fill the matron's eyes, but she was too well-bred to do anything other than offer

Lana her beringed hand and murmur something that was appropriate on such an occasion—some form of felicitation in accented English.

'Thank you,' Lana said, letting slip the Duchess's hand before repeating the gesture with the Duke.

Salvatore was telling her that he had the honour of presenting to her the historic owners of the grand villa, their hosts for the evening, complete with their high-ranking title, and she was smiling politely. The Duchess said something directly to Salvatore in Italian, which Lana could not follow, and Salvatore replied with a polite smile.

All Lana caught was 'London' and 'private wedding'. She kept her polite smile on her face and then they were moving on, into the throng. From then on, as Salvatore duly introduced her to all he spoke to, she got the distinct feeling that a ripple was passing through the guests. Heads were turning towards her, and she could hear Salvatore's name being uttered. Even though she did not follow Italian, she could tell it was with surprise and astonishment.

For herself, she did not turn her head at all, merely sailed forward with Salvatore, smiling politely, apparently unaware of the attention she was garnering.

Then, abruptly, their progress was halted. A middle-aged man and a much younger female at his side, newly arrived, were in front of them. Lana did not need an arrow over their heads to tell her who they were. She felt Salvatore's hand on her elbow tighten momentarily, but that was the only sign he gave.

He held out his hand. 'Roberto,' he said expansively, shaking the other man's automatically lifted hand. Then, dropping both the man's hand and Lana's elbow, he stepped forward towards the young woman at Roberto Fabrizzi's side.

Very young, Lana saw instantly, despite the full face of make-up and the over-sophisticated fuchsia-pink gown she was wearing by a Milanese designer notable for his opulence and extravagance. Although it suited the girl's darkly luscious looks, it was far too overpowering for her, making her look older than a girl who Lana was pretty sure was barely out of her teenage years, if that. Her full glass of champagne did not add any aura of sophistication either.

'Giavanna,' she heard Salvatore say, his voice fondly warm and with an avuncular tone to it that surely the teenager would detect. He went on in the same tone, his hands resting lightly on the girl's shoulders as if inspecting her. 'How spectacular you look!'

Even Lana could understand that in Italian, and she could hear the indulgent amusement in Salvatore's praise, almost as if she could hear him add *You look almost quite grown-up!*—which he tactfully did not.

But Giavanna's face was not displaying any pleasure at Salvatore's praise. Instead, she shrugged her shoulders free and glared at him. The expression, Lana thought, made her look a mere sixteen…or younger.

'You were going to bring *me* here, Salva!' she accused him. 'I *told* you Papa and I were coming—we were to arrive together! It was all arranged!'

'Only by you, Gia,' Salvatore said. The fond note was still in his voice, but with a slight tinge of reproof. He glanced at Roberto. 'I did let you know, Roberto, that I would be coming here almost directly from London. Speaking of which—'

Lana heard him say something briefly about what she

presumed were his business affairs in England, catching one or two references to banks and so forth. It was as if he were giving the other man a swift report on business, she realised, to emphasise what held the two together. Business. Not Roberto's voluptuous but demanding teenage daughter.

As Salvatore addressed Roberto, Gia turned her attention to Lana. If the glare she'd subjected Salvatore to had been open, the one she arrowed at Lana was positively slaying. Something sharp came out of the girl's mouth which Lana did not understand. She merely smiled.

'I'm so sorry, I don't speak Italian,' she said in English.

The girl swapped to the same language. 'I just said that you shouldn't get ideas about Salvatore! He has a new blonde on his arm every month!'

'Oh?' said Lana temporisingly. Then, quite deliberately, with a smile that she kept polite, if not quite pitying, she said, 'I don't think that will be the case now.'

She lifted her left hand to rest on the diamonds at her throat, both indicating her wearing of them—very obviously a family heirloom—and letting the matching bracelet on her wrist and the diamond betrothal ring catch the light…the light that also caught the wedding band on her finger.

She saw Giavanna's expression change. It was now one of mingled horror, disbelief—and fury.

'It isn't *true*!' she spat, first in Italian, then in English. 'I heard someone say it, but I knew it wasn't true! It isn't true—it *isn't*!' She reverted to her native language, giving vent to her emotions.

Lana could hear a rising note not just of fury but of outrage, even hysteria. She saw heads turn towards them.

Knew, with female instinct, that Giavanna Fabrizzi was not the kind to shy away from creating a scene when she felt like it. Already her father was saying something in Italian to her, his tone placatory and embarrassed.

Then Salvatore was speaking, cutting through Giavanna's dangerously rising tirade. 'Gia, I have done my best to convince you that I would make you the worst of husbands!'

He was speaking in English—presumably, Lana thought, so she would know what he was saying to the petulant girl. He was keeping his tone light, Lana could hear, but there was an implacable note beneath all the same.

'I am very fond of you—you are like my favourite niece, if I had one. And one day you will make a man the proudest in the world to call you his bride! But that day is not yet. Enjoy to the full these carefree days of being single, of slaying hearts wherever you go...'

Lana could hear the humour deliberately infused into the equally deliberate flattery.

'Enjoy your life before you settle down to the dullness of married life, keeping house, having babies. You are young, spectacularly beautiful, and you have the world at your feet! So—*enjoy*!'

He swapped to Italian, saying something to Roberto in a low voice. He nodded tightly. The older man's face was closed, and hard, and Lana did not like the expression in it. But it wasn't her business. Her business was to play the role allotted to her. So she went on standing there in a statuesque fashion, with a sympathetic look on her face, but nothing more than that.

Eventually Salvatore took her elbow again, and she knew he wanted them to move on. But suddenly, and quite viciously, Giavanna spat a word at Lana in Italian. It was coarse, and ugly, though Lana had no idea what the girl had just called her. A second later she had no more time to ponder. She felt a sudden cold splash on her face and neck and realised, in a moment of disbelief, that Giavanna had thrown the contents of her champagne flute all over her.

A sharp expletive broke from Salvatore. Even Roberto looked shocked. Lana could only blink away the beads of champagne on her mascaraed eyelashes.

A moment later Salvatore was handing her a silk handkerchief from his jacket pocket, and she was dabbing at her wet cheeks as best she could. She heard Giavanna say something in an angry, sulky voice, and gathered she was refusing to express even the slightest regret for what she'd just said and done. Lana was vividly aware that now heads were definitely turning in her direction, with shocked expressions on their faces.

Salvatore was saying something to her, but she waved her free hand. 'It's nothing,' she said dismissively. 'Champagne never stains, and the dress has caught very little of it.' She dabbed at the top of her bodice, then paid more attention to the necklace. 'I think these diamonds can withstand a little bath!' she said lightly. She turned to Salvatore. 'I'll just slip to the powder room to retouch,' she told him. 'Any idea where it is?'

He collared a server and made the enquiry, then pointed in the requisite direction.

'Thank you,' said Lana, using the same light tone.

She would minimise the incident—not just out of instinct, but out of an awareness that playing it down was the best thing to do. Already heads were turning away, and she was glad of it.

Squeezing the now damp silk handkerchief in one hand, she made her way to the ladies' room, gaining its privacy with relief. Bringing relief, too, a glance at her reflection showed that very little damage had been done. Her cheeks were splashed, eyelashes dewed, and a frond or two from her elegant upswept hair style were damp, but that was all.

Five minutes later she re-emerged, cheeks and diamonds dry, mascara and lipstick retouched, looking immaculate again. Salvatore was waiting for her outside in the quiet corridor leading to the powder room.

'I'm sorry about that,' he said stiffly. 'I didn't think she'd react quite that badly.'

'A teenager thwarted in love is unpredictable,' Lana said dryly. She handed him the rinsed out, wrung out silk handkerchief. 'I dried this as best I could with the hand drier, but it's a little damp still, I'm afraid, and very crumpled.'

He took it, stuffing it into his trouser pocket. 'Let's get out of here,' he said abruptly. 'The Duchessa will understand—'

Lana raised her eyebrows. 'So soon? Won't it look as if we've cut and run? Better surely to go back and show everyone how little it all meant?'

She spoke instinctively, forgetting for a moment that she was really no more than an employee of Salvatore Luchesi, and that she was there to do as she was told, not have ideas of her own, let alone express something contrary to him.

'Can you face it?' he asked, a frown on his face.

She gave an exaggerated roll of her eyes. 'If you had ever been backstage at a fashion show, you would know that Giavanna Fabrizzi's little outburst back there was a mere pinprick! I have seen full-blown hissy fits that would have given Mount Etna a run for its money when it comes to volcanic eruptions!'

She felt herself take Salvatore's arm, draping her hand over its smooth sleeve.

'Come on,' she said lightly. 'Show some backbone! I know men *hate* scenes—even Italian men, I dare say, though they probably see a lot more of them than Englishmen are subjected to in high society—but you can do this!'

Unconsciously—instinctively, even—she made her tone humorous. There was a darkness in Salvatore's eyes that might have been forbidding, but she would not let it be. And now the darkness changed to a glint.

'Stiff upper lip?' he contributed sardonically, but she could hear humour, reluctant though it was, in his voice.

'I'm sure the Duchessa will insist!' she answered, still lightly.

They walked back into the throng. It felt slightly odd not to have Salvatore's insistently guiding hand cupping her elbow, and instead feel the muscle of his forearm beneath her hand. And as they walked the Duchessa herself was gliding towards them, very much a ship in full sail, guests parting on either side to allow her approach.

'My dear, are you all right?' she asked concernedly.

'Perfectly, I promise you,' Lana assured her.

'*Bene, bene...*' intoned the Duchessa. She bestowed an approving smile upon Lana. 'Well done!' The look she threw at Salvatore was less approving. 'Your bride should not have been subject to that kind of thing!' she said tartly.

Lana intervened. 'Young love is so very painful, Duchessa,' she said. 'Salvatore's marriage must have come as a deep shock to the poor girl.' Her voice became sympathetic. 'She has such a huge teenage crush on Salva!'

'You are too kind to her,' came the Duchessa's still tart reply. 'She's been over-indulged and spoilt!'

'I'm sure she'll improve as she grows up,' Lana said

temporisingly. She wanted the subject changed. 'This is the most spectacular villa, Duchessa—it is a privilege to be here. The ceiling alone...'

She gazed upwards. As if on cue the Duchessa gave the name of the artist, and told her what the opulent scenes depicted by way of pagan gods and goddesses disporting themselves. Then she smiled at Lana.

'Come and lunch with me here one day, my dear, and I will be able to give you far more time than I can now.' The Duchess smiled benignly upon Lana, included Salvatore within it, and then she was sailing off again to attend to her other guests.

Lana felt Salvatore's hand fold over hers on his sleeve. 'You've found favour,' he said in a low voice. She could hear approval in it. Then something changed in his expression. 'I've announced you to the world—and to Giavanna and Roberto—as my bride. But perhaps...' Now his voice was changing as well. 'Perhaps I should give them a tangible demonstration of that fact.'

Before she realised what was happening—before she could even register his intention—Lana felt his hand catch her chin. He took a step towards her, closed the distance between them. His long fingers tilted up her face towards him, and her eyes, uplifted also, met his full-on.

Met them—and reeled.

They were dark, long-lashed, and drowningly deep...

And she was drowning in them...she absolutely was... Helpless to break his gaze, helpless to step away, helpless to do anything at all except know, with every female instinct in her, what was coming next.

And come it did.

As if in slow motion, Salvatore's sculpted mouth lowered to hers. His long fingers grazed the line of her jaw as his mouth touched hers. Lana's eyes fluttered shut, and sensation took over from vision.

Like velvet, like silk, like satin...

The sheer, blissful sensuousness of his mouth moving slowly, lingeringly on hers weakened every bone in her body. Did a sigh escape her? She did not know...could not tell. Could tell only that she did not want his kiss to stop. Did not want it ever to stop—

And yet it did. He was drawing away from her, his fingers releasing her, his hand dropping away. He was still close to her, though, so very close... The scent of his expensive aftershave was catching at her, making her feel faint.

Or something was...

Lana's eyes fluttered open to meet, once more, that drowning gaze, that gold glinting in the depths of his dark, dark eyes, pouring into hers. The rest of the world—the people in the room, the noise and the conversation—all had vanished. All gone. All that existed was his golden glinting eyes pouring into hers...

Her senses were reeling, the blood soaring in her veins. Her heart like a caged bird, beating wildly.

For one long, timeless moment she just went on gazing up at him. Helpless to do anything else at all.

And then—

A smile indented his mouth.

A smile of satisfaction.

'Well,' Salvatore said, and there was satisfaction in his voice, in his smile, in the gold glint of his eyes, 'I think we have just demonstrated very adequately that you are, indeed, my chosen bride.'

He tucked her hand into his arm, a proprietorial and masculine gesture, still smiling down at her. The rest of the

world reappeared. The women in their couture gowns…
the men in their dashing black and white tuxedos. The an-
imated chatter echoed off the high painted ceiling and the
marble floor. All of it snapped back into existence, despite
the reeling of her senses, the wild beating of her heart…

'Time to circulate,' he said.

He reached to lift a glass of champagne from a passing server, handing it to her. She took it nervelessly and
he helped himself to one for himself as well. Her blood
was still whirling in her veins, her heart still a wildly
beating caged bird. Her lips still echoed with his kiss…

Urgently, she tried to banish those lingering echoes.
Suppress the rush in her veins. Rationalise what had just
happened. Find an explanation for it.

The only possible explanation.

*It was for show! It was just for show! He said it was—
and that's all it was! For show—just for show!*

She heard the words like a litany, playing urgently
in her head, repeating themselves as, with a slight pressure on her hand, he led them both forward, resuming
his greeting of people he knew.

Were they smiling at them both, smiling at the newlyweds, smiling at having seen them kiss like that? She
didn't know, couldn't tell—couldn't do anything at all
except let herself be taken where Salvatore wanted to
go, standing at his side while in her head those urgent
words kept sounding.

Just for show! Nothing else at all!

That was what she had to keep telling herself all the time
they stayed in Rome. Keep telling herself that she was
glad—relieved!—that the man she had married for reasons that had absolutely nothing to do with the way she

had reacted to being in his arms would make no further 'tangible demonstrations' that required his kissing her.

After all, given the truth about their marriage, what else could she possibly be but relieved? It was the only appropriate reaction. Now all she needed to do was forget it had ever happened...

Something that, to her disquiet, she was finding disturbingly difficult...

Well, I just have to try harder then, don't I? she remonstrated with herself roundly as she stood, gazing sightlessly out of the window of her bedroom, trying not to remember the blissful sensation of his mouth moving on hers...

Trying, above all, not to let her eyes go to the communicating door. All that separated her from the man she had married.

All? The single word sounded silently in her head. She shook her head. No, much more separated them.

Much more.

With an impatient, resolute shake of her head she turned away from the window, padding to the bed in her jade satin pyjamas and tucking herself into its wide depths. She must get to sleep. Tomorrow they were leaving Rome, after a week of non-stop socialising, heading for Tuscany. It was a long drive, Salvatore had warned her, necessitating an early start.

The world would think them heading off on their honeymoon. But Lana knew better. Honeymoons were for real brides.

And she was not one of those.

CHAPTER FIVE

SALVATORE EASED BACK in the driving seat, increased the throttle, and felt the familiar and always satisfying power of the superb performance of the car—an exclusive model from an exclusive Italian marque. Also satisfying was looking back on the week in Rome that had just passed.

Despite the second thoughts about what he was doing that had assailed him on their arrival, the reality had proved his tension unnecessary. It had gone well—triumphantly so. Achieving just what he'd intended. Announcing to the world—to Giavanna and her father—that Salvatore Luchesi was no longer a single man.

And achieving more than that, too.

His expression changed and his glance went fleetingly to the woman sitting in the passenger seat, absorbed, so it seemed, by looking out at the passing scenery and countryside as they drove towards Tuscany.

Lana had been surprisingly forbearing about Giavanna's outrageous behaviour at the Duchessa's fundraiser. And, he acknowledged, she had been wise to do so. Rome loved nothing more than scandal to feast on, and the tale of how Giavanna Fabrizzi had hurled a glass of champagne over his bride would have lost nothing in the retelling. Everyone liked a tasty morsel of gossip. Had Lana reacted with outrage and hysteria it would have made the situation ten times worse! But her cool dismissal, playing down the incident and writing it off with a show of sympathy for 'teenage passion' had, he admitted freely, been masterly.

He threw another glance at her. He could only see her profile, as she was still gazing interestedly out over the passing countryside. But her averted profile was as beautiful and elegant as her full profile or her full face. She was, it seemed, incapable of looking anything other than breathtakingly beautiful, with her finely carved features, striking looks and those amazing green eyes of hers...

Memory pierced him. Those emerald eyes gazing up at him, seemingly helpless to break away. His hand tilting her face to his. His mouth descending on those perfect lips of hers, tasting their sweetness. Like softest silk beneath his own.

Oh, it had been for show, all right, that kiss—but also more than that. Much more.

Anticipation rose in him. Rome had been full-on, every day spent socialising, with no time for each other at all. But now—ah, now it would be different. In the privacy of his *palazzo* he would have this most beautiful woman all to himself, away from gazing eyes.

Away from all eyes but his.

He allowed himself the luxury of one last glance at her profile, noting yet again its absolute perfection. Then he dragged his gaze back to the autostrada. It wasn't wise to feast his eyes on her—not while he was driving.

Not yet.

But soon—enticingly soon.

The prospect was very pleasing.

His good mood increased and he accelerated towards their destination. His breathtakingly beautiful bride beside him.

Lana's eyes widened—it was impossible that they should not. They'd just driven through a pair of impressive gilded iron gates set in a curtain wall, and crunched down a long, curving drive set between tall, pointed cedars, slowing down as Salvatore's Tuscan *palazzo* came into view.

Her breath caught. It was magnificent! It was as if she'd stepped into a historical drama and at any moment people in full eighteenth-century rig would issue forth from the massive carved oak doors set in the centre of the golden stone frontage, with its huge sash windows and a balustrade around the roof.

'Oh, my word!' she breathed, her gaze riveted.

The massive front doors opened as Salvatore drew up, and an elderly, august-looking personage stepped through, followed by a middle-aged woman dressed in black.

'Giuseppe is steward here—he has been with the family many years. The housekeeper is Signora Guardi, and other staff will become familiar to you in due course,' Salvatore was murmuring. 'Remember,' he said, glancing back at her warningly, 'they will treat you as the new mistress, but as they know how to run everything here to perfection, if they should consult you on any matter leave it to their discretion.'

Lana did not need reminding, and as she got out of the low-slung car she kept her expression guarded. Salvatore was welcomed with a benign greeting from Giuseppe and a respectful nod of the head from Signora

Guardi. Then Salvatore was introducing her to them. She smiled, but stayed mindful both of her role and Salvatore's warning. She might appear to be the chatelaine of this stately pile, but in reality she was no such thing.

Then he was taking her elbow, guiding her inside. The interior of the *palazzo* was as impressive as the exterior, with a wide, pilastered, marble-floored hall, off which a series of double-doored rooms opened on either side. At the far end was a double flight of stairs arcing around to both sides, leading to the upper floor.

Her bedroom, so it seemed, had been created to look out over the rear gardens, set with three windows and furnished with beautifully painted and stencilled white wood pieces, including a huge bed covered in an exquisitely embroidered white silk quilt. The walls were a very pale eau-de-nil, with the same delicate floral stencilling around the ceiling's edge. Two crystal chandeliers hung from the ceiling, the lustres echoed in table and bedside lamps.

Lana gazed around with open pleasure as a manservant brought in her luggage—which had been plentifully added to in Rome after several sorties to the designer boutiques of the Via dei Condotti at Salvatore's behest. A maid was hovering, waiting to unpack. Lana let her do so, while she freshened up in the surprisingly modern en suite bathroom. When she emerged it was to hear the maid informing her politely that she was awaited downstairs.

Obediently, Lana headed down, to be ushered into a room opening off the long statue-lined central hall. It was a dining room, high-ceilinged and imposing, with oil paintings on the walls, but the long, polished mahogany table was not set for lunch. She was shown through

French windows to a wide terrace beyond. There, under the shade of a huge sail-like parasol, a glass and iron table had been placed, laid for lunch, and Salvatore was standing beside it.

For once, however, Lana did not have eyes for him—only for the vista in front of her. They were, it seemed, to one side of the *palazzo*, and the gardens beyond the wide terrace were sunken, reached by a set of stone steps and dominated by a large ornamental stone pond, in the centre of which was a sculpted fountain trickling water. Potted bay trees and olive trees were around the perimeter, the whole space girded by a sun-baked wall. Several carved benches were dotted about, each flanked by smaller bays and olives. It was both ornate and minimalist in its impact.

'The fountain is only turned on occasionally, to conserve water,' Lana heard Salvatore say.

'It's absolutely beautiful,' she said, taking the chair he was pulling back for her and seating himself at the head. 'As is the whole place!'

'It was mostly my mother's creation—both the gardens and the interior,' Salvatore told her. 'She spent a great deal of time here. My father was usually elsewhere.'

Lana glanced at him. There had been a tightness in his voice she had not missed. It dawned on her that it was there whenever he happened to mention his parents, whether to her or anyone else. She wondered why. It was sad that it should be so.

She found herself wondering more about him, and the family he came from. He was one of Italy's richest men, moving in elite circles, with a historic *palazzo* to call home, and yet—

Her own childhood and youth had been so happy,

with loving, warm parents—not rich, but owning their own house, sufficiently comfortably off, and so proud of their beautiful daughter becoming a successful model in a cutthroat world. Their tragic, untimely death had devastated her.

Making me vulnerable to Malcom—blinding me to his true nature. To the reason for his interest in me.

Her eyes went to Salvatore again as she shook a fine linen napkin out across her lap. She felt a flutter in her veins. He was nothing like Malcolm in looks.

Nor in nature, either. He's not devious or deceptive—he's completely up front with me about the reasons we've got married.

Mutual benefit. With the emphasis on mutual. Unlike Malcolm—

Darkly, she dismissed the man who had defrauded her. Stolen from her. She would not waste time thinking about him at all. Instead she would focus on the present.

Her gaze went to the two manservants, one of whom she recognised from the Rome apartment, who were now issuing forward with trays holding plates of a variety of salads. It all looked fresh and delicious, and Lana felt immediately hungry. She helped herself to a generous serving of leaves, plump tomatoes, cold chicken and a good dollop of oil-rich dressing and tucked in, savouring the taste. One of the menservants had poured wine, and she took a mouthful of the crisp white, savouring that too.

'You're definitely not eating like a model any longer,' Salvatore observed.

That momentary tightness as he'd mentioned his parents was gone. There was, she thought, a genial note to his tone of voice now. She looked across at him. Since setting out from Rome he seemed, she realised, to have set aside the reserved formality which she'd got used to when they were alone together.

In public he might smile at her, keep her close at his side—kiss her, even!—but that was only for public consumption. She sheared her mind away. Remembering that kiss was *not* a good idea! She'd been doing her very best to put it out of her head ever since it had happened, knowing perfectly well why he'd done it—he'd said as much to her straight out, after all. The two of them might as well be actors on a stage. In a way, they were—the glittering stage of Roman high society. With the key members of the audience he'd wanted to see the kiss being Giavanna and her father.

That was the only reason he kissed me.

There was absolutely nothing personal about it. How could there be?

You turned him down, remember? The first time you met him. Said no to his invitation. What you have now with him is a business arrangement—nothing more and nothing less. And there are implications that follow on from that. Implications you must not forget. Must not ignore.

She realised, with a mental start, that Salvatore's eyes were still resting on her, and that she should answer his remark. It was a safe subject, so she did so freely.

'Do you know?' she declared, cutting into the soft chicken breast with enthusiasm. 'I almost think this is the best thing about all this. Eating my fill after years of starvation. It's bliss!'

Salvatore smiled. 'But won't you have to starve all over again when you go back to modelling afterwards?'

'I'm not going back,' Lana replied. 'That is definite. I'm past my sell-by in modelling anyway. Once I can pay off that damn mortgage Mal saddled me with I'm selling up completely and getting out of London!'

'Where will you go?'

She wondered why he was in the least interested in what would happen to her once she no longer had to stand at his side and pretend to be his wife, but then she reckoned he was just making polite conversation.

'I'm not sure,' she answered, tucking in with a will to her delicious dressing-drenched salad. 'The seaside, probably, on the south coast. I might buy a place I can run as a holiday let, or maybe open a dress shop—that might be an idea.'

'I get the dress shop idea, given your experience of the fashion world, but why the seaside?'

Again, Lana wondered idly why he was bothering to ask, but since he had, she answered him. 'Childhood memories, really, from when I was much younger than now. Holidays with my parents. Until—' She stopped. It was still painful to think of them.

Dark eyes rested on her. She knew he was expecting something more after the sudden way she'd fallen silent. Too late to wish she hadn't mentioned them.

'They were killed in a motorway pile-up four years ago,' she said.

She swallowed, aware that he was taking a mouthful of his wine, then setting his glass down with a click.

'That's hard. To lose both at once.' His voice was short. 'Mine,' he said tightly, 'were killed when their private plane crashed off Sardinia. Twelve years ago now, but—' He stopped.

For a moment their eyes met. Something passed between them. Something that was nothing to do with the reason she was here in his beautiful *palazzo*, acting out being his wife when in truth she was no such thing. Something that was just between the two of them. Both with tragic memories.

'The pain stays,' Lana said quietly. She reached for her own wine, needing it suddenly.

'Yes.'

His voice was still tight. Lana knew why perfectly well. It seemed strange that both of them should have lost their parents in such similarly tragic and untimely ways. It seemed to link them, when in fact there was nothing linking them at all. Nothing personal.

Setting down her wine glass, she resumed eating. So did Salvatore. Was the silence between them awkward, or the opposite? She wasn't sure—knew only that it was safer to return to easier subjects.

'So, how old is the *palazzo*?' she heard herself asking. Her tone was conversational now, and that seemed safer, too.

He answered in kind, and that was better. 'Nearly three hundred years old,' he said. 'The family who originally built it sold it after the Napoleonic wars, and it changed hands again before my own family bought it.'

'May I explore?' she asked.

He frowned, as if her question were out of place. 'Of course. Unfortunately, I don't have time to show you around this afternoon—I must get some work done after my week of socialising in Rome. If you consider the weather warm enough, you might like to sit out by the pool—it's heated at this time of year, until summer arrives in full strength.'

'Thank you—that sounds very inviting,' Lana replied. 'What is our schedule for the time we'll spend here?' she asked. He'd set their schedule out in Rome, so she might as well discover what was expected of her here.

'As I say, I have a great deal of work to catch up with, but I see no reason why I should not show you something of the area. Would you like that? You mentioned you had never been to Florence, for example. Would that be of interest to you?'

'Well, yes,' she agreed, 'but I can easily visit on my own. Please do not feel obliged to—'

'Lana.' He cut across her. 'We are supposed to be on our honeymoon—newlyweds! What new bride goes off sightseeing on her own?'

'I simply don't want to make demands on you,' she replied.

'You won't,' he assured. 'I'll show you Florence, and there is so much more, of course. Pisa, Lucca, Sienna— the list goes on and on! Even after a year you won't have seen all that Tuscany offers.'

His mood seemed to lighten again, and he started to talk about Tuscany. Lana asked appropriate questions about its geography and history, just as if she were an invited guest, and it made the meal pass pleasantly.

As the staff emerged to clear the table, he got to his feet. 'I must go and get some work done,' he said. 'Have coffee out here, or down by the pool if you prefer. Feel free to do as you please this afternoon—pool, gardens, house, whatever. Dinner is at eight, but we'll gather at half-seven for drinks. Dress code is informal—I want to be comfortable after a week of tuxedos!'

He strode off back indoors, and Lana's eyes followed him. Moments later the two manservants had gone too, taking her request for coffee with them, and she was left sitting on her own. There was no sound except birdsong. It was very peaceful. Very beautiful. She looked out over the sunken garden with the stone fountain, its water playing gently, bathed in warm sunlight.

I could get used to this....

And not just to the lifestyle. Her thoughts flickered. She found herself wishing, as she had before, that the man she had married to lift the crushing burden of debt off her shoulders had been short, fat and old. It would have made things a lot, lot easier...

Her gaze flicked to the chair Salvatore had just been occupying. She saw him there again, his powerful frame dominating her vision, the chiselled planes of his face, the dark glance of his gaze on her.

She felt sudden heat beat up into her.

Heat that should not be there. That had no place being there.

Salvatore clicked off his computer and pushed the keyboard away. He was done for today. Time for something much more enjoyable.

An enquiry of Giuseppe confirmed that Lana was out by the pool. Ideal...

He headed out.

The warm air after the cool of his office was welcome. Though it was still spring, summer was on its way. He strode across the terrace, making his way past the rear of the *palazzo* where, to the right, the pool court was situated, sheltered in a walled garden that mirrored the sunken fountain garden on the other side of the *palazzo*.

He vaulted lightly down the steps, through the archway towards the aqua of the pool's water, sparkling in the late afternoon sunshine.

And stopped dead.

He'd known Lana would be there, but—

She was lying spreadeagled, face-down on a lounger, completely naked apart from a skimpy bikini bottom, her glorious hair like a swathe of shining gold waving over one shoulder. His eyes swept over her—over her long, bare body, the fabulous moulding of her shoulders and back, the soft round of her barely covered derriere and the long, slightly parted length of her thighs and legs.

Desire, strong and insistent, swept instantly over him.

Slowly, deliberately, with nothing whatsoever else in his mind, everything wiped out by the vision in front of him, he walked towards her.

Lana stirred. She'd been dozing on and off, conscious dimly of the sun's rays, stronger here than this time of year in England, and knowing that she must not overdo her first tanning session. But after the non-stop week in Rome simply lying here, lazy and resting, in this quiet, peaceful spot, with nothing more than birdsong and ci-cadas to accompany her, the faint hum of the water filter lapping the water gently, was just so blissful she simply didn't want to move.

Yet something had roused her. Had it been footsteps? Perhaps one of the maids who had earlier brought her out some iced juice and then water at her request, as well as rich, fragrant coffee, had returned to remove the empties.

She lifted her face slightly to see.

And froze.

It was not a servant. It was Salvatore. Standing a hand-ful of metres away from her and looking straight at her.

She knew exactly what he was seeing. Just about every square inch of her! And if she moved in the slightest, let alone sat up or turned over, he would see even more.

And he was enjoying the view of what he was already seeing, she thought, with a hollowing of her insides. Enjoying it a lot.

He didn't have sunglasses on, and his gaze was working over her slowly and deliberately. Though she was used to being looked at, it was usually for the sake of what she was wearing. Not for what she was *not* wearing…

Salvatore's lingering inspection was like a slow, burning flame licking over her body, heating it from the inside out, liquefying her…

Time seemed to stop, and her heart-rate began to thud within her, her blood quickening in her veins. Then, abruptly, he stopped looking. She could see it happen in his face, his eyes veiling. He resumed walking, raising a hand to her, but heading now for the pool house.

'I'm sorry for disturbing you,' he said casually, as he walked past her. 'I'm just going to change for a swim. You keep on sunbathing.'

Lana dropped her face again, still feeling the quickening of her blood. Willing it to subside. Conscious, with a silent gasp, that, even crushed as they were by her body weight on the lounger, her breasts had engorged, her nipples were cresting…

Oh, dear God—no! No, no and no!

She couldn't allow this. She mustn't! It was essential she didn't allow it! She buried her face in the towel and kept it resolutely there as she heard footsteps again, a heavy splash of pool water, then steady, rhythmic quieter splashing as Salvatore thrashed up and down the length of the pool. Eventually she heard him get out of the water, pat himself dry with a towel, and then bare feet approached her and a tall shadow fell over her.

'I really ought to put some after-sun cream on you,' he said, hunkering down beside her. 'Hold still.'

As he spoke, a dollop of cream, cold to her heated skin, was deposited between Lana's shoulder blades. A hand descended to anoint her.

'Relax,' Salvatore's deep voice admonished her.

It was an impossible command for Lana to obey—how could she possibly relax when the firm, smooth glide of his fingertips was working between her shoulder blades, down over the smooth expanse of her back? The cooling cream was soothing—but the stroke of his hands was the very opposite. A million nerve-endings fired simultaneously. She felt her hands claw into the towel, seeking self-control, willing herself not to react.

A moment later his hand was lifted from her, and he was straightening.

'All done,' he said. There was the slightest ragged edge to his voice. Then he was speaking again. 'I'll go and change in the pool house. You might want to turn over to protect your back.'

Now she fancied his voice was dry, not ragged. She heard him pad away, the pool house door open and shut. Instantly, her heart thudding hectically, she twisted her hands around her back to refasten the ties of her bikini top, then levered herself up to a sitting position, grabbing her wrap to tug it over her as quickly as she could. Before Salvatore emerged again.

When he did so, five minutes later, she was sitting up on the lounger, the back raised, demurely covered in the wrap, legs slanting sideways, dark glasses safely over her eyes, hair restrained by a ribboned tie. She was apparently absorbed in her paperback, reaching for her iced water. The image of cool, calm and collected.

A complete lie.

But one she had to hold to.

He paused by her lounger. 'Don't stay out too much longer,' he advised. 'There's still some heat in the sun.'

She gave an abstracted nod and he headed off. The moment he was gone she set down her book, swallowing hard. Staring helplessly out over the azure waters of the pool.

Heart still thudding.

Salvatore headed indoors. It had been sheer self-indulgence to put cream on her back as he had. But he didn't regret it. Why should he?

I know what I want of her.

Yes, he did indeed. And he would have a whole year of it. Unless, of course, he tired of her sooner. But that was for then. This was for now. And now was good.

He'd disposed of Giavanna, had been able to start the process of disposing with her father in his business affairs, and now he could focus on his other main purpose in bringing Lana out to Italy. Here, away from the non-stop social round in Rome, he could pursue his objective at his own pace.

It would have been preferable, obviously, simply to have been able to follow through on his initial intention to have an affair with her. Marrying her was a complication—but it was a necessary one. And now he'd achieved his purpose for marrying he could focus on Lana herself. The fact that she was his wife was to all intents and purposes irrelevant.

As he gained the landing his eyes went to the door of her bedroom, right next to his, just as it had been in Rome. And, as in the Rome apartment, her bedroom had once been his mother's and his, the master suite, his father's.

His expression changed. Became bleak for a moment.

Separated by a communicating door through which they did not communicate.

He pushed the bleak memory away, gained his own bedroom. He'd had it redecorated since his father's day, but it still brought a conflicting mix of affection and anger. His eyes went to the door that opened into Lana's room—his mother's bedroom. It felt odd to think of Lana there, making herself at home.

But she isn't—that's the point. She is merely passing through.

He dragged off his clothes, headed into the en suite bathroom. The vigorous swim had made him hungry for dinner. Putting cream on Lana's back had made him hungry to see her again.

Turning the dial to maximum force, he stepped inside the shower.

CHAPTER SIX

DINNER WAS SERVED in the elegant dining room, and although Salvatore had said the dress code was casual—something reflected both in her tunic-style rust-coloured dress with a dark scarf looped around her neck, and in Salvatore's fine cashmere sweater and dark trousers—simply sitting there at the polished mahogany table, surrounded by landscape paintings that Lana was pretty sure might equally be hanging in a museum, and being waited on by the two manservants overseen by the stately Giuseppe, was hardly, she thought, a casual experience. Nor was the meal itself, which consisted of the full panoply of courses—from an *aperitivo* served by Giuseppe himself, all the way through to the *dolce*, which was a delicate pear *sorbetto*.

'This is in your honour,' Salvatore murmured to her *sotto voce*.

Dutifully, Lana voiced her thanks, and determined to be vocally appreciative of every offering—which was not in the least hard to do, for everything served was delicious and she ate with gusto. She felt she was winning Giuseppe's approval, and felt a pang of guilt. He was treating her as the new mistress of the *palazzo*, when she was no such thing.

Nor will I ever be.

Her gaze went to Salvatore, sitting at the head of the table. Because of the table's length, she was not sitting at the foot but at his right-hand side, less than a metre from him, as if they really were a married couple. Something that was not an ache—it *couldn't* be an ache…there was no reason for it to be an ache, and certainly no justification—formed inside her.

Then he was speaking again, and the ache was dispelled. Discarded. It had no place, anyway.

She paid attention to what he was saying. He was no longer using the brisk, impersonal, imperious manner that he had during their first few days in Rome when had had been speaking to her alone, giving her instructions. He was more relaxed here—that much was obvious. Unless, of course, she realised belatedly, that that was simply for the benefit of his household.

For herself, though, she was not relaxed. She'd tried to hide it—again for the benefit of the household. But the incident by the pool still disturbed her. She must make sure, she resolved, that nothing like that could ever happen again.

'So, would you like to see Florence tomorrow?' Salvatore enquired.

'Tomorrow?' Lana echoed, slightly surprised. After all, he was under no obligation to entertain her.

'It would suit me,' he replied. 'The following day I have conference calls morning and afternoon.'

'Then, thank you, yes, I would love to see Florence,' Lana dutifully agreed.

The remainder of the meal was spent discussing their itinerary for Florence. Lana readily agreed to forego the

Uffizi this time around, to focus on a more general tour of the city's main highlights.

'There will be plenty of opportunity for you to visit as often as you wish,' Salvatore said.

She nodded in polite agreement. She was already thinking ahead to when she would be left to her own devices. She would use the opportunity of living in Italy for the duration of her marriage to learn the language. She would learn off the Internet…buy textbooks. It would be something to take away from her time here…

Her gaze flickered to Salvatore again.

She felt again, just for a fraction of a moment, that irrelevant tiny ache which had neither cause, nor justification, nor any business at all being there. So what if he was the most lethal-looking man she'd ever seen in her life? So what if he had eyed her up while she was sunbathing and put cream on her back? None of that had any place in the reason why she had married him.

That was all she had to remember.

Florence was everything its reputation said it would be and more. Lana was entranced, despite the crowds even this early in the season, and gazing about her avidly. Salvatore made an expert guide, his long familiarity with the city enabling her to make sense of all that she was seeing.

She'd worn a comfortable outfit quite deliberately—a crisply cut sand-coloured shirt dress and a loose jacket, which looked both casual and chic worn with day-proof flats that would cope with a lot of walking. Which they did.

They took in all the main sights, starting with Michelangelo's *David* and the basilica, and going on from there. Lana's head was reeling from all the information Salvatore was giving her, amplified by guidebooks and Internet. The weather was ideal—not too hot, and very pleasant. Even so, she was glad to stop for lunch, to be taken outdoors at an upmarket trattoria. Lana, still celebrating the end of her modelling diet, focussed on pasta—Salvatore on veal escalope.

Then they forayed forth again to cross the River Arno by the famous covered Ponte Vecchio bridge, where Salvatore regaled her with the tale of how the Medicis had had a secret crossing constructed within the bridge as a potential escape route from their city rivals, and how the disastrous floods a generation earlier had caused appalling damage to the city, from which it had now, thankfully, recovered.

Another break for coffee ensued, and then, as the afternoon sun lengthened, they ascended to the Piazzale Michelangelo above the city—the terrace that gave sweeping picture-postcard views over the whole panorama.

'Time for cocktails,' Salvatore announced, when Lana had had her fill of gazing. 'Then dinner. We're booked at the rooftop restaurant at the Falcone—you'll like it.'

Lana looked at him a little uncertainly. He'd spent the day showing her Florence—did he really want to dine out with her there as well?

'You don't have to,' she said. 'You've given up an entire day to me as it is.'

Salvatore's expression was unreadable. It was strange for her to see it like that again, for during the day he'd been more relaxed—more affable—than she had yet experienced. Perhaps, she thought, it was because there were no eyes on him…neither his staff's, nor his friends', nor his social acquaintances'.

We're anonymous here—I don't have to role-play, and neither does he. He's just a native Italian, showing Firenze off to an English tourist.

But now, somehow, that had gone.

'It's all arranged,' he said, as if brooking no contestation of what he wanted.

'Then of course…' Lana said acquiescently.

She wasn't dressed for somewhere as swanky as the Falcone was obviously going to be, but if that didn't bother Salvatore it need not bother her. He was casually dressed himself, in an open-neck shirt and linen jacket, with light trousers and, like her, comfortable walking shoes. She gave an inward sigh. He looked as drop-dead gorgeous in this outfit as he did in every other. Wearing dark glasses, as he had for much of the day, only added to it.

What am I going to do about this…?

The troubling thought plucked at her. She needed to stop being so aware of him physically the whole time. She had a whole year to get through, after all.

Perhaps, after a few weeks—a few months—the constant awareness would wear off.

It was a frail hope, but the only one available.

Salvatore sat back in his chair at their table on the roof terrace of the Falcone and looked across at the woman he was dining with. She looked as effortlessly beautiful as ever. Her dress might be casual, her hair drawn back in a plait that she'd wound around itself at the nape of her neck to keep it out of the way and her make-up nothing more than mascara and lip gloss. But that did not detract from her allure one iota.

She possessed a naturally bestowed beauty that had had male heads turning all day. She'd seemed oblivious to it—or perhaps, given her career, simply indifferent. He was glad of it. There was only one man he didn't want her indifferent to.

Except... His face tightened minutely. That seemed to be exactly what she was to him. Even after spending a day with her he saw nothing in her behaviour that had not been there before. She'd shown interest in what he was telling her, asked pertinent questions, displayed an informed level of general knowledge about the Renaissance. But nothing more than that.

She was civil and polite, but...

Guarded. Was that the word for the way she was with him?

Perhaps, though, he only had himself to blame for that. His state of tension when he'd first arrived in Rome had made him, he acknowledged, less than relaxed with her. He'd needed her to get it all right, what he required of her, to perform the way he'd wanted her to do.

Now, though, with mission accomplished—Giavanna stymied and her father perforce accepting his ambitions had been thwarted—away from the fishbowl and gossip hive of Rome, he could afford to be more relaxed.

And so could she.

He'd chosen the rooftop restaurant of the Falcone hotel for its famous vista over the rooftops of Florence, looking towards the basilica. The evening was warm, the lights low, and the candles on the tables were throwing a soft glow over the scene. It had been a long day, and both of them had been glad to sit down and make their choices from the superb menu. Now, as they sipped their *aperitivos*, Salvatore's eyes went to Lana, who was gazing appreciatively out over the city. For himself, he was gazing appreciatively over *her*.

'So, have you enjoyed today?' he asked.

She turned back at his question, a smile on her face. 'Yes, indeed. How could I not? It's been very good of you.'

He made a negating gesture with his hand. 'I was happy to do so,' he said.

There was a hint of brusqueness in his voice—impatience, even, and he was aware of it. Aware of why it was there. She didn't have to tell him it had been 'good' of him, as if he were doing her a favour he did not need to. Or want to.

'Next time,' he went on, 'you shall see the Uffizi. A private tour would be best.'

She shook her head. 'Oh, no, please don't. That's quite unnecessary. A timed booking to avoid the queues would be fine, and much less expensive.'

He raised an eyebrow. She came from a different world from him. It had been easy to forget that this last week, showing her off in Rome, couture-gowned and wearing jewellery she'd never be able to afford in all her life.

And now she is my wife.

Except that had it not been for the necessity of spiking Roberto's guns she would not be his wife at all. She'd be here as his latest *inamorata*—nothing more than that. He found his gaze slipping down to where her wedding band glinted in the candlelight as she lifted her glass to her lips. His own glinted too.

He drew a breath, not wanting to think about it. Marriage had been necessary—that was all there was to it. It was irrelevant, therefore, that it had not been by choice.

When would it ever be by choice?

The caustic words shaped in his head, long familiar to him.

'A private tour is far preferable,' he said, closing the subject. 'I'll arrange it for next time we come here.'

The waiter was hovering to take their order, and he turned his attention to that instead. The cuisine at the Falcone was first class, and never disappointed.

Nor did it tonight and nor did the company. Or the ambience. As the meal progressed he made a focussed effort to set Lana at her ease. To put aside the tensions that had inevitably surrounded their time in Rome, where it had been essential she play her part to perfection.

Here, now, it was different.

Not having to act—play the bride and groom to everyone. Just being ourselves instead...

Relaxing after an enjoyable day. Setting aside any consciousness of the fact that they were married, because here, and now, it was completely irrelevant. Because here and now, as dusk faded and night gathered, the city lights pricking out beneath the unseen stars, only one thing mattered. Just as it had from the very first.

The fact that he desired her.

And the fact that she was also, as it happened, his wife, for the purposes for which he'd married her and for no other reason at all, was of no account at all.

There was wedding her and there was bedding her— and they were completely separate.

Lana drained the last of her wine, setting the glass back on the damask linen tablecloth. Her mood was strange.

She had spoken the truth when she'd told Salvatore she'd enjoyed the day—how could anyone possibly not enjoy a day in Florence?

And with him to show it to me.

Her eyes went to him now, as he sat relaxed back in his chair, looking as lethal as ever. Somehow even more so, she thought, lounged back as he was, his wine glass held between long fingers, the open collar of his shirt framing the strong column of his neck, dark glasses casually pushed back on his sable hair. At his jaw the very faintest shadowing was visible, giving him a raffish allure. An allure of which two glasses of wine and an *aperitivo* was making her more than ever aware.

She was also all too conscious that it was enhanced by where they were—dining up here amongst the rooftops of Florence, beneath the stars. So ridiculously romantic...

Except that she must not think of it that way.

No, they were simply having dinner together, and the fact that they happened to be in such a ridiculously romantic location was nothing to do with them. Salvatore had chosen the spot because of the view and the excellence of the food. Their conversation over the meal had been innocuous, nothing personal—only about what they'd seen and what there was yet to see, both in Florence and in Tuscany further afield. It could have been a conversation between any two people, not herself and Salvatore. Not between two newlyweds.

But the marriage is irrelevant. It has nothing to do with us as people. It isn't real at a personal level—how could it be?

There was nothing personal between them at all.

She dragged her gaze away from him, back over the

rooftops of Florence. A much safer view than gazing at Salvatore.

She realised Salvatore was speaking again, diverting her thoughts from where it was pointless for them to go.

'Do you know the story of how the architect Brunelleschi won the competition for constructing what was then the biggest dome in the world for the basilica?'

She frowned slightly, looking across at him as she answered. 'My father explained it to me once—something about there being two domes, one inside the other, and the smaller one helped support the larger one?' she ventured.

'Essatamente,' said Salvatore.

'My father always wanted to come and see it for himself. He and my mother were planning a holiday here when—' She broke off, giving a slight shrug. 'Well, they never made it here.' Her voice was flat.

Her gaze went out over the rooftops again, towards the floodlit basilica with its famed octagonal *cupula.* Her throat had tightened. Painful emotion bit as she thought of her parents and their untimely deaths.

Then suddenly she felt her hand, lying on the table-top, being pressed lightly.

Sympathetically.

'Then they'll be glad, won't they, your parents, that you are here to see it for them?' Salvatore said quietly.

Lana turned her head back. The look on his face was one of understanding, and she felt herself blink unaccountably. Then it was his gaze that was looking away. Far away...

'My mother always loved Firenze,' he said slowly, automatically giving the Italian name for Florence, Lana realised. 'It gave her so much inspiration for the *pala-*

zzo. She loved to browse here in all the antiques shops, buying furniture and art. It kept her occupied when—'

He broke off, made a slightly apologetic face at Lana. 'I'm sorry. Ancient history.' He reached for the wine bottle, pouring a little into Lana's glass and into his, finishing the bottle.

'Please don't apologise,' Lana said, her voice low and full of emotion. 'Our memories are all we have and we must treasure them.'

She had heard the affection in his voice as he'd spoken of his mother, and knew without him telling her that she had been loved by him. She felt emotion come again— but this time for him, not for herself. Because he, like she, had suffered so grievous a loss.

He looked across at her. Was it the candlelight, or the wine, or the stars still dim in the sky above? Whatever it was there was something in his face, in his eyes, that had not been there before. Something in his gaze.

'You are right—we must,' he said. 'For their sakes as well as ours. The good memories—yes, those we must remember and cherish.'

He held her gaze. Then, lifting his wine glass, he titled it at her. The ruby wine caught the candle flame, reflected it in its depths. It was reflected in the depths of his dark eyes too, lightening them.

'And this will be one of them,' he said. His voice was different now. Lighter, like the expression in his eyes. 'So let's drink to it.'

She reached for her glass, not dropping his gaze, letting him touch her glass with his.

'*Saluti,'* he said. 'To a good day, a relaxing gourmet evening—and to all that is yet to come.'

For a moment—just a moment—she felt something

flicker deep inside her, as if the flame reflected in the wine and in his dark eyes were flickering inside her as well.

Then he was taking a mouthful of the wine, draining his glass. He lifted a hand, summoned a waiter to their table with an easy gesture, asked for the dessert menu.

'The *dulce* here are famed!' he told Lana smilingly. 'And since you are off your model's diet you can indulge to the max. Indulge,' he said, and his long lashes swept momentarily down over his eyes, 'in everything…'

Was there a husk in his voice? She was imagining it, surely. There was no need for her to hear one. No need for anything, in fact, except to take the gilt-edged menu card being presented to her by the returning waiter and put her mind to the tempting task of selecting something highly calorific and even more delicious.

The *dulce*, after all, were all that she must be tempted by.

Dulce… she thought driftingly, as she made her choice—a rich, caramel-based *crema* that Salvatore had recommended as a speciality of the house and which she had been happy to agree to—*dulce* meant 'sweet'. Her gaze went back to Salvatore as he relayed their identical choice to the waiter, who disappeared off.

And this is sweet—this whole evening with him. Sweet to sit here, high over this fabled city, wining and dining, just us, together, not on show, not pretending to be what we are not—just being who we are.

The wine was sweet in her veins, the air sweet in her throat, and the sight of Salvatore, so incredibly good-looking, so impossible to tear her gaze from, so sweet to gaze at…

She knew she was a little intoxicated—knew it and

didn't mind...didn't care. Knew that it was good
sweet—just to sit here, in this beautiful place, with
ambience, the view, the warmth all around her and S
vatore to gaze at...

He met her gaze. Smiled.

And it seemed very good to her.

Sweet.

I don't want this to end. The thought moved throu
her head. *I want to go on sitting here, gazing at him,*
cause it's all I want to do.

It was strange... Strange because a stranger was w
he was to her. What else could he be?

It was a question she should not have asked. Becau
it came with an answer that was impossible. Just i
possible.

He is no longer a stranger to me.

The lights of the *palazzo* were welcoming in the vel
night as Salvatore got out of the car, turning back to h
Lana out. She did not take his outstretched hand, mer
stepped out with the natural elegance with which she
ways carried herself. Salvatore closed her door and n
ded goodnight to his chauffeur. The car crunched slov
away around to the garages at the rear. As it depart
Salvatore glanced at Lana, ready to usher her indoc
but she was standing gazing upwards.

'What a glorious starry night!' she exclaimed. '`
couldn't see it nearly as well in Florence, with the c
lights.'

Salvatore followed her gaze. It was, indeed, a glc
ous starry night, with the Milky Way sweeping over
palazzo. Then his eyes dropped to Lana. Her uplift
face, the long, graceful line of her exposed throat a

the soft contour of the plaited coil of her hair at the nape of her neck were all dimly lit by starlight and the few lights showing inside the *palazzo*, giving her an ethereal quality.

Instinct took over. Impulse. He stepped towards her.

All evening his consciousness of her had been growing and growing. To sit with her on the Falcone's rooftop terrace, bathed in soft light, catching her fragrance in the warmth of the evening as the light dimmed and the city took on the glow of the night, its monuments bathed in iridescent up-lights… With no one but themselves to pay attention to, for all the other diners had only had eyes for each other in that most romantic of locales.

And I had eyes only for her—for her exquisite beauty.

And there had been something else too, he knew. Something that had come as they had touched upon the strange circumstances of their lives that were shared, each of them having lost their parents to tragic accident.

He felt emotion—alien, but present—move in him. Desire, yes, but something else, too. Something that had started to form, to flow between them. Something he was not used to.

Something that seemed to intensity her beauty…

His eyes shaped her uplifted face… He said her name. Wanting her to look not at the starlit sky, but at him. 'Lana…'

His voice was husky. Sitting beside her in the back seat on the journey home, with the wine from their meal warming his veins, the scent of her faint perfume had caught at him. Knowing she was only a hand's reach away from him in the dark interior of the car as it had hummed along the autostrada had been a torment.

They'd hardly spoken on the journey, only to make

inconsequential remarks about the events of the day, but Salvatore had been endlessly aware of her presence so close to him, so private, with the glass screen dividing them from his driver, who'd been focussing on the road ahead. He'd allowed himself the luxury of glancing at her from time to time, after conversation had ceased, and had seen that she had closed her eyes, as if in sleep. But he was pretty sure she had not been sleeping. One hand had rested on the door, and by its position he'd been able to tell that her muscles had not been relaxed. Nor had her breathing been that of someone dozing.

The thought had occurred to him that she was deliberately feigning sleep in order to withdraw from him. He did not want her withdrawing from him. Did not want her gazing up at the stars now.

The wine he'd drunk at dinner was accentuating his senses, his awareness of her.

His desire for her.

It rose in his veins, sweet and rich.

From the very first he had held back, knowing he must focus on the business of his marriage, on the reason he had undertaken it, on facing outward to the world.

But there was no more need for that. Now he could give free rein to what he had felt from the very first moment of setting eyes on her. No more delays, no more holding back. For either of them.

That kiss he'd taken from her the very first night he'd taken her out to show all of Rome his new bride had told him what awaited him. That she would return all he wanted of her.

She desires me, even as I desire her.

And now—oh, now that desire between them could blossom and flourish and be fulfilled.

As he said her name, his voice husky, she lowered her gaze from the star-filled sky to meet his. For a second—an instant, a timeless moment—he held her eyes with his. Then his hand reached out, folded around her upper arm as he stepped towards her, closing the distance between them. He said her name again, and his other hand—of its own volition, it seemed—cupped her cheek. She stood completely motionless, but there was something in her gaze as he poured his eyes into hers that seemed captive...helpless.

Wordlessly, he bent his head to hers, let his mouth do what it ached to do again—to feel the velvet touch of her lips beneath his, to softly press itself to hers. He heard the low, soft sigh in her throat as her lips parted for his, her body inclined towards his. His hand around her arm tightened automatically to support her pliant body...so pliant, and the fingers at her cheek speared into her golden hair, holding her for his deepening kiss.

Blood surged in his veins, desire flaring strong and insistent. This—*this* was what he had wanted, ached for, ever since he had first seen her...ever since that first tantalising kiss he'd drawn from her that night at the Duchessa's. He drew her against him, his kiss deepening, letting go her arm to fasten his arm around her slender waist, holding her for his desire and his sweet, sweet pleasure.

And for hers.

He felt it—felt her respond to him, felt her mouth open to his, her kiss deepen even as his did. Felt her hands lift to his chest, splaying out across it, and low in her throat he heard, with triumphant exultation, a low, helpless moan. Desire surged more strongly yet, released from the thrall he had imposed upon it—had had to impose

upon it. But now, gloriously, triumphantly, he could l
it loose upon her, let it loose within him.

He gave himself to it—to the arousal mounting with
him, the arousal he could sense with every long-hon
masculine instinct was possessing her too, binding h
to him, and he to her. Their bodies pressed against eac
other, her breasts peaking against the hard wall of h
chest. He wanted more—and yet more…

And then, like a douche of cold water, she wrench
herself free, jolting back. Stepping away.

'*No!*'

A single word. A single forbidding edict. A sing
denial.

He stared at her, disbelieving, while the bloc
pounded in his head, scythed through his veins. He sa
her hold up her hands, palms out, as if to ward him o
Her eyes were wide, distended.

'*No!*' she said again, and took a further step back. 'I
impossible—' Her voice seemed to shake, and she too
a shuddering breath, hands still held up. 'We *can't*,' sh
said, her gaze still stricken.

He stared at her. '*Can't?*' he echoed blankly. The wo
made no sense.

But she said it again. 'We *can't*,' she repeated, as v
hemently as the first time.

Her hands were still warding him off. She was bac
ing away from him now—backing towards the front do
as if trying to seek refuge from him by going indoor
He was still wordless with shock and incomprehensio
And with a frustration that was biting through him i
disbelief.

She was speaking again, throwing words at him
'Look, we've both drunk too much wine…spent too lor

alone together. We're acting under impulse. Because of the wine, the night, the stars, whatever—' She broke off, dropping her hands in a defeated gesture.

He was still standing there immobile, frozen. Uncomprehending.

'Why?' he heard himself say. 'Why are you saying *can't*? Do you think I don't know when a woman is responsive? You flamed in my arms just now—'

Her voice cut across his, urgent and denying. 'Of *course* I'm saying *can't*! How could it possibly be anything else! How could you *think* it could be anything else?'

He saw her shut her eyes for a moment, draw a ragged breath. Then her eyes flew open again, and her words were vehement and stabbing.

'How,' she said, her voice ragged, 'can it possibly be anything other than *can't* when you are *paying* me to be here with you?'

If he'd frozen before, he did so again now—totally.

'*Paying* you?' There was Arctic ice in Salvatore's voice.

He saw her face work in the dim starlight. Her hands raised again to ward him off. Heard the consternation in her face, her voice.

'What else do you call it? Salvatore, I'm only here— only with you at all—because you are paying me *four hundred thousand pounds* to be here!'

A hand slashed down through the air. He realised it was his own.

'*Como?* You say that to me? You say such a thing?' A furious breath was exhaled from him. His eyes flashed with outrage at the words she had thrown at him. 'That money,' he bit out, 'is the sum agreed in the prenup you

signed. It is a divorce settlement. It is *not*,' he groun
out, black fury in him, 'a *payment* to you for your pre
ence here!'

He could see her face working again, her hands drop
ping heavily to her sides, as heavy as her voice.

'Of course it is! What else can it be? It's the reaso
I married you—so you would pay off my mortgage fo
me! It's *money* that brought me here, Salvatore! I'm you
employee, or as good as! Nothing more than that. Yo
know our marriage is a lie as much as I do! It's a fictio
however legal it may be! And it doesn't matter wheth
you call that four hundred thousand pounds I'm goin
to get when you dispose of that fiction a divorce settl
ment or a pay-out—it's *payment* for my being here, fo
going through that marriage ceremony with you! So
I…if you…if…'

She lifted her hands again, stepping another pac
backwards.

'If there is *anything* else between us other than wh;
we've established so far…a…a working relationship,
you want to call it that, then what that amounts to…wh;
that makes me…is—'

She broke off. Looked straight at him, let her hand
drop again. Her voice changed. Became painful. Hal
ing. It hurt him to hear it. Appalled him.

'I'm spending a year of my life with you, Salvatore, i
the role of your wife. The *public* role of your wife. N(
personal—*never* personal. It can't be. *Nothing* can b
personal between us! Not beyond the remit of a workin
relationship! At the end of the year I walk away with fou
hundred thousand pounds. That's it, Salvatore—nothin
more. So it can't…*can't* be anything more. It just *can't*

She shook her head, backing further away from hin

'I'm… I'm sorry—'

Her voice broke and he saw her swallow painfully, chokingly.

'Sorry that I let you kiss me. I apologise if it…gave you ideas. Ideas that can't exist for the reasons I've given. I won't go down that path. I can't. I can't separate the money I'm being paid for marrying you from what you… what you want of me. Even…' she swallowed again, more painfully yet '… even if it's what I gave you the impression of wanting. The two don't go together. They can't. I'm sorry if you don't see it that way—but I do.'

She turned away, walking indoors. He watched her go. Ice in his veins.

But something quite different in his guts.

CHAPTER SEVEN

LANA STOOD BENEATH the pounding shower, water sluicing over her. She wished it would wash away her tormented thoughts, rinse the heated blood from her body. But it did no such thing. When she emerged, wrapped in a fleecy towel, she felt no less agitated than when she'd fled from him.

From Salvatore.

From the man who was her husband—in name only.

Because it has to be that way—and stay that way!

That was essential. Imperative. Because otherwise...

Memory, hot and humid, flared within her. In an instant she was back outside, hearing Salvatore say her name, hearing the desire in it, feeling her own response to it flare, standing there, quite motionless, with only the sudden thudding of her heart in anticipation...

If only I hadn't got out of the car and stared up at the stars as I did! If I'd just gone straight indoors! Said goodnight and thank you and headed straight upstairs! I could have... I could have—

Could have maintained the front she'd managed to preserve all evening, dining at that ridiculously romantic rooftop restaurant, letting that vintage wine seep into her veins, doing its disastrous work, lowering the defences she had erected from the very first moment she'd ever set eyes on Salvatore! Had had to erect.

Because anything else—

Is impossible—just impossible! Impossible because it's just so complicated! Being here, being his legal wife but not his real wife! Knowing I only married him to get my pay-off at the end. So I can't... I just can't...make things ever more complicated between us—

Her own desperate words to him out there under the stars burned in her head again, as her eyes went now to the door between their bedrooms.

Closed.

The way it had to be.

Salvatore stared at the screen in his office in the *palazzo*, but he wasn't taking in what was on it. He'd slept badly—restlessly—frustratedly. And he was frustrated not just physically, from being denied what his body had so blatantly told him it wanted. No, it was more than just physical.

Lana's outburst had shocked him—stopped him in his tracks, quite literally. He still could not believe what she had thrown at him.

How can she possibly think that I would take any notice whatsoever of the financial aspect of our divorce agreement at such a moment? And how could she think about it either? Neither the reason we married, nor the outcome of our eventual divorce, has anything to do with what there is between us—what has been there from the very first!

Somehow he had to make her see that. Had to make her see that the reason they had married was irrelevant to what had drawn him to her that very first evening… what had been in her lips when he had kissed her…

He drew a breath, reaching for his keyboard. He had a video conference to join. Work would distract him. And right now distraction was what he needed.

Tonight… Yes, tonight he would start to win Lana back after he had so disastrously scared her off. He did not want to make a mess of it a second time.

For a tantalising moment her image floated in his mind. How lovely she was—and how much he desired her! But his desire for her was not enough—*she* must accept hers for him. Accept that what drew them to each other was nothing to do with the artifice of their marriage.

It's between us personally—between her and me.

And that was the way he wanted it to be. Nothing to do with their marriage.

Because marriage—real, lasting marriage, to any woman—was not something he ever wanted to have anything to do with.

Cautiously, Lana made her way out on to the dining terrace. The warmth of the evening was balmy, but it was at odds with the tension inside her that had been there all day, even though she'd thankfully not set eyes on Salvatore at all.

Now, walking out on to the stone terrace in the balmy evening, she saw that he was already there, looking towards her. A bottle of champagne was in a cooler by the table which was set for dinner, soft candles already lit in their glass holders. She glanced warily at the open champagne bottle, smoking gently. What was going on?

Please, please don't let this be some kind of seduction scene! Not after the disaster of last night!

Her eyes went to Salvatore, her expression still wary. He was looking as gorgeous as ever, a loose-knit cotton sweater in moss-green and a pair of well-cut chinos emphasising his lean, fit build and declaring his innate Italian sense of style, but there was a look on his face that she'd not seen before. Apologetic.

He gave her a brief constrained smile. 'I'm sorry,' he said, 'about last night.'

Lana swallowed, her mouth dry suddenly.

'I don't want you stressing about it,' Salvatore went on. He was holding her gaze, his expression intent. 'I want you to be comfortable here—comfortable with me.'

He took a step towards her. His expression changed suddenly. Softened. Gently, with one finger, he touched her cheek—a fleeting moment only—looking down at her out of deep, long-lashed eyes, their darkness unfathomable.

'So—are we all right together?'

She swallowed again, feeling the trace of his fleeting touch on her cheek. Then she made herself nod.

He smiled. A warm, genuine smile. '*Bene*—I am glad.'

Then he moved towards the champagne cooler, lifted the bottle from it. Looked back at her. 'Let's drink to that,' he said.

His voice was lighter now, she could hear it, and she could see it in his expression too. She felt something lighten in herself as well. She watched him fill two slanted flutes in turn, judging the effervescence with practised skill, then he replaced the bottle and picked up the frothing glasses, handing one to her. She took it gingerly, not wanting their fingers to touch for reasons she didn't want to think about—for the reasons he'd just kicked into touch by what he'd said to her.

He lifted his glass, tilting it slightly towards her. 'To being comfortable with each other,' he said. There was a wry smile in his voice, on his lips, in his dark, unfathomable eyes.

She didn't reply, not sure what to say, but lifted her glass, let him clink his lightly against hers, then took a mouthful as he did from his. The mousse was chill, cooling the heat that had suddenly flushed her face—mistakenly, surely?

He set down his glass, smiled at her. A reassuring smile. 'And now, with our new understanding, we shall enjoy an excellent dinner!' he announced.

As if on cue, as they sat down at the table, one of the two manservants appeared, placing a bowl of plump olives on the table and a plate of crostini canapés. Salvatore exchanged pleasantries with the young man, who responded in kind.

He's polite to his staff...courteous and considerate, Lana could not but observe. Did that include herself? After all, she'd said last night that she was really nothing more than a kind of employee.

But even as she'd called herself that she had known it was not true. It was far more complicated than that. No employee would sit here like this, sipping champagne with him, dining with him, just the two of them...

She reached for an olive, plump and glistening with rich oil, taking a delicate bite from it to stop herself thinking about what it was, exactly, that she and Salvatore were to each other.

'What do you make of them?' Salvatore was asking,

helping himself to one of the large, luscious olives as well. 'They're from the estate here.'

Lana swallowed the rest of her olive. 'Oh, I didn't realise there was land attached to the *palazzo* other than the gardens.'

'Oh, yes, there's an extensive estate—olive groves, farmland, vineyards, woodlands… The wine is nothing spectacular, but I'm reserving an interest in wine-making for my old age! I'll do something about improving it then,' Salvatore replied lightly.

He started to tell her about the traditional grapes of the region, and Lana listened with half an ear, knowing little about wine but grateful that it was an innocuous subject. As she sipped at her champagne, nibbling the delicious olives and the equally delicious crostini, salty with anchovy and goat's cheese, she started—thankfully—to feel the tension that had racked her all day—and all the previous night—begin to ease from her.

Comfortable—that was what Salvatore had said he wanted them to be together. *And maybe we can be. However complicated the situation between us is—*

Her eyes rested on him momentarily as he waxed lyrical about Tuscan grape varieties. She felt her breath catch. He really was just so gorgeous…

She fought to clamp down on her reaction. What had happened last night had been a mistake—that was all. An impulse neither of them should have succumbed to. And now he'd apologised for it and put it aside.

So I don't have to think about it any more. Or feel awkward about it. Or feel awkward around him.

She made herself focus on what he was telling her, asking him a question she hoped wasn't too distracted. The young manservant appeared again, bearing a tray of more dishes, one of which he reverently placed on the table. Salvatore said something appreciative in Italian, and then turned to Lana.

'Black truffles,' he announced as the manservant took his leave. 'From our very own woods—but if I told you exactly where I'd have to shoot you!'

It was humorously said, and Lana gave the expected laugh, glad to do so. Glad to sip at her champagne, too, letting it help her set aside any obsessing about the complications of why she was here with Salvatore in the first place, the confusing tensions those complications engendered whenever she gazed at him in all his gorgeousness. She felt herself start to relax little by little, glad just to listen to him descant on the art of truffle-hunting, on the incredible noses of the trained dogs that sniffed out the prized treasures from under the earth and leaf mould.

As he did so, he shaved two of them into razor-thin slices, proffering them to her. 'Try them neat, before they go on the risotto,' he recommended.

She took a tiny sliver, tasting it somewhat tentatively. 'Oh, that is good!' she exclaimed.

'Isn't it?' he agreed, and then proceeded to scatter generous amounts on their respective servings of risotto.

With a will, Lana tucked in. The rich creaminess of the risotto was brilliantly offset by the musky earthiness of the truffle, and she ate with her eyes half shut to get the full impact. With a sigh, she set her fork aside, her dish empty.

'We'll save some truffle for the *secondo*,' Salvatore announced. 'It's going to be venison.'

It was—and, again, the combination of the strong-tasting meat and the distinctive truffle worked superbly, and the wine that was served alongside it was strong enough to withstand the robust flavours.

'Sangiovese grapes,' Salvatore informed her, lifting his glass to her. *'Saluti!'*

She murmured in reply. She was feeling easier now, she knew, and was glad of it.

We're just enjoying the moment, the delicious food, this beautiful place...just enjoying each other's company. Knowing—and accepting, both of us—that there can be nothing more between us.

Did a quiver of regret go through her? Her eyes lingered on him for a moment as the dusk gathered, as it had last night in that ridiculously romantic rooftop restaurant in Florence, drinking in the way it accentuated the planes of his face.

She suppressed a sigh, returning to her meal. Wanting no more complications.

Across the table, Salvatore watched her eat with lidded eyes. He had caught the half-suppressed sigh...caught the covert glance she'd given him. But he let them be. He was doing what he knew he must do now—focussing only on undoing the damage he'd inadvertently done last night, rushing her as he had.

His eyes moved over her. She was casually dressed in black leggings, with a loose, thigh-length charcoal-grey top. Elegant, but figure-concealing. Deliberately so, he surmised. Wariness had radiated from her on all frequencies as she'd emerged onto the terrace, and he'd known immediately that he must disarm it. The fact that he had succeeded was evident. Over the course of the meal she had visibly relaxed, and he was glad of it.

But there was a way to go yet before she yielded to

what he longed for and forgot all about the artifice of their marriage.

Made the reason that they were together simply… personal.

'Ready for the off?' Salvatore's tone was genial as Lana came down the grand staircase, attired for another day's sightseeing.

It had become the norm over the last week or more for Salvatore to intersperse the days he spent incarcerated in his high-tech office, commanding his business affairs, with expeditions designed to show Lana the glories of Tuscany. As well as Florence, she could now add Pisa, Lucca and Sienna to her collection. Today's expedition was to be further afield, so Salvatore had told her. They'd be heading up into the higher hills, a more remote part of Tuscany, off the standard tourist trail.

He'd made no attempt to be anything other than good, easy-going company, and Lana found she was being the same in return. What they talked about she was never quite sure, in retrospect. About the places he was showing her, yes, and ordinary chit-chat, but precisely about what was vague. Maybe that was a good sign, though, she thought. A sign of how comfortable they had become with each other. Almost unconsciously so, now she thought about it.

It's done us good, she thought, greeting him airily as they made their way outside on to the *palazzo's* gravelled carriage sweep.

Only as she felt the morning's heat envelop her did she feel a flickering thought fleeting across her mind.

Us? Is that what there is now? An 'us'?

But then it had gone.

Her eyes went to the rugged-looking SUV parked up for them—a far cry from either Salvatore's low-slung supercar or the sleek saloon they used when they were being chauffeured.

'Better for the steeper terrain,' he said, helping her up into the front passenger seat before vaulting in on his side and gunning the engine.

And so it proved as they reached what she thought was their destination—a walled hilltop town with vertiginous drops to the steep-sided valley below. But she discovered they were only stopping there for an early lunch, which they had at a quaint old trattoria in the small central *piazza*, while Salvatore told them of his plans for the afternoon.

'There's a lake nearby—higher up—that was formed by damming the river, with forest all around. It's very beautiful and I thought it would make a change for us,' he told her. 'A touch of "wild Italy", so to speak.' He smiled.

The lakeside was reached by a winding, unmetalled roadway which ended beneath a canopy of trees. They got out, and Lana was glad that Salvatore had advised sturdy shoes as well as comfortable leggings and a light sweatshirt. After a short walk through the thick trees, they emerged beside the water. A few metres back from the shore was a small chalet in log cabin style, with a shaded veranda at the front.

'Oh, how picturesque!' she exclaimed when she saw it.

Salvatore turned to her, a half smile on his face. 'Do you like it?' he asked.

'Perfect for the spot!' Lana confirmed with an answering smile.

He nodded. 'Good. It's where we're staying.'

CHAPTER EIGHT

'STAYING?'

Salvatore could hear the bewilderment in Lana's voice and hoped he'd made the right call. He wanted Lana entirely to himself, without anyone else around—not even the staff at the *palazzo*—and if she agreed to it this remote chalet, hired for the week, was ideal for that. Here, they could completely forget that they'd gone through a marriage ceremony that had absolutely no relevance to why they were together in this secluded hideaway.

'Come and see what you make of it,' he invited.

Lightly vaulting up the veranda steps, he opened the door. Inside it was rustically simple—a single room with a long, comfortable-looking settee, some woven rugs on the floor, a small dining table with two wooden chairs, and a log-burner stove set into a thick stone chimney breast. At the rear a kitchenette was tucked beneath what was little more than a ladder leading up to a narrow mezzanine beneath the rafters, the entire space of which was taken up by a bed.

He stepped back.

Lana, with a wary expression on her face, looked in, her gaze sweeping up to the mezzanine. Then she looked back at Salvatore. 'And where,' she asked, her voice deliberate, 'is the other bedroom?'

He was unfazed. 'The settee is long enough to sleep on—plus there's a camp bed that can be placed on the veranda. It's quite warm enough for me to sleep out, so don't worry about that.'

The look she threw at him was old-fashioned in the extreme.

He touched her wrist lightly. Made his voice encouraging. 'Lana, we've been on show ever since we tied the knot—first in Rome and then, yes, even at the *palazzo*, playing "the bride and groom" even if only for the staff. Even sightseeing there have been people everywhere! Here we can just—what's that English word?—chillax. Be ourselves…not what others think we are. Doesn't that appeal?'

He gestured sweepingly out towards the lake, where sunshine glanced off the water, dappled this tree-girt clearing by the shore, indicating the absolute peace and quiet of the place.

She was still looking at him, but less uncertainly, as if his words were getting through to her. Then a frown creased her brow.

'But we've brought no provisions! And I've only got the clothes I'm standing up in!'

'Not exactly,' he said. 'Follow me.'

He headed back along the path to the SUV, pulling open the tailgate. As Lana caught up with him he heard her give what sounded like a choke.

'This should keep us going,' he said cheerfully, and lifted out a large cardboard carrier containing dry foods. It was stashed neatly next to a couple of cool boxes, a portable barbecue and several sacks of charcoal, and two small suitcases.

'One of the maids, Maria, packed some suitable gear for you while we were having dinner last night,' he informed Lana, 'and you can always borrow some of my stuff. I'll take this to the chalet—can you manage one of the cool boxes?'

He set off, relieved that she was not objecting. That, with this impulsive decision he'd made to get away from Rome, away from the *palazzo*, he might, finally, be getting it right with her. The way he wanted it to be.

Lana hefted up one of the cool boxes. Maybe Salvatore was right. Maybe it would be good not to have to put on any kind of front at all—not even to the *palazzo* staff. She'd felt awkward, having them treat her as the *signora*, even more than having his friends and acquaintances think she was. Now she could have a break from it.

Inside the chalet Salvatore was unpacking the groceries, stashing them away in the wooden cupboards above the sink. It made him look very domesticated. Not the powerful businessman or the lordly *signor* of a *palazzo*. It was, she found herself thinking, reassuring…

'Do I leave the cold stuff in the cool box?' Lana asked.

'No, there's a fridge—the chalet has solar-powered electricity and, you'll be pleased to know, running water, fed by a spring from further up the hill. The bathroom, such as it is, is just behind the kitchen.'

Lana peeked through a half-open door, seeing a very simple shower room with toilet facilities that she would be glad of.

'We've got cylinder gas to cook on, plus the barbecue, and oil lamps and candles to supplement the solar electric lights,' Salvatore was saying now. 'Okay, let's get the rest of the stuff from the car.'

It took a couple more trips to empty the boot, then they were done.

'Coffee?' asked Salvatore, lighting the gas hob as Lana climbed, somewhat gingerly, down the ladder from the mezzanine. There had just about been space up there to place her small suitcase on the wooden floor and check to see what Maria had packed for her. Shorts, cotton trousers, tee shirts, a jumper or two, another pair of canvas flat-soled shoes, some underwear, a swimsuit—that was about it.

No nightwear, she noted with sudden suspicion. And then realised that Maria had correctly assumed that her glamorous satin pyjamas were hardly suited to roughing it in a primitive lakeside chalet. Well, she would wear a tee shirt instead. And she would sleep, *quite* definitely, on her own, up there on the mezzanine. She could even pull up the ladder to repel boarders if need be—

But she was given no cause to do so. No such attempt was made. And when Lana finally climbed up the ladder, bidding goodnight to Salvatore, who was stretching himself out on the comfortable settee below, she knew she was glad he had brought her here.

Glad that here, away from absolutely everyone else, they could—just as he'd told her—be themselves.

Not a married couple in a totally unreal marriage made for completely non-romantic reasons that has had its end date written into a contract from the off. Not pretending to people that it's a real marriage, made for the reasons a marriage should be made.

While they were here they could put all that aside.

'Chillax' and be comfortable. Just as Salvatore was u⸺
ing her to be.

Certainly the rest of the day had been relaxing. Af⸺
they'd unpacked and had a cup of coffee out on the ⸺
randa they'd gone for an exploratory walk along t⸺
shore. The narrow path wound along the lake's ed⸺
with more paths leading off it, up into the mixed dec⸺
uous and evergreen forest on the steep hillside. The⸺
returned as dusk gathered, and Salvatore had lit the ⸺
burner more for cosiness than warmth, before maki⸺
dinner.

It had been a simple affair—pasta in a *ragu* out ⸺
a bottle, with parmesan grated by Salvatore—wash⸺
down by a robust red. Dessert had been a chocolate ca⸺
freshly baked at the *palazzo*, rich with icing. The⸺
eaten in front of the fire, then finished off the bottle ⸺
red wine playing board games they'd found in a cu⸺
board, before going out to look at the lake in the st⸺
light. A crescent moon had just been clearing the hi⸺
thin in the heavens.

But Salvatore had made no attempt to take advanta⸺
of her. Scrupulously he had kept two metres from ⸺
as they'd paused to listen to the owls hooting in the d⸺
tance, and they had not stayed out long. Back indoo⸺
they'd time-sliced on the bathroom facilities, and La⸺
had just clambered up to the mezzanine to hurriedly ⸺
on the longest tee shirt she could find by way of ni⸺
attire, while Salvatore took his place in the bathroo⸺

She was asleep before he emerged.

She awoke to the aroma of coffee from the kitche⸺
ette below, and Salvatore bidding her to come down ⸺
breakfast. Pulling on shorts and a fresh tee, and a p⸺

of canvas shoes, plaiting her hair into a long tail, she shinned down the ladder to see Salvatore, in a checked shirt, jeans and trainers, frying bacon and tomatoes, and toasting rolls out of a packet.

Again, just as he had the previous day, he struck her as being surprisingly domesticated. Reassuringly so.

He turned and smiled at her. 'Sleep well?' he asked.

'Like a log,' she answered. 'How about you?'

'Another log,' he assured her, then suggested she laid the outdoor table, bathed in warm sunshine already.

Ten minutes later they were seated, demolishing a hearty breakfast.

He was easy company, obviously relaxed and obviously cheerful, talking about what they might do on this their first day here. They decided on an easy hike up into the forest, in green and dappled shade, which they did, not talking much, for it would have spoilt the wooded quietness all around them.

They descended back to the cabin for a lunch of ham, salami and strong cheese, with tomatoes and peaches and thick-cut bread—eaten, like breakfast, outdoors—and Salvatore, Lana discovered, had plans for the afternoon.

'The chalet comes with a rowing boat,' he told her.

It was pulled up just beyond the solar panels, and also came with fishing tackle. Salvatore, it seemed, was an enthusiastic fisherman.

Lana made no objection to lolling back in the rowing boat when he shipped oars and dropped his line, waiting for a bite at the bait. She did object, however, to gutting the fish after he'd despatched them with a sharp but swift blow to the head against the gunwale.

Watching him deftly make them barbecue-ready with a couple of neat knife-thrusts, she found it hard to think of him as either a high-powered businessman or the elegant man-about-town of elite Roman society.

'So, where did you learn to gut fish, then?' she enquired lazily, glancing at him curiously.

'My father,' he replied.

For a moment she thought he was not going to say any more. Then he did. Looking out over the sunlit lake as he spoke.

'He took me fishing sometimes. At sea—off his motorboat. We'd drop anchor and spend the afternoon and evening out on the water. He didn't talk much, but I didn't mind. It was good just to be with him. It didn't happen very often. Nor did the fishing expeditions. He only took time off when his life got too complicated—even for him.'

Salvatore hadn't tensed, but there was an acerbic tinge to his voice now.

'Complicated?' Lana echoed.

It seemed strange to think of Salvatore as a young boy. A boy with, it seemed, complications in his family.

'My father,' he said, his tone still acerbic as he looked away over the lake, 'would sometimes set up a new mistress without informing the current incumbent—who would then kick off. So he would take off out to sea, where neither could get at him, while they fought it out between themselves.'

She was silent a moment, and so was he. Then... 'It must have been difficult for you,' she said quietly. For all their wealth, his had not been a happy family. It saddened her to think so, to think of him growing up in that way.

His head turned, dark eyes going to her. They were shadowed, and she knew instinctively that he was veiling what he was feeling. That was something she knew all about. She, too, had learnt to hide her tearing grief at her parents' dreadful death.

'Not nearly as difficult as it was for my mother,' he said.

With a sudden gesture, he flung the extracted innards of the fish he'd caught out into the lake water. Then, dropping the gutted fish into the plastic box he'd brought for the purpose and rinsing his hands, he looked at Lana.

'Theirs,' he told her, looking straight at her again, with a shadow deep in his dark eyes, his voice clipped, 'you will appreciate, was not a happy marriage.'

Her eyes filled with open sympathy. 'It can't have been.' She shook her head. 'It must have taken its toll on you, too.'

He gave a shrug. 'I survived.' He looked away again, back over the dark lake water with its hidden depths below the sunlight glancing off its surface, frowning perhaps against its brightness—or for another reason. 'Yet despite all the unhappiness my father caused my mother I still loved him.'

His words came from deep within. She knew it, understood it. Without realising it, she stretched her hand out, just touched his, as if to comfort him.

'It's natural to do so,' she said, her voice low. 'Children hate to take sides when there's dissent between parents.'

He looked back at her. 'Oh, I took sides, all right! My mother's—she was the injured party. But...' His expression changed. 'I also knew my father should never have married. Not just never have married my mother, but never married at all.' His voice hardened. 'He wasn't cut out for it.'

'Why did he?' Lana heard herself ask carefully.

It was strange to be hearing such intimate things about him—and yet out here, in the middle of the lake, just the two of them in the little rowing boat, so isolated from the rest of the world, maybe it was not so strange...

'He fell for my mother—big-time,' Salvatore answered her. 'The trouble was—' he gave a shake of his head '—what he really wanted was just an affair with her—nothing as permanent as marriage. But she came from a family where that sort of thing wasn't approved of, so they got married instead.'

Now there was a hollow in his voice that Lana could hear distinctly.

'She went on loving him all the time. Even when he'd got tired of her devotion.' He took a breath, and his gaze slipped out over the water. 'He was never actively hostile to her, simply chronically unfaithful. Indifferent to her. Never around much. He never wanted a divorce—it would have been difficult, anyway—and he stayed with her for my sake, too. He simply wanted to be able to... to play around the way he liked. Enjoyed. It was all he was capable of.'

Again, Lana was silent a moment. Then... 'My parents were very happy together,' she said. 'I took it for granted. But it's only when you realise that isn't always the case that you truly value it.'

He looked at her. 'They were lucky. So were you.'

She nodded. 'Yes—they were lucky in each other. Lucky in love. They chose wisely. I only wish that I had been as—'

She broke off. Salvatore looked at her questioningly. She made a painful face.

'I only wish I'd been as wise around Malcolm,' she said. 'But I know with hindsight that I just wanted someone in my life after my parents were killed—someone to make me feel less alone.' She took a breath. 'That makes me sound pathetic, I know.'

Salvatore's dark eyes rested on her. 'It makes you sound human,' he said. 'And he's out of your life now—and you're well rid of him!'

He reached for the shipped oars and dipped them into the lake water, starting to pull towards the shore, the muscles in his bare arms flexing as he pulled the boat through the water with apparently effortless strokes. Lana tried not to be conscious of his powerful physique, focussing instead on the approaching shoreline.

His words echoed in her head.

'He's out of your life...'

One day Salvatore would be out of her life too...

The thought seemed to pluck at her. The time would come when she was back in England, picking up her real life again. A thousand miles and more away from here.

A thousand miles and more away from Salvatore.

Her eyes went back to him and she wondered why the thought was unwelcome to her.

Wondered why she was thinking it at all.

'Time for a swim before our sundowner?' Salvatore enquired of Lana as she stepped out from the chalet, a bowl of freshly chopped salad in her hands.

They'd beached the rowing boat and he'd taken the fish indoors to the fridge, got the barbie going while Lana prepared the salad.

His answer was a shake of her head and a rueful laugh. 'No, thanks—I felt the water from the boat, and it's freezing!'

He gave a grin. 'All the more exhilarating!' he told her.

It did not change her mind, and with a laugh h
stripped off to his trunks and plunged into the lake.
was indeed very cold, but he struck out in a fast, powe
ful crawl, warming up as he did so. Reaching the middl
of the lake, he duck-dived and headed back, emergin
with his whole body glowing.

'Wild swimming!' he exclaimed. 'Nothing to beat it

He seized up his towel, patting himself dry. Awar
that Lana's eyes were on him, though only sideway
Aware that he was glad they were. For all her stricture
that night when he'd succumbed to kissing her unde
the stars, she could not shut down her natural respons
to him.

But it must be what she *wants—what* she *accepts. Sh
has to accept that the reason for our marriage, the f
nancial benefit it will bring her in the end, has no rol
to play in what is between us!*

To him it was very simple. Their marriage, althoug
legal, was an irrelevance.

As marriage was to my father.

Affairs were all his father had ever wanted.

As do I.

His eyes shadowed.

I am my father's son.

He tossed the damp towel aside on to a chair, hi
mood darkening suddenly. Yes, he knew that! And h
must remember it, too.

His eyes went to Lana. In shorts and tee shirt, her ha
in a long plait, not a scrap of make-up, she looked ever
bit as radiantly beautiful as she did wearing a coutur
gown and diamonds.

Nothing can dim her beauty—lessen her allure. She

*as desirable now as she was when I first saw her, want-
ing her from the first...*

She had picked up the towel, was shaking it out and
draping it neatly over the veranda balustrade so it would
start to dry out. It was a simple, housewifely gesture, as
if she had done it a hundred times for him. As if they
were an established couple. It was a strange thought. At
odds with what he'd just reminded himself of. The fact
that transient affairs were all he wanted. That there was
nothing else it was safe for him to want.

She was smiling reprovingly at him. 'It won't dry
in a crumpled heap!' she reprimanded him with mock
sternness.

'Mea culpa,' he acknowledged in a penitential tone,
accepting her just criticism.

'Go and shower,' she told him. 'Then we can have
our sundowners and you can get on with grilling that
fish you caught! I'm starving! You must be too, after
that freezing swim!'

He gave a laugh, agreeing with her, and headed off
into the bathroom. Hunger growled in him. And not just
for his supper.

For much, much more.

But exactly for what, he was no longer sure.

Their sundowners were nothing more sophisticated
than a bottle of beer each, not even poured into glasses.
From time to time Salvatore tested the barbecue, turning the potatoes to cook them evenly. Slices of red pep-
per stood ready, beside the waiting fish. The salad was
dressed, and a packet of roasted nuts decanted into a
plastic bowl, each of them having a packet of crisps to
graze on as well.

Eventually Salvatore declared the moment right for grilling the peppers and fish, and proceeded to do so.

'For a man who enjoys the finest things in life,' Lana heard herself observe, humour in her voice, 'you're really very domesticated when you put your mind to it!'

He turned, giving a laugh. 'Do you think me one of those pampered playboys who fall apart if there's no one around to chef for them?' he riposted. 'I'm not quite so feeble, thank you!'

'No, but you're used to luxury,' she replied. 'Your world is so completely different from mine—'

He left the fish grilling, sitting down again and reaching for his beer, taking a mouthful.

'We're just people, Lana—you and I both. We're not so different.'

There was a smile in his voice, in his eyes—but there was more than just a smile in his eyes. Something that made her drop her own for a moment.

'We have a lot in common, really,' she heard him muse, and her gaze went back to him. He'd replaced his beer bottle on the table, was looking across the small wooden table at her. 'We have both had to survive tragedy, the untimely loss of our parents in traumatic circumstances. We've both agreed that marrying each other as we have, for very specific reasons, is not as insane as it might sound to others!'

There was a wry note in his voice at that, but then he went on, eyes holding hers.

'And we get on with each other well. We do, you know. It's easy for us to be in each other's company—I find it so, and I don't believe you don't. Look how we've got on when it comes to traipsing around the glories of Tuscany—and how well we're getting on here, now!'

He smiled again, warmth in his face, in his deep, dark eyes.

'Today has been good, hasn't it?' He gestured around him expansively. 'Basic this place might be, but what more do we need?' He lifted his beer bottle again, tilting it towards her. 'Let's drink to this place, shall we—because it's doing us both good?'

It was impossible to disagree with anything he'd said.

We do get on well—whether we're at the palazzo, or out sightseeing, or just chillaxing here in this uber-peaceful spot...

She wondered whether she should worry at it—but didn't. She just accepted it instead. It seemed the natural thing to do.

She made a wry face, tapping her beer bottle against his and taking a mouthful as he did, returning his *'Saluti!'* with a more British 'Cheers!'

Then the aroma from the barbecue distracted them, and Salvatore was standing up, removing the now nicely crisped fish and roasted peppers, plating them up. Then scooping up the soft-baked potatoes, putting one each on their plates.

Lana cut hers open, dropping a generous helping of butter into the steaming centre. Appetite speared within her. They settled down to eat companionably, both heartily tucking in to the simple but highly tasty supper.

We do get on well...he's right. And for people with such different backgrounds, we have more in common than one might suppose.

Her eyes rested on him as he reached for another beer, flicking open the top with practised ease, before taking a swallow straight from the bottle. In the dusk, and in the soft light from the storm lantern hanging from the balustrade over the veranda, the planes of his face were accentuated by the shadows cast on it. Enhancing—if enhancement were possible at all, she thought, giving an unconscious inner sigh—the sculpted perfection that was his.

He lowered his bottle, catching her gaze on him, slanting a smile at her. Something flickered in his eyes—something that seemed to quicken her pulse—but then his long lashes swept down, veiling it from her. But she had seen enough. He might be sticking to what he'd promised her that night after Florence, but she could not deny—however much she might wish to do so—the other searing and undeniable truth about what they shared in common...

The fact that, for all the complications between them, all the impossibility of what he wanted, their desire was as undeniable as it was unsuppressed.

She gave another sigh, inwardly this time. Knowing, as she dropped her gaze, that it was tinged with regret...

Regret for what surely was too impossible, too complicated to yield to...

'Ever rowed a boat before?' Salvatore was asking. 'No? Okay, so I'll teach you.'

He got her seated on the bench, an oar in either hand, and pushed the little craft out into deeper water before vaulting lightly in himself. Then he focussed on getting Lana to angle the oars correctly, before attempting to head off.

'Not bad,' he said approvingly as she did as he bade her. 'Shall we see if we can make it to the far side of the lake? See what's over there?'

They did, and beached beside a rocky promontory

which afforded them a perch on which to eat the picnic lunch they'd made after breakfast. Then they strolled off along another lakeside footpath, meandering along its gentle contours.

The day was passing easily, companionably. Salvatore was glad of it. Glad of a great deal.

Glad of that covert look she threw me last night, brief though it was.

But he would not—could not—rush her. Or pressurise her. It must come from her, the decision that he so wanted her to make. It must be right for her—completely right.

So that she can accept what is between us.

His eyes went to her as they settled themselves back in the rowing boat, with Salvatore doing the rowing this time. She sat back, hands resting widely on the gunwale on either side of her, lifting her beautiful face to the sunshine streaming down out of a cloudless sky, warm after the cool of the forest.

He felt something move within him, something he did not recognise.

How beautiful she is! How perfect—

Dimly, he knew that surely his desire for her would eventually pall, as all his affairs palled.

Just as my father's did.

No, he would not think about his father—about the serial womanising he'd spent his life pursuing. Never wanting to fall in love with anyone. *While the one woman who'd loved him he ignored. Left to pine, hopelessly, for him. A man who never loved her.*

He pulled his thoughts away from that, too. It was too painful. He'd witnessed his mother's pain at her husband's rejection of her, his indifference to her.

His gaze refocussed on Lana, drinking in her loveliness as he rowed her back to the simple chalet he'd brought her to. Would its peaceful remoteness, these peaceful days he was spending with her, far away from the world that had pressed upon them, bring him what he longed for?

He did not know. He could only hope.

And hope, for now, would have to do.

CHAPTER NINE

LANA FORKED THE last of the melt-in-the-mouth barbecued lamb fillet—richly marinaded since that morning with garlic, lemon and rosemary—and gave a sigh of repletion as she cleared her plate. It had been another good day of taking their ease in this beautiful remote spot. And another mouth-watering barbecue this evening, shared with Salvatore as she had shared the day with him.

'I hope you've left room for the roasted bananas.' He smiled at her, his own plate already empty. 'A shame we have no *gelato* to go with them, but the chalet doesn't run to a freezer. We'll make do with cream from the fridge instead. And douse them in amaretto for sweetness.'

They did, too, and as ever Lana lingered over the sheer luxury of eating guilt-free desserts. Around them night thickened, and the sound of owls haunted the forest around them. They were cocooned in the light from the oil lamp, which was throwing Salvatore's striking features into yet more striking *chiaroscuro*.

Lana was all too aware that she should suppress the thought, but it seemed too much effort. Her arms, her pecs and quads were tired from the unaccustomed exertion of rowing across the lake, and all she wanted to do was rest and relax. Not to make any effort. It would be an effort not to let herself do what she always seemed to want to do—let her eyes go to the man opposite her. The way they had right from the first...

Lingering over the glass of amaretto Salvatore had poured for her, in addition to dousing the barbecued bananas in it, feeling the rich liqueur's sweetness in her veins, she gave herself up to the indulgence of letting her gaze go where it wanted. It seemed easier, less effort, to do so.

They were no longer on the wooden chairs at the table below the veranda, next to the barbecue, but had repaired with their liqueurs to the bench on the veranda itself, padded with cushions filched from the settee. They sat there, not touching, keeping a space between them. The lightest of night breezes winnowed across the lake, refracting the starlight. The moon was riding high, silvering the dark waters of the lake. It was peaceful—balmy, even—and, replete and content, she went on gazing placidly out over the unchanging scene, catching the scent of the pine trees, the deep, earthy green smell of the forest all around, savouring the sweet, strong, almond liqueur warming her throat as it slid down in tiny sips.

Salvatore's long legs were stretched out in front of him and his head was turned towards her. He'd finished his amaretto, set the glass down on the veranda floor, under the bench. He was looking across at her.

'Another good day?' he asked.

She could hear the smile in his voice.

'Another good day,' she agreed.

She took another sip of her liqueur. It was sweet and warm in her veins. She let her gaze play on his face, knowing she wanted to, knowing she should not, half veiling her eyes and knowing she should make some remark about being tired after a good but long day, go inside, climb the ladder to her private bed.

Knowing that she should not go on sitting there, a mere cushion's space between them, while the wind blew across the dark lake and the moon dipped down towards the canopy of the trees on the far shore, painting the world with silver.

Knowing the veiling of her eyes did not disguise the fact that she was gazing at him, drinking him in as he sat there, his cuffs turned back, the vee of his throat exposed to the night air, the planes of his face perfected by the low light that touched the sable of his hair with gold.

Knowing he knew that she was gazing at him… That she could not help but do so.

For how could she help it? The question shaped in her head hopelessly, helplessly. She had always wanted to gaze at him. From the very first.

But I fought it—I fought it because…because…

Why had she fought it? There were reasons, she knew. Reasons she had run from him that night after Florence. Reasons she had told herself that his kiss at the Duchessa's had been for show only. Reasons she had insisted their strange marriage be entirely celibate.

Reasons. Complications…

I married for money—so I can't confuse why I married with all that I feel and want and yearn for…

Could she?

Here, away from the watching world, it was just him and her. Here, they were not some fictitious man and wife. Here, they were only man and woman. And very, very real…

Thoughts, feelings, longings rippled within her like currents of water…flowing in complicated eddies…finding no outlet. Another owl hooted, a breath of moving air rippled the lake water, a fish splashed far out in the centre of the lake then was gone.

'So, what are we to do, hmm?'

Salvatore's low voice broke the silence lapping all around them. His eyes were meeting hers, holding hers. She felt the breath still in her throat, her eyes searching his as if looking for the meaning in the words he'd just spoken. Words that echoed the confusion in her own mind.

But she knew their meaning. Knew it even before he reached his hand towards her in the shadowed light, meshing their fingers. She felt the strength of his, their warmth twining with hers. His eyes were still holding hers.

'Can you truly not see how very simple this is?' he asked her.

His voice was husky and it did things to her...things that echoed the sweet warmth of the almond liqueur, the warm pulse of her blood. Her gaze searched his almost pleadingly. The pulse of her blood grew stronger, her breath shallower. His strong fingers meshed so easily with hers...

'But it isn't,' she answered him, her voice low. Pained. 'It isn't simple at all!'

He shook his head. 'It is,' he contradicted her. 'So very simple.'

He drew a breath, inhaling slowly, never letting go of her eyes, his fingers tightening on hers, the thumb lying across her palm moving slightly, so very slightly, across its surface. His voice, when he spoke, was lower than hers, and still more husky. His gaze was intense, holding hers.

'Here…now…our marriage is very far away. And why we married—the reasons for it, so particular only to ourselves—are very far away too. Do not think about them—they have no place here. No relevance. They have nothing at all to do with what is happening between us! What has been there from the start. You have always known it—you know it now. What is here now has always been here. It is between *us*, you and me, the attraction we have felt for each other every day!'

A smile, half-rueful, half-sensuous, played about his mouth.

'Had we never married we would still be here, in Italy, under the stars,' he said. 'I would have come back for you even if I hadn't needed to do anything about Giavanna and her father! I would have come back, Lana.'

She felt him lift her hand…lift it and graze it softly, sensuously, with his mouth. It was like the touch of silk velvet.

'For you.'

His eyes were pouring into hers like wine she could not resist, and nor did she wish to. She could feel her blood singing in her veins, the breath catching in her throat.

'I would have come back, my most *bellissima* Lana, to make you mine. As I do now.' His eyes were holding hers…a silken noose. 'If you will have me,' he said.

He leant towards her and she caught the scent of his masculinity, potent and seductive…oh, so seductive… as his mouth found hers. Her eyelids fluttered shut. She gave herself up to the sensation. Could not help but give herself to it, so gentle, so arousing. It melted something within her. Something that had been knotted tightly… that confusing, complicated mesh that had bound her, trapped her, since the moment she had agreed to undertake their strange marriage.

Was she confusing money with desire?

But the money goes with the marriage. The desire is only within ourselves—

She heard his words in her head again—saying that even had he not needed to make their strange marriage he still would have come back to her. To make her his.

And I would have gone to him—I know that. I would have lain down my burden of endless work to try and pay my mortgage—would have thrown in the towel, accepted the loss Malcolm has imposed on me. Accepted, too, what flared between me and Salvatore from the very first time I set eyes on him.

She felt her mind move, her thoughts taking her to the place she knew she was meant to be.

I accept it now.

He drew away from her, but only a fraction, his eyes in the dim light warm and intimate.

'So will you?' His low voice was a question. 'Will you have me? Just as I am—just as you are? Here, now, under the stars? In this quiet and private place?'

He smiled, warm and intimate, like his eyes still holding hers, searching hers.

'It is so very, very simple. That we desire each other—'

His mouth found hers again, as softly sensual as before, tasting her lips for longer this time, not releasing her. And she did not want him to. Did not want to do anything but give herself to the moment, to the sensuous arousal he was inciting in her. She tried to think why it was that she should not be kissing him, but it was impossible. Impossible to do anything but yield to him, to let him part her lips, deepen his kiss, tighten his clasp on her hand pressed between them.

A million nerve-endings were firing in her, and the sweetness of his touch was melting her again. And then he was lifting his mouth away, gazing down at her with a rueful half smile playing on his lips.

'So what are we going to do, Lana? We're here, in this beautiful space, alone together, under the night. We desire each other. It is truly as simple as that.'

He held on to her hand, their fingers still meshed, as he drew back from her.

'This is a simple place, Lana, for simple truths.' He gestured all around him. 'It's why I brought you here. Away from anything that's complicated. That you think is complicated.'

He smiled an inviting smile, meeting her eyes, now lifted helplessly to his.

'This has been waiting to happen right from the first. We have both known it. And now...here...is the time.'

He brushed her lips with his again, lightly, softly, then drew back, taking her empty glass from her nerveless fingers to place it beside his own. Then he drew her to her feet.

As his eyes held hers, never letting them go, she felt the pulse at her throat thudding, the haze in her mind filling it. Beyond him, the dark waters of the lake stretched to the unseen forest beyond. It was so quiet, so far away from everything.

Just us—just here. Together.

And suddenly out of nowhere, rippling through her like the night breeze in the conifers all around, she knew that that was what she wanted. She heard his words again—'*So simple...so very simple...*'

And that was what it was. As simple as the moonli[g]
silvering the lake, the sweet night air, the call of owls
the forest, the quietness all around them.

So very simple.

He said nothing, and nor did she. There was no ne
to. And that, too, was very simple.

As simple as going indoors.

His hand still holding hers.

The mezzanine bed took them into its close confi[n]
and they took each other into an embrace. He laid [h]
down upon it, and she was pliant in the soft lowering
her willing body. The light was very dim up here, [b]
she did not need light to know him—to find him w[ith]
her hands lifted to his chest, pressed against its musc[le]
wall as he leaned over her. His body was warm and fir[m]
and she could feel the contours of his ribs through [the]
material of his shirt.

Her fingers found the buttons, slipped them one [by]
one. He let her do it, smiling down at her, his han[ds]
planted either side of her head as, little by little, she [re-]
vealed his body to her, slowly, carefully, sliding the sh[irt]
from his shoulders.

He shrugged it off, discarding it. 'Now my turn,'
said. He was smiling, his eyes holding hers, his gaze [in-]
timate and warm.

He eased her tee shirt from her, lifting it at her wa[ist]
to slide it upward. She wore no bra—not here in the [for-]
est—and as the high, small mounds of her breasts we[re]
exposed she heard him catch his breath.

'Por Dio, but you are so beautiful!' It was a sigh. [A]n
exhalation. A homage.

She felt his head lower—felt, with a rush of sw[eet]

pleasure, his mouth close over one breast. Felt it flower beneath his ministrations, its sensitivity increased a hundredfold, a thousandfold. She arched her neck in pleasure, offering herself to him, first one breast and then the other.

Then he was pulling away from her. She gave a cry of protest, but all he was doing was rapidly and purposefully shedding the rest of his clothes.

And hers.

And then he was coming down over her, and the weight of his body was on hers, his mouth seeking hers, finding it as her mouth opened to his, velvet upon velvet.

Her hands reached around the strong column of his back, glorying in its sculpted contours as his kiss deepened. She gave a sudden gasp of realisation. And glorying in the strength of his arousal, pressing against her.

Excitement quickened within her, an answering arousal, and heat beating up from the core of her body, flushing through her. She gave a low moan and then his mouth was leaving hers, sliding down the shallow valley between her ripened breasts, down over the sleek smoothness below…and further yet.

She gave a soft cry, eyes widening, as his hands lowered to her waist. His own body was arching now, to give him access to what he wanted…

Her thighs slackened. It was impossible to resist, because resisting—oh, dear God—was the very last thing she wanted to do. It was impossible not to want what he was doing now…not to want the incredible, delicate, tantalising, exquisitely arousing sensations he was drawing from her. They mounted and mounted and mounted. She felt the heat within her rise. The pleasure he was giving her was so intense, so incredible, that surely it was impossible that it should exist at all.

She felt her body melt, her head roll back, low moans breaking from her throat. She said his name,—an invocation...a plea. And at his name he lifted away, his hands sliding around her hips, tilting them upwards, opening her to him...

To his possession.

His complete possession.

She gave a gasp, a cry, her hands folding over his shoulders as his mouth found hers again, tasting and melding and fusing...even as his body melded and fused with hers.

He moved within her and she was folding around him, possessing him even as he was possessing her, and her body was melting...melting...

And then—as his slow, expert, ever-deepening thrusts within her aroused silken tissues brought her closer and closer still to what she ached for, to what she craved, what she sought with all her throbbing being—like molten metal her body became one single, all-consuming white-hot fusion with his.

She was drawing him deeper, closer, feeling her throbbing tissues convulse around him as wave after wave of a pleasure she had never known existed, never known *could* exist overwhelmed her. And she was crying out, her fingers clutching at him, clinging to him, clinging to his body now surging within her. And now it was him crying out, head bowed, low and urgent and guttural, as his moment came, matching hers as they were both fused in absolute union.

Her sated body gave one last long convulsion around him and then she was drawing his body down to hers, cradling it in her embracing arms, holding him within her, her heart hammering against his. Exhaustion swept over her, but her body was glowing in the flame, heat still in her tissues, ripples of pleasure still going through her. She did not want to let him go…did not want to lose him…could not bear to do so.

She wrapped her arms more tightly around him and he held her close against him, limbs meshed, their heartbeats gradually slowing. He was murmuring to her…soft words, sweet words…in his native language, his mouth gently kissing the column of her throat, holding her close in his arms. So very close.

It was the only place in all the world she wanted to be.

It was, she knew with absolute certainty as they held each other, as simple as that.

Salvatore turned to smile at Lana, his fishing line now cast, as the little boat bobbed gently on the lake water. She was lolling back, legs outstretched, one bare foot resting on his thigh with intimate, easy relaxation. She smiled when he smiled at her. An intimate, easy smile.

Idly, he wondered whether it might be possible to make love to her in the boat while waiting for the fish to bite.

As though reading his mind, Lana turned her smile to a laugh.

'No—don't even think of it!' she warned. 'I do *not* want to end up in that freezing cold water because we've rocked the boat too much! Wait till we get back to shore!'

'How do you know what I was thinking?' he asked with an answering laugh.

Her eyes glinted. 'Female intuition,' she said.

He slid his hand around her bare foot, lifting it to drop

a light kiss on the slender arch. Even her feet were the most beautiful he'd ever seen.

Everything about her is the most beautiful! Everything...

Including, most of all, the way she had given herself to him. Given in to what had been between them from the first. To what was now flourishing like a glorious flower opening to the warmth of the sun...

He let his lashes dip down over his eyes as he released her foot, which once again rested on his thigh. It was a dangerous place for it to rest, and he told her so.

'You might find I suddenly lose interest in fishing,' he warned her.

'I'll take that as a compliment,' she teased. 'Me versus fishing...hmm, tough call...'

'No competition,' he informed her. 'It's fishing every time.'

It was a lie. A blatant lie. And she knew it. It would have been impossible for her not to. In the remoteness of the log cabin they could do as they pleased, when they pleased—and it pleased him very much to demonstrate, comprehensively, just how much he desired her.

She was all that he had thought she would be, had known she would be. And more.

Much more.

Had he ever known a woman like her? It was a stupid question—one that had only one answer. An answer he did not need to give even to himself.

All he had to give himself was what there was between them. Now, here in this lakeside idyll, and way beyond. At the *palazzo*, in Rome, on business trips—it didn't matter. Lana would be with him by day and, of absolute certainty, by night. In his arms. His bed.

Just as he had wanted from the first. Married or not married—nothing would change that.

Lana glanced around her bedroom. It seemed strange to come back to the *palazzo* after their lakeside idyll. More complicated. Outwardly, nothing had changed, and yet everything had changed. Self-consciousness burned in her, as though all the household staff could see how very different things were now between her and Salvatore. But the only real change was that the communicating door between her bedroom and Salvatore's was now unlocked.

Yet for all that had changed between them since their stay at the lakeside chalet, one thing had not. Whenever a member of staff addressed her as *signora*, treating her as though she were mistress here, she still felt a fake. A fraud. Here under false pretences.

Her expression flickered as she stood looking out over the wide, beautiful gardens. Salvatore had said it was simple, their desire for each other—a desire they consummated night after night. But how could it be simple when the world thought their marriage real? When they themselves knew the truth? Knew that it was not designed to mean what marriage *should* mean—that it was not to last…was to end, before next spring turned to summer, in a divorce planned from the very outset.

She turned away from the window, her thoughts still troubled. And they would be more troubled yet, she knew. Today they were driving back to Rome. There were social engagements to attend, work meetings for Salvatore. Their honeymoon was over.

Except that it was never a honeymoon at all—because I am not a real wife to Salvatore. We are having an affair, that is all—whatever the world thinks, what-

ever his household here thinks, whatever his friends in Rome think.

She picked up her handbag, went downstairs. Salvatore was already in the car, waiting for her. She got in and he kissed her softly, eyes smiling.

'Looking forward to Rome?' he asked.

She bit her lip, unwilling to answer.

He started the engine and the car crunched slowly over the gravel towards the gilded gates beyond, now opening to let him pass.

'It will be easier for you this time,' he told her.

The expression in his eyes told her why he thought so. She wished she could agree with him. But it was impossible to do so.

So she said nothing. It seemed the easiest thing to do.

CHAPTER TEN

SALVATORE'S MOOD WAS good. It had never been better. It was impossible it should be otherwise. He had everything in the world he wanted. He had stopped Giavanna and Roberto in their ambitious tracks, his life was going just where he wanted, and right now that meant one thing only.

Lana...

Her name purred in his head. Her image was always there.

Beautiful, breathtaking—and *his*! Just as he had known she would be. Because how could it ever have been otherwise After desiring her so much?

It was impossible that such desire should have been denied any longer, for reasons that were as irrelevant as they were pointless. And hers was as strong as his—did he not know that now, with night after burning night in each other's arms?

The week they'd spent at the chalet by the lake had proved that completely. *He'd* proved it. And he would go on doing so now they were here in Rome as well. He was eager to show her off—not, this time, simply because she was a blocking move, to counter Giavanna and Roberto, but because he just wanted everyone to see him with her.

Why? Why do you want everyone to see you with her?

The question flickered in his head now, as he got out of the car, which then drove off into the busy Rome traffic, leaving Salvatore to stride the few paces to the fashionable bar where he was meeting Luc Dinardi.

Why? He answered his own question dismissively. Because he wanted to—that was all. He didn't have to justify it. Or explain it. Or even think about it. Let alone give any consideration to the fact that he'd never felt any need to show off the previous women in his life.

Well, he hadn't had to, had he? he thought impatiently. The women he'd had affairs with had come from the same social circles as himself—and in Rome everyone knew each other, and who was with who, or not. Whereas Lana was new to them.

But she's fitting in perfectly.

He'd already paid tribute to her in that first week of their marriage, telling her that she was playing Signora Luchesi flawlessly. And she still was. At all the glittering social events he had taken her to—showing her off—she'd been superb. She seemed to have made a hit with everyone—from his personal friends to old-school social arbiters such as the Duchessa, who had—as she had said she would that evening when Giavanna had shown off her spoilt brat credentials to perfection in chucking champagne over Lana—invited Lana to lunch. She was with the Duchess now, which was why he himself had agreed to meet up with Luc today.

He strode into the crowded bar, spotting Luc and heading towards him.

'Salva—*ciao*! It's good to see you again!' Luc greeted him warmly, with a cheerful slap on his shoulder. 'Let me look at you.' Eyes with a familiar worldly expression flicked over Salvatore. Then…

'Yes, marriage is definitely suiting you!' Luc said with an approving air, amusement in his voice. 'Who'd have thought?' he murmured, the amusement now more pronounced. 'Salvatore Luchesi—renowned bachelor of Rome, always playing the field—now a good and faithful husband!'

Salvatore tensed. 'Good and faithful' husbands did not run in the Luchesi family.

For a moment he felt an impulse to tell Luc the truth about Lana and himself—about the reason he'd married her. To disclaim any assumption that she was a permanent fixture in his life. But he bit his tongue. If he gave Luc any hint of the real reason for his marriage it would be all over Rome, courtesy of that one-woman gossip mill Stephanie, to whom Luc would be unable to resist passing on such a juicy morsel. And then it would reach Roberto and Giavanna, undoing all his efforts to get them off his case.

No, he had to keep up the fiction that Lana was going to stick around as his wife long-term.

Ruthlessly, he turned the tables on his friend, to avoid any further discussion of his own marriage, let alone the reason for it.

'And what about you, Luc? Are you ever going to make an honest woman of Stephanie?'

Luc gave a shrug. 'Oh, you know the score, Salva. She and I run around together when there's no one else for either of us. But it's out of habit as much as anything. I don't think anything will change. Well…' he made a face '…unless during one of our together periods she tells me she's pregnant, I guess!'

Salvatore looked at him. 'Would you know it was yours, though? Given your mutual lack of commitment to each other?'

Luc looked away for a moment, a strange expression on his face. 'That might not matter so much,' he said slowly.

Salvatore frowned. 'You'd raise another man's child?' His voice sharpened unconsciously.

'If the other man didn't want to be a father…then, yes, I possibly would. Unless, of course, Steph didn't want me any longer, only the other man.'

Salvatore took another mouthful of his martini. It tasted suddenly more sour than astringent. He put the glass back on the bar.

You're not wanted any longer…

The words echoed in his head. He knew the pain that could be inflicted when someone was told that.

'My darling boy, I have to accept—I have no choice but to accept—that your father simply does not want me any longer. Not in that way. As the mother to his son— yes, of course, and that will never change. But for himself? Ah, no, that has long gone.'

His father's rejection of his mother had hurt her so deeply. He had seen it, witnessed it as a young teenager when he'd started to understand just how unhappy his mother had been made by his father's constant infidelities. Yet she had not wanted to end the marriage either. Not just because she would not break up the family, but because, he had come to realise, his mother had constantly hoped that one day his father would turn away from all his other women and come back to the woman who'd loved him through thick and thin.

Instead, what had awaited his parents had not been

some fairy-tale joyous reconciliation but a devastating plane crash, cutting short their lives.

He pulled his mind away from such painful memories, realising that Luc was speaking to him.

'Talking of pregnancy, my old friend,' he was saying, looking straight at Salvatore, his voice half-humorous, half-cautious, 'you do realise that that was the suspicion Steph had about why you married so unexpectedly?'

'Absolutely not!' Salvatore refuted, tensing unconsciously.

He changed the subject decisively, to that of a recent football match, and Luc picked up the challenge for they supported opposing teams. With other sporting topics it served to take them through a long and convivial lunch.

Lana took a careful mouthful of her wine, conscious that she needed to be on her very best behaviour. She was lunching with the Duchessa in her private family apartments above the grandly magnificent *piano nobile*, where the charity fundraiser had been held.

The Duchessa was being very warm, very gracious, but she was also, Lana was aware, drawing her out. Thankfully, she seemed to accept at face level the fact that she and Salvatore had had a whirlwind romance and had acted on impulse, and there were no regrets.

'I am glad to hear it.' The Duchessa smiled. She looked directly at Lana. 'You are aware that Salvatore's parents were killed very tragically in a plane crash?'

Lana nodded. 'Yes, he has told me,' she said quietly. She took a low breath. 'Mine, too, were killed. In a car crash—'

'Ah,' said the Duchessa, and her eyes rested on Lana—she could almost feel it. A beringed hand was pressed lightly on hers in a sympathetic gesture. 'That is a bond between you indeed.'

Was it? Lana wondered. Her loss had driven her into the arms of Malcolm—an unwise reaction to the emptiness of her life. But her life was not empty any more. She had Salvatore—

She swallowed, her throat tight suddenly.

I've got him for a year, that's all. No more than that.

The Duchessa's hand was lifting from hers, and she was speaking again.

'Salvatore's mother was my goddaughter,' she was saying. 'She was very unhappy in her marriage.'

'He…he told me as much,' Lana replied.

'Yes. I've often thought that it was his father's philandering that made Salvatore avoid marriage,' the Duchessa mused. 'Because he did not want to risk discovering he was no better than his father.' Her voice changed. 'Which is why I am so glad that he has overcome that reluctance—thanks to you.'

Lana stayed silent. What could she say? She wished the Duchessa would stop talking about such things. They were really nothing to do with her. Discomfort filled her—both at the fact that she was being treated as though she were Salvatore's wife for real, and because it only emphasised to her that she was not.

I'm just his lover—his current lover.

Emotion twisted inside her. Though it should not.

I've known from the start how temporary our time is together.

He had been straight with her right from the off. Straight about the reasons he wanted them to marry and about when their marriage would end. Straight, too, about his desire for her. He had not deceived her in anything.

Malcolm had deceived her from the start—had had a malevolent hidden agenda up his thieving sleeve.

Salvatore's honesty set him totally apart from Malcolm. He was a far more worthwhile human being. One it would be very easy to come to feel more for than what held them to each other now merited…

She shied away from the thought—it was not a safe place for her mind to go.

What she had with Salvatore now was all she would ever have. She knew that—accepted it.

Because I must. Because his honesty from the start has spelled out all that we can ever be to each other. He's never pretended otherwise. I must be glad of that.

And yet gladness, suddenly, was not what she felt at all…

'You look troubled, my dear…'

The voice of the Duchessa pierced her thoughts—thoughts she did not want to have.

'But I am sure there is no need. Salvatore has eyes only for you!'

Lana's eyes veiled.

For now, yes.

For now, Salvatore was ardent in his attentions, his desires. But they had a shelf life—a time limit.

This time next year it will all be over. I shall be back in England, processing our divorce. Our pre-planned divorce.

How would that go down with his friends? His circle here in Rome? She didn't know. It was not her concern. Her only concern would be what she made of her life after Salvatore Luchesi had left it.

A sense of sudden bleakness filled her.

The Duchessa was changing the subject, saying something about an opera gala that was in the offing, and Lana was grateful. She could not take any more close examination of her marriage, her relationship with Salvatore, nor of her reactions to such examination.

Least of all any examination of those reactions…

'Have you been to New York often?' Salvatore asked, turning to Lana, sitting beside him in First Class, with an enquiring smile.

'Fashion Week—twice a year. So more often than I can count!' she answered.

She was glad to be accompanying Salvatore on a business trip. Glad to be out of Rome, where she was under constant surveillance, or so she uncomfortably felt, with everyone treating her as if she truly were the woman Salvatore Luchesi had chosen to be his wife—to make a life with—when she was no such thing at all.

It would be much easier being on her own with him, as they had been at the lakeside chalet. Far more honest. And after New York they would be flying down to the Bahamas.

'I want you all to myself again,' Salvatore had told her, his gaze warm and possessive.

'Me too,' she'd said, and smiled.

They got exactly that.

Their cabana at the exclusive resort opened onto a tiny secluded cove, private and for their own use, sheltered from the world by the palm trees waving in the cooling breeze. Their days were lazy, with their butler arriving on call with drinks, with gourmet meals, with anything they wanted.

But their wants were simple.

Each other.

Making love under the palm-thatched roof of their cabana. Making love in the plunge pool. Making love on the silver sand at midnight. Making love whenever desire swept over them and brought them into each other's arms, leaving them sated and fulfilled, still in each other's arms...

For Lana it was an ecstasy she had never thought possible. Had never thought existed. Malcolm, she now realised, had been incredibly selfish, pleasing only himself. Whereas Salvatore—

Sweet memory and eager anticipation mingled inside her like honey and cream...

In Salvatore's arms it was as if only they existed—nothing and no one else. Only the desire he aroused in her with the soft caresses of his hands, the skilled exploration of his fingertips, the velvet of his mouth, the lean strength of his body moving over hers...

Their limbs would mingle, her hands clutching his shoulders, her thighs winding around his, her spine arching. And then would come the low, pleading moans in her throat as he brought her ever nearer to that incredible, unbelievable moment when her blood would rush in her veins, her heart pounding as her body convulsed around his, and a tide of pleasure so exquisite she cried out would lift her to a heaven that she had never known existed—that could only exist in Salvatore's arms, in his strong embrace, in the passion of his desire for her. Of hers for him...

When she was lying in his arms, time stopped. All time. The sun rose and set and the days passed, slipping one by one into a past that existed as little as did the future.

She would not let there be a future. Not yet. Not when she wanted to embrace only the simplicity of what she had with Salvatore now, to embrace the bliss that came in his arms, the sense of ease and companionship that came just by being with him. The happiness…

They stood with their arms wound about each other on the silvered sand, still warm from the day's heat, watching the sun slip into the shallow turquoise sea, content to do nothing more than watch it set on another day of happiness.

And on their return to the *palazzo* they watched it set from the little stone gazebo at the far side of the garden, where once Lana had sat with her paperback, Salvatore still a stranger to her. He was a stranger no longer.

And they watched it set from halfway up a Swiss alp, when Salvatore took her with him on a business trip to Zurich. And then again from the penthouse suite of a high-rise hotel in Frankfurt… They watched as it bathed the Île de la Cité in Paris in golden light…watched it shine on the canals of Amsterdam and the lake of Geneva—wherever his business affairs took him.

There was only one business destination to which she declined to accompany him—London.

She would be there again soon enough…

When their sunsets had slipped from present into past.

She did not think about it. Would not. There was no point. She was with him now, sharing his life, his bed. When he no longer needed her to be his wife she would not be.

It was, after all, very simple.

Best to keep it that way.

The way Salvatore had told her it was.

Salvatore swung into the Viscari Roma, glad of the air-conditioning within. Rome in late summer was hot, and it felt even hotter after the rain London had been experiencing. He wished Lana had come with him, but she never came on his London trips.

'You only come abroad with me for the sightseeing!' he'd accused her with a laugh.

'I was never keen on London even when I had to live there,' she'd answered. 'I'll be selling up and moving out once I'm back in the UK permanently.'

He'd found himself frowning slightly at what she'd said. Then put it down to his disappointment that she didn't want to come with him. He didn't want to be away from her even for a handful of days.

And now he was back in Rome. He had flown in that very evening, in time to join Lana in celebrating Luc's birthday with a convivial dinner. It was to be here at the Viscari again, in the same private salon where he'd first introduced Lana to his friends in the spring.

He frowned again. Had so much time really passed since then? Had Lana really been part of his life that long already? It seemed to have flashed by.

Maybe, he thought, it was because disentangling his affairs from Roberto was proving easier than he'd been prepared for. And the main reason for that was that, far from obstructing him, Roberto was co-operating in the process.

For that, Salvatore thought cynically, he had Giavanna to thank. Thwarted in her ambitions for himself, she had set her sights on another prey. This time, much to her doting father's approval, the heir to a viscountcy. Salvatore wished them well of each other.

Now, making his way to the bar, where they were gathering before dinner, he let his eyes go straight to Lana, decorously sipping a cocktail, one fabulously long leg crossed elegantly over the other, looking, as ever, a complete knock-out in an iridescent mid-blue sheath that moulded her beautiful body. A stab of pride and proprietorship went through Salvatore, his eyes only for her.

And she had eyes only for him.

As she saw him her face lit, and she said his name in happy greeting. He kissed her cheeks, then greeted the others. Laura's pregnancy was advanced, and he could see Vito was being very protective of her.

Luc arrived shortly after, Stephanie with him, as exuberant as ever. She and Luc had had one of their periodic splits, each amusing themselves with a different partner, but were now back with each other again. It was a strange relationship, and one Salvatore could not fathom. The words Luc had said to him a while back came back into his head—that he would be prepared to stand by Stephanie if she ever got pregnant by a man who didn't want her. What would persuade a man to do that?

He gave a mental shrug, setting aside such a personally irrelevant question, settling down to an enjoyable evening.

A decisive glint formed in his eyes as he ran them over Lana. She was more beautiful than ever. Her figure, now that her model's ultra-low-calorie diet was long gone, was more rounded now, deliciously curvaceous in all the right places. He could not wait to celebrate his return to Italy that night with her...

Lana stepped out of the ferociously expensive famous-name boutique in the Via dei Condotti, and stopped short.

'Lana, *ciao*! Been spending more of Salvatore's money? What gorgeous gowns have you bought this time?'

The voice greeting her was friendly, the question humorously expressed, but Lana could hear the barb in it.

And she wasn't surprised. The person hailing her on the pavement was Giavanna Fabrizzi.

Lana schooled her expression into one of politeness. 'Hello, Giavanna,' she said in a friendly enough tone.

'You can wish me happy,' Giavanna announced, holding up her hand with an air of triumph to show off an engagement ring. 'It's been in Ernesto's family for centuries,' Giavanna confided with an air of smugness 'Every *viscontessa* has worn it—I shall be the next.'

Lana's smile was genuine. 'I'm really glad you've found your happy ending,' she said.

Giavanna smiled at her. Did the smile reach her eyes? Lana wasn't sure. She remained wary of the girl, for all her apparent friendliness now.

'Just like you did,' said Giavanna. 'And,' she added, 'that ex of yours.'

Lana tensed. Giavanna was lifting her phone out of her handbag, bringing up a photo.

'He certainly got lucky!' Giavanna was saying, holding up her phone for Lana to see.

Her eyes went to the photo, clearly from some celebrity's website. It was of one of Hollywood's top female movie stars, and at her side was Malcolm. Looking more handsome than ever. Bleached blond, and with a blinding smile of newly capped and whitened teeth. Looking incredibly pleased with himself.

The text below leapt out at her. The dominating phrase was: *Marriage plans with latest hunky leading man...*

A white fury filled Lana. So *that* was what he'd done with *her* money! Taken it to Hollywood with him to splurge on his career.

She forced her fury down. What did it matter what Malcolm had blown her money on?

Giavanna was looking at her expectantly, and now Lana could not mistake the gleam of malice in her eyes. She would not rise to it, though.

'Mal moved on a long time ago,' she said dismissively.

'As did you,' came the reply.

'Indeed,' Lana replied evenly. 'As did I.'

She made some polite remark, wishing Giavanna all the best for her wedding, and then made her escape, getting into the car she had summoned from the boutique when she'd finished shopping.

That encounter with Giavanna had disturbed her tranquility, reminding her of a time in her life she didn't want to think about any longer, even though the ramifications of it—the crushing debt Mal's perfidy had dumped on her—still cast a long shadow.

But Mal himself was out of her life. Nothing left of him but a photo.

One day all I'll have of Salvatore will be photos. Photos and memories. Nothing more.

She felt a hollow inside her as she heard the words inside her head, and she gazed out of the car window at the streets of Rome going by, wanting only to forget them. Not wanting to ask herself why that was.

'I have to fly to Milan next week. Will you come with me? You could refresh your wardrobe,' Salvatore remarked.

They were back at the *palazzo*, and he was glad. It was cooler here, and he and Lana made good use of the pool. How long ago it seemed since he had first seen her spread-eagled on that lounger, showing him nearly all of her fabulous body for his delectation…

It hadn't been his to enjoy then. But now… His eyes went to her across the dinner table where they sat out on the terrace. Now she was most definitely his to enjoy. Her beauty was richer, and riper than ever. Her Italian diet was enhancing her beauty every day. There even seemed to be a glow about her…

'My wardrobe is bulging at the seams!' Lana answered him with a laugh. 'How long do you need to spend in Milan?'

'A few days, no more.' An idea struck him. 'We could head for the Lakes—before the rains arrive in the autumn. How does that sound?'

'Better than Milan, I must say. To be honest,' she said, 'Milan doesn't really appeal—I've been there so often.'

'Join me on the last day, and then we can take off for the Lakes,' Salvatore said promptly. 'All we have to choose is which one. Como is the closest to Milan.'

'Como it is, then,' she smiled.

He smiled back warmly. It would be good to show Lana the Lakes. Have her at his side.

It's always good to be with her—to have her with me.

The thought in his head brought him the usual nod of satisfaction. But it was followed by another in its wake.

Will it always be good? And how long is 'always'? If you can get shot of Roberto in less time than you thought it would take, now that he's co-operating, what happens about Lana? You won't need her…

The question hung in his consciousness as his gaze rested on her. He set it aside. Reached for the wine bottle instead, refilling their glasses. Starting to tell her about Lake Como.

A much better subject to think about.

Lana walked into the pool house, pulling off her top as she did so. The heat was such that the only relief other than going indoors—which seemed a shame on such a lovely day—was the pool. She dropped her top on to the slatted wooden bench, peeled off her shorts and panties, reaching for her one-piece. She did not need to tan, she was quite brown enough—even her tummy.

She glanced down, frowning slightly. She had definitely become rounder and softer, since abandoning her low-calorie modelling diet. Salvatore was a big fan of her curvier figure, and she smiled reminiscently. He'd set off for Milan that morning, and she missed him already.

Perhaps she should have gone with him, even though Milan was not her favourite place—too many frenzied fashion shows. But spending some time at Lake Como sounded far more attractive. It would be their last chance to see the Lakes before autumn. And by spring she would be back in London.

Heaviness pressed at her. She did not want to think about the end of her time with Salvatore. Wanted only to go on enjoying this time with him. While she had him.

She shook her head to clear such pointless thoughts, tugging her swimsuit up her legs, over her hips and tummy. She had to stretch the fabric to do so, and looked down at herself again. The roundness of her tummy seemed accentuated, and she frowned again. She was definitely putting on weight—quite a lot, it seemed. She almost looked—

In mid-tug, she froze, eyes widening in shock. Something Laura had said to her that very first time she'd met Salvatore's friends was suddenly in her head.

'You won't ever get away with hiding even the tiniest baby bump!'

The words hung there, like a hammer suspended over her head. She was unable to un-hear them…

Instantly into her head came denial. No, of course she wasn't! She couldn't be. It was impossible. More than impossible.

Unthinkable.

Because it would change everything—everything!— between Salvatore and me…

Blindly, she pulled her clothes back on and walked back up to the *palazzo,* feeling her heart thudding in her chest. She had to know! She would go to a *farmacia*…buy at testing kit. Right now—this afternoon. Tension racked through her as she hurried indoors, seeing a maid, asking for a car to be brought round for her straight away.

I have to know. I have to know for certain. I just have to.

Salvatore put down his phone, frowning. Lana wasn't picking up. He texted her instead, saying he wanted to show her where they'd be staying on Lake Como, right at the lake's edge. She was going to be flying up to Milan tomorrow afternoon, and then they'd set off for the lake.

A bit less rustic than our last lakeside holiday!

He'd ended by attaching a photo of the luxury villa hotel with its ornate frontage and boat dock.

He waited for her reply. It did not come. He phoned her again. No answer. Only voicemail. He left a message, asking her to phone him back.

After forty minutes of fruitless waiting, he phoned home. Spoke to his housekeeper.

'But the *signora* set out this morning to join you!' Signora Guardi told him. 'She said she wanted to surprise you—'

Salvatore froze.

CHAPTER ELEVEN

HER FLAT SMELT musty after so many months left empty. Mechanically, Lana went around opening windows to let in fresh air, despite the damp chill outside, flicking on the heating, filling the kettle. She was going through the motions, but inside she was collapsing. Less than twenty-four hours ago she had been at the *palazzo.* Staring at that plastic strip with a hollowing of her insides.

I thought it would reassure me—not devastate me!

She had felt panic wash over her, but had fought it back. Fought to retain control of herself. Fought to *think…*

And she had done that all evening—thinking and thinking and thinking, until her head ached with it. Every thought piercing her like the thrust of a knife.

She was pregnant. Something that she had never envisaged as even a possibility. And something she never, *never* would have wanted—for one stark, implacable reason.

Because it was not part of the deal. The deal she had struck with Salvatore. The very simple, very unambiguous deal.

I play the role of his wife—he pays off my mortgage in our pre-planned divorce settlement.

And the fact that playing the role of his wife had turned into her having a searing affair with him changed nothing! Nothing at all.

She'd paced her bedroom at the *palazzo*, back and forth, trying to see it in another way. But it had been impossible.

He never signed up for this—me getting pregnant. He never signed up to anything more than a year with me.

She'd gazed bleakly out of the darkened window, seeing nothing of the night beyond, expression drawn. A year was all he wanted—he'd been up-front, honest, straight-up. That honesty of his—after Malcolm's lies and deceit—was what she had valued so much in her relationship with Salvatore. She had trusted him—and he had trusted her. They had both known they would abide by their agreement with each other. And so for her to tell him now that she was carrying his child…

Her face contorted in misery.

He'll think I did it deliberately—or carelessly. It doesn't matter which because the effect will be the same. He'll feel it's his obligation to stand by me—to make our marriage last in a way he never intended it to! It will chain him to me—chain him to a child he never planned for. Chain him in this marriage when I know how negatively he feels about marriage.

How could she do that to him?

She couldn't—that was all. She just could not.

And so in the morning, after a sleepless night, her head still aching, she had made the only possible decision. She'd packed a suitcase as if she were intending Milan to be her destination, and to account for why she wanted to get to Pisa airport that morning had told the

staff she was flying up a day early, to surprise Salvatore.
Then she had taken the first flight to London.

It had been agony to do so.

Agony to leave Italy.

To force herself to do so.

To leave Salvatore.

To know I will never see him again—

She felt that agony again, now, as she stood in the
kitchen of her flat, musty and empty and drear, a thousand miles away from where she longed to be, hearing
the kettle come to the boil. Sightlessly staring at the mug
she'd taken out of the cupboard, at the packet of fruit tea
she'd opened, filled with misery and anguish, her face
drawn and gaunt, she faced the truth about why it was
such agony to have done what she had. Leave Salvatore.
Faced the truth she had been trying to deny for so long
now, all through those glorious sun-filled days with Salvatore, in the ecstasy of their passionate nights together.

I've fallen in love with him! With Salvatore.

Too late—oh, far too late—self-knowledge pierced
her. Was that what she had feared all along? That she
would not be able to stop herself falling in love with him?

*Is that why I turned him down that first time we ever
met? Why I wanted our marriage to be in name only?
Why I told him, that night when we'd come back from
Florence, that I could not let it be anything else, saying
it was because he was going to pay off my mortgage that
I could not let there be anything between us?*

And when she'd been able to resist him no longer,
when it had become impossible to say no to him, then…
oh, then she had known. She had kept reminding herself
that they must part at the pre-appointed time, that she

must hope for nothing more, must give nothing of her self, want nothing more from him than what they had

In vain.

I went and fell in love with him... Knowing that could come to nothing...

Heaviness crushed her. And hopelessness.

Into her head came a memory from Rome, when she had first arrived there. How glad she had been that Malcolm had never broken her heart. And how she'd know she must make sure that she never fell for a man who did not return her feelings, who did not want to make his life with her.

Yet I've done exactly that!

Salvatore had never asked for love, nor offered it and he would not welcome or want it any more than he would their baby. A real marriage, let alone fatherhood had never been part of his plan. Just a year of her life, passionate affair—and nothing more.

She felt tears sting her eyes, heard his name a cry of heartbreak on her lips…a heartbreak that nothing could mend. For there was only one thing that she could do— that must be done. Cost her what it might.

I have to set him free and never tell him why. It's a that I can do for him.

Her silence must be her gift—the only gift of love she could give him. And he had given her a gift too—a gift he would never know.

Instinctively, protectively, her hand splayed out over her rounding midriff, her eyes welling with tears. She had been given such a gift—the gift of new life, growing within her… But she was paying such a price for it To have Salvatore's baby—but not Salvatore.

Her eyes closed in anguish and the pent-up tears seeped down her cheeks.

Unstoppable.

Salvatore stood in Lana's bedroom at the *palazzo*. His mother's room. Stared at the silver tray on the dressing table that had once been his mother's. Stared at the diamond ring lying on that silver tray, catching the sunlight from the window. The ring he had given the woman he had married. Who had now walked out on him, leaving her betrothal ring behind, just as she had left behind all the couture clothes she'd bought as his wife.

She had just…gone.

Why?

The question burned in him. She'd gone without warning, without explanation—without any reason! His calls to her had gone unanswered, gone to voicemail. She had never returned them, just as she had ignored his texts. There had been nothing—absolutely nothing.

Lana had not just disappeared—she had refused all contact.

Why?

The brutal question slammed again in his head. Why had she told his housekeeper she had decided to fly up to Milan to join him there and then, at Pisa airport, where she had been driven, had vanished into Departures. All contact lost.

He turned on his heel. There were no answers here. He drove to Rome, the devil on his tail, not wanting to be stuck in the middle of Tuscany. Had she returned to London? And if so, why?

When he was in Rome she made contact—but not with him. He got a call from his London lawyer, telling him she was filing for divorce and would not be taking a penny of their prenup agreement. Giving no reason for why she had left him as she had.

Frustration seized him, emotions writhed in him, but he did not know what they were—knew only that they were tormenting him like the biting of venomous snakes. He would fly to London, get answers from her—demand them!

But before he could book his flight he was given his answer. Courtesy of a visitor to his apartment in Rome—the very last person on earth he'd expected to see.

Giavanna.

Lana glanced one more time around the flat, checking everything was neat and tidy for the prospective purchaser about to look it over. She'd put it on the market the day after getting back to London—and already there was interest. She was relieved. She needed to sell as soon as possible, for the best price she could. Then she'd pay off the swingeing mortgage and head out of London with whatever was left.

She'd find somewhere to start over, where she'd stay for the rest of her life. Just her and her baby. The way it had to be. Living her life without Salvatore.

She tried to tell herself that her marriage—her time with Salvatore—would have ended anyway, just as Salvatore had planned. Her discovery that she was pregnant had only ended it sooner, that was all. But however much she told herself that, it made no difference to the pain she felt at losing him.

Yet she knew, with a chill inside her that ate into her bones, that a worse pain might have faced her. A worse destiny.

If I'd told him I was pregnant and he'd felt obliged to keep our marriage going, for then baby's sake, then—oh, dear God—I'd have ended up like his mother! Married to a man I loved—a man who did not love me...

It would have been worse than anything!

No... She felt her heart clench. This was the only way—selling up, clearing out. Making a new home for herself. A new life. In the time to come, in the long, long years ahead, her baby would be her comfort and her joy.

All that I'll have of Salvatore—

The sudden sound of the entry phone broke her stricken thoughts. With a start, she went out into the external hallway to admit the estate agent and her prospective buyer.

But as she pulled back the door she froze. It was the last man on earth she'd ever expected to see again.

Malcolm.

Salvatore climbed into the taxi at Heathrow and curtly gave the address, throwing himself back into his seat and yanking on the seat belt. The devil was driving him, he knew that, and had been since his return to the *palazzo* from Milan. But now the devil had pushed the accelerator button.

Courtesy of Giavanna.

He could still hear the false sympathy in her voice as she'd stood there in his apartment in a replay of her last visit. But this time her bombshell had not been that she wanted to marry him. It had been one that was still ripping his guts out.

'*My poor Salva... I think I may know why Lana has left you. Take a look at this—*'

She'd held out her phone to him and he'd seen the

photo—a man he had not recognised—but the caption had made his identity clear.

Giavanna's falsely sympathetic voice had trilled in his ears.

'Hollywood gossip says it's all over between Lana's ex and the A-lister he hooked, so he's going back to London. Who knows? Maybe he wants to get back together with Lana...'

Denial stabbed in Salvatore.

No! He would not believe it! It was just Giavanna making trouble, being vindictive! He would not believe that the reason Lana had left him was because she was rushing back to the man who had treated her so despicably!

Then his lawyer's words echoed in his head. Lana was refusing to take any of the money agreed in their prenup. Why would she do that? Unless—

Is Malcolm coming back to London to pay her back the money he took from her? And if he does will she forgive him? Take him back? Is it him she loves—has loved all along?

The thought was like icy water in his veins. He could feel it now, chilling him to the core, defying him not to believe what he so desperately hoped was just Giavanna's poison—what Lana herself would, surely, *por Dio!* prove was nothing but poison when he got the truth from her!

Of course she had never gone back to Malcolm!

And then she will come back to me! To me...

Emotions scythed within him, slicing and slicing at him. He could not name them, knew only that they were emotions he had never felt before—and that they were unbearable.

Agony.

The taxi ate up the miles into London, cutting through the streets towards Notting Hill, drawing up outside the white terraced house he remembered from so long ago, when he'd given Lana a lift back from the fashion show after-party. He moved to open the taxi door—then froze.

The front door was opening. Someone was coming out. Not Lana. A man with bleached blond hair, gleaming capped white teeth, a California tan, sauntering down the steps with a smile on his face that was a smirk of satisfaction. He walked by, taking no notice of the taxi at the kerbside.

A knife was skewering Salvatore. A knife coated with Giavanna's poison. Poison that was no lie but devastating truth. The evidence of his own eyes.

He slumped back in his seat, curtly ordering the taxi driver to drive on. Where, he didn't care.

Only blackness was in his heart.

Bleakness.

Lana carefully stepped into the shower, felt the warm water sluicing down over her. As she started to lather her hair she glanced down at her fast-growing bump. Memory stabbed at her of how she'd stood in the pool house at the *palazzo*, seeing her newly rounded figure.

So long ago now.

Summer was long gone. Autumn too. And by spring—

By spring I'll be preparing to receive my first visitors. Opening up for Easter. The start of the holiday season.

She hadn't moved to the seaside after all, but she wasn't that far away, in an attractive abbey town in Dorset, popular with tourists. The established B&B was an old, pretty stone cottage, part of a terrace in a quiet street, with hollyhocks in the garden and lavender along the path. She'd bought it after the rapid sale of her flat, and it was already well booked for next season. It would bring her in sufficient income, she reckoned, to make her living there financially viable.

A new start—a new life.

A new life that she would always have had. It had come sooner than she'd thought it would, but it would have come to the same thing anyway. That was what she kept having to remind herself. However painful it was to do so. Salvatore had had no objection to her leaving him as she had. Any hope that he might have not wanted her to leave had withered and died.

He's accepted that I simply ended the marriage earlier than we'd originally agreed, and thereby forfeited the prenup settlement. He hasn't objected. Hasn't tried to get in touch.

Because he didn't want her back. Was happy that she'd gone. Had ended it all sooner than planned. Their divorce was proceeding with no objections from Salvatore.

He doesn't miss me at all!

The cry was in her heart, but she crushed it back. She rinsed her hair, feeling her eyes stinging. It was the shampoo, that was all. Nothing more than that. Not tears—no, not tears.

There was no point in tears. No point in waking in the long reaches of the night, longing to feel arms around her, her own arms wrapped around Salvatore's strong body.

It was all over.

She turned off the water, reaching for her towel, wringing out her hair and stepping carefully out of the cubicle, wrapping herself in another voluminous towel.

Time to get on with things.

Time to get on with the rest of her life.

The life that would always have been waiting for me.

That was the only comfort she could take. And just one more thing other than that. One she had never looked to have but which had been given to her for all that by Salvatore himself. His beloved child, growing within her.

Salvatore jabbed at the channel changing button on the remote, indifferent to what programme he might watch. It would pass the time. Maybe make the long, empty evening which stretched ahead of him pass less agonisingly slowly than they always did now.

He should go and get some work done. That would blot up more time. Time that stretched endlessly now, whatever he did.

He no longer went out. The sympathy of his friends was unbearable. Even the Duchessa had written to him, expressing her regret at hearing that he and Lana were divorcing.

> *She was good for you, Salvatore, and I know how much your mother would have approved of your marriage, rejoicing that you had found such happiness. My heart goes out to you that you have lost it now—lost Lana...*

He had thrown the letter aside, not wanting to read it. Not wanting to hear what his mother's godmother had thought of his marriage...that she believed his mother would have approved of it.

He wanted to laugh—savagely. In a bitter mocking of himself.

He reached for the bottle of *grappa* sitting by his

elbow, refilled the glass he had already emptied. It did not help him—did not ease the hyenas tearing at his guts as they so ceaselessly did.

His eyes were bloodshot—and as bleak as polar ice.

He jabbed again at the remote, staring sightlessly at the huge screen over the fireplace. Some pointless documentaries, some pointless advertisements, some pointless programme about new film releases…

He let that last one settle, running out of programmes to surf. It finished by waxing lyrical about some new pointless blockbuster, then went on to something about a pointless Hollywood wedding…

And suddenly Salvatore straightened from his slump on the sofa, his eyes no longer bloodshot or bleak, but focussed, like a laser beam on what he was seeing.

As the item ended on a saccharine gush, in slow motion he set down his undrunk *grappa*. Got to his feet. Swayed slightly and then, with the force of will, straightened.

He had to sober up. And fast.

He had a flight to book.

Lana unpacked the groceries she'd just bought, neatly placing them in the kitchen cupboards. Memory stabbed at her of how she and Salvatore had unpacked their provisions in the lakeside cabin. She put the memory aside. Put them all aside. One day she would let them out. Tell her son or daughter as they grew up about the father they would never know.

Never could know.

She must not long for anything else.

I must not long for him with all my heart, with all that I feel for him. That is so, so hopeless! So pointless!

Yet memory came again, and she was lost in that unforgettable time with Salvatore at the lakeside cabin, out on the lake in the little rowing boat, as she'd asked about how he'd come to love fishing, and he'd told her about his father…about his indifference to his wife's love for him.

'He never wanted a divorce—he stayed with her for my sake…'

Pain twisted like a knife in her side.

That would have been her fate, too, had she told Salvatore about the baby. And it would have tortured her to know how much she loved him—and how indifferent to her he would have become when his desire for her finally died. He would have resented being married to her—or, worse, agreed to some 'civilised' divorce, some 'civilised' arrangement over shared custody and access…

Unbearable—just unbearable—

The knife twisted again, but she stifled the pain. There was no point feeling it—no point at all. It would be there all her life, she knew.

Her life without Salvatore…

Whom she would never see again…

Never.

The word tolled like a funeral bell in her head.

Then, as if thought had become reality, she heard the front doorbell ring. She started, wondering who was there—a late postal delivery, perhaps? She went to the door, opened it, blinking in the wintry sunlight that caught her eyes. Silhouetting the man standing there.

'Never' had been the wrong word. So she said his name instead, in a breathy gasp, as all the air left her lungs.

'Salvatore…'

CHAPTER TWELVE

HE STOOD THERE, motionless, for an endless moment.

Lana! I am seeing her again—here, now, in front of me!

She overwhelmed him, making his senses reel.

But she always had—she had always had that effect on him. From the very first moment to the very last.

His gaze swept over her. He was drinking her in like a man in a desert finding sweet, sweet water...

He looked her over from her golden hair, piled up loosely, to her perfect face—perfect even without make-up, for it was always perfect, could only ever be perfect—down over her fabulous body—

And stopped short.

'Dio mio...'

The breath was exhaled from him and shock—naked and brutal—punched him in the solar plexus. Her pregnancy was blatant—unconcealed. The long sweater over leggings outlined her fullness.

Shock detonated in him again as he took it in.

He heard her say his name, shock whitening her face. Saw her slump against the door...

In an instant he had her, catching her before she fell.

The weight of her body was heavy—heavier than he had ever known it. But then…

'You need to sit down.' His voice was brusque, terse with shock. Inside his head emotion was storming.

He guided her in, kicking the door shut behind him, going into a room opening off the hallway. It was a sitting room, warm from central heating after the chill of the English winter outdoors, and he got her to an armchair into which she sank like a dead weight.

He heard her say his name again, in the same faint voice, her eyes huge in her head, still blank with shock. Emotion was storming within him, and seeing her in that condition was like being inside a hurricane, turning him inside out. Everything he had come here to say vanished from him, torn away by the storm whipping through him.

He stood back, looking down at her. Then spoke, finding the necessary words. 'Let me get you some water—'

His voice was clipped, and he did not wait for a reply, just strode from the room. Behind the sitting room was a kitchen, and he seized up a glass from the draining board, filling it from the tap, coming back into the room where Lana still sat, her face ashen.

'Drink this,' he told her, handing her the glass.

She took it, sipping from it jerkily until he removed it again, setting it down on a nearby side table.

Then he stood, looking down at her. The hurricane was still inside him, or he was inside it—he did not know. But he was calmer now, forcing himself to be so. Finding the words he knew he now must say.

He drew breath, steadying his voice. But it still came out harshly. 'I should hate you for what you did to me—leaving me as you did, and for such a reason. But now—'

He stopped. She was staring at him, her beautiful face

still ashen. Something moved within him, crossing the whipping maelstrom of the hurricane inside him and finding the still, small eye where the maelstrom could not reach. Where he now was. Where everything was clear to him.

'I will stand by you,' he said. He drew a breath, like a razor in his throat, ready to say what he must say next, where only truth could be.

When he spoke again his eyes never left hers. His voice was no longer harsh. It was filled, instead, with all he knew he must say to her.

'Come back to me, Lana. It's what I came here to say to you…'

He had known it from the moment he'd realised that whatever kind of reunion she'd had with Malcolm it was over—he'd gone back to Hollywood to marry a film star. Leaving Lana alone. Alone for him to say what he had just said to her.

His eyes went to her midriff and emotion knifed within him. Emotion that filled him with a certainty that made everything else irrelevant. For a moment there was silence, only the ticking of a clock on the mantelpiece making any sound. Yet his heart was pounding such that surely it must be audible. As audible as the words echoing in his head now. The words he had said.

No man in his right mind would say them. What man could? In his head a memory flashed—seared—of his talking to Luc Dinardi about Stephanie. It had been unbelievable then, what Luc had said. But now—

Now I know. Know why he would say it. And why I have said it too.

And he knew why the words he would speak now were the only ones he wanted to say. Spoken out of that still, small space inside the hurricane where truth was. The only truth that mattered.

The certainty of it poured through him and his gaze poured into hers as she stared up at him, uncomprehending, stricken...

'I will stand by you,' he said, with indelible certainty, absolute promise. 'And I give you my word...' his eyes held all that he knew he must say '...no one will ever know your baby is not mine.'

Lana lurched to her feet and the blood drained from her again, making her legs collapse, her lungs collapse. For a second time Salvatore caught her, his hands gripping hers as her body sagged.

'No, don't faint on me! I didn't mean to shock you! Sit down—'

Once again he was propelling her into the armchair and she sank down. If she had been in shock before, now it was threefold. A million-fold. He let slip her hands and they dropped like weights into her lap as he stood there, looking down at her.

What was in his face was something she had never seen before.

He was speaking again, and in his voice was something she had never heard before.

'I do not talk of forgiveness,' he was saying, his eyes never leaving hers, 'for there is nothing to forgive. You knew him before you knew me. He hurt you badly and you hated him for it! So I understand—truly, I understand why you went back to him when he returned to London. And I understand your hopes, your thinking— believing—he might stay with you this time...'

And now his voice darkened, edged with an an[?]
contempt, that was not directed at her.

'But you were wrong to trust him—he let you [?]
again! Abandoned you again! Used you just as he [?]
you the first time around!' His eyes flashed with a[?]
'If he were here now I would pulverise him for wha[?]
done to you! Left you—again! Looking out for hin[?]
and only for himself, as he always did!'

She couldn't speak…couldn't think. Could no[?]
lieve—

But he was not done yet.

'For all that he has done to you, you are well sh[?]
him! He's worthless scum! Forget him! Forget hin[?]
come back to me.'

She took a breath. Deep into her lungs. Her w[?]
being seemed to be sucked into that breath. She lo[?]
up at him. She couldn't read his face. It had closed a[?]

'Are you telling me,' she asked slowly, with int[?]
care—because suddenly, out of nowhere, out of the [?]
strom that had stormed over her, it was the most in[?]
tant question in the world, in the entire universe, '—[?]
you would want me even if I was carrying Malc[?]
baby?'

His eyes were fixed on hers. His face still had[?]
expression she had never seen before, the one tha[?]
impossible to read.

'Yes.'

A single word to answer her.

She took a ragged breath. It seemed the words [?]
break from her now.

'But *why*?'

For a moment he did not answer her. Only stood [?]
his gaze still fixed on hers. That unreadable look st[?]

his face. She felt her heart start to thud, as if something were about to happen that she might not be able to bear.

She could see the tension edging his jaw, sitting across his shoulders, when he spoke next, as if his words were being forced from him. She heard them through the thudding of her heart, the tightness in her lungs. Sitting there, nerveless.

'All my life,' he said heavily, 'I have thought myself like my father. Feared it. I knew, therefore, that I should never marry lest I bring misery to my wife as he did to his. But then I discovered something about myself that I had never known,' he said, and his words were heavier yet. 'Giavanna came to see me after you'd walked out on me. Dropping poison in my ear. Giving me an explanation for why you'd left me. *Por Dio*, I did not believe it—did not want to believe it! Refused to believe it! Yet when I came to your house and saw Malcolm walking out of it…then I knew—'

Pain was in his voice—she could hear it through the thudding of her heart—and a hurt and wretchedness that reached out to her and gripped her heart like a vice.

'I knew, in that single moment, that it was not being my father's son that I should have feared…' He looked at her, and the pain that had been in his voice was in his eyes too. 'It was being my mother's.'

He was silent for a moment, and so was she, unable to speak, too full with what was inside her now. Then more words were coming from Salvatore. Halting, painful.

'I had come to know, as she did, the pain of being rejected for another. Because you…' his face was bleaker yet '…had rejected me for Malcolm, who wanted you back after he'd been dumped by his Hollywood star.'

Slowly…infinitely slowly… Lana found the words she

needed to speak. 'How could you *ever* think I would go back to Malcolm? After what he did to me!'

The tightness of his face made it a mask. 'I thought he must have repented…repaid you the mortgage money.' His mouth set. 'I thought that that was the reason you were turning down the prenup payment we'd agreed.'

Lana's eyes widened in disbelief. 'I refused to take your money because I'd broken the terms of our deal! I'd left you before the year was out. That was why!'

She felt her face work. Thoughts, feelings, emotions, words were tumbling within her, but she must make sense of them—she *must*. And above all she must say what she had to now.

'I *never* left you for Malcolm—even though, yes, he did repay what he owed me! You saw him leave my flat,' she said, her voice hollow, 'because he'd been sent there by his fiancée—who hadn't dumped him, whatever the gossip said! She discovered that I'd claimed he'd defrauded me, that I was seeking to press charges. She didn't want any scandal attached to him so she sent him there, gave him the money to repay the mortgage, in exchange for dropping all my accusations. Which I did.'

Salvatore was staring at her. Something different in his face now. 'So you got your money back, and you slept with him one last time, for old times' sake?'

There was no expression in his voice.

Nor was there in Lana's as she answered him.

'No,' she said again. 'It wasn't like that, Salvatore.'

She made herself look at him. The thud of her heart was deafening her. She gave a cry. Launching herself to her feet.

'Why do you think I left you?'

The words broke from her—impossible to halt them,

to silence them, to keep them locked within her any longer. Not a second longer. It was no longer possible to keep hidden the truth she'd had to hide.

He stilled. Utterly motionless.

'I left you because I found out I was pregnant,' she said, and each word was forced from her. They were the most important, the most vital words she would ever utter in her life, and her whole life now depended on them. 'And when I did, I knew I could not impose upon you what you had never agreed to. What broke our agreement into pieces. It…it would not have been fair on you.'

She took a breath before plunging on, saying what must be said—what could not be left unsaid. They had gone way beyond that now.

'You were always honest with me, Salvatore…' Her voice changed as she spoke now, and her eyes echoed the truth of what she was saying. 'Honest about the reasons we married, about when it would end, and why—honest when you said that we would only have a year together… honest about what you felt for me. Desire, yes, but nothing more. And, wonderful though our time was—and I am joyously glad that we had what we had together, and it felt right to be with you and to want you, be wanted by you—for all that… I always knew I was on borrowed time. That we would part.'

She shook her head.

'There was nothing…nothing that gave me any claim on anything else from you. Like…like being pregnant. So,' she finished, 'because of that I knew I could only do what I did. I left you. And although I would have given all the world not to have had to leave you, it was as simple as that.'

She fell silent, but she could hear each beat of her heart, each pulse of her blood.

'And when you did…when you left me,' he answered her, 'my world ended. It was as simple as that. And devastating to me.'

He shut his eyes for a moment, then they flashed open again, gold blazing in their night-dark depths. Gold that could melt her where she stood.

He took a step towards her. Halted. 'When I married you, Lana, I did so for hard-headed reasons—and I was honest with you, as you say, from the off. I wanted nothing more than what I'd planned—a year with you, no more.' He drew a razoring breath. 'I've never done long relationships because…' The razoring breath came again. 'Because I never…*never*…wanted to cause any woman the misery my mother endured because of my father. The father I thought I was like. *Feared* I was like…'

He was silent a moment, his face drawn. Then he spoke again, and now there was something different about him. Something clearer in his eyes.

'I thought all I wanted of you was an affair—that it would end like all my affairs end. That the time would come when I would stop wanting you, as has always been the case with me—as it was for my father. But it took your leaving—leaving me for another man, as I so insanely thought—to make me realise something that I had never known…something only the agony I felt when you left me could show me.'

He took a breath, but this time it was not razoring at all. Only resolute. As resolute as his voice when he spoke to her again.

'Show me,' he said, his eyes holding hers as if they were precious jewels he must never lose. 'Show me that

I am not my father's son, Lana, but that I am my mother's. And that as my mother's son I can know—as I did not when I thought I was like my father, incapable of emotional attachment—that all the time we were together I was falling in love with you, even though I had no idea of it.'

He took a breath from the very depths of his being, his eyes pouring into hers with such intensity that she reeled from it.

He shook his head. 'I did not know it…did not recognise it. But now…' He took another, deeper breath, his eyes still pouring into hers. 'Now I do recognise it—I know it for what it is. And even if it's only the sake of the baby…' his voice was diffident now, hesitant, unsure '…if you will come back to me, then—'

She cut across him instinctively, her words as heartfelt as everything that was in her. 'Then I will have found my paradise, Salvatore.'

She took a step towards him, reached out her hands to him. Her heart was singing, soaring to the very heavens.

'Oh, my most dearest one, I have known I loved you ever since I left you. It nearly killed me to have to leave you!' Her voice twisted, emotion breaking in it. 'But when I discovered I was pregnant I could not bear to make you resent me, make you feel that I was trapping you! I knew, for your sake, that I could not tell you I was pregnant! I could not do that to you. Not for your sake, Salvatore, or—' her voice broke '—or for mine.'

The words poured from her—all that had been stifled, all that she had not been allowed to say but now she could. She could speak at last.

'You say you are your mother's son—but, oh, Salvatore, I feared I, too, would be like your mother! Feared it for myself! Feared loving you so much and you never loving me—never wanting my love, never giving me yours, only staying with me for the sake of our child. I could not bear it! I knew I'd rather live out my life alone than that!'

He seized her hands, closing the distance between them. Clasping her fingers so tightly it was as if he would fuse flesh with flesh.

'And I knew,' he said, and there was something in his voice she had never heard there before, something that pierced her to the core, 'that loving you so much, as I do, I would rather have you in my life with another man's baby than not have you in it at all.'

She gave a little cry, unbearably moved, and lifted his hand to her cheek. 'If ever I wanted proof of your love, that declaration would be it! Oh, my darling, my dearest love—'

Tears were welling in her eyes, misting her face. He bent his face to hers, to kiss away the tears, and lowered his hand so that he could embrace her, hold her close against him.

For ever.

Then suddenly she gave a little cry, pulling back from him.

Consternation immediately filled Salvatore's face. 'Lana—no, don't pull away. Please—don't pull away from me! Not when I love you so much!'

She heard those words, so very dear to her, from this man who had once only wanted her for a year, no more than that, but who would now be hers, as she was his, for ever! Her hand had gone to the swell of her body, splaying over it. She lifted her face lifted to Salvatore's, amazement and wonder in her eyes, joy cours-

ing through every atom of her being after his declaration
of love for her.

'He moved! Salvatore, he *moved*! I felt him just now!
Like a butterfly inside me!' She gave another cry, a gasp.
'And again! He moved again. Oh, Salvatore…'

She reached for his hand, placed it next to hers, radiant joy in her face. And not just for the baby quickening
within her—but for all the joy that was pouring through
her now. And for ever and ever.

She saw his expression change, saw the same look of
wonder in his eyes as in hers, heard him give the same
gasp of breath.

'Si—il muovo!'

For a moment longer they just stood there, as the child
they had created between them made its presence felt.
Then Salvatore's free hand cupped her face. His eyes
poured into hers, telling her, without words, of his love
for her. Telling her that her joy was his as well.

'It's a wise child that knows his own father,' he told
her, and there was a catch in his voice that turned her
heart over.

She gave a cry of laughter, but there were tears in her
voice as well. Laughter, and tears, and a joy that could
light up the world.

For both of them.

'And it's an even wiser father,' Salvatore went on,
catching Lana back into his arms, 'who knows with
every atom of his being that he is in love with the woman
who is the beloved mother of his most precious baby.'

He kissed her then, and in his lips and hers was all
she could ever have desired and dreamt of.

He held her in the cradle of his arms as he released
her. His eyes held hers, glinting gold in the noonday light.

'I have a new business proposition to put to you, Signora Luchesi,' he said. 'I don't think a year of marriage is anything like enough. So I'm revising the end date of our contract.' His mouth skimmed hers, taking sweet possession, just to remind her, as her hands wound around his waist, of her possession of him too. 'I am setting it for a hundred years from now. 'That should be sufficient, I think,' he told her, kissing the tip of her nose, and then her forehead.

She shook her head. 'Let's go for broke,' she said, lifting her mouth to claim his again. 'Let's go for eternity.'

His arms tightened around her. 'Eternity it is, then,' he said. 'Sounds good to me.'

'And to me,' she whispered.

Their kiss deepened, and then, with an effortless swing of his arms, Salvatore was sweeping her up.

'This is a delightful cottage,' he informed her, with purpose in his voice, 'but right now there is only one room I want to find.'

She laughed, carefree in her whole being, as she would always be now. 'Upstairs, first on the right. And you'll be glad to know,' she said, eyes gleaming, 'that it's a king-size bed.'

She was right. Salvatore was very glad.

And so, she found, to her satisfaction, delight and incandescent joy, was she, as with all their passion and desire they proved their newly declared love for each other.

EPILOGUE

LANA STOOD BESIDE Salvatore, her emerald silk evening gown brushing the smooth black of his evening jacket, leaning against him as they both gazed down at the sleeping baby in his cot.

'He is simply the most perfect baby that ever there was!' Lana breathed, her gaze filled with devoted love.

Salvatore's arm came around her waist. 'Absolutely the most perfect,' he agreed.

For a few moments longer they stood there, gazing down in joint admiration of the son, who had been born in the early summer. Now it was August, and the *palazzo*, ablaze with lights, was preparing to receive its guests for the summer ball that was to take place that night. Already, through the open windows, they could hear the strains of the orchestra tuning up on the terrace, now bedecked with fairy lights, and the bustle of the staff as they made everything ready for the glittering occasion.

First, though, Lana and Salvatore were dining with their closest friends, who were staying with them at the *palazzo*.

Salvatore led Lana downstairs from the nursery, leaving their precious son in the reassuring charge of Signora Guardi's niece, who would babysit for the evening.

In the *saloni* opposite the dining room Giuseppe was opening the champagne, and Lana paused to thank and praise him and all the staff for their efforts tonight. He bestowed a smile upon her, and Lana returned it warmly. Now she truly felt herself the chatelaine of this beautiful *palazzo*, she thought fondly, her eyes going to Salvatore, the man who was the love of her life. It was her home for ever, and she was no longer the imposter she had thought herself when she'd first come here, uneasy at being treated as the *signora* and successor to Salvatore's mother.

Now I truly belong here!

It was a good feeling—a wonderful feeling…

The arrival of her and Salvatore's dinner guests into the *saloni* drew her attention. Laura and Stephanie— both, like Lana, dressed to the nines in couture gowns and diamond jewellery—hugged Lana, and then Vito and Luc, as resplendent as Salvatore in their evening dress, bestowed hand kisses with Latin gallantry. As the champagne circulated Lana was filled with a happiness that permeated every cell of her body. How happy she was…how perfectly, absolutely happy!

Lana's smile radiated from her and Salvatore's breath caught, his gaze fastening on her, his heart turning over with all that he felt for her. His Lana! His wonderful, beautiful Lana! His very own most beloved of women.

My wife.

His true wife—his one and only wife—his one and only love.

He closed his eyes for a moment. Had he really once thought it was impossible to fall in love, to want to spend all his days—and, oh, all his nights!—with one woman and one alone? Had he really thought that? Now every day, every night, every waking moment gave the lie to that.

Quietly, blinking suddenly, he raised his glass a little. Giving a silent toast.

But, slight though the gesture had been Lana caught it.

She met his eyes. 'How right she was,' she said softly, for him alone.

She knew what he was doing, and why, as the others chatted amongst themselves, laughing with the conviviality of good friends.

'Your mother knew you better than you knew yourself.'

She kissed him lightly on his cheek and he caught her hand, pressing it.

'And how happy she would be, seeing you so happy.' She paused for a moment. 'And I think, too, you know, that your father would be happy as well, knowing you have found a happiness in marriage that he never did.'

She bit her lip for a moment, throat tightening.

'One day you'll be taking *your* son off fishing, telling him how your father taught you and now you're teaching him.'

Salvatore smiled. 'It will be a year or two yet, I think. And who knows…?'

A sudden glint lit his deep, dark, long-lashed eyes, sweeping over Lana in a way she knew only too well. She felt her whole body quiver, the way it always did when he looked at her like that.

'Perhaps by then he'll have a younger brother for me to teach to fish as well.'

'Or a sister,' Lana said.

'Or a sister,' Salvatore agreed.

He raised his glass again, to her, his beloved wife. 'To our children and to us—and to our parents too.'

His gaze widened, taking in his friends.

'And to our friends!' He raised his voice and his glass.

Contentment filled him. Could life be better? He doubted it. He had his beloved wife, his adored son, and his beautiful home—created by his mother, purchased thanks to his father's business acumen. He had his health and his career—and his friends. And all the guests who would come later that evening.

The Duchessa and her husband would be there, bestowing their approval upon his renewed and so obviously happy marriage. And even Roberto would be there too. He gave a wry smile. They were on good terms now, with Roberto basking in his daughter's marriage into the aristocracy and Giavanna preening happily with her *visconte* heir.

'To friendship!' Vito echoed Salvatore's toast.

'Brava!' cried Steph enthusiastically. 'And,' she added, pausing for dramatic effect, to ensure she had all eyes on her, 'to one thing more!' She glanced at Luc, who smiled down at her indulgently.

'Go on,' he said. 'You can be the very first to announce this prime morsel of gossip, my treasure!'

Stephanie's eyes sparkled with delight. 'Then I shall!' She took another dramatic breath. 'I've decided, after *long* consideration, that it's high time I made an honest man out of Rome's favourite playboy. So...' She raised her glass. 'I hereby announce that Luc Dinardi is being taken out of circulation, to the tears and lamentations of all females everywhere, and is about to become my true and faithful husband. *Because...*'

She paused again, and exchanged a wicked glance with Laura and with Lana, who both silently gasped, as if they knew exactly what their incorrigible friend was going to announce, and that Luc had absolutely no idea of it.

'Because he's going to be a father too!'

A shout of delight broke from both Salvatore and Vito, followed by the back-slapping of a somewhat stunned-looking Luc.

His new fiancée patted him comfortingly on the wrist. 'Yes, Luc—and, yes, the baby *is* yours. Would I even dream of having a baby with anyone but you, my own beloved man of mine! How could you ever think such a thing of me?' she added demurely.

Salvatore and Lana exchanged glances and she felt him take her hand in hers, squeezing it. Both of them remembered how Salvatore had, in one heartfelt assurance, declared the extent of his love for her. Lana felt her eyes fill with tears now, at the very memory. How foolish she had been to think she must flee from Salvatore, to think he would not welcome their child! And how glorious had been the realisation of just how much he loved her!

Her fingers tightened on his as she gazed at him, love-light lambent in her eyes, glowing like the emerald silk of her gown. And for a moment…a timeless, eternal moment…there was no one else in the room, no one else in the whole world except herself—and the man she loved.

For all eternity.

Then, as Salvatore's mouth swooped down to steal a swift, infinitely tender kiss, the world returned.

Vito was raising his glass. His sweeping gaze encompassing them all. 'The toast, my friends, is to love, marriage—and babies!'

It was a toast they could all drink to.

So they did.

* * * * *

COMING SOON!

We really hope you enjoyed reading this book.
If you're looking for more romance, be sure to
head to the shops when new books are
available on

Thursday 18th August

To see which titles are coming soon, please visit

millsandboon.co.uk/nextmonth

MILLS & BOON®

Coming next month

INNOCENT UNTIL HIS FORBIDDEN TOUCH
Carol Marinelli

"Seriously?" His deep Italian voice entered the room before he even walked in. "I do not need a PR strategist?"

"A Liason Aide, Sir," his Aide murmured.

Beatrice stood as she'd been instructed earlier, but as he entered, every assumption she'd made about him was wiped away.

Prince Julius brimmed, not just with authority but with health and energy. It was as if a forcefield had entered the room.

She had dealt with alpha males and females at the top of their game – or rather – usually when they crashing from the top.

Not he.

He was, quite literally, stunning.

He stunned.

"It's a pleasure to meet you," she said and then added. "Sir."

"Likewise," he said, even if his eyes said otherwise.

God, he was tall, Beatrice thought, it was more than just his height, he was the most immaculate man she had ever seen.

Beatrice swallowed, not wanting to pursue that line of thought. The issue was that at most interviews she had found most people were less in the flesh.

He was so, so much more.

Continue reading
INNOCENT UNTIL HIS FORBIDDEN TOUCH
Carol Marinelli

Available next month
www.millsandboon.co.uk

MILLS & BOON

THE HEART OF ROMANCE

A ROMANCE FOR EVERY READER

MODERN

Prepare to be swept off your feet by sophisticated, sexy and seductive heroes, in some of the world's most glamourous and romantic locations, where power and passion collide.

HISTORICAL

Escape with historical heroes from time gone by. Whether your passion is for wicked Regency Rakes, muscled Vikings or rugged Highlanders, awaken the romance of the past.

MEDICAL

Set your pulse racing with dedicated, delectable doctors in the high-pressure world of medicine, where emotions run high and passion, comfort and love are the best medicine.

True Love

Celebrate true love with tender stories of heartfelt romance, from the rush of falling in love to the joy a new baby can bring, and a focus on the emotional heart of a relationship.

Desire

Indulge in secrets and scandal, intense drama and plenty of sizzling hot action with powerful and passionate heroes who have it all: wealth, status, good looks…everything but the right woman.

HEROES

Experience all the excitement of a gripping thriller, with an intense romance at its heart. Resourceful, true-to-life women and strong, fearless men face danger and desire - a killer combination!

To see which titles are coming soon, please visit

millsandboon.co.uk/nextmonth